# ANOTHER DAY

Eighteen years after being disowned by
her father, Kirsty Lennox returns to
Paisley. Inheriting her father's modest
cabinet-making business allows Kirsty to
restore the old family house. Her husband
Matt oversees the fortunes of the thriving
workshop and their sons, Alex and Ewan,
become apprentices. But there is a steady
stream of trouble for Kirsty. Matt's
stubborn ways remind her of her father.
Alex and Ewan squabble over girls and the
future of the business. Nothing, however,
prepares her for the loss of her youngest
child or the sudden reappearance of a
long-lost figure from the past.

# ANOTHER DAY

ANOTHER DAY

# ANOTHER DAY

*by*

## Evelyn Hood

**Magna Large Print Books**
Long Preston, North Yorkshire,
England.

British Library Cataloguing in Publication Data.

Hood, Evelyn
    Another day.

A catalogue record for this book is
available from the British Library

ISBN 0-7505-1077-3

First published in Great Britain by Little, Brown and
Company, 1996

Copyright © 1996 by Evelyn Hood

Cover illustration © Gordon Crabb, by kind permission of
Little, Brown & Co. (UK) Ltd.

The moral right of the author has been asserted.

Published in Large Print 1997 by arrangement with Little,
Brown & Co. (UK) Ltd.

All rights reserved. No part of this publication may be
reproduced, stored in a retrieval system, or transmitted in any
form or by any means, electronic, mechanical, photocopying,
recording or otherwise, without the prior permission of the
Copyright owner.

EATH PORT TALBOT
LIBRARIES

NOV

DATE 10|00 PR. 14.99

LOC. CS

Magna Large Print is an imprint of
Library Magna Books Ltd.
Printed and bound in Great Britain by
T.J. International Ltd., Cornwall, PL28 8RW.

*All characters in this publication are fictitious and any resemblance to real persons, living or dead, is purely coincidental.*

This book is dedicated to
Caitlin Rose Mitchell,
who allowed me to use her name,
and to her parents, Pauline and Rory,
with love.

# 1

As the train drew into Paisley's Gilmour Street Station pandemonium broke out in the Lennox family's compartment. Ewan had sulked throughout the journey because he had been made to travel with his parents and help with the luggage while his brother and sister, gloriously independent, had gone on ahead; now, impatient to be free, he lunged for the door and began wrestling with the handle. Kirsty, somewhat hampered by the weight of the baby fastened securely against her body by a large shawl, screamed at him not to open the door before the train stopped.

Stiff from a warm July day mainly spent sitting in crowded trains, Matt struggled to his feet and began scooping parcels and bags and a shabby, battered suitcase held together by half a ball of string from the overhead luggage rack.

'Lend a hand here, Ewan,' he barked, but the youth was more interested in the station as the train came to a standstill.

'There's Alex—and Caitlin.'

To her great relief Kirsty glimpsed her first-born's red head outside the window.

11

'They got here all right, then,' she said thankfully. She had fretted all day about Alex and Caitlin, who had been sent ahead early that morning to collect the house key from the lawyer and buy in some bread and milk.

'Of course they got here,' Matt said irritably. 'You fuss too much. If Alex cannae manage at eighteen years of age, God help us all. Ewan!'

The boy, struggling to get the window down, paid no heed.

'I'll help,' Kirsty said, but as she reached up towards the rack the engine of a train about to leave for Glasgow on the adjacent line proclaimed the fact by releasing a blast of steam. The triumphant shriek startled five-year-old Mary, who let out a shrill scream of her own and tried to bury herself in her mother's skirt. Kirsty reeled and almost lost her balance as her daughter's small body slammed against her thigh. She just managed to save herself by clutching at the edge of the rack.

Fergus, eight months old, slumbered on in the folds of the shawl, oblivious to the chaos all around him. Having driven his mother almost frantic by refusing to sleep all day despite his obvious exhaustion, he had finally allowed his eyelids to droop on the last leg of the journey from Falkirk, lying against Kirsty's breast like a hot, limp, soggy, and somewhat smelly, stone.

Alex opened the door from the outside and Ewan immediately jumped down onto the platform, shouldering his stepbrother aside, and made for the engine, deaf to his father's orders to lend a hand.

By the time they had all descended from the train most of their fellow travellers were disappearing through the door where the ticket collector waited.

As her feet touched the platform Kirsty was caught unawares by the wrenching memory of the last time she had been in this station more than eighteen years earlier, banished from Paisley by her father. For a moment her husband and family and even the great noisy, steamy iron train ceased to exist as her mind swept her back over the years to another life. She felt the ache of the bruises her father had inflicted on her, knew again the desolation and sheer terror of being forced, at sixteen years of age, to leave everything she had known behind and go alone into an uncertain future.

'God save us, the train'll be away and the things not out of the guard's van yet,' Matt fussed at her side, and suddenly the wintry days of early 1888 vanished and Kirsty was back in the summer of 1906 with her husband and her family, the ache in her shoulder caused not by the beating

13

her father had given her, but by Fergus's weight in the crook of her arm.

'Is Ewan down at the guard's van?'

'He's gone to look at the engine,' thirteen-year-old Caitlin informed her father as she helped Alex to gather up the parcels.

'He's got no more sense in his head than a sparrow,' Matt fumed at his wife. 'Now ye know why I'd not let him travel ahead with Alex—he'd have gone past Paisley and ended up down at Ayr at the very least. Mary, go and tell him tae get back here and give us a hand!' He snatched up the suitcase and started towards the guard's van, leaving Alex and Caitlin to deal with all the parcels.

'Go on, Mary—do as your father tells you,' Kirsty urged, anxious to save Matt's temper from further irritation. Mary's only response was to tighten her grip on Kirsty's skirt, burying her head in its folds.

'Ach, leave him be, Mam,' Alex advised, balancing the assorted parcels in his arms. 'He'll never hear us and we can manage without him.'

The shabby perambulator that had been second-hand when it was bought for Caitlin had been removed from the guard's van and stood on the platform. With some thought of putting wee Fergus into it so that she could take Alex's parcels and free

14

him to help with the trunk, Kirsty hurried towards it. It wasn't until she reached the perambulator that she recalled with dismay that it had been filled with all the odds and ends that couldn't be accommodated in the trunk or the suitcase or the many bags they had.

Inside the van the guard and Matt were struggling with the large trunk that held most of the Lennox family's belongings. The guard, using one knee to give it a final nudge from his van, reached for his pocket watch. Doors slammed up and down the train's length as embarking passengers settled down.

The trunk thumped onto the platform so hard that Kirsty feared for the china packed in it. She had wrapped each piece carefully in brown paper and had tried to surround it with clothing and bedding, but even so...

Backing across the platform, dragging the trunk two-handed, Matt almost fell over the perambulator. 'Someone take that damned thing out of the way,' he snapped irritably, and Caitlin bumped it aside with her hip while Alex put his parcels down on the platform and went to the other side of the trunk. Although he was lean, with scarcely a pick of flesh on him, he was strong; even so, he and his stepfather had a struggle to carry the large old trunk to the

15

exit. Watching them, Kirsty fretted about the strain Matt was putting himself under. He had been troubled with rheumatism throughout the previous winter, and to her mind he still wasn't entirely fit.

'That's too heavy for you, Matt—I'll get a porter.'

'I'll not pay good money tae a porter when I've got lads that can do the job for nothin',' he told her through gritted teeth. 'Caitlin, go and fetch Ewan!'

As she obeyed, the guard, who had disappeared into his van, emerged with a furled green flag. Throwing a swift glance along the length of the train to ensure that the new passengers were safely on board and the doors closed, he consulted his watch again and raised his whistle to lips already pursing to receive it.

Its piercing blast made Kirsty's ears ring and startled Mary into a fit of hysteria. Then, as the train began to lurch forward, a piercing scream came from the opposite platform. A woman stood there, horror etched on her face as she stared across the gap left by the departing train.

'My God,' she shrilled, 'the wean!'

The people on both platforms swung round to look in the direction of her outflung, pointing arm, then from up and down both platforms came wails and cries of anguish as the battered,

16

unattended perambulator rolled slowly but surely towards the edge of the platform, where it teetered for a breath-stopping moment before toppling over, showering the packages that had been packed carefully within its depths to right and left as it went.

It was halfway down when a small shawl-wrapped bundle soared from beneath the hood and spun into the air, shedding its covering as it went.

'The bairn! The poor wee bairn!' the woman on the opposite platform screeched.

A chorus of screams and shouts from the helpless onlookers rang out as the bundle landed on the rails with a sickening, soggy thud. The woman who had first raised the alarm collapsed into the arms of a porter, while the rest of the crowd rushed to the edges of both platforms to gaze in horror at the wreckage strewn over the tracks.

The pale, scrawny carcass of the chicken Kirsty had cooked the night before for her family's first meal in their new home lay on the cinders between the lines, its legs pointing pathetically towards the sky. Beside it the shawl it had been wrapped in for safekeeping flapped feebly in the air like a distress signal.

17

'Never,' said Matt grimly, limping along-side the cart, 'have I been so affronted! What sort of a way's that tae start a new life—makin' a spectacle of ourselves in front of everybody? And you laughin' like that.' His dark eyes scowled up at Kirsty.

'I couldn't help it,' she apologised for the third or fourth time, wishing, as the cart rumbled through Paisley Cross, that Matt had let her walk to their new home instead of insisting that she and the two little ones should travel in what he called, 'comfort'. She felt like a tinker woman, with all her worldly possessions lashed on behind her. The curved handles of the perambulator, which Alex and a porter had rescued from the railway line, nodded above the trunk as though acknowledging the glances of pedestrians on the pavement.

The cart lurched again and she slid towards the end of the bench until she was almost overhanging the drop to the street below. She clutched Fergus tightly in one arm, fearful that he might slip from her grasp, while the other arm encircled Mary who, when the cart rolled the other way, was in danger of being crushed between her mother and the silent, thickset carter.

Kirsty looked longingly over Matt's head at Alex and Ewan and Caitlin, striding along the footpath, laughing and

18

chattering together in the sunshine and looking incongruous in their thick, heavy clothing. Despite the pleasant July weather Matt had insisted on them all wearing their heavier clothes to save space in the trunk. Kirsty could feel perspiration trickling down the length of her body; she yearned to take off her long grey woollen coat and splash her face and neck with cool water, then unfasten her stays and have a good scratch.

After that she would like to make a cup of tea and sit down with it in a chair that stayed still instead of swinging and swaying and rocking like almost every seat she had occupied during that long day.

Matters were made worse when they left the Cross and started descending the short stretch of St Mirren Brae. Now the cart took on a forward tilt, and Kirsty, convinced that they were all going to topple from the bench and onto the horse's huge swinging behind, had to push the soles of her feet hard against the footboard to maintain her balance. A sudden mental picture of herself and the two youngest finishing their journey on the carthorse's back caused a bubble of laughter to spurt from between her lips. She turned it into a cough then swallowed hard, knowing that Matt would never forgive her if she started giggling again. To subdue her unseemly mirth she cast about for more sobering thoughts and found, as the brae levelled out into Causeyside Street and she began to look around the once-familiar place, that her amusement had already vanished.

She had last travelled through Causeyside Street in a tramcar, but going the other way, towards the station. It had been January, a cold, wintry day that suddenly became so real in her memory that she shivered, caught up again in the heartbreak of her mother's sudden death and the subsequent daily struggle of trying to please her father.

She had known loneliness since, before Matt had come into her life, but it hadn't matched the terrible loneliness of those days, when there had been nobody to care about her except her maternal grandfather, Alexander Jardine, and Sandy, the orphan her father had taken on as his apprentice. In the months following her mother's death they had come to care for each other, she and Sandy, both too young and naive to realise the dangers of caring too much. When Kirsty had fallen pregnant with Sandy's child her father had beaten them both, his rage so great that Sandy had had to be taken to the infirmary, more dead than alive. What had become of him Kirsty didn't know; she herself had been packed off in shame to her aunt in Stirling to await the birth of her baby, which was then to be given for adoption.

She glanced again at Alex, tall and lean, laughing as he strode along the pavement. She had known from first sight of him that she couldn't let him be taken from her and given to strangers. She had run away, fleeing with only the clothes on her back and Alex, named for her grandfather as well as for his own father, in her arms. She had been very fortunate; instead of dying with her baby in a ditch, she had found work with a kindly, childless couple willing to let the two of them live in. Five years later, she had met and married Matt Lennox, a widower with a son, Ewan, a little younger than Alex.

'Ye're away in a dream, woman!' Matt's voice jolted Kirsty back to the present and the heat of the sun through her clothes.

'What?'

'I'm askin' ye has the town changed much since ye were last here?'

'No, not much.'

He grinned up at her. 'We're goin' tae do well here, lass. I can feel it in my bones,' he said, then faced front again, tramping along the gutter by the side of the cart. He was elated—she could tell by the set of his chin and the way he held his shoulders back and his head up despite the exhaustion of the journey.

21

It was Matt who, when she had finally told him the truth about herself, had nagged her into writing to her father. She had resisted for a while, then, worn down by his insistence, had written a brief note. To her surprise Murray Galbraith had replied and in the ten years since they had exchanged a few scribbled words once a year. But to Matt's disappointment and Kirsty's relief, Murray Galbraith had not invited his daughter and her family to Paisley or expressed any interest in seeing them.

The news that he had died and had left his house and his cabinet-making business to Kirsty had come as an unwelcome shock to her. Paisley and the sad memories it held for her were locked away in her past, and she had had no desire to return to the place. But Matt had reacted angrily to her suggestion that her father's lawyer should be asked to sell the property.

'Of course we're movin' there. After all those years of workin' for other folk I'm finally gettin' the chance tae run my own business. I'd be daft tae let it slip from my fingers!'

'But you're a joiner, Matt, not a cabinet-maker.'

'What's that got tae do with it? Alex is a time-served cabinet-maker, and Ewan's only got another year tae go in the same

22

trade. I'll learn tae be the master easy enough. Now d'ye see how right I was tae put both lads tae that trade?'

He had insisted on apprenticing Alex to a cabinet-maker when the boy left school in the hope that when Murray Galbraith heard of it he would offer the boy employment.

'It would only be right for him tae take his own grandson on and make him his heir,' he had told Kirsty, and had even apprenticed his own son, Ewan, to a cabinet-maker a year later. But to his disappointment, no invitation had come from Paisley. Secretly, Kirsty had been relieved, horrified by the prospect of her Alex suffering under his grandfather's domination as she herself had.

Now, though, just as Alex had finished serving his time, and Ewan had gone into his final year's apprenticeship, Matt had got his reward, she thought sadly. Just then he started sniffing the air. 'What's that smell?'

On the pavement, Alex and Ewan and Caitlin were also sniffing, their brows furrowed as they tried to identify the sweet, tangy, mouth-watering smell. To Kirsty, lifting her face to the sun, it was part of the smell of childhood. She felt her lips curve in a smile. 'It's Robertson's marmalade factory in

23

the Neilston Road. That's Canal Street Station we're just passing—Causeyside Street turns into Neilston Road at the turning just ahead.'

'D'ye tell me? Marmalade?' Matt said, fascinated, and sniffed again. 'It makes me feel hungry. I'll be glad tae get somethin' in my belly.'

They had almost reached the wide junction where Causeyside Street gave way to Neilston Road, with Espedair Street off to the left and Stevenson Street and Calside coming in from the right. The carter pulled on the reins and as the horse swung round into Espedair Street the happy memories the rich aroma of orange marmalade had brought to Kirsty fled at the sight of the tobacconist's shop on the corner. It looked as it always had, but surely, she thought fearfully, Mrs Laidlaw, the scourge of the local children, couldn't still be behind the counter? The perspiration chilled on her at the mere thought of the woman, with the cold merciless eyes that had recognised sixteen-year-old Kirsty's pregnancy even before she knew of it herself and the vicious tongue that had given the news to Kirsty's father even as she and Sandy had feverishly been making plans to run away together.

'Mam, I want to go home,' Mary whimpered. 'I want a drink of water.'

24

Kirsty pushed her fears aside, reminding herself that even if Mrs Laidlaw was still alive, she herself was a grown woman now, not to be intimidated, and she used a corner of her shawl to wipe the sheen of sweat from her daughter's upturned face.

'We are home, pet. See—there's our new house, the one with the pend at the far side.'

A strip of board was fastened above the pend, the writing on it so faded by time and weather that it was impossible to read unless you stood as close as possible. But Kirsty knew that the faint lettering said, 'M. Galbraith, Cabinet-Maker.'

Even after all those years everything was so startlingly familiar that she wouldn't have been surprised if her father had appeared at the mouth of the pend, wearing his sacking apron with its big pocket for tools, and ordered her to stop dawdling and make his dinner.

# 2

The cart stopped and Alex produced the key from his pocket while Caitlin reached up to take the baby. Kirsty had been holding Fergus for so long that when she handed him down to her daughter she felt oddly unbalanced.

Matt whistled softly as he surveyed the two-storey building. 'It's finer than we're used tae.'

'Are yez goin' tae take all day?' the carter asked from above their heads, and Matt, prodded into action, started barking orders at his family while Kirsty, clutching Mary's hand, went into the house. A waft of stale air, still bearing a hint of her father's strong pipe tobacco, met her in the narrow hall. She hesitated, and Matt, following behind with the roped, handleless suitcase in his arms, said impatiently, 'Let's inside, for any favour. The sooner we bring everythin' in the sooner the carter can get away.'

He nudged the case against her bottom, urging her towards the foot of the stairs.

'I want a drink of water,' Mary whined again, and Kirsty led her past the stairs and into the small, dark kitchen. Alex and Caitlin had brought some of the dishes with them and had unpacked them; Kirsty found a cup and filled it from the tap over the sink. Mary buried her small face in it, drinking deeply and noisily as Kirsty looked around.

This was where it had happened. This was where her father, fresh from hearing her secret from Mrs Laidlaw, had slammed his way into the house and started beating her to make her tell him who had fathered the child she carried. She turned blindly to the door, wanting only to escape back into the street, and came face to face with Caitlin, who was carrying Fergus in at arm's length, her nose wrinkled against the strong smell of urine.

'He's wringing wet—and he stinks!'

The sight of her daughter, and of the baby dangling in midair blinking, his round little face still crumpled with sleep, calmed Kirsty. 'So did you when you were his age.' She took the baby and followed Caitlin out of the kitchen and into the front parlour.

'It's awful dark in here!'

'My mother used it for special occasions, and she kept the curtains drawn so's the sun wouldn't fade the carpet and the furniture.'

'I couldn't be doing with that.' Caitlin wrestled with the window shutters. 'When I'm grown up and married I'll let the sun flood in whenever it chooses. And if it spoils the furniture, I'll buy more.' The stiff shutters finally submitted to her impatient young hands and let the July daylight grope its way through the dirty windows. Caitlin looked about and again wrinkled her nose, this time against the air of neglect about the room. 'Let's go upstairs.'

In the main bedroom the double bed

had been stripped and the sagging mattress and two yellowed pillows looked naked and obscene without covering. They would have to be replaced tomorrow, Kirsty thought, shivering at the prospect of spending the night on the mattress her parents had once used.

'Alex and Ewan'll have the room across the passageway, and you and Mary can have the wee room over the pend. It used to be mine,' Kirsty added, remembering how much she had loved that room, especially in the mornings when she had lain snugly in bed listening to the clatter of hooves and the rumble of iron-shod wheels as a cart passed through the pend below on its way to or from the workshop at the end of the yard.

Caitlin had put their own sheets and pillowcases on the washstand. Kirsty put Fergus, now struggling in her arms, down on the floor to crawl and made up the bed swiftly, then went to the window, which was thick with dirt. With childish pleasure she wrote her name in the grime, then added 'Lennox' to make it clear to the house and the street that although she might have left the town in disgrace, she had returned as a wife and mother, a match for Mrs Laidlaw and others of her ilk.

She heard the trunk thump onto the

hall floor, then the boys' feet thundering up the stairs and onto the small, square landing.

'We've got a real bath!' Ewan whooped. 'And a privy inside the house!'

In Falkirk they had shared an outside privy with two other families and bathed in a hip bath in front of the kitchen fire. Kirsty, who had quite forgotten about the bathroom, her mother's pride and joy, picked Fergus up and arrived in the doorway in time to hear Alex say, 'There's spiders, too.' Mary fled to her mother's skirts while Caitlin, who had been hanging over the edge of the claw-footed bath, retreated, shuddering.

'Is nobody goin' tae get some food ready?' Matt shouted from below. 'My belly thinks my throat's cut!'

Already, Kirsty thought as she went downstairs, the ghosts were being laid. Perhaps there was nothing for her to fear here after all.

The battered chicken had been rescued from the railway lines by Alex and a porter. Kirsty was doubtful about the wisdom of eating the bird after all it had been through, but Matt, brushing cinders and tiny stones from the carcass, shrugged her objections aside. 'It's not as if a train ran over it. In any case, it cost good money and I'm not lettin' it go tae waste.'

When the meal was over, they poured out of the back door to explore further. The tiny drying green resembled a small meadow, with the three metal poles that held the washing lines rising from the grass. The border where Eliza Galbraith had lovingly tended flowers as well as vegetables for the table was overrun with weeds, and the once low and well-kept hedge separating the drying green from the workyard was tall and shaggy. A stone building containing the wash-house and coal store and outside privy, now used only by the men in the workshop at the end of the yard, stood at right angles to the house.

Kirsty, with Fergus jiggling about in her arms, followed slowly as her family moved beyond the hedge to the large cobbled yard where a sturdy sawhorse stood against one wall and a great pile of timber was stacked against another to allow air to get to all the planks. At some time in the past, beyond Kirsty's memory, her father or perhaps his father before him had bought the end part of the yard belonging to the house on the other side of the pend so that the work yard could be enlarged to accommodate the delivery carts that came and went. In the L-shape thus created stood the two-storey workshop. Matt made for it at once, longing to explore his new domain. The interior, smelling strongly of glue and wood and varnish, was immaculate. The windows sparkled, and the tools were clean and oiled and well cared for, some laid out neatly on the bench, others hanging to hand on the wall. A half-made chair stood to one side, ready for the next day's work.

'We've met the journeyman—his name's Todd Paget,' Alex said. 'He's been looking after this place—and doing it well,' he added, his hands moving deftly over the tools.

'He's nice,' Caitlin put in, and Matt's mouth tightened.

'I'd as soon we'd the place tae ourselves. The four of us'll be fallin' over each other.' From the first he had criticised Murray Galbraith's stipulation that although the house and business would be owned by the daughter he hadn't seen for more than half of her life, his current journeyman should be kept on for a period of at least two years.

'It's mebbe as well to have someone here who knows the customers and the suppliers,' Kirsty said. 'I just wish the house had been as well cared for as this place.' She thought of the stained old mattress on the double bed and the dusty cushions on the shabby fireside chairs in the kitchen and shuddered. 'It'll need a deal of work.'

'We'll manage.' Matt looked around the place with satisfaction. 'Our own business!'

Kirsty saw Alex flick a glance over his shoulder at his stepfather. From the moment the lawyer's letter had arrived Matt had felt slighted at not being co-inheritor of the business. Since that day he had resolutely referred to it as 'ours' and even, on occasion, 'mine'. Kirsty had not corrected him.

A sudden rapid tattoo of feet on the floor above made her jump. Caitlin's black-stockinged legs, then the hem of her skirt, appeared on the top step of the flimsy wooden stairs at one side of the room. Her face appeared next, upside down, the ends of her silky auburn hair drifting beneath it.

'There's a wee room up here—'

'Come down at once!' Kirsty knew by Matt and Alex's surprised faces that her voice was too sharp.

'Don't fret yerself,' her husband told her as Caitlin, subdued, came down the stairs, followed by Ewan. 'If she falls it'll teach her tae be more careful the next time.'

'If she breaks her neck on these rickety stairs there won't be a next time!'

'You fuss too much.'

It wasn't fear that had prompted her sharp reaction but memories. 'I'm tired,' Kirsty said by way of apology to her family. 'We're all tired, after the travelling. We'll have an early night.'

'But there's still that other room by the pend to look at,' Caitlin protested. 'There's some strange stuff in it.'

'Let me see.' Ewan was out of the door at once, Caitlin and Alex at his heels.

'Can it not wait till the morning?' Kirsty appealed to Matt, who plucked Fergus from her arms and carried him out of the workshop.

'It won't take long. Ye want tae see the storeroom now, don't ye, my wee mannie?' he asked the baby. 'One day ye'll be workin' here along with yer brothers an' yer daddy. Lennox and Sons, eh?'

A door set in the wall of the pend led into the large storeroom that ran the full length of the dwelling house's parlour and kitchen. It was meant to be lit by two small windows, one at the front of the building, the other at the rear, but Kirsty had never seen the window shutters open. She recalled her mother telling her that in Paisley's heyday as a weaving town this very storeroom had been a weaving shop.

'There's a step down,' she suddenly remembered as her husband handed Fergus back to her and lifted the latch.

'Alex fell down it already,' Caitlin informed them with a chuckle as Matt probed about in the gloom with one foot. 'A man could twist his ankle in this place if he didnae know better. Is there a lamp?'

'There might be spiders,' Mary quavered, staying close to her mother.

'There was always a lamp on a shelf to the right of the door, and matches beside it.'

'I've got them,' Alex said almost at once, and they all blinked in the sudden spurt of flame from a struck match. Within moments the oil lamp's steady glow illuminated a collection of tables and chairs and two small chests of drawers neatly placed against one wall.

Alex ran a hand over a table. 'They're good pieces of work.'

'See.' Caitlin's voice came from the far corner. 'There's funny-looking strips of wood here, tangled up with string.'

'It's just rubbish,' Matt said dismissively.

'I don't think so.'

Carefully, Kirsty picked her way over. 'Alex, bring the lamp here,' she said, then as he obeyed, 'hold it nearer.'

'And risk settin' the place on fire?' Matt wanted to know. 'I've told ye—it's just rubbish tae be thrown out.'

'Caitlin, take the bairn.' Once Kirsty's

arms were free she stooped to examine the jumble of timbers lying against the wall, then straightened.

'It's not rubbish.' Her voice was thick with excitement and emotion. 'It's a loom. It must have been brought here from my grandfather's weaving shop in Kilbarchan.'

'A loom—like the one you told us about?' Caitlin asked excitedly. She had always loved Kirsty's stories about her grandfather's two-loom shop in Kilbarchan and the early days of her childhood playing amongst the looms while her grandfather and her mother wove cloth.

'It is the one I told you about. Look.' Kirsty dropped to her knees, heedless of the chill of the hard-packed earthen floor, and ran her hands over the timbers. 'Hold the light closer, Alex. There, on this upright—AJ. That's him—Alexander Jardine. And this rounded piece is the beam, and this narrow strip that broadens out at one end's a treadle. And that's not string—it's the web.'

'It looks like old rubbish tae me...' Matt began, then was caught unawares by a massive yawn. 'Whatever it is, ye can have a good look at it in the mornin', when the light's better,' he decreed when he got his voice back. 'Right now, I'm for my bed.'

For the time being, Fergus had to sleep in

35

his perambulator, while Caitlin and Mary squeezed together into Kirsty's old narrow bed and Alex and Ewan made do with mattresses on the floor of their room.

'We'll have to get a decent bed for the boys, and a crib for the wee one,' Kirsty said when everyone else was settled and she and Matt were finally free to go to their own bed.

'Ye can go out tomorrow and get what ye think best. Use the money we got from sellin' our own things. I told ye that'd be for the best, didn't I?'

Kirsty, anxious to sweep every trace of her father from the house, had wanted to refurnish it with the few pieces from their Falkirk home, but Matt had insisted on selling what they had, thus saving on the cost of moving.

He took his jacket off and opened the door of the big old wardrobe. 'There's still clothes in here.' His voice echoed in the wardrobe's depths. 'They must be yer father's.'

Kirsty, investigating, was enveloped in the stale smell of pipe smoke. 'It's his best Sunday suit and his winter coat. I'll sell them tomorrow.'

'That's good material.' Matt rubbed a lapel between finger and thumb. 'Ye could mebbe alter some of these things tae fit me.'

Kirsty said nothing but decided that she would find a second-hand shop first thing in the morning. She couldn't bear the thought of her husband wearing her father's clothes.

Her body almost cried out with relief as she unlaced her stays. She hated them but had no option but to wear them, for to her great sorrow Kirsty had never been slender, and motherhood had rounded and softened her body even further.

Although she was weak with fatigue she delayed the moment when she would have to lie down on her parents' bed, taking time to brush her long fair hair, hearing it crackle as she drew the brush through it. She had inherited her father's fair hair instead of her mother's rich auburn tresses, but when the light caught her hair a certain way there was just a hint of red. Murray Galbraith had had deep-brown, almost black eyes, while his wife's had been a brilliant, startling turquoise. Again, Kirsty had inherited her colouring from her father, though her eyes were lighter than his, more of a hazel shade.

Although he looked very like his true father, Alex's hair owed something to his maternal grandmother's colouring and was a deeper red than Sandy's had been. But Caitlin was the fortunate one, for she had inherited Eliza Galbraith's tresses as well as her beautiful blue-green eyes.

Matt started snoring, and Kirsty turned out the gas mantle and crept into the bed, deciding that she would replace it on the following day, no matter how much Matt might protest.

The knowledge that the very loom her grandfather had owned lay close by warmed and comforted her. Alexander Jardine had always represented warmth and love and security in her world, especially after her mother's death. She would never forgive herself for leaving Paisley without saying goodbye to him, but during her final days at home her father had turned a deaf ear to her pleas to be allowed to see the elderly weaver, and Mrs Laidlaw had cruelly given it as her opinion that, since the old man was already ill and frail, a visit from the granddaughter who had brought such shame on him would probably kill him.

Kirsty had written to her grandfather from her aunt's cold, comfortless house in Stirling. She had longed to spill out all her fear and anguish and worry about Sandy but had smothered her instincts in order to spare the old man further grief, sending only a brief explanation of why she had been sent away. She had begged his forgiveness and promised to do all she could to see him again, if he so wished.

She still had his reply and would always

treasure it, a small scrap of paper with a few words scrawled over it, assuring her that he would ask God every day to watch over her and her child. Six days after giving birth to her son, she had received a second note, this time from one of her grandfather's neighbours, telling her that he had passed away. She had taken Alex from her aunt's house on the following day.

Even if the loom couldn't be put together again, she thought as sleep began to close over her, she would keep it. As long as it existed, even in its present sad condition, her grandfather and her mother wouldn't be forgotten.

# 3

Kirsty woke to the sound of a cart rumbling along the roadway outside and the whistling of an errand boy on his rounds. Matt still slept soundly, close against her back, and the house was silent. Even Fergus, worn out by the previous day's excitements, hadn't stirred all night.

She slid quietly out of bed and gathered up her clothes then went downstairs, avoiding the treads that creaked just as she had years before in order to keep from disturbing her father when she rose to prepare his breakfast and heat his shaving water.

She could have wept at the sad picture the kitchen presented in daylight. The wooden fireplace, large table and big dresser badly needed polishing. The varnish that had once protected the two wooden fireside chairs was worn away and the spars and arms looked shabby and neglected, while the cushions were stained and torn.

In her mother's time the kitchen had been fragrant with the mingled smells of fresh baking and the promise of a good meal in the making, and the hearth had always been swept clean and the fire well tended. 'My Eliza could make a home out of four bare walls and a wooden crate,' her father had been known to say of his wife in a rare moment of affection.

After Eliza Galbraith's death Kirsty had done her best to keep the place bright and welcoming in her memory, but it was clear that once she had left her father had made no attempt to look after it.

She blinked, realising that she was staring at the corner where she had last seen Sandy, motionless on the floor, his face a mask of blood. He had burst into the room to save her from her father's rage but, thin and undernourished as he was, he had been no match for Murray Galbraith's iron-hard fists once the man realised that this was the lad who had got his daughter 'into trouble'.

Wrenching her gaze away, she was calmed by the sight of the cups and plates still lying on the big table from the previous evening's hurried meal, reminders that the past was over and the present had need of her attention.

After filling the kettle and putting it on the greasy gas cooker, she dressed swiftly before washing the dishes and resetting the table. She had brought enough oatmeal with her to make porridge—a lot of it, she decided, tossing generous handfuls of meal into the pot, since there was only enough bread for Matt. She and the children would have to make do with porridge and tea, both without milk.

The debris of the last fire her father had built still lay in the grate. Down on her knees, cleaning it out, Kirsty suddenly noticed his pipe and tobacco pouch on the little wooden table by his fireside chair. She snatched them up at once and threw them into the bucket she was using, hurriedly piling more ashes on top to hide them. If this must be her new home—and Matt was determined that it would be—she would at least remove every trace of her father from it.

Outside the morning was still and cool, the sky a soft pearly grey with a flush of warm peach over to the east heralding the sun's approach. Kirsty emptied the bucket into the big metal container that stood, as ever, against the outhouse wall, then set it down and walked through the long grass, which soaked her feet and legs and skirt with dew, and round to the yard behind the hedge. There were still ghosts to be laid, and it was best to deal with them while she was alone.

In the workshop, she went up the wooden staircase leading to the garret. Lit only by a skylight, it was a place of shadows and secrets, even on a clear morning. This was where Alex had been conceived, where she and Sandy had discovered the comfort of loving and being loved and had briefly escaped from the misery and loneliness of their lives. Standing in the middle of the room, she half expected to hear his voice saying, 'Kate,' the name that only he and her mother had given her, and to feel his bony hands, marked with the scars of his trade, drawing her down onto the pile of sacking used to protect completed furniture from harm while it awaited collection.

There was no voice, no Sandy—but there was still sacking in the corner. She knelt beside it then sat back on her heels,

42

grunting a little. She was thirty-four years old now, and the passing of time and the birth of four children had made her less agile than the sixteen-year-old she had been then. Laying a hand gently on the rough sacks, she knew from memory how they would cushion the hard floor a little if she lay on them and that if she rested her cheek against them they would smell of linseed oil and wood and dust.

'Sandy...' She shaped the name soundlessly with her lips. At first, in the long weeks and months between her last sight of him and Alex's birth, she had hoped and prayed that he had recovered from the terrible beating her father had given him and would come looking for her. But the pain of seeing day after empty day pass by without any word from him had become too much to bear, and she had let hope go. Remembering how he had looked when the passers-by she had summoned frantically from the street had carried his limp body out to the ambulance wagon, she accepted that he had probably died from his injuries.

Below her feet the workshop door opened. Kirsty froze, her mind scrabbling for the right words to explain to Matt why she was in the garret when she should be in the kitchen, seeing to his breakfast.

She must have moved slightly, for a

plank creaked beneath her foot and a voice from the workshop below said sharply, 'Who's there?'

It wasn't a voice she knew. The journeyman must have arrived.

'It's only me,' she called back, hurrying to the top of the steps, embarrassed at being caught. The man in the workshop was tall and well-built, with smoky grey eyes looking up at her from under a thatch of dark-brown hair.

'I'm Kirsty Lennox,' she said from halfway down the stairs. 'I was just looking round. You'll be Todd Paget.'

His face was lit by a smile, and his hand, hard and calloused from work, clasped hers firmly for a few seconds as she stepped off the final tread. 'I met yer lad Alex yesterday—and his sister.'

'They said. Have you been managing on your own since...' she paused, then said carefully, 'my father's death?' The word, rarely spoken aloud since she had last seen her father, felt alien in her mouth.

'Aye, mistress.' Like many local people, he still used the old title when addressing a woman. 'There were some orders that had tae be seen tae, so the lawyer told me tae keep workin'. There's more orders come in since.'

'You've kept the place neat.'

He glanced round the workshop. 'It's

a good wee business, Mistress Galb—
Lennox.'

'The old loom in the store by the pend
—when did that come here?'

'It was there when I started as an
apprentice. Mr Galbraith talked of throwin'
it out, but he never got around tae it.'

Kirsty nodded, then remembered her
domestic duties. 'I must get back to the
house. Come to the kitchen in a wee while
for a cup of tea and meet my husband and
my sons,' she invited, and he ducked his
head in agreement.

'I left some kindlin' by the back door
yesterday, and there's wood waitin' tae be
chopped in a corner of the yard. I'll see
tae it now and bring it tae the house.'

She found the neat bundle tucked into
a corner by the door and carried it into
the kitchen, then dealt with the neglected
kettle, which was filling the place with
steam. Footsteps and voices could be heard
overhead, followed, just as Alex and Ewan
came down the stairs and into the room,
by the panic-stricken wail of a baby newly
wakened to find himself in an unfamiliar
place.

Leaving the boys to see to the porridge
and the fire, Kirsty went up to the bedroom
where Caitlin, still in her nightdress, walked
up and down with Fergus roaring over
her shoulder, outraged tears pouring down

45

his scarlet face. Mary trudged by her sister's side, clutching a fistful of Caitlin's nightdress, still unsure of the house and unwilling to venture downstairs on her own, while Matt, in shirt and trousers, sat on the side of the bed, seemingly oblivious to the noise, carefully turning one of his socks the right way out.

'Here—I'll take him.' Kirsty laid the baby over her own shoulder and the roars eased to a damp wail, then stopped as she sat by Matt's side, unfastening her blouse and easing her petticoat down to give Fergus's hungry mouth access to her breast. 'Caitlin, get yourself and Mary dressed then see to the breakfast. Todd Paget's coming in for a cup of tea.'

'The journeyman? Comin' in for a cup of tea?' Matt propped one ankle against the other knee so that he could pull on his sock. 'Is the man a worker or an honoured guest?'

'I met him in the back yard,' Kirsty said glibly. She couldn't tell the truth, for then he would have wanted to know why she had been in the workshop instead of in the kitchen, getting the breakfast ready. 'I thought he might as well come in and meet everyone. It'll not be happening every morning.'

'I should hope not.' He dusted the sole of his foot before reaching for the second sock. There had always been something about her husband's long naked feet, narrow and pale skinned with delicate toes, that pulled at Kirsty's heartstrings. They were the most vulnerable part of him, not rugged like his face, or calloused like his hands or muscular like his lean body.

'We'll have to go and see the lawyer,' she remembered. 'We'll do that this afternoon—that'll give me time to brush your good clothes and iron a shirt.'

Matt slid his feet into his boots and stood up, stamping hard on the floorboards as he always did to settle his feet in place before tying the laces. 'I'd best get downstairs, then, and be ready tae meet this man.'

Kirsty had fed and dressed Fergus and gone down to the kitchen before Todd Paget arrived. 'I left a pile of logs in the store for ye, mistress. Any time ye need more, just let me know.'

He had removed his canvas work apron with its tool pocket and donned his cap for the short journey between the workshop and the house. As soon as he stepped indoors he took the cap off, rolling it up and twisting it between his hands.

Matt didn't get up or offer his hand to his new employee. He eyed the young man thoughtfully from where he sat, then said shortly, 'Sit down. The wife'll give ye some tea.'

Todd nodded his thanks as Kirsty put a cup before him. 'We've no milk,' she apologised. 'I'll have to get some provisions in.'

'Ach, it's no hardship,' Matt said brusquely. 'Milk's for bairns.' Startled, she looked along the table at him then realised, from the way he gripped the handle of his knife as he scraped the last of the margarine on to the last slice of bread, that he was as tense and nervous as the young man facing him. Matt had never been an employer before, and at that moment he was floundering in deep water.

Alex and Ewan had no such problems. By the time the four men went off to the workshop the two of them were talking easily with Todd, while Matt, working hard at being a master, was still aloof.

Once they had gone Kirsty started making plans. The whole house needed cleaning, Alex and Ewan needed a new bed, Fergus would have to have a proper cot—the list grew as she moved from room to room, leaving Caitlin, always reliable, to wash the dishes and see to Mary and Fergus.

The large drawer beneath the wardrobe was filled with spare sheets and blankets, just as her mother had left them. Kirsty spread a sheet over the bed then emptied the contents of the wardrobe onto it, the smell of stale pipe smoke almost choking her. She tossed all her father's clothing on to the sheet then she knotted its corners together, just as determined as she had been the night before that she wasn't going to let Matt wear clothes that had been on her father's back.

Kirsty's best friend at school had been Jean Chisholm. Jean's widowed mother had owned a second-hand clothes shop in Causeyside Street, and to Kirsty's surprise the shop was still there. When she lifted the bundle of clothing from the perambulator and went in it was like stepping back into the past. The same cracked bell gave a flat clang as the door opened, and she remembered the one step down into the dim interior. Even the clothes hanging on the walls and the overflowing boxes left on the floor for customers to hunt through seemed to be the same.

'Yes?' A woman hovered in the shadows behind the wooden counter, itself covered with clothing. It wasn't Mrs Chisholm, who had been elderly when Kirsty knew her.

'I was wondering,' she negotiated her way between boxes and put her bundle down on top of the things already on the counter, 'if you'd be interested in these?'

'Mmm.' The hands that sorted through Murray Galbraith's clothing wore woollen gloves with the fingers cut off at the knuckles. The shopkeeper was smaller than Kirsty, and with her head bent over the bundle, all Kirsty could see was the top of a felt turban pulled well down over the woman's hair. 'I don't usually deal with men's clothing. What price would you be lookin' for?'

She glanced up, fixing large brown myopic eyes on her customer. With a sudden stab of astonishment, Kirsty recognised her.

'Jean? Jean Chisholm?'

'Aye, that's me. Who wants tae know?'

'I'm Kirsty Len—Kirsty Galbraith. D'you mind me?'

'Kirsty?' Jean Chisholm stared, then scuttled around the end of the counter, moving with a familiar rolling gait. Her body was solid and quite squat, her legs bowed. Jean had had rickets as an infant and would carry the legacy to her grave. She peered up at Kirsty, then her round face broke into a wide grin. 'Kirsty Galbraith, back in Paisley at last!'

'It's Kirsty Lennox now.'

'You got married? I thought you would, for you were a bonny lass. I was that upset

50

when you left without a word,' Jean said. 'Your father said you'd tae go and look after an aunt, but he never said when you were comin' home again. D'you have any weans?'

'Five—though one of them's my stepson. The youngest's outside in his pram.' Kirsty beamed down at her former friend. 'Oh, Jean, I'm so glad you're still here!'

'Where else would I be? I took over the shop when my mam died five years back, and I still live upstairs. Where've you been? Are you back tae stay?'

'I've been living in Falkirk. My father left the house and the business to me, so we've moved to Paisley.'

'Let me see the bairn.' Jean waddled towards the door. 'Oh, he's bonny,' she crooned a moment later, bending over Fergus, asleep in his perambulator. 'Like a wee angel! Come and have a cup of tea and tell me what's been happenin' tae you.'

'I haven't time,' Kirsty said regretfully, following her friend back into the shop. 'I've got things to buy for the house, but I'll be back as soon as I can.'

She left Jean's shop equipped with advice on the best second-hand furniture shops to visit, and a suspicion that Jean had paid her more for her father's clothes than she would have given a stranger. Promising herself that she would make it up to the woman for her kindness when she could, she set off along Causeyside Street.

Half an hour later she turned towards home, well pleased with her purchases. She had bought a cot and bedsteads, complete with mattresses. None of her purchases was new, but everything was in good condition. And there was just enough money left to buy some pipe tobacco for Matt.

She hesitated, tempted to go back down Causeyside Street in search of a tobacconist's, then gripped the perambulator handles and advanced on the corner shop. It was time to lay another ghost to rest.

The name 'Laidlaw' was still over the door and the interior of this shop, too, was just as she remembered it, but to Kirsty's relief the young woman behind the counter looked nothing like old Mrs Laidlaw.

She was breathtakingly beautiful; beneath arched brows her eyes were a clear, pale green, with an almost Eastern slant to them. Her glossy black hair was drawn back to lie in a coiled plait at the nape of a long, slender neck, and her skin was creamily flawless. When Kirsty went in, the girl was dealing with a male customer, laughing up at him. The hands wrapping the man's purchase were small and dainty, the nails perfectly rounded. She watched him leave the shop before turning to Kirsty, the smile vanishing as though it had never been.

'Yes?' she asked crisply.

Kirsty scanned the shelves and saw Matt's favourite pipe tobacco. The girl unwrapped the solid black cake and put it on the chopping board Kirsty had always admired.

As she handed over the money she summoned the strength to say casually, 'Old Mrs Laidlaw used to run this shop, didn't she?'

'My grandmother.' The girl rattled the coins into a drawer and picked out change. 'She died a while back.' Then, as a wave of relief broke over Kirsty at the news, 'My father owns the shop now.'

Kirsty looked closely at her, remembering the pretty little girl, the joy of Mrs Laidlaw's life, who had often been in the shop when she went in to buy her father's tobacco. 'You're never Beth, are you?'

One perfect eyebrow was raised in cool surprise. 'I am.'

'I mind you as a wee girl, when I lived across the road. My father was Murray Galbraith,' Kirsty explained.

The girl's head snapped up and for the first time she looked fully at Kirsty. The eyes that had smiled at the last customer were hard and cold, and so was her voice when she said, 'Is there anything else?'

Outside Fergus wakened and gave a loud impatient wail. 'Nothing else,' Kirsty said, and left, suddenly chilled by the girl's attitude. Bumping the perambulator across the cobbled street and onto the footpath, she puzzled over the coldness in the girl's lovely eyes. Surely, she thought uncomfortably, Beth Laidlaw couldn't know anything about what had happened to Kirsty all those years ago?

# 4

When she and Matt returned from their visit to the lawyer that afternoon, Kirsty enlisted Caitlin and Mary's help and set to work in the house. They carried all the rugs into the back yard and hung them over the clothesline, beating years of ancient dust out of them, then leaving them to air while they marched upstairs. Fergus was wedged with pillows and blankets into an empty drawer from the big cupboard in the main bedroom, and Kirsty tied a rope to the handle so that she could drag him from room to room as she worked. He clutched at the sides of the drawer as he was pulled along the oilcloth, screaming with excited laughter and well pleased with this new form of transport.

All the curtains were stiff and sticky with grime. They would have to be taken down and washed; some of them would disintegrate in the washtub, which meant that Kirsty would have to make new ones. Fortunately her father had left some money—not much, but enough to buy what was needed to make the house habitable again, if she was careful.

The lawyer hadn't had much to tell them, other than that her father had died in the Royal Alexandra Infirmary in Neilston Road. Kirsty was grateful for the information, relieved to know he hadn't died at home.

Looking through the chest of drawers in the small room over the pend, she found that everything she had had to leave behind when she was banished to Stirling—a few precious books, her favourite wooden doll, the teddy bear that had been hugged almost bald—had disappeared. Her father had stripped the house of her presence, just as she was now stripping it of his.

The room was lit by two small windows, one overlooking the street, the other overlooking the work yard. Kirsty recalled standing at that one after her mother's death, hoping to see Sandy come out of the workshop. She rested her forehead on the glass and narrowed her eyes, half convinced that if she looked hard enough she might manage to magic him into being there, glancing up at the window as he usually did and smiling at the sight of her.

'The beds have arrived,' Caitlin shrilled from downstairs, shattering the moment.

'Go and ask your father if he and Alex and Ewan can spare a few minutes to help the carter,' Kirsty called back, turning away from the window. There was work to be done.

Within a few weeks the house was well on its way to becoming a home again. Every inch of the place had been scrubbed and polished, and new curtains hung in the bedrooms.

Murray Galbraith's sign had been taken down and Alex, who had some artistic talent and enjoyed drawing and painting, made a new square board to set on the wall by the pend. Against a yellow background, 'Lennox & Sons, Cabinet-Makers' stood out in bold white edged with black. After reading about the art of decorating furniture in a book borrowed from Paisley Library, he volunteered to refurbish the shabby old fireside chairs in the kitchen, painting them a deep oyster colour and finishing each one off with a spray of intermingled flowers and leaves along the top bar of each backrest to match the new cushions Kirsty had made from a large floral-patterned skirt bought from Jean Chisholm's shop.

Kirsty was delighted with the result, for it not only gave the chairs a new lease of life but helped to brighten the kitchen. But when she suggested to Matt that some of his customers might be interested in painted furniture he huffed into his moustache then retorted, 'We make good solid furniture and that's what folk want—not fancy nonsense.'

Todd Paget, who saw the chairs when he brought in some logs for the fire, was as impressed as Kirsty had been. 'They're bonny. I know my Beth'd like somethin' like that for our house, when we get one.'

'Beth?'

'My intended,' he told her proudly. 'Ye'll have seen her, surely—she works in her father's shop at the corner.'

Kirsty gaped at him. 'You're marrying Beth Laidlaw?'

'Aye, though I cannae see what a lass like her sees in a big lump like me when she could surely have any man she chooses. There's times I have tae pinch myself tae see if I'm dreamin'.'

'That's not what I meant at all,' Kirsty hurried to assure him, though it was true that she couldn't see Beth Laidlaw's cold beauty as a match for gentle, likeable Todd. 'I just thought that you were young for marriage.'

'Young? I've just turned thirty.'

Again, she stared at him, taken aback for the second time. 'I'd thought you to be a good few years less than that.'

'So do most folk.' he said ruefully. 'My mam always said I was tryin' tae hold on tae childhood, and mebbe she was right.'

'Why don't you bring Beth here on Sunday afternoon to see the chairs?' Kirsty said on an impulse.

'Ye mean that?'

'Of course I do.' After he had gone, beaming with pleasure at the invitation, she recalled the girl's cool demeanour each time she went into the shop and wondered if she had spoken too swiftly. Then she reminded herself that the invitation had been extended for Todd's sake, not Beth's.

But on Sunday, pouring tea for her visitors in the parlour, Kirsty wished that she had never made the invitation. Beth, in a green muslin dress elaborately trimmed with primrose-yellow ribbon and small knots of artificial primroses, was cool and reserved, twitching her full skirt aside ostentatiously whenever Fergus crawled within a yard of where she sat. A wide-brimmed straw hat lavishly decorated with more artificial primroses and yellow ribbons was tipped elegantly over one eye.

She had admired the painted chairs, studying them with a gleam of avarice in eyes that matched the colour of her gown, but since then the conversation had faltered. Beth Laidlaw seemed to be more interested in the house and its furnishings than in the people who lived there, Kirsty thought, willing the hands of the clock to move faster.

Todd, dressed in his Sunday best and uncomfortable in a stiff, high-collared shirt, was perched on the edge of an upright chair, his large hands dwarfing the china cup they held. He had tried to persuade Beth to visit the workshop, but she had declined, protesting that the rutted lane was too difficult to negotiate.

Matt, horrified at the prospect of entertaining his own journeyman, had retired upstairs before the guests' arrival, leaving Kirsty to make excuses for him. At that moment, she thought enviously, he would be stretched out on the bed, enjoying the Sunday afternoon doze he usually had in his chair. Ewan and Alex had opted for a walk over the braes beyond Paisley; only Mary and Caitlin had stayed to greet the visitors. They were both fascinated by Beth's elegance and entranced at the sight of Todd in his Sunday best.

'Mary, offer Miss Laidlaw another sugar biscuit.'

Mary, who had been sitting on the floor, scrambled to her feet and very carefully lifted the plate of biscuits, mincing across the floor with small steps in order to avoid spilling her precious cargo. Beth watched her approach unsmilingly then said, when Mary arrived by her side and offered the plate, 'No, thank you.'

Mary swung round to face her mother, and the biscuits almost fell to the floor. 'She doesn't want one—and I carried them all that way, too!'

'Put the plate back on the table—and have a biscuit yourself,' Kirsty said hurriedly, then, to Beth, 'and when do you and Todd hope to marry?'

For some reason the question appeared to offend the girl. Her chin came up sharply and as she opened her mouth to speak, Todd, shifting uncomfortably on the edge of his chair, broke in, 'Mebbe next year. We're savin' towards gettin' someplace to live.'

Beth's green eyes shot a cold look at him, and he freed one hand from the saucer he clutched so that he could run a finger round his collar to ease the pressure on his neck.

'What sort of place would you like?'

Kirsty asked, and was taken aback when Beth retorted, 'This house would have suited us fine.'

'This house?'

'Beth...' Todd almost dropped his cup in his agitation, and Caitlin rescued it just in time.

His fiancée swept on, ignoring him. 'Did Todd not tell you that we'd hoped to live here?'

'No.' Kirsty shot a puzzled look at the journeyman, who had gone scarlet.

'When Mr Galbraith took ill it was Todd who did all the work and kept the place going.' Beth's voice managed to put a sharp edge on every word, as though flicking small knives across the room at her hostess. 'And when Todd visited him in the infirmary Mr Galbraith told him that the business was to be left to you, but he'd made sure that Todd would be kept on because of all he'd done to help.'

'Beth, will ye—'

'It's as well spoken of, Todd,' the girl snapped. 'Folk should know the truth.' Then, turning back to Kirsty, 'Mr Galbraith said that he didn't think you'd want to come back to Paisley, so Todd would probably manage the place for you and live here, in this house.'

'I see,' Kirsty said faintly. And now she did. No wonder Beth had been cold towards her—she had taken over the house that the girl had coveted as her own.

'It was only in the master's mind, Beth—I said so all along,' Todd protested to his betrothed. 'Mrs Lennox had every right tae—'

The door opened and Ewan came surging into the room, jacket and tie discarded and shirt collar open, his handsome face flushed with exercise and fresh air, and his thick brown hair tousled. At the sight of the visitors Alex, following his stepbrother, hurriedly ran a hand over his own hair and rolled his shirtsleeves down, but Ewan merely said, 'I didn't realise you still had company, Mam,' and scooped up a handful of small sugared biscuits, surveying Todd, who had scrambled to his feet, with amusement. 'You must be hot in that outfit,' he said, and stuffed the biscuits into his mouth, mumbling through them, 'any tea left?'

'Ewan, don't speak with your mouth full,' Kirsty scolded, annoyed with him but at the same time relieved that he had arrived just in time to put an end to a difficult scene.

His mouth was still full, but his blue eyes, darker than Alex's, laughed at her. Although he was only seventeen, Ewan could charm the birds from the trees if he so chose, and he knew it.

'Caitlin, go and make a fresh pot of tea—and bring two of the big cups,' Kirsty said, then, to Beth, 'you'll have to forgive my sons' sudden intrusion.'

'Not at all.' The girl rose, smiling, and advanced on Ewan, one gloved hand outstretched. 'How do you do, Mr Lennox? I thought that your painted chairs were delightful. I shall insist on having some made and decorated for me once Todd and I find a home of our own.'

He swallowed down the last of the biscuits, jerking his head in Alex's direction. 'They're not mine—he's the artist in this family.'

'Oh—I was so sure...' Her smile faltered slightly, then rallied as she withdrew her hand from his and turned to Alex. 'They're quite charming,' she said, then, picking up the half-empty plate, laughingly offered it to Ewan. 'Do have another biscuit.'

It was just like the shop, Kirsty thought, watching him grin cheekily down at her as he swept the few remaining biscuits up in one hand and tossed them into his mouth. She had seen it happen more than once on her visits to buy Matt's tobacco. When Beth was serving her, or any other woman, she was expressionless and businesslike, but let a man enter the premises and the girl immediately became charming and flirtatious.

63

It was a relief when Beth, having decided that she would like to see the workshop after all, went away with the others in attendance, leaving Kirsty on her own. Putting the empty biscuit plate on a tray with the cups, she wondered if Todd knew what he was taking on.

'I can't see what she sees in the likes of Todd,' Ewan said flatly once the visitors had gone. 'She's too lively for him.'

'That's for Todd to worry about, not you.' Alex's voice was heavy with meaning. 'She's his sweetheart.'

'I know that—no need tae fret,' Ewan said easily, a smirk playing round his mouth. Since leaving school at thirteen he had been 'walking out' with girls. Alex, who had his fair share of feminine company, had stopped bringing his girlfriends to the house because on more than one occasion they had been charmed away from his side by Ewan.

'She's very beautiful, but...I'm not sure about her,' Caitlin's voice was thoughtful. 'She's more like a doll than a person.'

'She didn't like the biscuits.' Mary was still suffering from rejection.

Ewan ruffled her hair. 'I did, pet—lucky you kept them for me. Are there any more, mam?'

On the following morning Todd came to the back door, nervously twisting his hands in his canvas apron. 'About what Beth told ye yesterday,' he began as soon as Kirsty opened the door. 'She shouldnae have—'

'It's all right, Todd. I'd no idea that my father had given you reason to think that you might live here.'

'He didn't, not really.' The man couldn't meet her eyes. 'He was failin' fast by the time he went intae the Infirmary and I didn't think seriously of anythin' he said then, though I'm grateful tae him for seein' that I was kept on. I should never have told Beth, though.'

'I can understand her disappointment when we decided to come to Paisley and spoiled your plans.'

'Ye didn't,' he said at once. 'I just wish she hadnae said anythin', after you makin' us so welcome, too.'

'Put it out of your mind, Todd. You'll get a suitable place soon, I'm sure.'

'Aye, and when we do,' he said, cheering up, 'Beth'll be wantin' some of these painted chairs. She was right taken with them.'

Watching him stride down the lane, Kirsty wondered if it was the prospect of getting the house that had prompted Beth to agree to marry him. She dismissed the thought as unfair, but it lingered. The house was certainly finer than the three small rooms she and her father occupied above the tobacconist's shop, or anything that Todd's wages could buy or rent.

Jean's shop, untidy and disorganised as it was, had turned out to be a treasure chest. As she regularly collected unwanted clothing from the big houses in the area, everything in the shop was of good quality and in good condition, though mainly old-fashioned and far too elaborate for the women who frequented the shop. During one visit, Kirsty unearthed two very large gowns, one in flowered silk, the other of fawn velvet with a voluminous waist-length cape.

'These belonged tae old Mrs Naismith,' Jean told her as the two of them spread the velvet gown out between them. It took up all the space in the shop, and little Mary stared up in wonder at the rich canopy it made above her head. 'She was that big she'd tae have a special carriage made for her with wide doors.'

Kirsty stroked the velvet. 'It's beautiful. How much d'you want for this—and the flowered silk, too?'

Jean eyed her doubtfully. 'Ye're mebbe a wee bit on the sonsy side, Kirsty, but three of you'd be lost in one of they dresses.'

'There's some lovely material there. I could make a dress for Caitlin from the silk and bonny winter coats out of the velvet for Mary and Fergus, and have plenty left over for cushions or the start of a patchwork quilt.'

'I mind you were always good with a needle—not like me. You can have them both with my blessin',' Jean said, 'for there's nob'dy round here big enough tae wear them. I only took them because I couldnae refuse. Imagine the likes of me turnin' up her nose at the chance tae get pickins from the Naismiths—they'd be fair scandalised. I'd never get as much as a rag from them or their neighbours again if I did that!'

Kirsty insisted on paying, and they haggled amiably for a few minutes before coming to an agreement.

'Would ye be lookin' for a wee sewin' job?' Jean asked, bundling the purchases into crumpled brown paper.

'I could do with the money. I'd expected to do the books for Matt the way I did them for my father, but he's insisting on seeing to them himself.' Kirsty had strong doubts about Matt's ability as a book-keeper but kept them to herself, knowing that it was his constant sense of insecurity that had made him insist on taking the books on in the first place. 'D'you know of someone looking for a sewing woman?'

'I've heard that Mrs Hamilton's sewin' woman's off tae Ayr tae look after her old father, and she's not been replaced. You mind the Hamiltons, surely—you worked there after we both left the school.'

'Is Mrs Hamilton still alive? She was a nice old lady, a good employer.'

'The one you knew's long dead. It's her son and his wife that have the house now. It might be worth yer while havin' a word with her.'

Kirsty thought it over as she walked home. With the children growing so fast and continually needing clothes and shoes, it would be useful to have some money of her own. Although Matt was a good provider he felt that he had the right to know how every penny of his money was spent, and sometimes Kirsty longed to have even a few coppers of her own to spend as she wished.

A year after Caitlin's birth Matt had been badly hurt in an accident at work, and Kirsty had had to take on a cleaning job in order to pay the rent and keep food on the table. Although the work was hard, she had enjoyed the independence and had insisted on keeping the job when

Matt was fit again, much to his annoyance. His opposition had been vindicated when Kirsty suffered a miscarriage, then a few months later, although she had stopped work by then, there had been another loss.

'Ye see?' he had harangued her each time as she lay in bed, weak from the loss of blood, 'This is what happens when ye try tae take on too much. Your place is in the house, looking after me and your bairns.'

The heartbreak of losing the children had been hard to bear. On the advice of an older and wiser neighbour, Kirsty had resorted to various ploys to avoid any further pregnancies for a year or two to give her body a chance to recover. Matt, who believed in letting nature have its way, would have been furious if he had known, but Mary's uncomplicated birth, followed, after a secretly planned wait of a few years, by Fergus's safe arrival led Kirsty to believe that she had been right to take control over her own body.

Matt would probably object again to her going out to work, but there was no danger this time. As far as Kirsty was concerned, five children between them was enough. Her child-bearing days were over.

# 5

'Mistress Lennox—what're ye doin'?' Todd Paget asked in astonishment.

Kirsty sat back on her heels. 'I'm cutting the grass,' she said, and a chirrup of agreement came from Fergus, crawling about the back yard.

Todd came in from the lane and dropped to crouch before her, putting the box he had been carrying on the ground and taking the scissors from her. 'With those?'

'The mower and the shears are all rusted.'

'Ye should have told me. I'd've oiled an' sharpened them.'

'You've got enough to do.' She had spoken to Matt once or twice about the shears, but nothing had been done. Knowing from the tension round his mouth that he was finding it hard to grasp all the facets of running his own business, she hadn't pressed him.

'I'll see tae them before I go home,' Todd said, then lunged after Fergus, crawling at surprising speed towards the lane. 'Not yet, my mannie,' he told the baby, swinging him above his head then depositing him in Kirsty's arms. 'Ye're too wee tae go out intae the world on yer' own.' He tickled Fergus's neck, then said, 'Ye should mebbe get a wee fence put up tae keep him away from the road and the work yard. I'll see tae it for ye, when I've got a minute.'

He must have arrived for work early the following morning, for when Kirsty went into the wash house to use the copper, the shears and the lawnmower were gleaming with oil and, as she discovered when she tested them cautiously with the tip of one finger, well sharpened. Todd and Ewan were alone at the bench when she went to the workshop to thank him.

'It was no bother. I brought a scythe with me, for the long grass'll have to be cut down before you do anything else. I've got a minute or two free now, I'll just start on the grass for ye.' The curved blade flashed as he lifted the scythe from a corner.

'I'll do it,' Ewan offered at once. He had served most of his time with a large and successful workshop employing quite a number of men and was finding the Paisley business restricting. He also disliked working with his father and stepbrother. 'I feel like a wee laddie when they're beside me all the time,' he had complained to Kirsty. 'I can't be myself.'

Now he reached eagerly for the scythe, his face falling when Todd shook his head.

'If ye've never used one before it could have the legs off ye, laddie—then what would Mr Lennox have tae say?'

'He'd find a low bench for me and make me work on my stumps,' Ewan muttered, scowling.

'I don't want to take you from your work,' Kirsty protested as they went up the lane.

'It'll take but a minute or two. Is the wee lad in the house?' he asked. 'This thing could cut him in two.'

'Him and Mary both, with the door latched.' She stood back as Todd took a firm two-handed grip on the scythe handle, setting his feet apart. He swung the blade smoothly along at ground level, and a swath of grass toppled and fell. A step, another swing, and more grass was laid low by the shining blade. It was fascinating to watch.

'Where did you learn to do that?'

'I've got a wee allotment,' Todd explained without breaking the rhythm of his work. 'It means I can help my sister with fresh vegetables. I bide with her and her man now that my mam and da are gone,' he explained as another strip of grass fell before the blade. 'I like tae do what I can tae pay them back for their kindness.' He had reached the far side of the patch in no time. 'There's nothin' like new tatties cooked in their jackets. I'll bring ye some if ye want.'

'That'd be kind.'

'When Beth and me get wed we'll be able tae eat our own home—'

'What's this?' Matt asked from the pend.

'I'm takin' the worst of the grass away for the mistress,' Todd told him easily, flipping the scythe around with practised ease to bring the wicked-edged blade uppermost. He ran one broad hand carefully over the metal to clear away strands of grass and nodded at the lane. 'And I'll put up a fence tae keep the bairn safe by the house now that he's gettin' around so well.'

'I'll see tae that,' Matt's voice was sharp. 'It's my concern—yours is in the workshop.'

Todd shrugged easily. 'I'd a minute while I waited for the glue pot tae heat. It'll be ready by now,' he said, and went off whistling, the scythe over his shoulder.

That night in the privacy of their room, Matt gave his wife a lecture on how employees should be treated.

'He was just trying to be helpful,' Kirsty protested. 'And that scythe made a difference to the grass.'

'But he's my journeyman.' She noticed that Matt's stiffening fingers were having some difficulty unfastening the buttons on his shirt.

'Let me do that,' she suggested, but he twitched away, in no mood to accept it. 'I can manage fine. As I was sayin', how am I expected tae keep the man's respect if my own wife treats him like one of the family?'

'I don't think Todd Paget's likely to stop respecting you that easily.'

'Just tend tae the house, Kirsty, and let me tend tae my workshop and those in it,' Matt said huffily, wrenching one of the buttons so hard that it came off and bounced against the washstand. He muttered a curse. 'The thread can't be up tae much.'

Kirsty retrieved the button. 'I'll sew it tomorrow morning.'

Her father, she thought, as she released her hair from the bun she kept it in during the day and began to brush it, had objected just like Matt when her mother had taken an interest in Sandy, fresh from the orphanage and alone in the world.

'The laddie's never known a mother or father, or a proper home,' Eliza Galbraith had protested. 'And he's that thin. If you'll just let me give him his dinner every day it'll strengthen him, then he can work all the harder for you.'

Her husband had been adamant. He would not, under any circumstances, allow his apprentice to share his table, but Eliza had finally persuaded him to let her send the occasional bowl of hot soup to Sandy in the workshop on cold days.

'Men seem to need self-respect more than women do,' she had explained to her daughter. 'Women have the comfort of knowing who and what they are, but for some reason men have to keep proving that they're men. It's best to humour them.' Then, her lovely turquoise eyes lighting up with amusement, she had added, 'And even though it means letting them win the big battles, we women can aye use the wits the good Lord gave us to make sure that we always win the wee ones.'

Eliza Galbraith was never to know it, but her efforts on behalf of the shy, undernourished apprentice had set in motion events that would reach far into the future. It was during her visits to the workshop at her mother's request, carefully negotiating the stony lane without spilling a drop of the hot soup, that Kirsty had got to know Sandy, first as a friend, then later, after Eliza's early death, as a confidant and lover.

It was strange, Kirsty thought as she put the brush down and got into bed, how even an occasional bowl of soup could alter people's lives.

Caitlin and Mary jostled for a place at

the window as the tramcar rocked its way through Paisley. Even Fergus, who normally fell asleep when in motion, sat bright-eyed on Kirsty's knee as she pointed out the handsome library and museum and, a little further along, the Coats Memorial Church.

'Look at all these steps up to the door,' Caitlin marvelled. 'I've never seen so many steps!' While Mary wanted to know, 'Why do they have a church just for coats?'

'It's named after the Coats family. They own big mills in Paisley, and they built the church—and the library and the museum. See that hill we're passing? That leads up to the John Neilson School. If you squeeze against the window and look up above the trees you can see the dome on top of it, like a porridge bowl turned upside down.'

The tram rocked through the town and out into the countryside, past the big tramcar workshop at Elderslie, then through the tiny village itself before rattling downhill into the engineering town of Johnstone.

They were fortunate; until two months before, the terminus had been in John-stone's main square, and travellers wanting to get to Kilbarchan had faced a three-mile walk. Now, much to Kirsty's relief, they were transported in comfort to the foot of Steeple Brae, the hill that linked the village's two levels.

Instead of walking up the brae, Kirsty started up a narrow, steep road off to one side. It rose a little, then levelled off into a cool, shaded lane running between the high walls bounding two small estates. At the other end of the lane, where it opened onto a green, sun-filled park, Caitlin and Mary raced ahead while Fergus chattered in a language of his own, pointing at everything with his chubby little hands. At the other side of the park the path rose again, towards double gates leading to a road. Kirsty called the girls to her, pointing at a row of neat two-storey stone houses facing the park.

'One of these houses used to belong to my grandfather. The rumbling noise comes from the stone quarry on the other side of the park.'

A few minutes later they had reached the house. The minute patch of grass in front of her grandfather's former home, the pansies edging the stone path, the rambling roses smothering the trellis by the door were just as they had been. Kirsty went up the path and, from force of habit, lifted the latch. The door swung open to reveal a long, cool, dark hall, running from front to back of the building. From behind a door halfway along the hall she could hear the steady familiar beat of looms at work, the click of the treadles beneath the weavers' feet, the rattle of the overhead harness, the rhythmic crack of shuttles speeding back and forth, carrying the warp thread.

The place and the sounds were so familiar that when Kirsty opened the door she fully expected to see her grandfather's sturdy body swaying on the saytree—the weaver's bench—his bald head shining in the sun from the window behind him. But the man at the big loom was as thin as a rake, with spiky dark hair, well dusted with grey, thick over his narrow skull.

The dark-haired girl operating the smaller of the two looms was the first to see Kirsty and the children hovering at the door. 'Faither,' she said in a soft, pretty voice, and the man looked up, then stopped work.

'Aye, lass?'

'I'm—' she stumbled over the words. 'My grandfather, Alexander Jardine—'

'You're never Mr Jardine's grandwean! Come in, come in—and welcome!' Beaming, he got to his feet.

'You knew my grandfather?'

'Knew him? I was his 'prentice once.' Like the girl, he had a soft, lilting Highland accent. 'When I became a master weaver I went back home tae work in the islands.'

He caught up a broom handle from

its place against one whitewashed wall and thumped the end of it against the ceiling. 'I'm just callin' the wife,' he explained, putting an arm about the girl, who had come to his side. 'This is Ellie, my daughter, and these'll be your own bairns.'

'There are another two at home.'

He nodded at Caitlin. 'This one's got the look o' Mr Jardine's daughter. She used tae work that wee loom when I first came here.'

'She was my mother.'

'Aye, well, she would be.' His smile faded. 'I heard she'd passed on.'

'Nineteen years ago.'

'And awful young tae be taken.'

'Now what is it, Geordie Bishop?' a voice demanded from the doorway. 'Can a body never have a minute's peace?'

'Morag, ye mind me mentionin' Mr Jardine that I was 'prentice tae? Here's his daughter and grandweans come tae visit.'

'Mentionin'?' Mrs Bishop's smile almost split her round face as she shook Kirsty's hand. Her voice had the same lilt as her husband's, and although she radiated energy, her hair, wound round her head in a long plait, was white as freshly fallen snow. 'In all the years I've kenned him Geordie's never stopped talkin' of Mr Jardine. I'm pleased to meet ye, Mrs...?'

79

'Mrs Lennox—Kirsty. I wanted the children to see where my grandfather used to live.'

'It's not changed since then,' Bishop said, 'though the loom's my own. I don't know what became of yer grandfather's.'

'It's in a storeroom at the house we're living in now,' Caitlin told him. 'But it's all broken.'

'Now that's a great pity, for a loom's only content when it's working.'

Caitlin looked puzzled. 'How does it know? It's only wood.'

'Some folk'd agree with ye, pet, but looms are more than they seem.'

'Can we see yours working?'

'To be sure ye can.' The weaver moved back to his saytree as Mary tugged at Kirsty's sleeve and said in a loud, clear whisper, 'Mam, I need to go to the privy.'

'I'll see tae the wee one,' Mrs Bishop took Fergus from Kirsty, 'while you take the lassie to the privy at the back. Then you'll come upstairs and have some refreshments.'

The kitchen above the weaving shop was warm and bright, with patchwork cushions on the armchairs by the fire and copper pans and spotless hand-painted dishes set in rows on the dresser shelves. Fergus was chewing contentedly on a crust when

Kirsty and Mary arrived, while Mrs Bishop buttered warm scones.

'My Geordie thought the world of your grandfather—and his daughter,' she said as they drank tea. 'That'd be your mother?' She fed a piece of scone to Fergus. 'He said she was always lively.'

'She was.' Kirsty thought of her parents, one brimming over with her love of life, the other dour. Perhaps folk were attracted by opposites. Perhaps that was the secret of the romance between Todd Paget and Beth Laidlaw.

'Is Ellie your only child?'

'Dear me no, she's the youngest of eight. The others are all over Scotland, all wed and with bairns of their own. She's a grand wee weaver—Geordie's pleased that she's still workin' with him.'

Fergus fell asleep and they put him on the Bishops' big bed, wedged in with pillows and cushions, then went to the weaving shop, where Caitlin was still watching the looms at work.

'Mr Bishop says he'll come to Paisley to see the broken loom,' she announced as soon as her mother appeared.

'I'd said I'd like tae have a look at it, if yer mam and da don't mind,' the old man corrected her mildly.

'I'd be very pleased if you would, Mr Bishop.' Kirsty was certain that sooner or later Matt would throw out the remains of the old loom, and she wanted to know, before it was too late, if it could be saved.

Listening to the beat of the looms, she recalled playing on that same earthen floor while her mother and grandfather worked. There were usually others in the weaving shop—local men who looked in for what her grandfather called 'a good crack'. He loved taking part in the nonstop talk and the arguments, which usually centred round politics or religion.

'My mother used to make clothes for me from the dumps—the ends of cloth that weren't needed,' she told the Bishops. 'Good, sturdy cloth it was too. It wouldn't wear out, no matter how roughly I treated it.' She laughed, memories flooding back. 'I remember telling her that I didn't want to wear dumps any more—I wanted clothes bought in shops, like the other girls at school.'

Morag chuckled. 'Ellie knows what you mean,' she said, and as her shy daughter laughed and agreed, she lifted a pile of cloth from a shelf in one corner. 'Here.' She handed the material to Caitlin, 'These are dumps. Mebbe you and your wee sister can use them to make clothes for your dollies.'

Caitlin fingered the cloth, her eyes round

with pleasure. 'Was this made on these looms?'

'Every bit of it, lass,' Geordie assured her.

A carter called to deliver pirns and collect finished cloth, and Kirsty, reminded of the passing time, announced that they must go home.

'Jamie'll take ye back tae Paisley on the cart,' Geordie Bishop said. 'Will ye not, Jamie?'

The carter nodded. 'If ye don't mind cuddlin' up beside the cloth I'm takin' over tae Barrhead.'

It was an improvement on the last time Kirsty had been on a cart, bumping uncomfortably through Paisley Cross. They were tucked snugly in among large bales of cloth, a bag filled with home-baked scones and a piece of fruit cake beside them.

'Mind and come back soon,' Mrs Bishop called from the gate, while her husband waved his pipe at the departing guests.

'Can we?' Caitlin asked as the cart jolted off.

'If you want.'

Caitlin hugged her precious cloth. 'I'd like to be a weaver when I leave school,' she said, and Kirsty put an arm around her. She herself had wanted to take up weaving, and eventually work with her grandfather, but her father had refused to consider it.

'Weaving's a dying craft,' he had said. 'Best tae go into service an' get a trainin' that'll stand ye in good stead. If ye're not fortunate enough tae find a man willin' tae marry ye,' he had added, 'there'll always be a rich woman wantin' a servin' lass.'

# 6

'It's fit for nothin' but firewood,' Matt said, indicating the ruckle of timbers and yarn lying in a pathetic heap against the store's stone wall.

Geordie Bishop stooped and put a hand on one of the wooden rollers, touching it gently, as though soothing a sick animal.

'It's worth trying to make it better, isn't it?' Caitlin asked anxiously, then, as her father gave a soft snort of derision, said, 'Mr Bishop says that looms are more like people than machines.'

'I think it'd be worth tryin' tae get it together again,' Geordie said slowly. 'There's not that many looms left, though once they numbered in their hundreds in this very town. It's a shame tae let this one go without tryin'.'

'I've no room for it in here,' Matt told him impatiently. 'I've got orders tae fill—I need the space.'

Geordie sucked on his pipe, and its tobacco fragrance floated through the air. 'There's an old weavin' shed in our back yard. It's got bits an' pieces in it, but I can clear them out easy enough.'

Caitlin's face shone. 'Could we send it there, Father?'

'One of the carters could mebbe bring it over tae Kilbarchan when he brings pirns,' the weaver went on placidly. 'He'd need payin', mind.'

'I'll see to that,' Kirsty offered.

'Father?' Caitlin went to Matt, standing before him, taking his hands in hers. 'Please?'

His face softened as he looked down into her pleading eyes. He had always had a soft spot for Caitlin, though he would have been the first to deny it. 'As long as I get it out of here, I don't care where it goes.'

'I don't know what ye think ye're at,' he grumbled to Kirsty that night, 'payin' out good money tae get a clutter of old wood taken tae Kilbarchan. Ye're daft, woman, that loom'll never work again.' He slid his nightshirt over his head, pulled his trousers off and sat on the edge of the bed, rubbing at one of his knees.

'It matters to Caitlin.' It mattered to Kirsty as well, but she kept quiet about that. 'If Mr Bishop can't restore the loom, at least she knows he tried. Is your knee sore?'

'Aye, confound the thing. I cannae understand it, it's not as if the weather's cold.'

'It'll be the rain we've had over the past few days.' Kirsty fetched the jar of wintergreen. 'That's why the west of Scotland suits textile manufacturing; the dampness in the air is good for the yarn.'

'It's not so good for folk, though,' Matt said as she knelt before him and began to rub the strong-smelling ointment into his knee, working at it until her palm burned with the friction.

'I'll wrap a piece of flannel round it to keep it warm.' The strong smell of wintergreen stung at her eyes and caught her throat as she put the lid back on the jar and washed her hands thoroughly in the basin before wrapping the flannel round his knee.

He rolled into bed with a grunt of satisfaction. 'That stuff can warm like a dram of whisky in yer belly,' he said, and was asleep and snoring before she got into bed.

In September Caitlin and Mary started

attending the South School in Neilston Road. For Caitlin, it was the beginning of her final year, while it was Mary's first taste of education. She clutched at her sister's hand as they left the house and hurried along the pavement, her plain little face set with the sheer effort of leaving babyhood behind and becoming a 'big lassie'.

Until then, Kirsty had been too busy to apply for the post of sewing woman that Jean had mentioned. On the day the schools started she walked to the Hamiltons', where she discovered to her surprise that the cook was Bessie Mac-Intosh, who had been a kitchen maid when Kirsty worked for the family. She recognised Kirsty at once and insisted on giving her a cup of tea and bringing her up to date with all that had happened since.

'I've not done all that much,' Kirsty said evasively. 'I married and raised a family—and here you are, in charge of these big kitchens!'

Bessie simpered and smoothed her apron and launched into her own story. While Kirsty had travelled along a road beset with disgrace, banishment, motherhood and marriage, Bessie had stayed on with the Hamiltons, gaining the post of cook when the only son of the house and his new bride had taken over as master and mistress.

'It's fortunate that you came when you did,' she finished. 'Another sewing woman was taken on, but she didnae suit the mistress one bit, and she's just been dismissed.'

'Is this Mrs Hamilton difficult to get on with, then?'

Bessie shrugged massive shoulders. 'She's no' easy, but ye just don't let her bother ye. If ye're good at yer job, she leaves ye alone. And as I mind, you were always the best seamstress in the class. If ye'd stayed on here, ye'd probably have been Mrs Hamilton's lady's maid by now. I'll let her know ye're wantin' a word and I'll keep the wee chap company while ye're talkin' tae her.'

The present Mrs Hamilton, plump and fussy and not at all like her late mother-in-law, who had been both elegant and serene, agreed there and then that Kirsty should spend two mornings a week in her sewing room.

'It's difficult to get good reliable servants these days, and I need someone as soon as possible. You'll be on trial, of course, for a month.'

'Yes, Mrs Hamilton.'

'The last sewing-woman claimed to be good, but she was quite impossible, and there's a lot of work waiting to be done. Can you start this week, Mrs er...?'

Her face fell when she heard that Kirsty would have to bring Fergus with her each morning.

'He's very well behaved,' Kirsty pleaded. 'He'll be no bother.'

'Well, I really do need a sewing woman. You can bring him,' Mrs Hamilton said reluctantly. 'But if he makes a noise or gets into the rest of the house, you'll have to go.'

'Daft woman,' Bessie scoffed when she heard. 'The bairn can play in the sewin' room, and if he gets tired of that, or milady's in talkin' tae ye, I'll see tae him.'

As it happened, Fergus coped with the new arrangement very well. For most of Kirsty's time at the big house he played contentedly in a corner of the room, and when he tired of that, Bessie was happy to take him into the kitchen, where she and the rest of her staff made a fuss of him. Sometimes one of the yard staff took him out to see the horses. Fergus adored animals and had no fear of them, not even the large horses that drew Mrs Hamilton's carriage. Soon he was a favourite with the entire staff, who became adept at whisking him out of sight when the master or mistress happened to appear.

Mrs Hamilton didn't believe in paying

her servants well, but even so there was enough, with what was left of the money inherited from her father, for Kirsty to buy an old sewing machine from a second-hand shop. She carried it home triumphantly, and after cleaning and oiling it she used it to make a stylish winter coat and bonnet for Mary from the huge velvet gown she had bought from Jean Chisholm's little shop. There was enough material left over to make a little coat for Fergus, too, and for two velvet cushions for the chairs in the front room. The remaining scraps were cut into shapes then sewn into a ball for Fergus, who celebrated his first birthday in November with a traditional home-made dumpling.

By that time he was toddling about the house, drunk with the sense of power that his newly learned method of transport brought. In order to curtail his travelling Kirsty knitted a harness to go round his chest and back and over his shoulders, with long reins that could be used to tether him to her sewing table when she was working at Mrs Hamilton's or, in the house or the wash house, the table leg or the leg of the deep stone sink used for rinsing clothes. If she was hanging up her washing in the back yard, she tied him to the clothes-pole furthest from the pend, for he knew that it led to the street and was continually making a bid for freedom.

'He's an adventurous one,' Jean said in the shop one day as Kirsty stopped him from making yet another dash for the door. 'He's going to grow up to be a sailor or a soldier.'

'A tinker, more like,' Kirsty said in despair.

'This is bonny enough tae grace a lord's bairn.' Jean was examining the velvet coat and bonnet Kirsty had brought in to show her. She turned the coat over in her work-reddened hands, holding it close to the window so that she could study the lining. 'Where did ye get the pattern?'

'Out of my own head. I can't afford patterns, but I've learned a lot just trying to keep all of us dressed on Matt's wages.'

'What about the other gown ye took?'

'I've not had time to start on that, now that I'm working at the Hamiltons'. It'll make a dress and jacket for Caitlin and the bits left over'll make more cushions.' Kirsty peered round the small dim shop, wishing that there was more light. 'D'you have any bits of fur I could use to trim the coat and bonnet?'

The old bell fixed above the shop door signalled a customer's entry with the toneless clack that was all it could muster. 'Have a look for yersel' in the back shop,' Jean said.

The tiny room behind the shop was crammed with boxes and bags of clothing. Kirsty began to rummage through a box while Fergus plunged into a great pile of clothes stacked in one corner.

By the time Jean came in Kirsty had found a fur stole. 'This might do. There'll be enough left over to make a nice wee muff once I've done the trimming. And I'll take this too.' After a tussle she pulled out a fawn and blue striped dress. 'I could make it over for myself.'

'Ye'd need tae take the whole thing apart.'

'That's no trouble.' Kirsty set the things aside and went to untangle Fergus, who was squalling for help after burrowing into skirts and blouses and jackets and getting lost. 'You should sort all this stuff out properly, Jean. You'd probably sell most of it if the folk could just see it. What you don't need could be sold to the ragman. It'd bring in some money and make space for the better stuff to be hung up properly.'

Jean looked round helplessly. 'I know, but there's so much of it. I don't know where to begin.'

'You'll have to make a start one day, for it'll not sort itself out. Before you give anything to the ragman you should cut off the buttons first, for some of them are bonny. They're probably expensive too. And take off any ribbons and bits of fur or lace you find,' Kirsty went on, her enthusiasm rising. 'You could put them into wee boxes in the front shop. Folk who make their own clothes would be glad to buy them.'

'It all sounds like more trouble than it's worth.'

'I'll help you,' Kirsty said without stopping to think. Jean brightened at once.

'Would ye? I could never do it all on my own—I'd not know where tae start.'

It had been a rash promise, made on the spur of the moment. Kirsty already had enough to fill her time, but her fingers itched to set the place to rights and to find any treasures that might be lurking undetected among the untidy piles of clothing.

When they started work on the back shop Kirsty began to understand why Jean had put the task off and thus let the stock get out of hand. The place was so full of clothing that there was no room to sort out what was to stay and what was to go to the ragman. Finally they resorted to tossing the contents of every box and bundle into one corner, a method that gradually cleared half the room, while creating a colourful mountain of muslins, tarlatans, flannels, taffetas, silks, bombazines and velvets against the opposite wall. The sturdier boxes were retained and the others banished into the tiny back yard.

The hours they spent together revived the close friendship they had once shared, until finally Kirsty felt comfortable enough with Jean to tell the truth about her sudden departure from Paisley. She half expected the other woman to react with shock and perhaps censure, but instead Jean said, 'I'd not have wanted tae lose a bairn if I'd been fortunate enough tae have one.' Then, an edge to her voice, she added, 'If ye ask me, yer father treated ye cruelly. Ye were little more than a bairn yersel'. I wish ye'd thought tae come tae my mother, Kirsty. I'm sure she'd have helped ye.'

'I didn't have time to think of that, but even if I had my father would have fetched me back. He'd not have wanted me to stay in Paisley, where everyone knew that I was his daughter.'

'Still,' Jean said, 'it all worked out for ye, and I'm glad ye finally found yer way back.'

It took a week to empty all the boxes. Kirsty and Fergus returned home each afternoon sneezing from the dust and fluff they had inhaled. When the first rough sorting was over, the boxes that had been retained were each assigned to a different type of garment, with RAGS crayoned on the largest. Then the two women began to dismantle the great pile of clothes, garment by garment.

Buttons were snipped from clothes deemed to be too stained, torn or worn to be of use, and at Kirsty's insistence other forms of ornamentation, such as ribbons and flowers and strips of velvet and lace were also kept back.

'We could mebbe use them to improve some of the clothes you're selling,' Kirsty told Jean when she tried to argue. She paused to mop her face and fold her sleeves back. It was a bitterly cold day in November, and chilly draughts blew into the unheated shop through the ill-fitting doors and windows, but the two of them were working so hard that perspiration stood out on their foreheads.

'I'm not in the business of improving things, Kirsty. I just take in stuff that folk don't want any more and try tae sell it tae other folk that do want it.'

A customer came in and she bustled into the front shop while Kirsty, glad of a respite, sank down onto the pile of clothing still awaiting attention. If the shop was hers, she thought, she wouldn't settle for just receiving and selling castoffs. There was surely more to running a business than that.

# 7

By the beginning of December Jean Chisholm's back shop was cleared of the tumbled mass of bundles and boxes that had annoyed Kirsty. A row of boxes against one wall held stock to be sold, and Jean was a few pounds richer, having struck a lucrative deal with one of the town's ragmen.

As far as Jean was concerned, matters could be left like that, but Kirsty, fearful of seeing the little back shop slowly fill up again, tried to persuade her to turn her attention to the shop itself.

'It's too cluttered, Jean.'

'How else dae folk know what I've got if they cannae see it?' Jean argued.

'You can always bring other things from the back shop if they ask to see more.'

They were standing together behind the counter, watching as two women picked their way through piles of clothing, tossing each rejected article aside. One of them had taken out several pretty but impractical gowns, then dropped them on the floor. Now she held a more serviceable dress up in front of her scrawny, undernourished body and asked Jean, 'D'ye think it's too big for me?'

Jean narrowed her eyes thoughtfully. 'A wee bittie, mebbe—but if ye put a belt round it and fold the sleeves back it'll do ye fine. It's good material and it'll last for a long while.'

'I suppose ye're right,' the woman said doubtfully. Kirsty knew that she was probably younger than she looked, still young enough to like pretty clothes and to want to look her best, even though she had been prematurely thrust into middle age by hard work.

'What's it for?' she asked.

'I wanted somethin' nice for the kirk on Sundays. My best frock's that worn ye could spit peas through it. It'll no' take another washin'.' The woman looked again at the dress, chewing at her lower lip, then said, 'I thought I could mebbe find somethin' in here.'

'That'll hang on you like an empty sack,' Kirsty told her bluntly and heard a sharp intake of breath from Jean. 'Here, let me look.'

Well aware that Jean was seething silently at her for throwing away a possible sale, she went through the box herself and found a sturdy cream-coloured dress. 'This'd fit better.'

Disappointment spread over the once-pretty face. 'It's awful plain, though.'

'There's a nice bit of red velvet in the back shop, enough to make a collar and put a strip of velvet down each side of the bodice—here and here, see?' Kirsty suggested, then, as interest dawned, 'Mebbe the velvet could stretch to a narrow belt and strips round the wrists and the hem. You've got a nice slim waist; a narrow belt would suit it. Come into the back shop and try the dress on while I look for the velvet.'

By the time she found it in the box of pieces saved from rejected clothes, the woman had stripped off her shabby blouse and skirt. The skinny body beneath her much-darned petticoat bore indications of the fullness it would have had if its owner had not been born into a life of drudgery and malnourishment. She had probably never had pretty clothes, Kirsty thought with compassion. She deserved one nice dress.

'Here it is.' She held the velvet up. 'There's just enough to do everything I suggested. And here are some pretty wee pearl buttons—a row of them down the velvet strips on the bodice would look bonny. Try the dress on and I'll hold the velvet against it.'

The different colours and materials went well together. Kirsty looked round in vain for a mirror, then led the customer through the shop and out onto the pavement. Jean's small-paned window was no use, but the large window in the butcher's shop next door provided quite a good reflection.

'If you sewed the velvet on here, and here...' Kirsty held the ribbon against the dress, ignoring the stares and sniggers of passers-by. The woman nodded eagerly, her face flushing with pleasure.

'It'd look braw,' she agreed. 'I'm no' a great hand at the sewin', though. I'd probably spoil it.'

'I'll do it for you—for threepence more than the price of the dress.' Kirsty already had more than enough to do, but she was eager to see what the altered dress would look like. When they had returned to the back room she ferreted around for a pair of scissors and a box of pins then started pinning the velvet to the dress.

'You could pay half now and the other half when it's finished,' she said through a mouthful of pins, 'and I'll try to have it ready next week.'

The customer was glowing when she left, but Jean's mouth was tight with annoyance.

'There was nothin' wrong with the first dress she picked out. It would've done her fine. And it was hard-wearin'.'

Kirsty was picking up the scattered clothing, grunting slightly each time she stooped. She straightened up, easing her back. 'Just because folk are poor it doesn't mean that they can't look nice, Jean. If you showed the clothes off to better advantage on rails folk wouldn't need to dig into the boxes and make such a mess.'

'Ye were never as bossy as this when we went to school together, Kirsty Galbraith!'

'I've learned an awful lot since then,' Kirsty said dryly.

The red velvet and pearl buttons made all the difference to the dress. When the young woman saw her reflection in the butcher's window a week later her stooped shoulders seemed to lift and straighten.

'It's the bonniest gown I've ever had,' she whispered, touching the velvet gently with the tip of a finger, basking in the inquisitive, interested glances of the women queueing in the shop. 'Even bonnier than my weddin' gown was!' Pleasure smoothed years of hard work and worry from her face, giving a glimpse of the pretty girl she had once been.

'You need a good mirror, Jean,' Kirsty said when the customer had departed, walking on air, her new Sunday dress in a brown paper package beneath her arm. 'It's not seemly for folk, standing on the footpath and trying to see themselves in a window reflection mixed up with cuts of meat and plucked chickens.'

'Ye should have used the window of the empty shop on the other side,' Jean told her. 'Anyway, most of the folk that come in here don't need tae try the clothes on. This isnae a dress shop.'

'It is, for the folk that live round here. Mrs Hamilton's maid sometimes brings fashion papers she's done with down to the kitchen for the servants to read, then they're thrown out. I'll ask if I can have them. We could hang them on the counter to let folk have a look through them.'

'You're going to be the ruination of me,' Jean said in despair.

While Christmas was celebrated in England, north of the border Ne'erday, the arrival of the new year, was considered to be the more important of the two festivals. To mark the family's first New Year in Paisley, Kirsty invited Jean and the Bishops to share in their New Year dinner.

'The place'll be a madhouse,' Matt grumbled when he heard her intentions. 'It's supposed tae be my holiday—I cannae

101

be doin' with all those folk in about me.'

But Kirsty was adamant. Jean had nobody else to celebrate the New Year with, and the Bishops had been good to Caitlin, who had taken to visiting the weaving shop every week to watch the looms at work, sometimes taking Mary with her. Geordie and his wife always made them welcome, and as often as not the girls returned with gifts of garden produce or home baking or pots of honey from the bee skeps Morag kept in the long back garden behind the house.

Kirsty would have liked to invite Todd as well, but that would mean asking Beth too, and she was in no hurry to repeat the experience she had gone through on the girl's last visit. She asked Jean's advice and told her what had happened during Beth's last visit.

'She always was an uppity lassie, that Beth Laidlaw,' Jean said with a disparaging sniff. 'Her grandma spoiled her, and so does her father.'

'I never see him behind the counter.'

'That's because he believes himself tae be a religious man.' Jean gave another sniff. 'He doesnae believe in drinking, gambling or smoking. He's a worshipper—he worships the Lord three times every Sunday, and worships Mammon all the time. You can laugh, but it's true. That's why he kept the shop on instead of sellin' it. But Beth works behind the counter so's his hands can stay pure. How can the lassie be anythin' else but uppity, raised by folk like her granny and her da?'

'Poor Todd! He's a decent man who deserves a good wife.'

'Beth may not be the wife you'd want for him, but she's bonny, an' sometimes men cannae see the wood for the trees. As tae invitin' her for Ne'erday dinner—I'd leave it be, Kirsty. She'll only spoil the day for the rest of us.'

With Caitlin's help, and a little assistance from Mary, Kirsty cleaned the entire house in readiness for the New Year, paying particular attention to the parlour. During her childhood the room had only been used occasionally, when her mother entertained friends to tea. But there had never been visitors at Ne'erday because Murray Galbraith, like Matt, disliked having other people in his home.

Jean was the first to arrive on the day, in her best dress of grey watered silk with a pale lilac turban in the same material covering her grey hair. The Bishops knocked on the door just as she was accepting a small glass of sherry, their arms full of gifts including pipe tobacco for Matt, who thawed noticeably as he accepted it.

Ewan had made no secret of his interest in meeting Ellie Bishop, who was his own age, but the girl's natural shyness was even more evident among strangers, and he soon gave up his attempts to start a conversation. He lapsed into a sulky silence as he saw that Alex, with his more gentle approach, fared better with the girl, and once the meal was over and everyone had settled down in the parlour, he slipped out and went off to seek the company of his own friends.

'That Bishop lassie was awful quiet,' he complained the next morning. 'Ye get more crack from our Mary than from her.'

'She's nice enough,' Alex said defensively. 'Just young, and not used to meeting folk.'

'Going tae see her again, then?' Ewan teased, and Alex flushed slightly.

'She said she'd go out walking with me next week.'

'Can I come?' Caitlin asked at once.

'No, you can't.'

'Might as well let her, since the two of you'll only be walking,' Ewan jibed, and Alex flared up.

'There's nothing wrong with just walking and talking. You should try it some time.'

'And mebbe you should try—'

'Ewan!' Kirsty said sharply, while Matt rumbled, 'That's enough—I'll not have talk like that in my house.'

Ewan laughed and shrugged, but the exchange made Kirsty feel uneasy. Although Ewan and his father were very similar, and the boy's good looks showed what Matt must have been like as a youth, their natures were completely different. Ewan was more adventurous than his father had ever been, and he certainly hadn't inherited Matt's strong views on morality.

Since coming to Paisley the youth had been restless, though he had made many friends among the young men in the area and rarely spent any of his free time at home. He liked dancing, and visiting the theatre in Smithhills, and Kirsty knew from the smell of his breath when he came home most evenings that he enjoyed a drink, though he held it well and she had never seen him the worse for it.

He was very popular with the girls. There were plenty to choose from; Coats' and Clark's huge mills mainly employed female workers of all ages, and it was a common sight, particularly at the end of the mill shifts, to see great numbers of laughing, chattering girls and women march along the streets, arm in arm, their clothes and hair flecked with white clumps of cotton from their workplace.

Recalling Alex's words and reminding herself that Ewan had reached eighteen years of age in October and was no longer a mere boy, Kirsty began to worry. If he ever got into trouble or, worse still, got a girl into trouble, Matt's fury would know no bounds.

She was glad, on reflection, that Ewan had found Ellie Bishop uninteresting.

During January the front shop was cleared and tidied and more of the clothes were hung on the walls instead of being left in boxes. Kirsty had coaxed some fashion papers from Mrs Hamilton's personal maid, and Jean insisted on boring holes in the corner of each one so that they could be hung on a string from the counter.

'Some folk round here have sticky fingers,' she explained, watching Kirsty push the string through the rough holes. 'Best not tae put temptation in their way.'

'I wish there was a bit more room. Then folk could try on the clothes.'

'God save us, Kirsty Lennox, what'll you think of next? I'm not givin' up my room upstairs for anyone, so you neednae think it!'

'I'd not expect you to. That shop next

door's still empty,' Kirsty said slowly. 'It's a shame you can't take it over.'

'Have you gone clean daft? Where would I find the money to rent another shop?'

'You could mebbe get a loan from a bank.'

'And lie awake at nights worryin' about bein' in debt—no, no,' Jean said firmly. 'I'd not consider it.'

'I suppose you're right,' Kirsty agreed, and concentrated on getting another magazine onto the string. If the shop was hers, Kirsty would have ventured to try for a loan to improve it. But it wasn't, and Jean had already given in to so many of her ideas. She resolved, since it was the start of the new year and the right time for resolutions, to guard her tongue in the future, and she cast around for a change of subject.

'There's ructions in the Hamilton house just now. The youngest daughter, Rose, is home for the holidays from that finishing school of hers, and she and her mother don't see eye to eye on anything.'

'I thought I saw the lassie at the Cross the other day. She was always the cuckoo in that nest. Tall and gangly, and dresses more like a man than a woman.'

'She likes her clothes to be plain,' Kirsty agreed. 'But that's because she's mostly outside anyway, walking or bicycling. Mrs

Hamilton's maid says that she's determined to get Miss Rose into pretty clothes now that she's almost old enough for marriage, but the lassie hates frills and ribbons.'

'Her two sisters were the pretty ones. They were both married off with no trouble, but Mrs Hamilton's goin' tae have trouble with this last one,' Jean said sagely. 'You wait and see. When does she finish that fancy school she's at?'

'In the summer. The maid says she's dreading it, for the girl'll be home all the time then. There.'

Kirsty tied several large knots in the end of the string and pulled it to make sure that it was well nailed to the counter. 'Folk'll enjoy looking through them.'

'And if they don't,' Jean said, 'the papers'll always come in useful in the privy.'

# 8

Contrary to Jean's prediction, the fashion papers attracted so much attention that she herself began to ask for more at the houses she collected clothing from. The box of bits and pieces cut from discarded clothes also proved to be popular; as often as not women who bought a dress or jacket then went on to choose ribbons or buttons or artificial flowers from the box to embellish their purchases.

Some of the women now sought Kirsty out to ask for her help in choosing clothes or her advice on alterations. Kirsty enjoyed it, and Jean no longer objected, realising that the new service offered by her friend was encouraging more women to come into the shop.

'You've got a rare way with the customers,' she said admiringly. 'You should've been a shop assistant instead of a maidservant.'

'I'd not have been able to care for Alex when we were on our own if I'd been working in a shop.'

'I suppose not, but what's meant'll no' go by, and you were meant for this sort of work.' Jean hesitated, then said tentatively, 'I don't suppose you'd be willin' tae work here with me?'

Kirsty was tempted, but common sense prevailed. She had become dependent on the little she earned at the Hamiltons', and Jean couldn't afford to match it. 'I've not got the time, what with the house and my wee sewing job.'

'Right enough, I couldnae expect you tae give that up. But mebbe you could do some sewin' if it's needed,' Jean said hopefully, 'the way you did for that woman. You could make a wee extra charge for it.'

'Ye've got enough tae dae without takin' on more,' Matt grumbled when Kirsty told him that she had agreed to Jean's suggestion.

'It'll just mean an hour each day in the shop, and I can do some of the sewing in the evenings when I'm seeing to the darning anyway.'

'If the house or the bairns suffer it'll have tae stop.'

'They'll not suffer, and neither will you.' Kirsty was determined not to let this chance slip by. To her mind, there was potential in the little second-hand clothes shop, and she was keen to develop it in any way she could.

Snow fell in early February, turning the industrial town into a different world overnight. Even the work yard was beautiful, with the piles of timber like mountains beneath a spotless white blanket and sunlight glittering on the icicles suspended from the workshop roof. Horses' hooves on the road and in the pend, where snow had been blown during the night, scarcely made a sound.

Fergus, enchanted, wanted to spend the entire day outside, and Kirsty was hard put to keep him indoors so that she could get on with her work. Another heavy snowfall came as she made the midday meal, so she filled an extra bowl with hot soup and handed it to Alex when he and his stepfather and stepbrother came in.

'Take this to the workshop for Todd before you sit down to your own meal.'

'Todd's got bread and cheese tae eat,' Matt growled as Alex, snow still clinging to his hair and eyelashes, went out again. 'There's no need for you tae feed him.'

Kirsty lifted Fergus onto her knee and started spooning soup into him. 'It's bitter cold in that workshop.'

'There's the stove that keeps the glue-pots goin'.'

'That doesn't make much difference, as you know from your rheumatics.'

'Todd's a good bit younger than me,' Matt snapped. 'He doesnae feel the cold the same.' Without thinking, he rubbed at the ache now gnawing continually at his knee joint.

'And where d'you think your rheumatism started? Working in cold shops when you were his age. One bowl of soup's not going to turn us into paupers.'

While Kirsty washed the dishes and made preparations for the evening meal, Fergus

111

clamoured to get out to run about in the soft white world.

'If you're a good laddie and play with your bricks for a minute we'll go to Auntie Jean's shop later,' Kirsty promised, settling him on the rug with his wooden blocks and making sure that the guard was secured in front of the fireplace. Gathering up some clothes to be soaked in the wash house, she hurried out of the back door before he realised what she was doing. Ignoring the howl of realisation and rage, she pulled the door shut behind her, listening for the click of the latch falling into place. The snowfall had passed, but a few flakes drifted down from the lightening sky, and the footprints she and Fergus had left that morning in the back yard had almost been obscured beneath the new fall.

Kirsty had built a fire beneath the copper that morning and the whitewashed room was pleasantly warm. Dropping the last garment into the bubbling water, Kirsty pushed it well down with the wooden tongs. As she went out again, shivering as the sudden cold hit her, she heard a cart rumble into the pend from the street and saw that the ghostly footprints beneath the previous snowfall had been replaced by a line of small, fresh hollows leading in a wide curve from the back door, now swinging open, to the pend. Even as she took in their meaning, a man's hoarse shout came from the pend and was drowned out almost at once by the shrill squeal of a frightened horse.

Kirsty, screaming Fergus's name, dropped the empty basket and started to run. A stone hidden beneath the snow tripped her and threw her to her hands and knees. Pain stabbed through her ankle as she fell. Plunging her hands into the snow to the wrist, she tried to get up, but her body had locked with cold or fright or both, and she could only crouch like an animal, screaming Fergus's name over and over again while within the hidden recesses of the pend the horse kept squealing, and the man kept shouting.

Alex and Todd Paget came running from the yard, staring into the pend at something Kirsty couldn't see and shouting, their eyes and mouths gaping wide.

Ewan followed, a hammer still clenched in one fist, with Matt limping behind as fast as he could. Ewan forced his way between the two men in front of him, his shoulder slamming into Alex and sending him flying. Kirsty, still kneeling in the snow, still screaming, heard the dull thud as his forehead collided with one of the metal poles holding the drying line.

Tossing the hammer away with such force that it clanged on the wall, dislodging stone chips as well as a shower of snow crystals, Ewan threw himself into the pend, his hands reaching forward and down towards something on the ground, something that Kirsty couldn't see. Todd leaped out of her sight too, reaching up instead of down, while Matt, panting, half fell against the wall dividing the lane from the adjoining property. Later Kirsty was to learn that the journeyman had managed to catch the terrified horse's bridle, saving Ewan, at least, from the animal's slashing ironclad hooves.

Alex lay motionless where he had fallen, a line of red blood spreading across his forehead and spilling into the white snow beneath, while Matt, his face grey and his eyes glazed with horror, cast a glance into the pend, then folded in the middle like Mary's favourite rag doll and vomited on to the dirty, slushy lane.

Matt carried Fergus's small coffin through the streets in his arms, followed by Ewan and Alex, who insisted on going although he was still white and shaken, his badly cut and bruised head bandaged.

Kirsty, following tradition, stayed at home with her daughters. Jean was with her, and Morag; Caitlin helped the two of them to prepare food for the mourners who would return to the house, while Kirsty sat by the fire, Mary huddled in her lap. She was unaware of the warmth of the coals, or the others' hushed voices or Mary's face, wet with tears, against her neck. All she could see was the windswept cemetery and the open grave, a slash of bitter black earth against the white snow. All she could hear was the thud of cold wet earth falling on the wooden casket that cradled her bairn.

She blamed herself bitterly for not crediting Fergus with the wit to open the latched door. It was clear from the way the sturdy box that housed his wooden bricks had been found lying empty on its side that the little boy had clambered onto it in order to lift the latch.

Mary whimpered, and Kirsty automatically rocked her to and fro. 'I knew he never liked being shut in the house,' she said aloud. 'I should have thought...'

'Nobody can read a bairn's mind.' Morag came to sit opposite, putting a work-worn hand over Kirsty's.

'Did you ever lose a child, Morag? I don't mean a stillbirth or a death before you got to know the wee soul, but a child you had long enough to know?'

'Two of mine went that way, hen. One from the diphtheria, the other drowned in a burn. I know how it is, and I know that ye'll survive it. My Geordie believes that looms have souls,' Morag said with a faint, affectionate smile. 'As for me, I think folk's lives are as true and as sure as patterns on the woven cloth. What's meant tae happen's already planned, and what's planned'll happen.' She got to her feet as the street door latch was lifted. From the hallway came the shuffle of feet and the subdued murmur of voices.

'Ye'll not make much sense out of what I'm sayin' for now, lassie, but one day ye'll know that I'm right. Now,' Morag lifted Mary from her mother's knee, then helped Kirsty from the chair, 'come and greet your visitors.'

In the weeks following the funeral Kirsty threw herself into work in the house, at the Hamiltons' and in Jean's shop, where she willingly took on more alteration work. She felt as though Fergus's death had somehow made it essential for her to find, or to make, new purpose in her life.

Although the house had been cleaned thoroughly when they had first moved in, she started again, first the bedrooms, then the parlour, and last, on a mild day heralding the end of winter and the arrival of spring, she dragged the chairs and rugs from the kitchen out to the drying green.

She had hung the rugs on the line and was attacking them with the carpet beater when a deep voice said from the lane, 'Aye, ye're in fine fig the day, Mrs Lennox.'

Startled, Kirsty swung round. 'It's yourself, Mr Gregg.' Embarrassed at being caught in such a mess, with her hair wisping about her face and her working apron on, she waved the beater. 'I thought I'd take advantage of the better weather and give the kitchen a good turnout.'

As a little girl, she had regarded Thomas Gregg, the merchant who had always supplied her father with timber, as a giant of a man, heavily built and loud voiced. Now, although he must have been nearing seventy, his voice still boomed, and his back was as straight as ever, though he had lost some weight and furrows had dug themselves into his face as the fat had melted from beneath the skin. She had heard that even though he was now a wealthy man he still worked alongside his employees when he had the time.

'Ye sound just like my wife—and my daughters,' he said, then, with sudden interest, asked, 'what have we here?'

Stepping off the lane, he examined the kitchen chairs, running his blunt, work-calloused fingers over the painted sprays on the back of one of them. 'That's bonny. Who did it?'

'The chairs are old, but Alex—my son—painted them and decorated them for me.'

117

'A pattern like that'd fairly brighten a room,' Gregg said thoughtfully. 'Yer man's already makin' a kitchen set for me. I think I'll ask the lad tae paint it when it's done, for I know the wife'd like fine tae have some pretty pictures like that in her kitchen. Is he asked tae do many?'

'These were done just for me, Mr Gregg. I don't think he's given a thought to decorating furniture for anyone else— though I know he'd be happy to do it for your wife,' she added hurriedly.

'Hmmm.' The man ran a hand thoughtfully over his chin, his eyes still on the chairs. 'I was hearin' recently about a big furniture exhibition comin' up in Glasgow this summer. He should exhibit some of his work in it.'

'D'you think folk would be interested?' Mr Gregg was known to be a shrewd businessman, with a good eye for anything that might make a profit.

'The womenfolk certainly would. I'll have a word with yer man—and the lad.'

The sun glanced on his bald head for a moment as he lifted his hat to her, then he strode off down the lane.

Alex was exultant when the men finished work for the day. 'Mr Gregg wants me to paint the furniture we're making for him—and put it into an exhibition!'

'What I want tae know is who put him up tae it?' Matt glowered.

'He saw our chairs in the passing. I'd put them out on the green to get room to wash the kitchen floor. Are you not pleased for Alex?' Kirsty asked.

'Pleased tae see good wood painted like a loose woman? The man's gone daft. He's a timber merchant himself; he should know better than tae encourage such nonsense.'

Alex flushed. 'It's not nonsense. I've told you, it's popular all over the world. There's no reason why we shouldn't supply it if it's what folk want.'

'If it was what folk wanted they'd ask for it—and they don't.'

Kirsty could tell that Alex was holding in his temper with an effort. When he was angry, his red hair seemed to take on added colour. Tonight it almost lit up the kitchen.

'They don't ask because they don't know we can provide it. That's why Mr Gregg wants us to put his furniture into this exhibition when it's done.'

'Where's the harm in it, Matt?' Kirsty asked, and Matt, who had been taking his jacket off, shrugged it back on again.

'I'm away out for a breath of fresh air.'

'But what about your dinner?'

119

'I'll have it when I get back.' He threw the words over his shoulder, slamming the door behind him.

Mary, who had been jumpy and suffering from nightmares since Fergus's death, burst into tears and ran to her mother, while Caitlin, who had just come in to the room, asked, 'What's Father angry about?'

Alex gave a short, mirthless laugh. 'He's angry because someone likes something that I did.'

'Alex.' Kirsty glared at him over Mary's head. 'That's no way to speak of your father!'

Alex made for the door to the hall. 'I'm only telling the truth, Mam. Nothing any of us does in that workshop pleases him!' he said, then he too stormed from the room, while Ewan, who had taken no part in the argument, asked plaintively, 'Are we never to get our dinner?'

When Mary had been soothed and soup had been ladled out, Kirsty took a bowl upstairs for Alex. He was sitting on the edge of the bed he shared with Ewan, staring at the opposite wall and clenching and unclenching his fists.

'I brought your soup, and some bread. You can come downstairs for your next course.'

He looked up at her, and for a moment,

it was like looking at Sandy. 'I don't want it.'

'Of course you do. You've put in a day's work and there's no sense in punishing your stomach just because your head's angry.'

He shrugged, but accepted the bowl and the hunk of bread.

'You should have seen his face when Mr Gregg said he wanted that furniture painted and shown to folk,' he said at last, when the edge had been taken off his hunger. 'But there was nothing he could do but agree to what the man wanted. Mam, what's wrong with a wee place like ours branching out and trying something different—something that might bring in more work?'

Kirsty thought fleetingly of Jean's shop. It seemed that she and Alex were more ambitious and adventurous than Jean or Matt. 'I don't see anything wrong with it.'

'He's not even a cabinet-maker,' Alex said through a mouthful of food. 'If he'd just be content to see to the ordering and the customers and leave the work to the rest of us we'd manage fine. But he's always poking his neb into everything we do and treating us as if he's the craftsman and we're the 'prentices. There's no reason why he should be so opposed to me decorating furniture, except that it's another skill that I have and he hasn't.' He dug the spoon into the soup again. 'Todd's as tired of his pettiness as I am. I'd not be surprised if he found work elsewhere.'

Kirsty felt a flutter of alarm. 'Todd wouldn't do that.'

'I'd not blame him if he did,' Alex said bluntly.

'Mebbe your father needs to feel important. Is that so wrong?'

Alex stuffed the last hunk of bread into his mouth. 'If he does,' he said indistinctly, 'he can't be much of a man.'

She put a hand on his arm; beneath her fingers it felt strong and hard. 'He'd be upset if he knew how you feel.'

'Would he? I'm not his blood kin, remember.'

'He never thinks of that!'

Alex gave her a long, level look. 'Lennox and Sons. It's not me he wants to take over after him, mam. It's Ewan. The thing is,' his mouth took on a wry twist, 'Ewan can't wait tae get out of that workshop. It's me that'd like to take it over one day, not him. But it's him that'll get it.'

'That can't happen.'

'Can it not?' He got up and went to the door. 'We'd best go downstairs.'

# 9

As usual, Ewan went out after his evening meal, and when he finally returned Matt was with him. The two of them had obviously met in a public house, for they were cheerful and swaggering, more like drinking companions than father and son, and the stink of alcohol was strong on their breath.

Without comment, Kirsty set out Matt's dinner, now dried out from the oven. He wolfed it down without complaint, then settled into his usual chair by the fire with his pipe and the newspaper.

'You should see the doctor about that knee,' Kirsty said later in the bedroom. The business of rubbing wintergreen into his bad knee had become a daily routine, but tonight the swelling was worse and the skin of his knee was hot against her palm. 'Is your hip as bad as ever?'

'Aye, but I'm managin'.' His hand landed on her head, trailed down over her ear and her cheek to cup her chin and raise her face to his. His open mouth, still tasting strongly of drink as well as tobacco, lingered on hers for a long time while his free hand fumbled with her blouse buttons.

She drew her head away from his. 'Matt...'

His breathing had quickened, his eyes were half closed, his mouth slack. 'Hush, bonny bird,' he whispered. He had unfastened the first two buttons, and his fingers were rough against her skin as they probed beneath her blouse and petticoat then moved lower. She heard the pop of a button giving way and felt the sudden lack of resistance in her clothing as his fingers gained their objective, curving round below her left breast, then lifting.

'No, Matt...'

He stopped mouthing at her neck and drew his head back to survey her blearily. 'Why not?' he wanted to know, a belligerent note creeping into his tone.

'It's too soon.'

'For God's sake, Kirsty, it's been more than a month. How long am I supposed tae wait? I'm a married man—I'm used tae my comforts. I cannae just go without at your whim!' He caught at her wrist, pulling her hand down, forcing it against his groin. 'Ye cannae deny that I've strong need of ye.' Beneath the nightshirt he was hard, pulsing. He buried his face in her throat, nuzzling her, his lips hot on her skin.

'At least let me put my nightdress on and get into bed.'

'An' hope I'm asleep by the time ye're ready?' he mumbled against the curve of her breasts. 'No, no, bonny bird. I know yer tricks, and ye're not tryin' them tonight.'

'But it's not seemly this way!'

'There's a ring on yer marriage finger that says whatever way I want it's seemly,' said Matt, pushing her back onto the bed, following her down, stopping her mouth with his.

When Matt finally rolled away from Kirsty he fell into a deep sleep with the suddenness of a child, his arm lying heavily across her breasts, his unshaven face scratching her neck. Carefully, Kirsty eased out from beneath his embrace and got out of bed, locating her nightdress and feeling her way downstairs in the darkness to the kitchen.

She lit the gas mantle then hastily stripped off her disordered clothing, noting that two buttons would have to be found and sewn back on before she could wear that blouse again, and slipped the nightgown over her head. Working quickly and silently, she gathered together the things she needed—a bowl of clean water, a small dish of vinegar, a towel, and the carefully cleaned sponge she kept hidden away from the family's sight. She dropped the sponge into the vinegar, then lit a candle and carried everything out into the night.

The flagstones were cold beneath her bare feet and so was the cold stone floor of the wash house. Shivering, Kirsty closed the door then set the candle by the sink and put the bowl on the flagged floor. Squatting over it, she pulled her nightdress up to her waist and sluiced herself with clean water again and again, crouching like some primitive witch in the flickering, dancing shadows. She could have used the bathroom instead of going out into the cold night air but, being unused to such a luxury, none of the family felt comfortable there. In any case, Kirsty needed, that night, to be right out of the house where her children slept and to be sure of privacy.

Finally, after dabbing herself dry, she squeezed out the vinegar-soaked sponge and inserted it into her body. It should have been put in place earlier, but there had been no warning, and no time. She could only hope that as it had protected her against unwanted pregnancy before, it could still do so.

For the present, at least, she couldn't bear the thought of conceiving and birthing, and possibly losing, another child.

'What've ye done tae yer hair?' Jean asked in surprise a week or so later. The usual loose knot at the back of Kirsty's head had gone, and instead her fair hair was rolled up all around her head and knotted loosely on top.

'I got tired of wearing it the same way. And I finished making this blouse last night,' Kirsty took her coat off to display the plain white blouse, high necked and with deep cuffs. She had tied a piece of black silk round her throat as a cravat. 'I'm going to wear it and this black skirt in the shop from now on—and I'm making a blouse and skirt like them for you.'

'I keep tellin' ye—this isnae a high-class gown shop!'

'The customers'll enjoy seeing us both look a bit smarter.'

'I'll admit that ye suit havin' yer hair piled up like that,' Jean acknowledged. 'An' the blouse is smart. Ye look very...capable.'

Kirsty eyed herself in the full-length mirror Jean had bought. The severity of the blouse and black skirt did give her an efficient air, and the new hairstyle made her hold her head high, which was all to the good.

When the spring-cleaning was over, Kirsty

still felt restless and filled with untapped energy. Turning her attention to the shop, she persuaded Jean to let her whitewash the back room, then the shop itself. She experimented, buying some red dye and stirring it into the bucket, so that the walls, took on a faint but warm blush of colour.

Once that was done, it was easy enough to coax Jean, who was impressed by the difference the whitewash made, to go with her round the pawnshops. In one they were fortunate enough to find some rails to hang dresses from, and in another they wrangled over a section of garden trellis Kirsty discovered in a corner.

'We can whitewash the outside wall and fasten this to it. Then we can hang clothes outside in the good weather,' she explained to Jean, who replied witheringly, 'What good weather? It's more often wet than dry in Paisley, summer or no'!'

'We have our good days. A few nice dresses hanging outside'll tempt folk to come in and look around,' Kirsty coaxed.

'I've got a pot of green paint ye can have for tuppence if ye buy the trellis,' offered the shopkeeper, who had been listening with interest.

'We'll take the both,' Kirsty said, while Jean groaned and raised her eyes to heaven.

The tobacconist's shop was busy when Kirsty went in. Todd Paget and Beth faced each other across the counter, while Ewan, who had recently taken to smoking a pipe, lounged at one side of the shop, idly eyeing a selection of tobaccos.

Beth's mouth was sulky, and drooped even more when she saw Kirsty, though Todd greeted her with a smile. 'I was just sayin' tae Beth, I've heard of a wee place nearby in Mary Street for rent. We're goin' tonight tae look at it.'

'We're mebbe going.' Beth sliced off a piece of Matt's favourite tobacco with a vicious slam of the knife.

'If we don't go tonight we'll mebbe lose it.'

'You don't want that to happen, Beth,' Ewan put in, and the girl shot him an irritated look.

'It's only two rooms, and Mary Street's not what I had in mind at all.'

'It'd do tae start with,' Todd said hopefully. 'We'd look for somethin' better once we were in.'

'And have to keep moving from one place to another? Where's the sense in that?'

He shuffled his feet. 'But if we find somewhere tae live, even if it's not what we really want, we could fix the weddin' date.'

'Settle for Mary Street and have the wedding,' Ewan drawled. 'I'd like to dance at a good wedding.'

'What makes you think you'd be invited?' Beth snapped at him, and he laughed and clapped Todd on the shoulder.

'We're workmates, me and Todd. He'd want me to dance at his wedding. Wouldn't you, Todd?'

'I'd want ye all tae come,' the journeyman agreed, beaming at Kirsty.

'You see? I'd wear my best clothes, Beth. I'd not shame you.'

'We'll see.' Beth spread the coins Kirsty gave her over her palm, counted them, then threw them into the brass bowls in the till drawer contemptuously.

'Ye'll meet me in Mary Street at eight o'clock, then?'

'Aye, I suppose so.' The girl shut the drawer with a bang. She asked Ewan tartly, 'Are you in here tae buy or just tae make a nuisance of yourself?'

'To buy, but I'm not sure which mixture I should use. I'm new to pipe-smoking.'

'And I don't do it at all, so there's no use in asking me, Ewan Lennox. I just sell the stuff.'

Kirsty put the small packet in her bag. 'Come away, Ewan, and stop bothering the lassie.'

'I'll come over when I've bought my

tobacco. If the old man starts his complaining, Todd, tell him I'll not be a minute.'

'I'll see tae yer basket, Mistress Lennox,' Todd offered when the two of them paused on the footpath to allow a large brewery cart piled with barrels to lumber past. He took the heavy basket and put a guiding hand beneath Kirsty's elbow as they crossed the road.

'You're quite the gentleman, Todd.'

'I got intae the way of helpin' my mam across roads, for she was near blind before she died,' he said, then added hurriedly, 'not that I'm sayin' you're old and helpless, of course.'

'Women of all ages appreciate a gentleman's assistance,' she assured him, amused. 'I'm certain that Beth does.'

'My Beth knows what's what,' he agreed proudly. 'I know Mary Street's not where she'd like tae live, but it'd be a start for us.'

'If we hadn't come to Paisley and claimed the house you'd be wed by now.'

'No, no, you've got far more right tae this place than I have.' Todd paused at the street door.

'I'll come through the pend with you,' Kirsty said. 'Todd, are you content working for us?'

131

'Of course I am. It's where I served my apprenticeship, where I've always worked.'

'Alex tells me that sometimes things can be...difficult. I'm sorry if you're finding that too.'

She hadn't mentioned Matt, but glancing up at the journeyman, she could tell by the look in his steady grey eyes that he knew what she meant. 'I'm no' complainin', Mistress Lennox,' he said. 'It must be awful hard on the master, with his hands gettin' tae be so bad. Bein' in pain all the time'd make a saint bad-tempered now and again.'

'He probably shouldn't even be in the workshop at all now, but he'll not listen to me.'

'The rheumatics might get better.'

'I don't think they will—not now.' The pain had been going on for too long, and Matt's hands were so misshapen now that Kirsty suspected that they would never improve.

'He's best left tae make the decision himsel'. It's hard for someone who's worked all their lives tae feel that they're no longer able.' Todd followed her into the kitchen and put the basket on the table. 'There ye are. We'll just have tae look out for him all we can, me and the lads,' he said as he turned back to the door. 'As for mysel', I've no mind tae leave.'

'I'm glad of that, for we need you—all of us.'

He coloured and shrugged the compliment off awkwardly. 'I'm right pleased about young Alex gettin' that order from Mister Gregg.'

'You approve of painted furniture, then?'

'I like well-made furniture, painted or not. The laddie's got a skill there, an' he deserves tae be free tae use it,' Todd said.

Watching him go past the window, Kirsty wished that Matt could realise how fortunate he was to have Todd and Alex working for him.

# 10

'I'm not wearing that!'

'You are.'

'You can't make me!'

'Indeed I can.'

'We'll see what Father says.'

'Your father,' Mrs Hamilton told her daughter icily, 'will agree with me, Rose—and he will be very cross if he hears of this disobedience. I don't know what that finishing school taught you, but it certainly isn't good manners.'

The girl's vivid blue eyes flashed. 'If you don't approve of it, you and Father should never have made me go there.'

'Rose, don't be impertinent!'

Kirsty longed to shout at both of them to be quiet and behave themselves, but instead she had to sit silently at her sewing machine, looking from one to the other of the squabbling women, one on either side of her, like a child at a Punch and Judy show.

Once, the Hamiltons' sewing room had been a quiet haven, but with Rose home for good, and on the verge of her eighteenth birthday, her mother was bent on launching the youngest, most difficult and least attractive of her daughters into society as soon as possible. Discovering that her sewing woman could do more than darn and patch and sew on buttons, Mrs Hamilton had shamelessly decided to save money by getting Kirsty to make a dress for the girl to wear at some social occasion. Since Rose and her mother could never agree on anything, Kirsty's former refuge had become a battleground.

'Look at it!' Rose scooped up the paper pattern from among the mass of pink silk lying on the cutting table and thrust it under her mother's nose. 'It's the wrong shape entirely—and the colour's dreadful!

I'm not a pink silk person. I shall look like a—a French doll!'

'Nonsense! Phemie Sanderson's Margot looked very fetching in this exact colour at her engagement party.'

Rose tossed the pattern, mercifully still intact within its packet, at her mother's feet. 'Margot Sanderson only comes up to my shoulder, Mother. And she's plump—and she has curly black hair and dimples and a silly simpering face. Of course she looked fetching, but that doesn't mean that I will!'

Mrs Hamilton made an attempt to retrieve the pattern, then realised that her girth prevented her from bending. 'Pick it up, Mrs, er, Lennox, there's a dear,' she said airily, then to her daughter, 'take off that blouse and skirt. You can't be measured in those clothes.'

'Mother...'

It was difficult for Kirsty, too, to pick up the pattern, but she managed to get to her knees, wincing as her stays dug into her ribs.

'The more you protest, the longer the task will take. For myself,' Mrs Hamilton said, ignoring the fact that it was almost time for Kirsty to go home, 'I'm willing to stand here all day, and so is Mrs, er, Lennox.'

There was a moment's silence, during

which Kirsty had to bite her tongue, then Rose said sulkily, 'Oh—if you must!'

Now that Kirsty was on her hands and knees, the hem of Mrs Hamilton's skirt swung just before her nose, and she could see the woman's fat ankles and the tops of her feet bulging over the stylish strapped shoes she wore. No wonder she always walked with little mincing steps, Kirsty thought as she groped for the pattern. Each step in those tight shoes must be agony for the woman.

Just as her fingers brushed the packet Rose's brown skirt collapsed into a pool on the floor, creating a puff of air that wafted the pattern beneath the big cupboard that held bolts of cloth and drawers full of needles and thread and thimbles and tape measures. Only a corner of the pattern was left poking out.

Rose stooped effortlessly and picked it up, then put her free hand beneath Kirsty's arm and hauled her to her feet. 'Let's get it over with,' she said in a voice heavy with gloom.

The girl was quite right, Kirsty thought as she started work while Mrs Hamilton wrote down the measurements in the tiny notebook she carried wherever she went. That pattern was all wrong for her. She was taller than fashion decreed for a young woman of her social standing, and thin to the point of gawkiness, with practically no bosom.

She held herself rigidly throughout the measuring, forcing Kirsty and her mother to move her around as though she was a jointed wooden doll. Resentment emanated from every pore. As soon as the ordeal was over she slid swiftly into her clothes then stalked from the room.

'I'll not wear it!' Her voice floated back as the door closed.

'You will!' her mother screeched after her, then said to Kirsty, 'Now then, Mrs, er, Lennox, do you think there's enough material here?'

'Yes, madam. If you don't mind, madam,' Kirsty ventured, 'it's time for me to finish for the day.'

Mrs Hamilton glanced at the clock. 'It's only ten minutes to noon!'

'When I agreed to change to three mornings instead of two, we arranged that I could go home in time to see to the midday meal for my family,' Kirsty reminded her. The woman frowned; she hated to pay servants a penny more than she had to, and at the same time insisted on getting full value for what she did pay. This meant that all members of her staff usually had to work at least five minutes over their correct time.

'Can't your family see to their own

137

meal?' suggested Mrs Hamilton, who had never in her life had to boil a kettle. 'Or eat bread and cheese?'

'My husband works hard, and he's used to eating a proper meal. That was our arrangement,' Kirsty said again, anger clenching like a fist inside her.

'Oh, very well, though I'm sure that there are plenty of sewing women who would be glad of the chance to work here without making such a fuss about stopping times!'

It was people like Mrs Hamilton, Kirsty thought as she walked home later, that caused working-class resentment towards the wealthy. The woman was shallow, selfish and had no idea of life outside her own pampered existence. In Kirsty's view it was unfair that someone like that should have so much while others, decent and honest folk like Matt or the customers who came into Jean's shop in the hope of finding something nice for themselves among other people's cast-off clothing, had to struggle all their lives simply in order to survive.

'You'll get yourself into trouble with that sort of talk, Mam,' Alex teased when on occasion she voiced such thoughts.

'But it's true! Folk that don't have to work for their money don't appreciate it.'

'And folk that do have to work for it

are supposed tae be humble and keep their thoughts to themselves,' he pointed out, while Ewan often chimed in, laughter in his voice, 'Think of the shame you'd bring on us, Mam, if you were taken off to prison for stirring working folk to rebellion!'

Waiting her turn in the grocer's, Kirsty recalled that once, when she had been particularly incensed about what she had considered to be mindless extravagance on the part of the Hamiltons, Alex had made her a paper hat like those the French revolutionaries had worn in the last century. He had painted it red, white and blue and pinned a pleated cockade in the same colours to one side. She smiled at the memory as her turn came.

'That's what I like tae see,' the bearded shopkeeper boomed as she stepped up to the counter, fumbling in her pocket for the shopping list she had written out that morning, 'a happy, smilin' customer!'

She arrived home from Jean's shop that afternoon to find a dark-haired girl hesitating before the door. As she and Kirsty came face to face the girl burst into speech.

'Are you the lady o' the house? Would ye have a wee morsel o' food for the bairns, ma'am?' Although she looked little more than a child herself, a baby was tied to her body by a shawl and a toddler clutched her hand. 'Just a crust or a bit of broken biscuit would do, for we've been walkin' all the day, and me with nothin' tae give them.'

Her voice was soft and wheedling, the words flowing in a singsong way into each other. It was a speech she repeated day after day, hour after hour, Kirsty knew, for she had heard it often enough before from the great band of tinkers that roamed the country in all seasons.

The baby stared solemnly at Kirsty with large wondering eyes, and so did the little girl, from under a thick mop of matted hair.

Matt, like Kirsty's father, strongly disapproved of encouraging tinker folk, claiming that they were shiftless and lazy. But her mother had never turned any of them away empty-handed, nor could Kirsty, especially when there were children involved.

'Wait here for a minute,' she said, and went into the house, prudently closing the front door behind her. When she opened it five minutes later the girl-woman was sitting on the scrubbed white step, the baby suckling at her breast, while the little girl squatted patiently beside her.

As soon as the door opened the tinker

readjusted her clothing and rose gracefully. The baby was clearly used to interrupted meals, for it accepted the situation without complaint, a trickle of milk at one corner of its small soft mouth. When Kirsty handed over a bag containing a few vegetables, some hastily made slices of bread and jam and a bottle of milky tea, a radiant smile lit the girl's face, revealing a gap where a tooth had fallen out, or been knocked out. 'Bless ye, lady,' she said, and began to turn away.

'Wait—could you do with some clothes for the wee ones?'

The girl's eyes narrowed for a second, then opened wide. 'I could that, lady. Ye've bairns of yer own?' The singsong plaint returned. 'Ye'll know then how hard it can be tryin' tae clothe them and them growin', growin' every day the good Lord sends.'

'Is your man nearby? Has he a cart?'

'He has, lady, in the next street, just.'

'Go and find him and tell him to fetch it here,' Kirsty said, and closed the door. She ran to the wash house, noting with relief that Mary was still playing happily with her doll in the back green, and fetched a clean sack from the pile that lay in a corner, then hurried back into the house and up the stairs. Bundling Fergus's clothes into the sack willy-nilly, she was keenly aware that part of her, like another self, was standing by and watching with horror.

Even so, everything went into the sack—the soft woollen shawl she had knitted while waiting for Fergus's birth, the larger shawl used to bind him to her body so that she could carry him about, his flannel gowns and tiny shoes, and even his toys. It was time for them to go; she knew that instinctively. Fergus would never be out of her thoughts, but the continual hard work of the months since his death had blunted the immediate pain of her loss and made it bearable. As Morag would say, Fergus had been woven into her life's pattern; he was—and always would be—part of her. Because of this she no longer needed material reminders.

Scooping the bedding from the cot, Kirsty stuffed it in on top of the clothing, then, hearing the clop of a pony's hooves in the roadway she ran downstairs to the front door, motioning to the man on the cart.

'Up here,' she said when he came to the door, and ran up the stairs before him, driven on by a fever that suddenly consumed her. 'Take that cot downstairs and put it onto your cart,' she ordered when the tinker came into the bedroom, fumbling nervously with the cap he had pulled from his black greasy hair and ill at ease within the room's confines.

Nervousness faded and avarice lit his eyes as he looked at the sturdy cot, then suspicion washed over his features. 'Are ye certain, missus? I'd no' want for the polis tae throw me intae the jail for theft because ye'd changed yer mind.'

'I'll not change my mind,' she told him impatiently. 'Will you just do as I say?' Responding automatically to the sudden snap of authority in her voice, he hurriedly moved towards the cot as she dragged the sack to the stairs, anxious, now that she had made her mind up, to get the matter over before Matt discovered what was going on and put a stop to it.

All was calm in the back yard. The sound of hammering could be heard from the workshop, and Mary, deeply involved in some game of her own making, paid no heed as Kirsty wrestled the shabby perambulator from where it had been stored in the wash house. She tossed the full sack into it before wheeling it hurriedly through the pend and out onto the pavement.

The tinker woman was waiting by the horse, her baby in her arms and the little girl clinging to her skirt. 'Where's my man?' she wanted to know anxiously.

'He'll be out in a minute. See.' With trembling fingers Kirsty pulled the mouth of the sack open. 'There's clothes for

143

the bairns, and some toys—and the perambulator too.'

The girl's eyes rounded. Just then the man struggled out of the front door, laden with the cot. Kirsty went to help him, certain that at any moment Matt would burst through the pend and make her take everything back. Her tension and sense of urgency communicated itself to the tinkers, already uneasy about her orgy of giving. They were more used to closed doors and unwelcoming faces than to having goods pressed on them.

'Missus, are ye sure?' the man said again.

'I've no need of the things now. Take them.' Kirsty swung the full sack up onto the back of the cart as she spoke, and to her relief he followed suit with the cot without any further argument.

Once everything was lashed on, he bundled his woman and their children up onto the bench and leapt up beside them.

'God bless ye, lady,' the girl said as the tired, thin horse, startled from its reverie by the sting of reins on its back, burst into action.

Watching the roped perambulator nodding and shaking as the cart rattled along the street, Kirsty suddenly remembered their own arrival a year earlier. For a moment her arms seemed to be weighted down, as they had been on that day, by Fergus's warm, solid, soggy little body, and such a rending pain came into her chest that she felt as though her very heart was struggling to tear itself loose so that it could follow her dead baby's possessions.

Then the cart made the turn that took it out of sight and the pain eased away, replaced by a great calmness and a sense of acceptance.

# 11

'Ye've done what?' Matt's voice was low, but his fury was so strong that for a moment Kirsty thought that he might strike her.

'I've given all Fergus's things to some tinker folk,' Kirsty repeated as calmly as she could. To her surprise, she had managed to keep her secret all evening, until Matt decided to go to bed. She had followed him up within the minute, to find him staring in confusion at the spot where Fergus's cot had stood that morning.

'Tinkers!' Her husband spat the word out as though it was a foul-tasting stone he had found in his mouth. 'Tinkers! How often have I told ye never tae give those scoundrels anythin'?'

'They'd two wee bairns, Matt. They were in more need of the things than we were.'

'In need?' He gave a derisive laugh. 'Ye don't think their bairns'll get the good of the things you handed over, do ye? It'll all have been sold by now tae buy drink!'

'Mebbe, and mebbe not. It's their business what they do with what I gave them. They were of no more use to us.'

'Those things belonged tae our Fergus!' She was astonished to see sudden and unexpected tears sparkling in his eyes. He turned away quickly to hide them. Matt rarely showed such signs of weakness; involuntarily, appalled by his reaction, Kirsty went to him and put her arms about him, her face pressed close to his back.

'Fergus has gone, Matt,' she said into his heavy work shirt. He turned to face her, breaking her hold, blinking rapidly and fighting against his tears.

'There'll be another bairn tae take his place.'

'No!' The word was so hard that they were both startled. 'No,' she said again, this time softly. 'No more children, Matt.'

'But we're young enough yet...'

'It's not that. I couldn't bear to lose another child.'

146

'It wouldn't happen again, pet.' He reached for her, but she stepped back.

'I mean what I say, Matt. We've still got four bairns—we should be content with that,' she said, and saw his expression change as he grasped her meaning.

'So it's like that, is it?'

'It's like that. We're not old, but we're not young either. I'll not risk another child—or myself. You shouldn't ask that of me, Matt.'

He bit his lip, thinking, then his anger began to return. 'Ye'd no right tae give the wee lad's things away!'

'I had the right. I made the clothes, and the bedding, and most of the few toys he had. I bore the bairn and I cared for him.'

'Ye werenae carin' for him that day, were ye?' Matt asked deliberately. He might as well have pushed a knife into her chest.

For a moment the pain was so strong that the breath went out of Kirsty. When it returned, she took no time to consider before she rapped back, hurting as she had been hurt, 'And if you'd put up that wee fence as you promised he might still be here!'

The blood drained from his face, and he picked up his nightshirt then went out of the room without another word.

Kirsty lowered herself carefully, like an invalid, onto the edge of the bed. She couldn't believe that after all they had been through together they could have injured each other with such deliberation and such malice. At some point during their short angry exchange, Fergus had stopped being the issue; all they had wanted to do from then on was cause pain in whatever way possible. And they had both succeeded.

Changing into her nightgown, Kirsty wished with all her heart that she had never given in to Matt's coaxing to write to her father. If she had kept silent as she had wanted and intended, Murray Galbraith wouldn't have left the house and business to her. She and Matt would still be living in Falkirk, content enough in their marriage, and Fergus would still be alive. Now, by giving away all Fergus's things, she had come to terms with her loss—and had neglected to think of Matt's loss.

When Matt finally returned from the bathroom she was in bed, pretending to be asleep.

He put the light out and she felt the mattress dip as he slid beneath the covers, settling as far away from her as he could.

The tension between the two of them the following morning seemed to permeate the house like an acrid smell. The rest of the family couldn't miss it; Caitlin was puzzled, looking from one to the other of her parents, unspoken questions in her vivid eyes, and Mary was silent and ill at ease. Ewan was indifferent, while there was concern in Alex's gaze when he looked at his mother, and censure when he looked at his stepfather.

Kirsty was glad to escape to Jean's shop in the afternoon. Walking along Causeyside Street, she remembered an ornament owned by the woman she had worked for before Matt had come into her life. It was a ball of very fine glass, sitting on a stand, a fragile thing that caught the light on its curved surface and reflected it in rainbow colours. Kirsty had loved that beautiful thing. When she lifted it carefully from its stand to dust it, it was as light as a feather within the careful cradle of her palms, almost as though it was a figment of her imagination. Today she felt strangely like it—brittle and weightless and dreamlike and fragile. In her case, though, she was certain that should she break, the shattering would release not trapped air, but a multitude of tears.

It was a warm, bright summer's day, so she set herself to hanging clothes outside the shop on the trellis, which Alex had secured to the shop frontage. When it was done she stepped back and considered it, head to one side. It looked very fine, but there was something missing.

On an impulse, Kirsty fetched an old tailor's dummy she had found during their excavation of the back shop and dressed it in an elaborate cerise and gold striped costume from among the stock. When she stood it outside the door, passers-by immediately stopped to look at it.

Jean was scandalised. 'Ye're makin' a laughin' stock of me!'

'Not a bit of it. With luck, it'll bring some of them in to see what else we have. It's attracting attention already. See?' she finished as the broken bell clacked and the door opened to admit a woman wreathed in smiles.

'I like yer new assistant,' she said blithely, 'the one standin' outside havin' a crack with all the folk.'

Jean glared. 'It's her doin', not mine,' she snapped, jerking a thumb in Kirsty's direction.

'I call her Aggie,' Kirsty informed the woman from the corner where she was sewing a new hem on a skirt.

'It's a grand idea—folks need a laugh now and again,' the woman said. 'Ye'll need tae keep an eye on her, though, or some laddie'll be runnin' off with her her bein' so bonny,' she added, going into a peal of laughter at her own wit.

'She's right,' Jean said gloomily when the woman had gone, after making a purchase. 'The wee rascals round here cannae keep their hands off anythin'. It'll disappear within the hour—and the dress, too!'

'If it does, it'll be a small loss. It's old, Jean, and not many folk round here'd want the outfit it's wearing. That's why I chose it.'

Jean looked at her closely. 'Is somethin' botherin' ye?'

'What could be bothering me?' Kirsty asked brightly. She could tell Jean a lot, but never about the destructive quarrel between herself and Matt.

'Ye're...different. It's as if ye're tryin' tae cover up bad news.'

'It's just that terrible dress I'm making for poor Rose Hamilton,' Kirsty lied. 'I'm so sorry for the girl, for she'll look a right fright at this party she's going to.'

The bell clacked again, and again, and for most of the afternoon. Every customer came in to ask about the dummy, and not one of them left empty-handed.

'Mebbe that dummy wasnae such a bad idea after all,' Jean admitted grudgingly as Kirsty brought it in before going home. 'I suppose'ye might as well put it out again tomorrow, if ye've a mind tae.'

'I'll dress her in a different outfit then.

151

Mebbe it should be something folk might want to buy.'

'And have good clothes stolen along with it when it goes?' Although the ever-changing small crowd around the dummy had kept thieves at bay, they had had to go and rescue it from barefoot, ragged urchins twice during lulls.

'I'll try to think of a way of tethering it tomorrow,' Kirsty promised.

'You might be in much better condition than poor old Aggie, and have a better pedigree than her,' Kirsty said to the dummy in the Hamiltons' sewing room the next morning, 'but I must say, milady, that she's got better taste in clothes.'

She laughed aloud, then composed herself hurriedly and set the sewing machine whirring as she heard footsteps in the corridor.

Rose Hamilton must have been out bicycling, for she wore a grey flannel skirt and mannish jacket, and a peaked cap was jammed over the brown hair. 'I thought my mother was here.'

Kirsty, sighing inwardly, stilled the machine. 'She's not been in this morning, Miss Rose.'

'Did I not hear voices as I came along the corridor?'

'No, Miss Rose,' Kirsty said blankly.

'Oh.' The girl's eyes fell on the dummy, swathed in pink silk. 'Are you still wasting your time on that?'

'Mrs Hamilton says it must be finished for next week, miss.'

'You might as well save yourself the trouble,' Rose said shortly, pulling the cap off.

'But it's nearly done, Miss Rose. I'm working on the overskirt now, then there's only the rib—'

'I—won't—wear—it!' Each word was snapped out, sharp and clear, as though she was talking to a small child, or a cretin. She had rolled her cap up and used it to underline the words by slapping it against her thigh.

'I must take my orders from your mother, Miss Rose.'

Kirsty's head began to ache, the result, she knew, of sitting in a stuffy room for two hours, watching the needle flash in and out of the material travelling beneath it.

'Here.' The girl fished in her skirt pocket and brought out a banknote. It fluttered from her hand onto the mass of silk frothing across the sewing machine table. 'This'll help you to make some sort of mistake, so that I can't possibly wear the dress.'

As Kirsty stared at the note, sudden rage at the girl's condescending audacity swept through her. It was all she could do to hold it in check. 'I don't take money I've not earned, Miss Rose.'

'You will earn it, by doing what I ask,' Rose pointed out, then, suddenly shedding her usual arrogance, 'have a heart, woman. You must know that I'll look like a—a parcel in that dress,' she said, in genuine misery. 'I'll be a laughing stock!'

Anger gave way to sympathy. The girl was right, and it was unfair of her mother to put her in such a difficult situation. 'It might be possible to do something with the gown,' Kirsty said slowly.

'The only thing anyone could do with that,' a long bony finger pointed at the dummy's finery, 'is burn it.'

'I'd something else in mind,' Kirsty said, going over to the cupboard covering one wall. Mrs Hamilton, blessed with more money than sense, was addicted to buying yards of any material that took her fancy just in case she might need it one day. Kirsty often looked longingly at the bolts of cloth that might never be used, wishing that she could have such riches in the shop.

She found the dark-blue lace she was looking for and took it to the dummy, unrolling a yard or two so that she could hold it against the skirt.

'An overdress of this lace would tone the

pink down,' she explained. 'I could do a cummerbund of the pink and a short cape of the lace round your shoulders. See...' She gathered an edge of the lace between her fingers and held it against the bodice. 'Artificial flowers in this same dark blue would look well on the bodice in place of that knot of pink ribbons. And the blue matches the colour of your eyes.'

Interest began to temper the anger in the girl's eyes. 'You're right. How clever you are.'

'I'm used to matching materials and trying to think what's best for folk. I help a friend who runs a second-hand clothes shop in the town.'

'You mean she sells clothes that have already been worn by someone else?' Rose's nose wrinkled with disgust. 'Why would anybody want to wear someone else's clothes?'

'There are plenty women in Paisley who can't afford new gowns, Miss Rose. My friend Jean sells good second-hand clothing that comes from—' Kirsty stopped suddenly, realising that she would have to choose her words carefully, 'from rich folk that don't want them any more.'

'Really?'

Aware that the girl's interest had been caught and that she was on the brink of accepting the offered compromise, Kirsty hurried on. 'Most of the clothes need to be altered to suit, so I've got used to matching materials and colours and mebbe—'

The words died in her throat as the door opened and Mrs Hamilton bustled in. 'What are you doing in here, Rose? And what,' she added sharply, taking in the dark-blue lace, 'is that?'

For once Rose was enthusiastic rather than mutinous in her mother's presence. 'Look, Mamma—an overdress of this lace would be a great improvement to the gown. Don't you think so?'

The older woman's eyes narrowed and she drew her breath in sharply. 'I most certainly do not think so! Whose idea was this?'

'Mine, Mrs Hamilton. I thought—'

'My good woman, if you had the capacity for thought, you would know that dark lace is far too mature for a girl of my daughter's age!'

The animation immediately drained from Rose's face. 'Mamma, I am not an empty-headed ninny like most of your friends' daughters. I want the overdress.'

'It would look ridiculous on you,' Mrs Hamilton snapped. She was a head smaller than her daughter and considerably rounder. Their confrontation looked almost comical, but Kirsty had no desire to laugh.

'Not as ridiculous as that will look!' Rose's outflung hand smacked against the dummy so hard that it rocked precariously on its solid circular stand. 'Mamma, you're treating me like a child, and I'm not—I'll be eighteen in September, and then I'll have my inheritance from Grandmamma and be independent.'

'That is not a subject to be discussed before servants, Rose! As you say, you can choose your own clothes once you are eighteen, but until then you will be guided by me.'

'I will not wear that nasty, ugly dress, and you can't make me!' In her rage and frustration the girl was rapidly reverting to nursery behaviour. Her mother immediately reacted in the same way and began to treat her like a child.

'Go to your room and change for luncheon. You look like a—a hobbledehoy!'

For a moment it looked as though Rose was going to refuse, then she shrugged and spun towards the door, head held high, just as Kirsty, smoothing out the folds of material on the sewing table, found the treasury note that the girl had tossed at her.

'Miss Rose.' She held it out, 'This must be yours.'

Blue eyes, blazing with anger, surveyed the money then flicked up to hold Kirsty's gaze. 'You're mistaken.' Her voice was heavy with meaning. 'It's your money.'

Kirsty held the look, refusing to submit. 'I know it's not, miss. Mebbe you dropped it when you came in.'

'For goodness' sake, Rose.' Mrs Hamilton plucked the note from Kirsty's hand and pushed it into her daughter's. 'Clearly the money is yours. You shouldn't be so careless with it—you know how hard Daddy has to work to earn it for us.'

Rose cast an angry, unforgiving glance at Kirsty. 'I won't wear that pink monstrosity,' she said, and swept out.

'You will!' Mrs Hamilton said just before the door slammed. Then, rounding on Kirsty, 'And as for you, Mrs, er, Lennox, I don't know what you think you were doing, encouraging my daughter to defy me.' She held up a podgy hand as Kirsty tried to speak. 'All I require of you is to follow the pattern I gave you. If you find that too difficult you need only say so. I'm sure I could find plenty women willing to take your place.'

She paused, her raised eyebrows inviting comment. Kirsty closed her lips tightly over the tongue that longed to speak, and stared at a point just beside the other woman's left ear.

'Very well,' Mrs Hamilton said triumphantly, consulting the little enamelled watch pinned to her bosom. 'You've wasted a good fifteen minutes this morning. I shall expect you to make that up before you go.'

# 12

As the door closed behind her employer, Kirsty spun the wheel and set the treadle rocking furiously and the pink silk racing beneath the needle. She had been hired as a sewing woman, not a seamstress; she shouldn't have to spend more time here than she could afford—and more than she was being paid for—making clothes for a spoiled brat. She seethed as she stitched, turning the material, turning it again, the machine whirring beneath her deft fingers.

There was a brisk tap at the door, and one of the kitchen maids looked in. 'Cook says d'ye know it's gone quarter past, Mrs Lennox?'

'Already?' Kirsty stopped treadling, and the wheel whirred into blessed silence. When she eased herself from the chair she enjoyed the luxury of a good stretch then covered the sewing machine and tucked a white sheet over the pink silk to protect it until her return. Then she left the room without a backward glance and made her way to the kitchen.

Despite the bustle as the kitchen staff prepared the family's midday meal, Bessie MacIntosh had a cup of tea waiting for Kirsty.

'I've no time to drink it, I'm late as it is.'

'Get it down ye before ye set off,' Bessie insisted. 'Ye've been workin' hard all mornin' without a bite or a sup. What kept ye?' she wanted to know as Kirsty swallowed the tea down in quick gulps, one eye on the kitchen clock. 'Ye should have been gone a good twenty minutes since.'

'Miss Rose and her mother had one of their spats about the new gown.'

Bessie clicked her tongue. 'That lassie! Her sisters werenae half the trouble she is. We'll all be glad when she finds herself a man and a place of her own. Here.' She thrust a bulky brown paper parcel into Kirsty's shopping bag. 'There's half a roast chicken and a pair of chops for ye.'

'I can't take the Hamiltons' food!'

'Away ye go,' the cook said vigorously. 'She owes ye for the extra time ye put in. Since she'll no' pay ye what ye're worth, ye're surely entitled tae some of her food.'

When Kirsty got home Matt and Alex were confronting each across the big kitchen table, which was strewn with the debris of a makeshift meal.

'I'll decide what happens in that workshop, not you,' Matt was shouting. 'I'm the master, and by God ye'd better—'

'What's going on here?'

'A lot of noise about nothing,' Alex said tightly, then ducked back as Matt swiped at him across the table.

'Ye cheeky bugger, ye—ye're not too old tae get a good hidin'!'

'But I'm old enough to hit back—and I will, make no doubt about that!'

'That's enough!' Kirsty dropped her shopping bag on the table. She had already been forced to witness one domestic quarrel that morning, and she was in no mood to suffer another. 'Will one of you tell me what this is about?'

For a moment the two men glared at each other like dogs being held back from a fight, then Matt said contemptuously, 'Let him be the one tae dae it, seein' as he's always got so much tae say for himsel'.' He threw himself down in his usual chair and hawked deeply in his throat, then spat a gob of phlegm into the kitchen fire. It sizzled noisily on the red hot bars.

'Matt!' Kirsty protested, then as he

ignored her asked, 'Alex, what's happened?'

Alex glanced at his stepfather as though expecting to be interrupted, then when Matt remained silent said, 'It's Mr Gregg's furniture. The exhibition's coming up soon, and if the order's not finished within the next two weeks I'll not have enough time to paint it.'

'But surely you've already started.' Kirsty knew that Matt had refused to let Alex carry out any decorating during normal working hours, claiming that the workshop was too busy to spare him. Instead Alex had been working on the furniture in the store by the pend every evening.

'I've started, but I can't paint furniture that's not been made yet,' Alex said impatiently. 'The order should have been finished by now.'

'That's Gregg's fault,' Matt said at once. 'He got it intae his head that he wanted a dresser as well, so it's takin' longer.'

'That's because you've put us onto an order that came in since Mr Gregg's. His should have been seen to before the other!'

Now that they were back at the nub of the argument, the tension in the air began to thicken again. 'It's me that decides these things,' Matt barked at his stepson. 'And you work for me, not for Gregg. You do as I say!'

'But surely finishing Mr Gregg's order in time for the exhibition is for the good of the business, Matt,' Kirsty offered.

'You mean it's for the good of Master Alex here. That's all he's thinkin' of!'

Hot colour flew to Alex's long face. 'Ye're haverin'!'

Matt scrambled to his feet and lunged across the table, pushing his chin belligerently at Alex. 'Am I? You're the only one in that workshop that decorates furniture. Ye think if ye dae well in that fancy exhibition and we get enough orders for yer rubbish, it'll be easier for ye tae edge me an' Ewan out an' take over yersel'. And that's the truth of it!'

The skin seemed to tighten on Alex's face. He started to speak, but Matt drove on, emphasising the words with stabs of one thick-knuckled finger in the air.

'But yer plottin's not goin' tae work, lad. My Ewan's got as much right tae be master here as you...mebbe even more.'

For a moment Kirsty thought that Alex was going to throw himself across the table at his tormentor. Matt thought it, too—she could tell by the way his broad shoulders tensed in readiness. Then with a disgusted snort, Alex whirled away and slammed out of the back door.

'Leave him,' Matt ordered as Kirsty made to follow him.

'He's upset.'

'He's no' the only one. What sort of time d'ye call this tae come in? We'd tae get by on bread and cheese for our dinners because you weren't here.'

'I had to stay behind to finish some work.'

'It's not good enough, Kirsty. Your place is here, not working at that big house...'

She went out, unable to listen to his ranting any longer, and caught up with Alex in the work yard, catching at his sleeve so that he had to turn towards her. 'Your father didn't mean what he said, Alex.'

'He's not my father!' She could feel him trembling with rage beneath her fingers.

'He's the only one you've ever known. And he's been good to you—to both of us.'

He wrenched himself free. 'When I was wee, mebbe, but now I'm in his way. You heard him, Mam—it's Ewan he wants tae leave this place tae. I might as well get out of it now.' He paused, breathing heavily, glaring at the kitchen window, where Matt stood watching them. 'It'd be safer for him if I did go,' he said at last. 'For if I don't, I'll mebbe end up swinging for the bastard!'

In the morning every joint in Matt's body

was locked with pain, and he couldn't stir from his bed. Caitlin was dispatched to fetch the doctor while Ewan and Alex helped Matt, groaning through gritted teeth every step of the way, to the bathroom. When he had been settled back in bed Kirsty sent the others downstairs to break their fasts while she eased her husband's nightshirt off and replaced it with a clean one.

'The doctor'll be along soon.'

Though grey with pain, Matt was mutinous. 'I don't need a doctor. Fetch the wintergreen ointment and some hot flannels and I'll be fine by noon.'

'Matt, you've never been so bad before. This is what comes of working in that cold workshop,' Kirsty fretted. 'I've told you time and again that you don't keep yourself warm enough.'

'Ach, stop fussin'!' He couldn't even hold a spoon or a cup. Kirsty fed him as if he was a baby, then left him to rest while she poured herself a cup of cooling tea in the empty kitchen.

Only Todd and Ewan were in the workshop when she went down the lane a little later.

'How's the master?' Todd asked at once.

'The doctor gave him something to ease the pain.'

Ewan shrugged. 'We'll manage well enough without him,' he said indifferently, and made for the garret.

'Did the doctor say how long Mr Lennox'd have tae stay in his bed?'

Kirsty looked round the workshop that had been the realisation of Matt's dream just one year earlier. 'No, but I doubt if he'll be working in here again, Todd,' she said, then pushed the unacceptable prospect from her mind. 'I meant to ask you about that house in Mary Street. Are you and Beth taking it?'

He was at the bench, dipping a small brush in the glue pot. 'It didnae suit, so I'm lookin' for somethin' else now.'

'I hope you find something soon.'

'So dae I,' Todd said fervently as Kirsty wandered over to a sturdy broad-seated fireside chair in the corner. It had been painted pale yellow, and bright cornflowers and poppies rioted along the length of one armrest. The flowers seemed to stand out from the wood, real enough to be picked.

'Is this one of Mr Gregg's chairs?'

'Aye. With the master not comin' in today, Alex thought he'd do some paintin' in here where the light's better.'

'It's bonny.'

'The design's from Mrs Gregg's best china. She's goin' tae set it all out on the dresser.' Todd drew the glue brush

166

carefully along one edge of a shaped piece of wood, 'I'm goin' tae get Alex tae paint a dresser for my Beth once we've found the right house.'

'What do you think about Alex exhibiting the furniture in Glasgow?'

He tossed a sidelong glance at her, then went back to his work. 'I'm no' paid tae have opinions, Mrs Lennox.'

Kirsty moved to stand beside him at the bench. 'I'm asking you as a friend, not an employee.'

Todd laid the wood aside carefully, then replenished the brush. 'Since ye ask, I think it's a grand idea.'

Kirsty nodded slowly. 'We're of the same mind, then.'

Silence fell between them. The wooden beams above their heads creaked, measuring Ewan's movements in the garret. Todd ran his brush along a second piece of wood, then fitted it to the first and carefully put both pieces into a vice. He moved unhurriedly but with confidence in his ability. Kirsty, her eyes on his hands, was reminded of something she had once heard her father say about wood needing to be treated with respect and never hurried.

The tension brought on by worry about Matt began to drain from her. Todd was a craftsman, and it was such a pleasure to watch him at work. Alex was a craftsman too—he should be allowed to display his talents.

He came in just then, the sawdust rippling over the floor like waves on a beach as the door opened. 'The doctor's been, then,' he said at the sight of his mother.

'He's given Matt some laudanum to ease the pain. It seems that he's got arthritis, not rheumatics. It's some kind that can get worse all at once for no reason.'

'No reason?' Alex shrugged out of his jacket and took his apron from the hook where it hung. 'The man's filled to the brim with malice and it's started poisoning him. That's the reason.'

'Alex!'

Todd carefully laid down his brush and left, mumbling some excuse about checking the timber piled outside.

'You shouldn't speak like that in front of Todd,' Kirsty said as soon as they were alone.

'He knows full well what's going on in this family.'

'The doctor says Matt'll not be back at work for a good while. Mebbe never. That means you'll be running this place.'

'Aye, I know.'

She hesitated, then said, 'Give your father his place, Alex. Talk to him about what's happening and let him give orders.

If you don't, he'll just lie in that bed and fret and make himself worse. Do it for my sake if not for his.'

He gave her a level look. 'And am I supposed tae follow his orders to the letter—for your sake?'

'As to that, you must do as you think best. I just want Matt to feel that he's still master.'

He shrugged, then called Ewan's name. When his stepbrother appeared on the stairs, Alex said, 'You can stop what you're doing—we'll be working on Mr Gregg's order now.'

Matt's illness meant that Kirsty was forced to spend more time in the house and less at Jean's shop. She kept going to the Hamiltons' because she needed the work and the hated pink silk dress had to be finished. She saw to it before she left for work that Matt was comfortable and that everything he might need was to hand, and while she was away Todd and Alex and Ewan took it in turns to look in at the house and make sure that he was all right.

To Kirsty's relief, Rose Hamilton stayed away from the sewing room, so there were no more tantrums and no more attempts to bribe her. The family were about to leave for their six-week summer holiday within days of the party at which Rose was to wear the dress, and as a result the big house was in turmoil.

'How's yer man?' Bessie asked, as she always did now, when Kirsty arrived that morning.

'He still can't get down the stairs, but at least he can manage to get himself to the bathroom with the help of a walking stick.'

'It's an improvement. Mebbe things'll get better week by week.'

'I hope so, for he's not taking kindly to being an invalid. When he's not grumbling, he can be so quiet that I worry about him, Bessie. It's not in his nature just to sit about and be looked after. I think not being able to do things for himself hurts him more than the swollen joints. At least,' Kirsty added, cheering a little, 'Miss Rose's dress'll be finished today. I'll be glad to see that over and done with.'

'And I'll be glad when the whole jing-bang of them go off tae the seaside next week.'

'Are you going with them?'

'No, no. They hire some other poor soul tae cook for them when they're away. I'll get a holiday with my cousin in Dumfries, then I'll be back in time tae get the kitchens all readied for them comin' home.'

Kirsty, too, was going to have two weeks free of her duties in the sewing room before returning to repair bed linen while the Hamiltons were out of the house.

'I hope the mistress is goin' tae give ye a bit extra for all yer hard work,' Bessie said as Kirsty left the kitchen.

'I doubt it.' But as Kirsty went along the corridor leading to the, sewing room she wondered if Mrs Hamilton might, after all, decide to be generous for once. An extra shilling or two would help to pay for the delicacies she had been buying in an effort to tempt Matt's flagging appetite.

'What's the sense in a man eatin' when he's not earnin'?' he had started asking, turning away from the meals she and the girls carried up to him.

To her surprise, the sewing room door was ajar, although she was certain that she had closed it behind her when she had last been there. She pushed it open, then stared in horror.

The window, which she had also closed, was partly open, and the protective cloth she always used to cover the silk material lay on the floor. A small bottle of oil on the sewing table had tipped over, its contents spilling out to cover the pink silk overskirt on the table with a dark, ugly stain.

# 13

'Carelessness!' Mrs Hamilton's double chin shook with rage. 'Sheer carelessness! How could you have allowed such a thing to happen?'

'I left the silk well covered. I don't see how the covering could have fallen off.' To her own ears, Kirsty's voice sounded distant and unreal. The sight of the terrible stain on the half-finished overskirt seemed to have taken the wits from her and she couldn't think straight.

'Look at the window, woman! You should have known better than to leave it open and the door ajar. Clearly a gust of wind blew the covering off—if it was ever on in the first place,' her employer added scathingly, 'and blew the bottle over. You didn't even put the stopper on properly!'

'Mrs Hamilton, I always make sure that the door and window are latched when I leave this room. And I would never leave a bottle of oil so close to material—'

'Don't argue with me! What else could have happened? This is what comes of being more interested in rushing home to your family than in remembering your duty to the people who pay your wages! Now what am I going to do?' the woman moaned. 'The party is tomorrow evening and the gown's ruined—ruined!'

'The dress itself is unspoiled, ma'am,' Kirsty ventured. 'It could still be used. There's the blue lace I showed Miss Rose—'

'Will you be quiet about the blue lace?' her employer shrieked, then reeled dramatically against a cupboard and fumbled in the small cloth bag that always hung from her wrist.

'Ma'am?' Kirsty, moving forward to help her, staggered and almost fell when Mrs Hamilton pushed her away, showing surprising strength for a woman on the verge of fainting.

'Don't come near me!' She produced a small bottle of smelling salts, opened it, inhaled deeply, then went into a fit of coughing. 'Out!' she choked. 'Out of my house! Out of my sight!'

'But Mrs Hamilton—'

'One more word and I'll make you pay for the material you've ruined. Get out!'

There was no reasoning with her. Kirsty gathered up her things with shaking hands and went. Mrs Hamilton's final words, 'And I shall see to it that nobody else in this town employs you as a sewing woman!' followed her down the narrow passageway.

In the kitchen Bessie looked at her in surprise. 'What are you doin' back here?'

'I think you'd best fetch Mrs Hamilton's maid to the sewing room.'

'Has the mistress taken ill?'

'No, there's b-been an accid-dent.' Kirsty's tongue stumbled over the words. 'Some oil spilled on Miss Rose's new g-gown. I don't know how it could have happened. Oh Bessie—I've been d-dismissed.'

'Sarah, ask Miss Hastie to go to the sewing room at once,' Bessie ordered one of the maids, then as the girl disappeared through a door in a whirl of black skirt and white apron strings, the cook pulled a kitchen chair forward.

'Sit down before ye fall down, woman,' she ordered, 'ye're as white as a sheet.' Then to the others, who had stopped what they were doing and were listening, agog. 'Well? The work won't do itself—get on with it!'

Kirsty was desperate to get away from their inquisitive eyes to somewhere where she could be alone to try to make sense of what had just happened. Ignoring the proffered chair, she said, 'I have to go,' and blundered towards the back door, bursting out of the house just as the hot tears started spilling down her cheeks.

She tried to dash them away as she half ran round the side of the huge house towards the tradesmen's drive, but they kept coming, blinding her, so that halfway down the drive she was forced to step in among the trees and lean unseen against a sturdy trunk and give way to them. When the worst of the weeping was over she started walking back to the town, her body shaken with involuntary hiccuping now and again, like a child's after a paroxysm of weeping.

She couldn't face the thought of returning home and admitting to Matt that she had been dismissed. Instead, keeping her face averted from the people she encountered, she went to the only refuge she knew—Jean Chisholm's wee shop.

Jean, busy with a customer, looked up in surprise. Knowing that if she tried to speak she might start weeping again, Kirsty lifted the hinged section of the counter and pushed past her friend and into the back shop without a word. She was rinsing her face with cold water when Jean hurried in a few minutes later.

'What's wrong? Is Matt worse—or has something happened tae one of the bairns?'

'No, it's—' To her horror, Kirsty felt the tears well up again. 'Oh, Jean!'

The Paisley folk weren't ones to touch or

embrace each other, but on this occasion Jean took Kirsty into her arms without hesitation. Her tenderness reminded Kirsty of her mother's comforting arms years before and sent a wave of self-pity through her. By the time she had brought it under control her face was in ruins again. Jean put her into the big chair that had to be used with care and respect because of its broken spring and wrung a cloth out in cold water.

'Hold that tae your eyes while I make us a cup of tea. I've locked the door, so we'll not be disturbed.'

'But folk won't get in,' Kirsty objected, her voice muffled by the cloth.

'That's why I locked it. I don't want tae be bobbin' in and out all the time.' Jean settled the teapot on the gas ring. 'We'll let it mash for a minute tae get nice and strong.' As it began to boil briskly, throwing out a steady plume of steam, she took a chair opposite Kirsty's, surreptitiously wiping wet tears from her neck. 'Now, tell me what's happened.'

Her sympathy changed to fury as the story came out in a series of gulps and chokes and broken sentences. 'The nerve of the woman, speakin' tae you like that after all you've done for her! Money doesnae always bring good manners with it!'

'It was the humiliation that hurt the most, Jean.'

'And no wonder. She's treated you like a dog, with not even the chance tae defend yoursel'.' Jean dashed strong hot tea into their cups so vigorously that drops and splashes flew in all directions, then added two spoonfuls of sugar and a generous dollop of condensed milk, which she adored, to each cup. 'Drink that down,' she instructed.

The tea was scalding, and very sweet, but it was also comforting. Drinking it down as she had been commanded, nearly burning her mouth in the process, Kirsty felt strength flow back into her rubbery limbs.

'I'd never have left that silk uncovered, Jean—never!'

'Of course you wouldnae!'

'And I'd never have left the bottle of machine oil beside it, or forgotten to put the stopper on securely.'

'Or left the door and the window open,' Jean agreed. 'You'd be as likely tae cut your own throat as tae do that.'

'I haven't even used the oil for a week. It should have been on a shelf in the cupboard, where I always keep it. But she'd not listen when I tried to explain.'

'God forgive me for sayin' this about another human bein', but that woman's a right cat.' Jean refilled both cups. 'Now listen, there's no sense in frettin' about it, for it'll no' change what's happened. Best put your mind tae what you're going tae do next.'

'I'll have to find more work.'

'D'you think she will tell her friends not tae take you on?'

'Probably, knowing Mrs Hamilton. If she does, I'll have to look further afield—Barrhead, mebbe, or Johnstone. There are some big houses there too.'

'I wish there was enough work for you here. I'd like it fine if there was, but I couldnae pay as much as you got at the Hamiltons.'

The broken spring had been pressing painfully into Kirsty's backside for the past few minutes. She rose and began to rinse her cup out at the single-tap sink in the corner. 'Something'll turn up, I'm sure.' She sniffed, scrubbed at her nose with the back of her hand and forced a smile at her friend. 'My mother always said that tomorrow's another day. Mebbe tomorrow'll bring something better than working for Mrs Hamilton.'

'It's for the best—ye've got enough tae do here,' Matt said when told of his wife's dismissal. Ewan, always caught up in his own interests, shrugged the news off without comment, while Caitlin, who had left school in April and was now working behind the counter of a grocer's shop, promised to keep her ears open for any word of an opening in one of the big houses.

'Sometimes the cooks or the house-keepers say something when they're in the shop. You'll find work easily, Mam, for you're the best sewing woman in the town.'

'Will you be sent to the jail for spoiling the dress?' Mary asked anxiously. Mary had always tended to be a worrier, and she had got worse, Kirsty knew, since Fergus's death.

Alex, who was fond of his timid little half-sister, scooped her up and deposited her on a seat at the table. 'Of course not. It's more likely to be Mrs Hamilton in the jail for tellin' wicked lies. Mam didn't spoil the dress, it was someone else that did it. Here.' He tore a sheet of paper from his sketch pad and gave it to the little girl along with some coloured pencils. 'Draw me a nice design to paint on a chair. Mebbe it was that girl herself that damaged the frock,' he added to Kirsty as Mary settled down happily to her task.

'Miss Rose? She'd not do a thing like that.'

'Would she not? You told us yourself

that she didn't want to wear it. I'm certain it was her. She got into the room and ruined it, then left you to take the blame. Mrs Hamilton should set herself to finding out the truth instead of turning you off when she's got no proof at all!'

'What's done's done, Alex,' Kirsty said wearily, sick of the entire matter. 'I'll start looking for another place next week.'

'You shouldn't have to go out to work, Mam. You've done your fair share already.'

'I like to be independent,' Kirsty told her first-born, and meant it.

He said no more, but as he passed behind her chair later she felt his hand touch her hair in a swift token of affection. The small, unexpected gesture sent a warm flood of pleasure through her. She would have laid her life down for Caitlin and Ewan and Mary, and she would always miss wee Fergus bitterly, but there was something special about Alex.

She reached up, and for a brief moment their fingers met.

On Monday Kirsty visited three of the big houses in Carriagehill Road, which was closer to home and ran along the back, of the Royal Alexandra Infirmary's imposing red-stone structure. It had occurred to her over the weekend that as Mrs Hamilton and her family were leaving Paisley in a day or two for six weeks, the woman might not have time before then to make good her threat to blacken Kirsty's name among her friends. If she could find work quickly, Mrs Hamilton would probably have forgotten the matter by the time she came home again.

There was no work available at the first two houses, but at least, Kirsty thought as she walked down the second driveway, the ladies she had spoken to showed no indication of having heard anything amiss about her. But the mistress of the third house, who interviewed her in the drawing room because, she said, she had need of a good sewing woman, suddenly cooled when Kirsty gave her name.

'You worked for Mrs Hamilton at Thornly Park, didn't you?'

Kirsty's heart sank. 'Yes, Mrs Brodie.'

'And she dismissed you.'

'Because of an accident that wasn't my doing.'

Mrs Brodie's face suddenly looked as though it had been carved from marble. 'I would prefer to seek elsewhere,' she said, and pulled the bell rope hanging close at hand. A uniformed maid arrived almost at once, and Kirsty was shown out, humiliated and close to tears.

There was nothing else for it, she thought

as she went to the butcher's and the grocer's, she would have to look further afield, though the cost of a tram or bus fare to and from Barrhead, Elderslie or Johnstone would eat into her wages.

'Mebbe ye should try the west end of the town,' Jean suggested. 'There's big houses there too.'

'I'd not thought of that.' Each district in Paisley tended to keep itself to itself, and folk from one area rarely had friends or interests in another, as though the town had split itself up into a collection of villages.

'You'd only need tae walk up the length of George Street then, instead of payin' fares tae get tae work. An' mebbe if you worked there,' said Jean, with gathering interest, 'you could start collectin' old clothes for the shop.'

# 14

'You there, is this where Mrs Lennox lives?'

Alex, about to go into the house, turned as a young woman in a plain, tailored costume marched up to him, taking strides

182

almost as long as a man's. She was tall for a woman, her eyes on a level with his, and beneath a straw boater clamped over a severe hairstyle her features were sharp and uncompromising.

There was something about the girl that he disliked at once, and his own voice was curt when he said, 'Who wants tae know?'

Her eyes narrowed with irritation. 'My business is with Mrs Lennox. Is she at home?'

He suddenly realised, from her arrogance and her educated accent, who the caller was. 'She's out,' he said abruptly.

'When will she return?'

'I don't know. I don't own her—nobody owns my mother.'

Her clear blue eyes blinked. 'You're her son?'

'I am. And you're Miss Hamilton.' He took satisfaction in knowing that he had managed to discomfit her twice.

'How did you know?'

Alex looked her up and down, making no attempt to hide his dislike, and she reddened. Normally he wouldn't have dreamed of embarrassing anyone in this way, especially a female, but to his mind, this particular female didn't deserve to be treated with courtesy. 'It wasn't hard tae guess.'

She gathered herself together. 'When your mother returns, perhaps you would be so good as to tell her that I would like to see her.'

Alex folded his arms across his chest, standing straddled before the door as though protecting his home. 'You may want tae see her,' he said bluntly, 'but I doubt if she'll want tae see you.'

'How dare you speak to me like that!'

His temper began to spill over. 'I dare, Miss Hamilton, because my mother's a hard-working woman, and the most honest person I know. She's been treated unfairly by you and your family, and she doesn't want tae set eyes on any one of you again. I'm telling you this,' he added, 'because she's too much of a lady tae tell you herself.'

The girl's high, strong cheekbones were glowing and her eyes snapping with rage during his tirade. 'I'm aware that she's been treated...unfairly. That's why I have to see her.'

'What's done's done.' Alex used his mother's own words. 'Just leave it at that.'

'As you said yourself, you don't own her.' She began to lose her self-control. 'Nor do you have the right to make decisions on her behalf!'

Alex was more than ready to have a

full-blown row with her, right there on the pavement. 'Folk like you believe that folk like us shouldn't have any rights at all, don't you? But we do, and I'm speaking for my mother when I tell you tae just go away and leave us alone. Goodbye, Miss Hamilton!' he said, and turned his back on the girl, stepping into the house quickly and shutting the door in her face. He leaned back against it, listening, and released his breath in a long sigh as he heard the click of well-shod feet fading away along the pavement.

Rose Hamilton, he thought as he went along the hall, was as pleasant as a mouthful of vinegar. He hoped that she had taken heed of what he had said and would stay away. In his view, the girl was nothing but trouble.

'There.' Kirsty settled the dummy against the shop wall. 'Behave yourself and you'll be quite safe.' Today Aggie was matronly in an elderly brown silk two-piece dress, complete with bustle. She had already become a familiar sight on the pavement, and whenever the weather was fine enough for her to be outside people made a point of passing to see what she was wearing. At least once every day someone came in to ask about her, and most of them stayed to look around and buy.

Kirsty now tied a rope round the dummy's ample waist beneath the clothes. The other end was looped to a hook once used to hang clothes on inside the shop. After a particularly determined raid by a small clutch of lads, she had bought a bell in a pawnshop and fastened it to the pedestal beneath the skirt. The entire street had been alerted the first time boys tried to make off with Aggie after the bell was installed, and the culprits had almost collapsed with the shock. Now the other shopkeepers looked out for Aggie as well, and the would-be thieves had more or less given up.

Once Aggie was well anchored, Kirsty stepped back into the shop to collect the basket of clothes waiting just inside the door and began hanging them on the trellis, humming under her breath. The sting of Mrs Brodie's haughty rejection faded away. It was a lovely day, far too nice to fret about stuck-up women in big houses.

'Mrs Lennox, may I speak with you?' Startled, Kirsty turned to see Rose Hamilton hovering by her side. All at once, the day stopped being lovely. Her first impulse was one of flight, then, realising that if she ran into the shop the girl would only follow, she said coolly, 'I'm very busy.'

'Let me help, then you'll be free to

talk to me.' Rose swooped down at the basket and brought out a skirt, holding it fastidiously at arm's length and trying, using only the tips of her gloved fingers, to locate the waistband. Two women passing by on the pavement nudged each other and grinned.

'It wouldnae fit ye, hen,' one called, and Rose swung round, fixing her with a cold look.

'I beg your pardon?'

The women yelped with laughter and moved on. Rose stared after them, the skirt still dangling from her hands. 'What did they mean?' she asked Kirsty, who snatched the skirt from her and tossed it into the basket. Tucking the basket against her hip, she urged the girl towards the shop with her free hand.

'We'll go inside.'

'But the clothes...'

'I'll do them later. Mind the step,' Kirsty said just as Rose stumbled and almost fell down it, arriving in the shop at a clumsy run. Jean and the customer she was serving turned to gape, their faces like pale moons in the dim interior.

'We'll go into the back shop,' Kirsty said hurriedly, and as Jean, mouth still open, automatically lifted the counter flap for them, she steered her unwelcome visitor through the gap and into the back, where she put the basket down. 'What are you doing here?'

'You sound just like your son.'

'My son?'

'A...person,' Rose said coldly, 'with red hair. I went to your house first and met him there.'

'Was it him who told you I'd be here?' If it was, Kirsty thought, she'd have a word or two to say to Alex when she got home.

'He wouldn't tell me anything.' Rose's face was stiff with disapproval. 'He was most rude to me. He even said that you wouldn't want to see me. Then I recalled you telling me once about helping in a friend's shop, so I looked for it, and it was easy enough to find.' She looked round with open curiosity at the old sewing machine on its rickety table in the corner and the clothing hanging on the walls or stacked on every available surface. 'You've not got much room here.'

'We manage.' Kirsty was beginning to lose her patience. This girl had caused her nothing but trouble. She had had to suffer in silence at work, but why, she asked herself, should she have to put up with Rose Hamilton on her own ground? 'Mebbe you'd be best to go back home, Miss Hamilton, and leave me in peace.'

'At least listen to what I have to say.'

Rose's eyes had become accustomed to the poor lighting. Fastidiously, she lifted a pile of clothing from a chair, laid it on top of another pile on the table and sat down in the chair with the broken spring.

'What could you have to say to me?'

'I only discovered this morning that my mother had dismissed you because of what happened to the gown you were making for me.' Rose took a deep breath, and looked at her intertwined fingers, then at Kirsty. 'It was I who spoiled it,' she admitted. 'I only wanted to make sure that I wouldn't have to wear it. I thought my mother would believe it to be an accident. I opened the window and the door and laid the bottle down to make it look as though a breeze had knocked it over.'

She stopped, then said feebly as Kirsty kept silent, 'It didn't occur to me that Mamma would blame you and dismiss you.'

'If I'd left the bottle of oil beside the material, and if I'd left the door and window open as well, I would have deserved dismissal,' Kirsty said stonily. 'I was responsible for everything in the sewing room. That meant that if anything went wrong, I'd be the one held to blame.'

'I—I didn't think of it that way. I'm sorry, Mrs Lennox. Truly very sorry.' The words came out jerkily. Clearly Rose

189

Hamilton wasn't used to apologising—especially to her social inferiors. 'I'll tell Mamma the truth, of course, and you'll get your job back.'

Without stopping to think, Kirsty heard herself say, 'You needn't trouble yourself, Miss Rose. I don't want to work for your mother any more.'

The girl's head lifted sharply. 'But I've said I'm sorry—you must come back now!'

Kirsty's curt reaction had surprised herself as much as Rose, but now that the words had been spoken, she realised that she meant them. Much as she craved the independence of earning her own money, she loathed the thought of submitting to Mrs Hamilton's narrow-minded bullying again.

'Your mother will find another sewing woman easily enough. She told me so several times during my employment.'

The spring must have discovered Rose, for she shifted uncomfortably in the chair. 'Please.' She had probably never pleaded with anyone in her life. 'If you don't come back you'll be on my conscience for the rest of my life!'

'I'm sure you'll have forgotten the whole matter by next week, Miss Rose. I know I will. I've no wish to be at your mother's beck and call again, always wondering if I'm going to be turned off because of something that was no fault of my own.' Kirsty could scarcely believe that she was talking like this to Rose Hamilton of all people.

'But what will you do?'

'Mebbe I'll just work here, doing something I enjoy. At least I'll be among friends and helping my own kind.' Kirsty turned towards the door. 'If you'll excuse me...' She had made her decision, and now she wanted the interview to end.

Rose struggled out of the armchair's clutches. 'If you won't come back to work for us, at least let me give you some money to make up for...' Her voice faltered into silence as she met Kirsty's eyes.

'I wouldn't take your money before, Miss Rose, and I'll not take it now. Good day.'

The girl's face flamed. She dipped her head, and fled from the room.

'Was that not Rose Hamilton?' Jean asked, hurrying into the back room to find Kirsty busy with kettle and teapot.

'It was. She wanted me to go back to work for her mother.'

'They've realised you weren't at fault?' Jean's face lit up. 'That's grand news! Now you won't have tae worry about findin' another position.'

191

'I will, for I told her I wasn't going back.'

Jean's jaw dropped. 'You said no?'

'I said more than that,' Kirsty admitted. 'I think I might have said a bit too much altogether.' She squared her shoulders. 'But on the other hand, it was grand being able to speak my mind for once.'

'Will you sit down and tell me what she said—and what you said—and let me try to make some sense of it before I lose my wits altogether?' Jean screeched.

'Och, Kirsty,' she protested ten minutes later when she had heard the whole story, 'should you not just change your mind and go back? There's still time—think of the wages Mrs Hamilton paid!'

'That's not much to think about.' Kirsty poured a generous dollop of condensed milk into her cup and discovered, when she lifted the hot drink to her lips, that her hand was shaking. 'Think of the misery the woman's caused. I'd rather do without than work for her again.' She took a second sip of tea, feeling stronger already. 'Sometimes it does you good to face up to folk instead of letting them have their own way. Morag Bishop says that folks' lives have patterns. If so, mine's just taken a new turn.'

Alex flushed with anger when he heard

about Rose's visit to the shop. 'I told her tae leave you alone!'

'Rose Hamilton was never one to take a telling. Anyway, she wanted to get a confession off her mind, for it was her that spoiled her own gown.'

'Did I not tell you that?' he exploded. 'Her sort have more money than decency!'

'At least she said she was sorry. It cost her dear to have to say such a thing to the likes of me.'

'Not as much as she cost you in the first place. I'm glad you sent her away, Mam. We can manage without the likes of the Hamiltons.'

# 15

Matt had refused from the beginning to let Kirsty handle the firm's books, despite her protests that her mother had done them for her father and she herself had taken them over after her mother's death.

'You see tae the house, and I'll see tae the business,' he had insisted all along. It had hurt to watch him toiling over the ledgers and the order books, knowing that he didn't understand book-keeping but that any offer of help would be spurned. She could only try to concentrate on her own sewing work while he sucked furiously at the end of his pen evening after evening, alternately mumbling and staring into space. Every now and again he laboriously wrote something, hunching over the book and holding the pen clumsily in his fist.

But illness had broken his resolve. At first he was determined to keep that part of the business, at least, under his control, ordering her to bring the books to the bedroom and making a show of working on them. But holding the pencil hurt his fingers, and the weight of the ledgers on his knees was more than he could bear. Then there was the worry of the inkwell toppling and spilling over onto the bedclothes.

When Kirsty tentatively suggested that she should do the books for him, 'Just until you're able again,' he finally agreed.

'Ye might as well keep them for the time bein'—but just till I'm better, mind.'

Turning the pages was like looking back over her family history. First came her paternal grandfather's faded copperplate writing, then her father's hand, clumsier but legible and meticulous. This was followed by more copperplate, indicating the point where her mother had taken over the books. Much as she would have liked to write as well as her mother, Kirsty had

194

never quite mastered the art, and her own earlier contributions to the ledgers were in the round, childish style that she still used. After her banishment to Stirling, Murray Galbraith had taken on the task again. Kirsty turned those pages quickly, then gave a soft exclamation of dismay at the sight of Matt's work, a confusion of scrawls and blots and scoring out. Reaching for the workbook, which itemised incoming materials as well as outgoing orders, she found the same mess and confusion.

'What are you doing?' Alex wanted to know that evening when he came in to find his mother at the table, surrounded by ledgers.

'I'm writing the figures from the ledger into this exercise book I've bought, so that I can see things properly.'

He glanced over her shoulder and whistled softly. 'He's made a right mess of them! No wonder he's so jealous of me being able to draw neatly.'

'Alex,' she indicated an entry in Matt's handwriting, 'I think you should start buying your nails from Jackson's again, instead of that shop in the Back Sneddon.'

'I didn't even know we'd changed merchants. We've had no need to order more since he fell ill, though I'll be ready to put in an order by the middle of next month.'

'Look.' Kirsty indicated an entry she had made in the exercise book. 'The new people must have made Matt a special offer to get his business. They gave good value at the beginning, but once we started ordering regularly from them, they began adding a penny or two each time, not enough to be questioned—'

'Unless the book-keeper knew what he was about,' Alex put in, but she ignored him.

'But enough to help their profits. Now they cost more than Jackson's ever did.'

'And we've been payin' it over without a word. I'll go and see them tomorrow,' Alex said grimly. 'They're not gettin' away with that. You'd think he'd have noticed!'

'It's easy enough to overlook wee things,' Kirsty said in swift defence of her husband. 'And a man should have a right to trust folk he trades with regularly.'

'Nobody's got a right to trust anyone in business, Mam. It's a lot to ask when you've got enough on your hands, but would you see to all the paperwork for me? It'd be a help, and I'd pay you for it.'

'Of course I'll do it, but I'll not take money for it.'

'And I won't have you working for nothing just because you're blood kin,' he said firmly. 'It'll not be much, but I'll see that you get something.'

The small gardens fronting the terrace where the Bishops lived were brilliant with colour and poured a heady mixture of fragrances over the low stone walls as Kirsty, Caitlin and Mary passed by.

Morag and Ellie were working in their little front garden. They waved when they saw their visitors, and Morag called in at the door to her husband. Caitlin ran ahead, Mary at her heels, and they were all waiting when Kirsty arrived, delicate blue smoke from Geordie's pipe mingling with the perfume of the red roses climbing over the front of the house.

'We've interrupted your evening, but Caitlin was so insistent—' Kirsty began, and was interrupted by Geordie.

'We were expecting ye, lass. It was all arranged with Caitlin.'

'Was it?' Kirsty raised an eyebrow at her daughter, who had the grace to look slightly embarrassed.

'Come and see what we've done with the loom, Mam.'

'Mebbe yer mother would like a cup of tea first,' Morag suggested, but Kirsty, seeing her daughter's face fall, opted to visit the weaving shed first.

The old shed lay almost at the end of the long, narrow back garden. Her grandfather had loved gardening in his spare time, and most of the plants and bushes growing there—the redcurrant bushes with their clusters of small, shiny, bead-like red berries, the hydrangeas he had so loved, the raspberry canes—had probably been planted by him. The very sight of the raspberry canes reminded Kirsty strongly of the fruit's perfumed flavour bursting in her mouth when she had been Mary's age.

Geordie and Morag had green fingers too, and the rich black earth had been well tilled and well planted with vegetables and flowers. Bees hummed around the flowers, gathering the day's last pollen collection before returning to their skeps at the far end of the garden. Some of the bushes blossomed with shirts and sheets. Morag liked to dry her washing in the old way, spreading it over the bushes and leaving it there for days at a time so that the rain could soften it and the sun bleach it.

Kirsty knew that when it was finally gathered in it would be spotlessly clean and soft, with the mingled scents from the garden held fast in every fibre.

'Come on, Mam,' Caitlin shouted impatiently from the shed, where she and Ellie waited hand in hand.

'I wish Alex and Ellie had taken more of a liking to each other,' Kirsty said thoughtfully. To her disappointment, the romance that she had hoped would blossom between the young couple had come to nothing. They had gone walking over the braes above Paisley several times and enjoyed each other's company, but Ellie was too shy and Alex too caught up in his interest in art for the relationship to develop.

'They took pleasure in each other's company for a while, and that's what matters,' Morag said comfortably. 'Ye've got a fine lassie in Caitlin. We've all enjoyed her visits.'

'She's wasted in that grocer's shop. I'm hoping to get her into Cochrane's sewing room when she's older.' Kirsty was referring to the large and very grand shop opposite Paisley Abbey, patronised by the wealthy members of the town.

'Whatever she turns her hand tae, she'll do it well—like her mother. That lassie's pattern's strong and bright.'

At the shed, Caitlin drew Mary to one side and motioned to Kirsty to go in first. She did, then stopped short, staring.

'Is that—?'

'It's great-grandfather's loom, Mam, all mended.' Caitlin almost sang the words in her excitement. 'That's why I wanted you to come here tonight. Go on in and look at it.'

The loom almost filled the shed; Kirsty walked round it, stopping to touch a beam here, fondle the curve of a roller there. It was solid beneath her hand, solid and strong and brought back from the dead. When she sat on the saytree her haunches settled exactly into the hollow created through the years by her own grandfather's backside. She stretched her feet out towards the treadles, remembering, as she felt them beneath the soles of her shoes, that her dearest ambition as a child had been to reach those same treadles.

Caitlin could contain herself no longer. 'Are you pleased, Mam?' she wanted to know, sliding onto the saytree beside her mother. Mary, not to be outdone, came scurrying to the other side.

'Pleased?' Kirsty put her arms about both girls, holding them tight. 'I've never been so pleased about anything in my life!'

'I didn't tell you how it was coming along because we wanted it to be a surprise. Mr Bishop found a man who used to repair looms, and another man who used to be a weaver himself helped. A lot of folk helped.'

'And they all had a grand time.' Morag gave a rich chuckle. 'All men that used tae be in the weavin' business, an' that pleased tae be dealin' with a loom again.'

Despite Caitlin's optimism, Kirsty hadn't really believed that the broken loom could ever be made whole again. But here it was, proof that miracles could happen—or rather, proof that faith and determination such as Caitlin's, coupled with the skill of dedicated craftsmen, could make miracles happen.

'Can it—will it work?'

'There's no reason why not,' Geordie told her placidly. 'There's a man in Houston who used tae be a dresser, and he's goin' tae try tae set it up. If he can, I'll try a bit of weavin'.'

Caitlin stroked the loom lovingly and took a deep breath. 'It's come back to life,' she said, and Geordie beamed down on her from behind his pipe.

'Didn't I tell ye that it would, lass?'

A faint mist rose from the basketful of warm, damp clothes as Kirsty carried it from the wash house. The air was cool, but a pearly grey sky with a rosy flush to the east promised a warm day, though it was almost September. A hush lay over the still-sleeping town, and she felt as though she was the only person awake.

She hummed a tune and even broke into a little dance step as she pinned one of Ewan's heavy work shirts on the line. A bird foraging in the vegetable bed halted and cocked its head at her.

'Aye, I'm daft, but sometimes it's

allowed,' Kirsty told it. Apparently deciding that, daft or not, she was harmless enough, the bird continued its search, keeping a bright eye on her as it worked.

When the basket was empty she began emptying the copper. Todd Paget, a canvas sack dangling from one hand, came whistling through the pend as she brought out the first pailful of warm water, and he hurried along the path by the house to put the sack down and take the pail from her.

'Here—let me.'

'I'm not in my dotage yet,' she protested.

'It never hurts tae get a wee hand from someone. Were ye goin' tae put it on the vegetable bed?' When she nodded, he began to trickle the water, a little at a time, around the plants. 'I brought ye some vegetables from the allotment.' A nod of the head indicated the bag by the back door. 'There's more than my sister can use.'

'That's good of you, Todd, but what about Beth?' Todd's allotment was thriving, and he had supplied almost all the vegetables the household needed over the past few months.

'She's got some,' he said, and went into the wash-house to fill the bucket again.

'What's happened about the flat you found?' Kirsty wanted to know when he returned.

A shadow passed across his normally cheerful face. 'Beth didnae like it, though I thought it was just right, myself. She said the close was too dark.'

Kirsty opened her mouth to say something, then closed it again. Todd was tireless in his hunt for a suitable place that he and Beth could rent, but every time he found one, there was something about it that Beth disliked. It seemed to Kirsty that Beth just didn't want to get married, but even if that was the truth, it was no business of hers.

'So, you'll be looking for something else then?'

'It's the only way. One of them'll be just right for us, you'll see. Is Alex all set for the exhibition?'

'I'm just going to waken him now.'

'Then I'll not hold ye back. Give him my good wishes,' Todd said, and went off to work.

Alex was already in the kitchen when Kirsty brought in the sack of vegetables, wearing only his drawers and washing himself at the sink.

'I was just going to wake you.'

'I scarcely slept,' he confessed, glancing

203

vaguely around, droplets of water cascading from his chin and dripping from his fingers onto the floor. 'I forgot to bring the towel over.'

'Here.' She handed it to him, then mopped at the floor as he dried himself vigorously. 'It's a grand day.'

'Just the right sort of day for success,' Alex agreed. He was rubbing at his wet hair, the smooth skin on his chest and arms moving easily across the sheet of interlocked muscles overlying his skeleton. He had grown to full manhood, his formerly thin, boyish body now lean and sinewy.

'Are you nervous?'

'No,' he said briskly, then followed the denial almost immediately with, 'and that's a lie if ever I've told one. Mam, I'm scared tae death. What if the Glasgow folk don't like what I've done with the furniture?'

'Of course they'll like it.'

He ran his arms into the shirt she had carefully ironed the night before and buttoned it, then tried several times to get his tie to lie correctly, tutting and muttering annoyance at it. 'I'll do it,' Kirsty offered at last, unable to stand by and watch any longer. He was much taller than she was, and she had to reach up. His teeth were worrying his lower lip, a sign of inner anxiety stretching back to his earliest childhood.

'I hope the furniture arrived safely.' The pieces being put on show had gone off to Glasgow the day before on one of Gregg's carts, and Alex was following by train.

'I'm sure Mr Gregg's seen to that very efficiently.' Kirsty gave one final tug to the tie then stepped back to study the overall effect.

'How do I look?'

'Grand—and you'll look even better when you cover your shirt-tail with your trousers,' she said, and he glanced down at his legs, puzzled, then gave a muffled exclamation and hurried upstairs.


# 16

The other three were eating their breakfast when he came back and asked anxiously, 'Will I do, Mam?'

Glancing up from the stove, Kirsty experienced a glow of maternal pride so strong that she was sure it must be radiating from her like beams from the sun.

He was wearing a grey flannel suit that she had found in Jean's shop and had carefully altered to fit and steamed and pressed. His shirt was snowy white, with a high cellulose collar, and the tie, also from Jean's, was soft blue speckled with grey. His curly red hair had been plastered to his skull with oil; the severe style gave his longish face a distinguished look.

'Mam?' he prompted, panic beginning to glitter in his eyes. 'Is there something wrong? Is it the tie, mebbe, or—'

'You look just right,' she said simply, and he relaxed, then laughed when Mary, whose mouth had fallen open to reveal a half-chewed lump of bread to all and sundry, swallowed hard then said in a breathless squeak, 'You look just like a gentleman! Can I walk to the station with you before I go to school?'

'I'd be honoured by your presence, my lady!'

After a swift glance at his stepbrother, Ewan returned to his breakfast without comment. Kirsty, who had happened to catch his look, recognised a sudden flash of jealousy in it. Ewan made no secret of the fact that he was bored by his work and by everything else in his life. He would no doubt have given a great deal to be going to Glasgow in Alex's place, Kirsty thought, feeling sorry for the boy.

'I never realised how handsome you are,

Alex,' Caitlin said. 'Now I know why Ellen Forsyth likes you.'

'Who's Ellen Forsyth?'

'One of the girls in the shop. She's talked about you quite a lot.'

'Ellen Forsyth's easily pleased, then,' Ewan jeered, and Kirsty's sympathy shrivelled somewhat. Caitlin turned on her half-brother with a sudden and rare flash of anger.

'She must be—she's walked out with you often enough,' she snapped.

He glared at her, then at Alex, who said, 'Is there a lassie in this town who's not walked out with our Ewan?'

'That's more than anyone can say about you.'

'Has your father seen you?' Kirsty broke in swiftly.

Alex shrugged. 'He'd not be interested.'

'You must go up to him before you leave, Alex. He'll be offended if you don't.'

He gave her a sidelong look. 'D'you think so?'

Too excited to eat, he only managed to swallow half a cup of tea and a slice of bread and margarine before going upstairs, at Kirsty's request, to see Matt.

'I was right,' he said tersely when he returned. 'I needn't have troubled myself. He just grumbled about me expecting the workshop to run on its own while I'm gallivanting in Glasgow.' His face was shadowed.

'Me and Todd can manage fine,' Ewan said at once. 'He knows that.'

Alex ignored him. 'I'd best go,' he said, then offered his arm to Mary and forced a cheerful note into his voice. 'Her Royal Highness's coach awaits—and if her prince doesn't catch the train and get to Glasgow in time he'll turn into a toad for ever. Come on.'

'You might have wished the laddie well,' Kirsty said when she went up to give Matt his breakfast.

'Wish him well when he's jauntin' off on some daft ploy and leavin' Todd and Ewan on their own?' Matt had aged noticeably in the past month or so. There were more lines on his face and more grey in his hair and in the stubble over his chin.

'They can manage fine.'

'I wish I wasnae stuck here, of no use tae anyone,' he railed.

'There's no sense in fretting; it'll only make you worse. D'you want to come downstairs? I'll fetch Todd and Ewan. You should come down, Matt,' she added when he shook his head.

'What's the point in exchanging one prison for another?'

208

He was in continuous pain, and at night he still needed laudanum, which Kirsty carefully measured out, to help him to sleep. But now he could manage the stairs with assistance, although once down them he was more or less confined to his chair in the kitchen. Kirsty worried over the way he seemed less and less inclined to make the effort.

'It'd be a change of scene. If it gets warm enough, you could sit out at the back.'

'And have everyone who goes up and down the lane stoppin' tae pity me? Ye can tell Ewan tae come up tae discuss the day's work.'

'D'you not mean Todd?'

'I said Ewan, and I mean Ewan,' he flared at her. 'It's my bones that've gone wrong, woman, not my brain. If one son isnae interested in how the workshop's doin', then I must depend on the other.' He tossed his newspaper aside petulantly and it slid over the side of the bed to land on the floor like a broken-winged seagull. 'Ewan can fetch Todd if I decide tae go downstairs.'

Kirsty walked round the bed to pick the paper up and folded it properly. 'I'll fetch Ewan,' she said.

Going out to the workshop, she thought longingly of the peaceful days when

Alex and Ewan, growing up together and much the same age, had been close friends. As often happened with brothers, the friendship had weakened as they neared maturity and developed different characteristics—Alex quiet, Ewan with his love of activity and companionship. But even so, there had never been any antagonism between them. That had come after the move to Paisley. Kirsty didn't know why or when it had first appeared, but she felt that Matt, with his habit of favouring Ewan over Alex, had had a hand in it.

Alex shifted the chairs, table and dresser from one position to another, wishing that Mr Gregg had stayed with him instead of hurrying away to see to other business he had in the city. Most of the exhibits in the large hall were attended by two or three or even four people who had, he suddenly realised with alarm, brought various items with them to highlight their wares. Lengths of material were being pinned to the walls as backcloths, or draped over stands. Bright Spanish shawls with long silky fringes were tossed over the backs of handsome chairs, and lush green pot plants or vases of dried flowers were being placed on polished surfaces. One exhibit even boasted a live model, a smartly dressed young woman stretched nonchalantly on a chaise longue with a magazine in her lap.

If only, he thought in despair, he had asked Mrs Gregg to lend him the china he had copied the design from, to display it on the dresser. But it was too late now, and his work would have to speak for itself.

He studied it, trying hard to see it with a stranger's dispassionate gaze. The poppy and cornflower spray had been painted across the top bar of each of the four chairs that went with the table, and the same flowers swarmed up the table legs. They appeared on the dresser as formal posies on the doors and the drawers, and in a spray along the top. On the two fireside chairs they covered the armrests generously, as well as decorating the backrest.

Mr and Mrs Gregg had been delighted with the furniture, but what, Alex wondered with a clenching feeling in the pit of his stomach, would other folk think? Was it all too much, too garish?

Strolling casually to the far side of the hall he glanced across and saw with relief that the cream-coloured plaster walls in the corner allocated to him displayed the furniture well enough, though an extra splash of colour would have helped. He returned to move the pieces around for the last time, then, for want of any other embellishment, dug into his bag and brought out the large book of patterns he had brought with him to study if time permitted. Opening it at a favourite page, he propped it on the dresser, then tore some half-finished pages from his sketch pad and scattered them carefully over the table.

Another stroll to the far wall satisfied him that the sketchbook and drawings fitted into the overall picture. There was nothing more he could do, and in any case, the exhibition was about to be opened to the public. Returning to his corner, Alex sat down at the table and brought out the crayons he always carried in his pocket. He might as well work as sit there doing nothing.

The day passed fairly swiftly. Alex became quite intent on his work, relaxing as he began to get used to the place and the people. Now and again someone came over to look at his furniture and ask him about it. He got one small order, which elated him, and another two people said that they would return later.

During a lull, he became so involved in the sketch beneath his hand that when one of the organisers approached he had to give a little cough to attract Alex's attention. Crimsoning, he jumped to his feet, almost knocking the sketchbook to the floor.

The man referred discreetly to the list in

his hand. 'May I introduce Mr Alexander Lennox, Miss MacDowall? Mr Lennox, this is Miss Fiona MacDowall...' He paused, then added with subtle emphasis, 'whose father owns one of the city's most successful furniture emporiums.'

'Mr Lennox, I am most taken with your furniture.' Fiona MacDowall held out a gloved hand, and Alex took it carefully in his own. She was the most beautiful woman he had ever seen. Her face, small and neat, was dominated by wide brown eyes flecked with gold and thickly lashed. Beneath her corn-flower-blue hat—the same blue as the flowers on the furniture, he noted—her hair was a smooth sweep of pale gold.

'And this is...' The official looked at the older woman, then said again, 'This is...'

'Mrs Dove, our housekeeper.' Fiona MacDowall's voice was as clear and as pure as spring water. Alex suddenly realised that he was still clasping her hand and released it hurriedly as the housekeeper bowed her head in acknowledgement, her own gloved hands remaining folded at her waist.

'Will you sit down, Miss MacDowall, Mrs Dove?' he invited.

'If you'll excuse me, Miss MacDowall?' the official said when both women were seated.

'Of course. You must have a great deal

to do, and I'm sure that Mr Lennox will look after us very well.' As the man hurried off Fiona MacDowall spread her fingers wide over the painted rests of her chair. 'I feel as though I'm dipping my hands into a field of flowers,' she said with delight.

'That was my intention. You don't think it's too much?'

'Oh no, not at all.' This girl, Alex thought, was the best embellishment his furniture could have; better by far than china, or Spanish shawls or vases of flowers. The deep blue of her dress and neat-fitting bolero jacket and the pale-blue straw hat with its froth of creamy feathers round the brim, almost the shade of the furniture itself, were quite perfect.

'Do you always decorate your furniture with flowers?'

'I can do any pattern the customer asks for.' Alex dipped into his bag and brought out a smaller sketchbook. 'Perhaps you would care to look through some of my ideas.'

She and Mrs Dove bent together over the pages, while Alex went on to explain that the furniture was made in his father's workshop.

'These are beautiful,' Fiona MacDowall said, 'but I think that I like the flowers best. My father has just bought a new house, Mr Lennox, and I'm furnishing my own bedroom. Could you make a set of furniture for me?'

'It would be my pleasure, Miss MacDowall.' Alex turned to a blank page in the sketchbook. 'Tell me something about the rooms and the style you would like,' he invited, while the hall and all the people in it, including the housekeeper, faded into the background, leaving only the two of them—Alex Lennox and the exquisite young woman who had just walked into his life.

Kirsty jerked awake and scrambled to her feet, the darning she had dozed over falling from her lap to the floor, as the latch was lifted on the back door and Alex came in.

'I thought you'd be in your bed, Mam.' Although it was late, he didn't look in the least tired. Instead he was glowing and filled with energy, the hair he had oiled so carefully that morning framing his face like a blazing halo.

'I wanted to find out how—' The words ended in a muffled squeak as he surged across the little room and swept her into his arms, spinning her round. 'Alex, put me down, you'll have the two of us on the floor!'

'Not a bit of it, you're light as a feather,' he said breathlessly, setting her back on her

215

feet. 'Mam, I'd a wonderful day! There was so much tae see, and so many folk.'

'Did they like the furniture?'

'I got three orders, and some other folk showed an interest.' He pulled his jacket off and wrestled with his high shirt collar. 'I wasn't the only one with painted pieces, but those that looked at mine seemed tae like them well enough.'

'I'm glad—not that I'd any doubts that you'd do well,' Kirsty added hastily. 'I kept some dinner hot, but it'll be dried up by now.'

'I'm not hungry.' He dropped the collar on the table then stretched out in Matt's chair, rubbing at his neck where the collar had chafed. 'That's better—I couldn't be doing with having tae wear one of these things every day. It made me feel as if my head was being cut off.'

'You'll have some tea, at least. I thought you'd be home earlier than this,' she said over her shoulder as she picked up the teapot.

'I walked about Glasgow for a while tae see something of the place while I was there. Mam,' he suddenly burst out, 'there was a lassie—I mean, a young lady—that was awful taken with my work. She's given us an order for chairs for her own bedroom, and a washstand and two chests of drawers and a wardrobe.'

She handed him his tea. 'That'll cost her a fair bit.'

'Her father can afford it.' He lifted the cup to his lips, then lowered it untouched. 'He owns one of the big furniture shops in Glasgow, yet she wants us tae make the furniture and me tae decorate it. She's called Fiona MacDowall.' He said the name reverently, as though reciting a poem.

'Oh aye?'

'She invited me to her house when the exhibition ended, so's I could see the room for myself.'

'Just the two of you, on your own?' Kirsty asked, shocked.

'No, no, her housekeeper was with her.' Again the cup was lifted then set down. 'It was the grandest house I've ever been in.'

'And what does her father say to her ordering furniture from us instead of using his own shop?'

'Not a word, for he's away somewhere just now, seeing to a new shop he's opening in another town. Anyway, she says he doesn't sell decorated furniture, and that's what she wants.'

'Alex, son, are you sure of this order?' Kirsty asked gently, reluctant to spoil his elation. 'Her father'll mebbe get her to change her mind when he comes home.'

'I'm quite sure. She's not the sort of

lassie tae say a thing if it's not true, and the housekeeper seemed tae think that it was all right.' He got up and emptied his untouched tea into the sink, saying as he rinsed out the mug, 'You'll meet her yourself on Monday, for I've invited her and the housekeeper tae come and see the workshop.'

'Monday?' The shock of his announcement brought Kirsty upright in her chair. 'This Monday coming?' Then, as he nodded, she cried, 'Oh, Alex, could you not have given me more warning?'

'What for? She only wants tae see where her furniture's going to be made.'

'But they'll expect to be invited into the house and given refreshments!'

'Just a cup of tea after their journey, and mebbe a bit of shortbread. I'd tea and sandwiches at her house,' Alex said happily, oblivious to his mother's dismay. 'Wee dainty things they were, not even big enough for a decent bite at them.'

'Alex Lennox! Men have no idea of what's right and proper! I'll have to turn the place out—and do a baking...'

Surprised, he cast a look round the crowded, shabby kitchen. 'It looks fine to me, and she's not one to fuss. You'll see that for yourself when you meet her. You'll like her, Mam—you'll not be able

218

to help but like her,' Alex said, then went off to bed, beaming as though he didn't know how to stop, leaving Kirsty to panic over the impending visit.

# 17

Matt reacted with predictable derision to the news that his stepson had done well at the exhibition, and when he heard that one of the customers was coming to the house, his temper flared.

'I've never heard such nonsense—if we start allowin' everyone who puts in an order tae come an' see the workshop first we'll never get anythin' done!'

'This is a special matter, with the lassie's father selling furniture himself,' Kirsty tried to soothe him. 'You never know, we might get orders from him one day. Anyway it's been arranged, there's nothing we can do about it now.'

'One thing's for sure—I'm havin' nothin' tae do with it. I'm staying in my bed while she's here!'

The decision was a great relief to Alex, who, Kirsty knew, had been worried about what his father might say in front of the visitors. But on Monday morning Matt suddenly changed his mind.

'When all's said and done, I'm still the master here, even if that laddie is puttin' on airs an' graces an' tryin' tae make folk think otherwise,' he announced, sitting up in bed, his grey hair awry and his chin thick with stubble. 'I'd best be there, tae keep an eye on things.'

Kirsty, worn out after a weekend of cleaning and baking, looked at her husband in despair. The visit would be a lot easier for her as well as for Alex if Matt stayed where he was. 'Are you sure? It'll mean getting shaved and washed, and having to wear your good suit...'

'In my own house? And me an invalid? A shirt and trousers, and a blanket about my shoulders'll do.'

'If you come downstairs while we've got visitors, Matt Lennox, you'll be dressed in your best and that's final. I'll press your good suit.'

'Can you not make him change his mind?' Alex asked in despair when she went downstairs with Matt's suit over her arm.

'You know your father—once he's decided on something he'll not be moved from it.'

A broad grin split Ewan's face. 'That'll spoil your nice wee afternoon tea with your young lady.'

'She's not my young lady, she's a customer!'

'I've never seen you put on your best suit and oil your hair for Mr Gregg,' Ewan retorted. He himself was annoyed because he was expected to work as usual instead of being included in the welcoming party.

'At least you'll see Miss MacDowall when she visits the workshop. She'll not be coming to the grocer's shop,' Caitlin said. 'Remember, Mam, I want to know all about what she wore.'

'I'm going to wear my best dress and say please and thank you,' Mary said smugly. She wasn't due to return to school for the new term for another two days, so she would be there to see the visitor. Ewan and Caitlin both glared at her.

Alex had arranged to be at nearby Canal Street station that afternoon to meet Fiona MacDowall's train and escort her and the housekeeper to the house. By the time he left, in his good grey suit, Matt had been washed, shaved, dressed and settled in an armchair in the parlour.

'He'll ruin everything,' Alex said gloomily on the doorstep. 'He'll say—God alone knows what he'll say, but it's sure to be something tae embarrass me!'

'It'll be fine—your father wouldn't spoil things for you,' Kirsty soothed. Then, nervously, her hands smoothing her brown skirt and fluttering among the frills on her pale-green blouse, she said, 'D'you think I look all right? I'd not want to let you down.'

His worried frown melted into a smile. 'You look fine, Mam. You'd never let me down,' he said, and strode off to the station, holding his shoulders back stiffly, like a brave soldier marching to possible doom.

Fiona MacDowall disarmed Matt from the start by saying, as she took one of his swollen hands gently in both of hers, 'I was so sorry to hear that you suffer from arthritis, Mr Lennox. I can feel the inflammation's heat in your poor joints—it must be a great trial to you.'

'It comes an' it goes,' Matt said gruffly, making no attempt to draw his hand from hers. 'There's no' much I can do but thole it.'

'That's very brave, but courage doesn't make the pain any easier to bear.' The girl gave his hand a final pat before releasing it. 'My poor grandmamma had very bad rheumatics, I remember. There was an ointment that she swore by. I'll ask our housekeeper about it when I go home, and send it to you.'

Kirsty could understand why her serious, level-headed son had been captivated by this girl. Although everything about her indicated wealth and comfort, her manner was natural and friendly, and her expressive brown eyes sparkled. Instead of the housekeeper, she was accompanied by a smartly dressed middle-aged man who was introduced as Mr George Gavin, the manager of her father's furniture shop.

'Mr Gavin was interested in hearing more about your painted furniture, and he's willing to stand witness to the fact that although I'm a mere woman I have the authority to order furniture for my own use. I felt that you were unsure about that,' Fiona MacDowall said solemnly to Alex, then laughed when he began to splutter out denials. 'I know how men's minds work—my father would have thought just the same.' She laid a hand on his arm, and Kirsty saw her son's eyes glow at the brief contact.

'What d'you think of her?' he whispered when the two of them left the room, Kirsty to bring the tea tray from the kitchen, Alex to fetch some sketches to show to the visitors.

'She's a nice lassie—and a pretty one, too. Best not to leave Matt alone with them for too long, though,' she warned, and they went about their business.

To Kirsty's relief the atmosphere was still calm when she returned to the parlour.

Matt, more animated than she had seen him for a long time, was talking to George Gavin about the business, while Mary showed Fiona MacDowall her doll.

'Her drawers can't come off, but her dress can—and her petticoat,' she was saying in her clear, composed little voice. 'And her bonnet. My sister, Caitlin, made them all. She makes lots of clothes for my dolls.'

'Your sister must be very clever.'

'She is. She makes her own clothes, and some of mine. She made this.' Mary stepped to the centre of the floor and turned round to display her square-necked cotton dress, frilled at the neck and sleeves and hem.

'It's very pretty.'

'It's my best.' Mary eyed the guest's yellow jacket, decorated with bands of dark-green lace, and her dark-green skirt trimmed with yellow rosettes. 'Did you make your clothes?'

'No, I didn't. I'm afraid I'm not good at sewing.'

'Princesses like you don't have to sew, do they? They have servants to do that for them.'

'I'm not a princess, dear,' Fiona said.

'You look very like the princess in my book. P'raps you really are, but you don't know it yet,' Mary suggested.

Kirsty, listening and watching, saw Fiona glance up at Alex, who had just come into the room, from beneath long thick lashes. 'Perhaps I won't know it until the right prince comes along,' she said.

The conversation flowed easily enough while they drank their tea, but when George Gavin showed a keen interest in Alex's sketches of decorated furniture and expressed his view that his employer might take a professional interest in them, Matt stiffened.

'Tae my mind, Mr Gavin, a chair's a chair an' a chest o' drawers is a chest o' drawers. Furniture's made tae be used. If ye want something nice tae look at, ye can put pictures on the wall.'

Alex shot to the edge of his chair, his lean body tense. 'What's wrong with furniture that's serviceable and looks bonny at the same time?'

'Turnin' a good piece of work intae a sideshow's an insult tae the man that made it,' Matt snapped.

'It's not an insult—it's just a way of helping the furniture to fit in better with the decor of the room!'

Matt took in a noisy mouthful of tea, shooting a withering glance at his stepson over the top of one of Kirsty's good china cups. 'Decor, is it? That's a word for lassies, no' skilled craftsmen!'

Alex, scarlet to the tips of his ears, opened his mouth to reply, but Fiona spoke first. 'I can understand your meaning, Mr Lennox, but isn't it usually the woman who chooses furniture for her home? And women put great value on pretty things. What do you say, Mr Gavin?'

'I'll admit that in my experience the ladies usually have the last word.'

'Although my father sells very fine furniture,' Fiona added, with a warm smile at Matt, 'I know full well that he has no great idea of how to make a place homely. That task has fallen to me.'

'Aye, well,' Matt humphed, determined not to give in but reluctant to offend her.

'I knew that you'd understand my meaning.' She gave him another sweet smile and put her cup down. 'I would so like to see your workshop, Mr Lennox. Would you allow your son to take us there?'

Kirsty took advantage of the visitors' absence to wash and dry the cups and make a fresh pot of tea in case it was needed. She was putting the last dried piece of china back on the tray when the door from the yard opened and Alex ushered his guests into the kitchen, announcing cheerfully, 'Miss MacDowall wants to see the chairs I painted for you, Mam.'

While the visitors enthused over the chairs, Kirsty glared at her eldest son, who looked back at her with puzzled innocence, quite unaware of any wrongdoing.

An hour later Alex swung out of the station and turned towards the Cross, too elated to think of going back to Espedair Street. He knew full well that he should return to the workshop, but he needed to walk, to be free to dwell on every moment he had spent in Fiona MacDowall's company that afternoon.

She had liked his family, and the chairs he had painted for his mother, and the workshop. She had invited him to call on her on Thursday evening with preliminary sketches for her furniture. And Mr Gavin had said, shaking Alex's hand before stepping onto the train, that he was certain that his employer would be interested in meeting Alex and seeing his work when he returned to Glasgow.

At that moment Alex Lennox wouldn't have changed places with any man on earth except George Gavin, now sitting opposite Fiona—in his most private thoughts, he allowed himself to call her by her Christian name—in the enclosed intimacy of a railway carriage, free to look at her lovely face, hear her voice and, at the end of the journey, able to take her hand in his and help her to alight from the carriage. Remembering the touch of that small gloved hand against his palm as he had assisted her to board the train, Alex's heart sang, while the fingers of the privileged hand curled slightly by his side as though enfolding hers again.

At the foot of St Mirren Brae he came face to face with Beth Laidlaw, who inclined her head slightly and swept past. Now there was a stuck-up besom, Alex thought. He'd seen Beth often enough to realise that her smiles and her charm tended to be reserved for men she considered to be blessed with either looks or money. He hoped that Todd might come to his senses before he went to the altar with Beth, for the man deserved better. Not that there was any sense in trying to say so to Todd, who was too besotted by the woman's looks to give much thought to the calculating creature beneath the surface. She was pretty enough in her own way, but not a patch on Fiona when it came to beauty and good manners.

Fiona. As he crossed the road to walk up through the public gardens that ran alongside St Mirren Brae, Alex gloated over the way Ewan's eyes had widened when Fiona had walked into the workshop. Because young women tended to forget Alex when his handsome, charming stepbrother was around, he had been nervous about bringing the two of them together. But Fiona had been different from the rest—pleasant enough towards Ewan, as she was pleasant towards everyone, but staying by Alex's side throughout the visit, asking questions of him and not of Ewan.

He emerged from the gardens into Paisley Cross and turned along the side of the imposing George A. Clark Town Hall, built with a handsome donation from a member of one of the town's leading textile-manufacturing families. At the corner he turned right again along Abbey Close, the narrow thoroughfare between the town hall and Paisley Abbey.

The close was quite busy on that pleasant afternoon, but because of her height he saw Rose Hamilton almost at once, walking along the pavement towards him, a step or two behind a middle-aged couple. Even in his euphoria Alex, felt his hackles rise at the sight of her and saw, by the way she drew herself upright, that she had seen and recognised him. Stepping aside to let the couple pass, he gave Rose a brief nod, which she acknowledged with a dip of the head.

A sharp voice floated in his wake. 'Rose, did I just see you acknowledge that...that person? Who...?'

Alex smiled to himself and strode on.

'How could you?' Kirsty stormed at Alex when he finally arrived home. Matt, worn out by the afternoon's events, had gone back to bed and Ewan, his day's work finished, was washing his hands at the sink, his sleeves rolled up to the elbows.

Alex looked at his mother, confused. 'How could I what?'

'You know fine and well what! Bringing these people into the kitchen, and it in a mess!' Kirsty wielded the potato masher vigorously in the big pot. 'I didn't know what to do with myself when they walked in without warning.'

'They only wanted to see the chairs I'd painted for you—and there's nothing wrong with the kitchen.'

'Alex Lennox—!' she began, just as Caitlin burst in at the back door, wanting to know all about the afternoon's visitor.

'She was like the princess in my story book.' Mary spread a handful of cutlery on the table and began to set it out.

'She was the most beautiful lady I've ever seen.'

'If you like those sort of looks,' Ewan drawled, reaching for a towel. Alex stiffened.

'What does that mean?'

Ewan turned, resting his backside on the edge of the sink, a slight smile on his face as he dried his fingers one by one. 'I'm just sayin' that a glass of spring water can be pleasant now and again, but I prefer somethin' with more bite to it, myself. Like a good whisky.'

'You keep your tongue off Fiona MacDowall.'

'I never mentioned her name,' Ewan protested. 'I was talking about different drinks—wasn't I, Mary?' His eyes were wide and innocent, but there was a smirk at the corners of his mouth.

'That's enough,' Kirsty said sharply, sensing trouble.

Alex ignored her. 'We both know who you were talking about,' he said tightly to his stepbrother. 'You're jealous because Fiona MacDowall wouldn't bother herself with the likes of you!'

'What makes you think she'd look at you either?'

'Nothing—Miss MacDowall's a customer, that's all.'

'Oh aye?' Ewan's faint smirk broadened

into a grin. 'I've never seen you simpering and blushing when Mr Gregg comes into the workshop.'

Caitlin gave a yelp of laughter at the thought, and Mary started to giggle. Alex, his face almost as red as his hair, stared at Ewan for a moment, then said slowly and clearly, 'Going back to what you were saying about drink, at least I'd not stoop so low as tae sip from another man's glass when his back's turned.'

The grin vanished from Ewan's face as though it had been struck off by a blow. He whitened, then tossed the towel down. 'You...' he began, all the amusement gone from his voice as he advanced on Alex, who moved willingly to meet him.

A swift step brought Kirsty between them. 'I'll have none of this in my kitchen!'

'We'll go outside then.' Alex's voice was hard and flat.

'You'll do nothing of the sort! If there's any blows being struck today, they'll come from me—and this!' Kirsty brandished the heavy wooden potato masher at them. 'Ewan, pick up that towel and sit at the table. As for you, Alex, go upstairs this instant and take that good suit off. The food'll be on the table in a minute.'

For a moment she thought that she might have to carry out her threat and use the masher, then Ewan threw himself sulkily into a chair and Alex, the threat over, marched from the room. Looking at her daughters, Kirsty saw that the merriment had flown. Caitlin was ashen faced, and Mary's eyes were bright with frightened tears.

'Caitlin, you put the soup out while Mary helps me to finish these potatoes.' When Mary came to her, she lifted the little girl onto a chair and put the heavy masher into her hands, covering them with her own so that her arms were about her daughter.

'You're getting to be too heavy to lift, milady—you've been eating too many potatoes. Now, push down hard, that's it...'

She realised that she was shaking inside. Ewan and Alex had always had squabbles, even fights on occasion. That was only to be expected from two boys growing up together and less than a year apart in age. But this had been different—this had been a confrontation between two grown men. It had blown up so quickly, too. She was confused as to exactly what they had said to each other, but it was clear that they both understood it.

Something had gone wrong between them, and she hoped that it could be resolved before it went too far.

# 18

It was to be a full month before Angus MacDowall, Fiona's father, returned to Glasgow. By that time Alex had completed the first piece of furniture for the girl, a chest of drawers painted a light stone colour, with a design of roses in all hues —cream, yellow and every shade of pink and red from shell-pink to crimson—edging the top. A full deep-pink rose decorated each drawer, its heart the brass handle.

'It's lovely, Alex,' Kirsty said when he showed her the finished piece. 'Mr MacDowall'll surely be impressed.'

'We thought—Fiona and me—that it was best tae complete a small piece first, tae let him see it. The rest should be finished by the turn of the year.' He started to rewrap the chest of drawers carefully in sacking. 'Mr Gavin's cart should be here within the hour tae take it to the house.'

Detailed technical drawings of each of the other pieces of furniture had also been completed, with the planned decorations clearly shown. Alex had worked hard at the sketches in his own time—when he wasn't in Glasgow with Fiona.

After the quarrel with Ewan, he hadn't invited the girl back to Paisley but visited Glasgow at least once a week, sometimes calling on Fiona in her home, sometimes going out walking with her or listening to band music in one of the city's many parks. From what Alex said, Kirsty gathered that the housekeeper was always in attendance; from what he didn't say, she had a shrewd idea that he and Fiona managed to spend a fair bit of time on their own.

'It'll end in tears,' Matt prophesied gloomily. 'That lassie's father'll be lookin' for a wealthy son-in-law, not a cabinet-maker who has tae work hard for every penny he can get.'

'It's just a friendship between the girl and Alex,' Kirsty protested, and her husband gave a disbelieving snort, then winced and barked, 'Will ye watch what ye're about, woman!'

'I'm sorry. It's hard to rub the stuff in properly without hurting.' Matt's health had deteriorated again, and Kirsty was rubbing the ointment Fiona had sent into his swollen knuckles, trying to loosen them.

'Just good friends?' he returned to the subject when the pain in his hand had eased. 'A lad, and a lassie their ages don't just have friendships. If ye've got any sense ye'll warn him tae put an end tae it before there's trouble.'

'Does that feel any better?'

'Aye, a bit.'

When he nodded, she went to wash her hands in the bowl of water on the stand, breathing in the rose-scented fragrance of the small tablet of soap she kept on the washstand. It made a pleasant change from wintergreen. She was sick of the smell of the ointment; the bedroom reeked of it these days.

It had been agreed between Fiona and Alex that he should wait until her father had settled back home before their meeting. To his surprise, when the summons finally arrived, it was an invitation to call on Angus MacDowall at his office, and not in his home.

'You're discussing business,' Kirsty pointed out, although she herself was surprised. 'He'll want it to be man to man, without Fiona there. Mebbe it means that he's going to give you an order for his big shop. Perhaps he'll ask you to the house afterwards.'

'Mebbe.' Alex's teeth worried at his lower lip, then he shrugged. 'I'll not know till I get there, will I?'

Bathed, and dressed in his good suit, his hair oiled down and his sketchbook under his arm, he went off to Glasgow and returned three hours later.

'He doesn't like the furniture,' Kirsty said as soon as she saw the look on his face.

'Oh, he liked it well enough—it's me he didn't like.' Alex tossed the sketchbook on the table and sank into a chair.

'You? Did you have words with the man?'

'I didn't spend enough time with him to have words about anything. Most of the time I was with George Gavin, being shown round the place.'

Kirsty sat down opposite him, confused. 'Start at the beginning. What did he think of the furniture?'

Alex kept his gaze fixed on his clasped hands. 'He said he liked it, and so did Fiona, and it was fine to go ahead with the rest of the order. He asked me about the workshop—if it was a big place, and who I worked for, and if I'd served my time there. I told him about Falkirk, and your father leaving it tae you, and I invited him over tae see it.'

'When?' Kirsty asked nervously, and he looked up at her, smiling faintly.

'You've no need tae worry, Mam, I've not landed you with a visitor again. He said that he'd like tae see the place sometime, but he said it in that sort of way that tells you a person's not telling the truth.' He suddenly slammed a fist on the table. 'Mam, I don't know what I've done tae annoy the man, but it seems that I must have done something.'

A cold feeling in Kirsty's chest hinted that she knew what Alex had done, even if he didn't. 'Was Fiona mentioned?'

'He said that she'd been taken with my work, and she'd apparently enjoyed visiting my home.' He gave a short laugh. 'That's just the word he used—"apparently", as if he didn't believe that she really had enjoyed coming here. Then he said that she'd been invited to visit friends in Fort William and she'd be gone for a while. And that was that. George Gavin was waiting in the other office. Mr MacDowall said he'd a lot tae see tae, after being away, and he'd asked Gavin tae show me round the shop.' He turned his right hand over on the table, uncurling the fingers and staring down at his palm. 'He could scarce bring himself tae shake hands with me when I left, Mam. It was as though he thought I was a leper!'

'Alex,' Kirsty began tentatively, 'have you thought that mebbe it's something to do with this friendship that's grown between you and his daughter while he was away?'

His head came up. 'What's wrong with friendship?' he asked at once, on the defensive. 'The lassie was lonely on her own with her father away. We like each other, that's all.'

'Mr MacDowall might have thought that you were becoming more than just friends.'

'You mean he's decided that I'm not good enough for his daughter?' he said bitterly. 'We've already talked about that, her and me. She told me that her father came from ordinary stock himself and he believes in judging folk by what they've done with their lives. She was certain he'd like me, and instead of that—'

Again he banged a fist on the table, then got to his feet abruptly. 'I'd best change into my work-clothes.'

The dull thump of the stick Matt kept by the bed echoed through the ceiling.

'One of these days,' Alex said, 'he'll come right through and you'll not have tae bother going up tae see what he wants.'

'Did I hear Alex?' Matt asked as soon as she went into the bedroom.

'You did. He's getting ready to go back to work.'

'How did he get on with the man?'

'Fine,' she lied, rescuing the newspaper, which had fallen off the bed, and restoring it to him. She didn't feel strong enough at that moment to tell him the truth and have to put up with his inevitable gloating.

'I'll have tae visit the wee room soon.'

Matt hated having to use a chamber pot, but when his hips and knees were bad, as they were that day, it was almost impossible for him to get to the bathroom unaided. He refused to allow Kirsty to help him, preferring to rely on his sons and on Todd, who had helped to nurse his own father in his final illness and, big as he was, had revealed a talent for providing steady and reliable support without causing added pain. He had taught the rest of them how to handle Matt more gently.

'I'll get Alex to give you a hand before he goes along to the workshop,' she said. But when Alex came downstairs and she passed the request on, he said abruptly, 'I'll send Todd and Ewan,' and went out.

A letter arrived for Alex on the following morning after he had gone to the workshop. Kirsty, seeing the Glasgow postmark, waited until after the midday meal, then called Alex back as he and Ewan prepared to leave for work.

'This came for you.' She handed the envelope over and was glad that she had waited until they were alone when she saw the naked emotion and hunger in his face as he took it from her. Alex had lied when he had claimed mere friendship with Fiona MacDowall. Kirsty turned quickly away and busied herself at the table, giving him privacy to tear it open and scan its contents.

'She's not going away tae Fort William at all!' His voice was exultant.

'I thought her father said—'

'He was right about her getting an invitation from friends there, but she's not going. She says it was him that wanted her tae accept.'

'Does she say anything about him being cool towards you?'

'Only that she had expected him tae invite me to the house after our meeting. She's as confused by the man's behaviour as I am—and she's known him all her life.' Beaming, he folded the letter and put it back into the envelope.

'Are you going to see her again?'

'Why not?'

'But Mr MacDowall—'

'As Fiona says, if he can't give either of us good reason why we should stop being friends, then why should we do what he wants? She says he's always wanted them tae be truthful with each other, and now he's the one who's broken his word.'

'Alex—'

'It's between me and Fiona, Mam,' he said, tucking the letter into his shirt pocket. 'I'd best get back tae work.'

Kirsty fretted about the matter all the

way to the shop and would have gone on fretting if Jean hadn't been waiting for her on the pavement, rocking from one foot to the other in an ungainly dance of impatience.

'I'm that glad you've arrived at last!' She seized hold of Kirsty's sleeve. 'It's that Hamilton lassie—she's back again.'

'Rose Hamilton? Am I never going to get rid of that girl? Tell her I'm not interested in going back to work for her mother,' Kirsty said in a panic, and turned to flee. Jean's fingers held her, digging painfully into her arm.

'I've already said you'd be here any minute. She's in the back shop. She's your problem, Kirsty, not mine. You cannae leave me with her!'

Rose Hamilton had avoided the chair with the broken spring and was perched on the edge of an upright chair. She bounced to her feet as soon as Kirsty appeared.

'I've had an idea.' Until then, Kirsty had only seen her animated by anger, but today the sparkle in the girl's eyes and the set of her shoulders spoke of excitement and a sense of purpose rather than frustration.

'What has any idea of yours got to do with me?' Kirsty was too worried about Alex and Fiona, not to mention Matt's health, to care what she said to this nuisance of a girl.

Rose didn't seem to notice the rudeness. 'It has everything to do with you—you're the reason I had it in the first place.' She sat down again, but Kirsty stayed on her feet to indicate to the girl that her unwelcome visit was going to be brief. 'When I came here to ask you to come back and work for my mother again I noticed that this place was too small for all the clothes you have in store.' Rose indicated the garments hanging on the walls and the pile of clothing Jean had brought in that morning, waiting on the floor to be sorted out. 'I also noticed that the shop next door's for rent.'

'I cannae afford tae rent that one as well,' Jean immediately chimed in.

'I could.'

'You?' Kirsty and Jean spoke together, and Rose beamed and settled herself more comfortably in her chair, sure now of their attention.

'When I reached my eighteenth birthday a few weeks ago I inherited some money from my grandmamma. I want to do something useful with it—and what better than helping you to expand this place?'

Jean gasped and sat down abruptly on the arm of the broken chair, while Kirsty said at once, 'It's out of the question!'

'Why? You told me yourself that this shop is popular with the local women. It would make sense for them and for you to improve it.'

'Your parents would never agree to it.'

The girl's chin jutted in an all too familiar gesture. 'The inheritance is mine, to spend as I wish. It has nothing to do with my parents.'

'Even so, I'm sure your father'll expect you to save it towards your future.'

'He wants me to invest it.' With a sweeping movement of the arm, Rose indicated the small room. 'I could invest it here.'

'I doubt if that's what he meant,' Kirsty said irritably. She had alterations to see to, and after all that had happened at home, she had been looking forward to a quiet hour or so with her needle. 'And what about your mother? She'll say you should spend your money on yourself'

'This would be for myself. I'm not just proposing to hand the money over to you and go away. I would become a partner, and I'd hope to make more money out of it eventually. That's what investments are all about,' Rose explained smilingly.

'But you could just as easily lose every penny of it,' Kirsty argued, keeping one eye on Jean, who had slid from the arm into the chair itself and flopped there, mouth open like a fish.

'My dear woman,' a flash of the old, arrogant Rose came through, 'I didn't just wake up this morning with the idea in my head. I still feel guilty about what happened to you. After you refused to take your job back, or let me give you money to make up for my...' she paused, then said flatly, 'my childish, selfish stupidity, I started thinking of other ways to make up for what I did to you. And one day the answer just came to me. I've come down here every day this month, ever since we got back home, to watch the people coming in and out of the shop. You do quite a brisk trade. If the place was larger you might very well do better. I'm sure my father would call that a sound investment.'

'But this isnae a dress shop, miss,' Jean quavered. 'We only sell second-hand clothes. The folk don't pay much for them.'

'A shilling here and a shilling there can mount up,' Rose Hamilton said briskly. 'I've taken advice on the matter. I spoke to the junior partner in my father's lawyer's office, and he has confirmed that my inheritance is mine to use as I wish. He took the trouble to listen to what I had to say,' she added pointedly, 'and he would like to speak with you both.'

She paused, looking from one of them

to the other, then when they said nothing, 'Please don't turn my suggestion down without considering it,' she said, her voice suddenly losing its force and shaking slightly. 'Think what you could do to this place with a little money behind you.'

'I don't know what tae say,' Jean faltered, and Rose nodded.

'It's all very sudden, I know.' She got to her feet, gathering up her bag and her gloves. 'I should leave you to talk about it. I'll come back tomorrow afternoon for your answer.'

At the door she turned and said directly to Kirsty, 'You probably think that I'm just looking for another toy to play with, but that's not true. I know that my parents think I'm fit for nothing but marriage then running some man's home, like my sisters. But I want more than that. I want to do something with my life while it's still mine.'

# 19

'Have you got any brandy?' Kirsty asked when the girl had gone.

'No.' Jean was still lolling in the chair, heedless of the way her skirts rode up to expose her short, bowed legs.

'In that case I'm going to the public house along the road to buy a wee bottle of the stuff.'

Jean shot upright. 'You can't go intae a pub! Someone might see you!'

'I don't care, I need something to steady me. I've heard that spirits are a good help for shock.' Kirsty turned to the door, wondering if her shaky knees would carry her as far as the public house.

'Wait—if you're that determined, there's some whisky in the wee cupboard by the grate in my room. For hot toddies,' she added hastily. 'I get terrible throats in the winter.'

When Kirsty had located the small bottle and returned down the dark, rickety staircase, she poured a generous amount into two cups then topped them up with tea.

Jean downed half a cupful in one swallow, then erupted into a bout of coughing. She banged her chest with a clenched fist and said, when her voice returned, 'It seems tae do the trick.'

The sharp sting of the whisky made Kirsty's throat muscles contract, and for a terrible moment she thought that she was going to vomit. Then the contractions eased and a warm glow began to spread through her stomach.

'What d'ye think we should do about the lassie's offer, Kirsty?'

'It's your shop.'

'Mine?' Jean snorted. 'It stopped bein' my shop the day you walked in with all yer fancy plans about hangin' the gowns up an' puttin' them on display outside an' doin' alterations. You cannae leave me tae decide things for myself now!'

'Rose Hamilton can't be trusted. Look what she did to that gown I was making for her birthday party.'

'Give the lassie her due, Kirsty. She apologised for that, an' tried tae put things right.'

'You're right,' Kirsty had to admit. 'But even so, you'd be taking a terrible risk, letting her get her hands on this place.'

The broken bell over the shop door indicated the arrival of a customer with its usual dull 'chunk', and Jean drained her cup then got to her feet. 'She doesnae seem tae be as empty-headed as most of her kind.'

'Even so, I'd not trust her.'

'You're probably right,' Jean said, and disappeared into the front shop.

When Kirsty arrived the following afternoon, though, Jean had changed her mind. 'I think we should go and see Rose Hamilton's fancy lawyer.'

'I thought we decided against it yesterday.'

'I know what we decided,' Jean interrupted with unaccustomed asperity. 'But I couldnae sleep a wink last night for thinkin' about it. My mother, rest her soul, worked herself tae death tae scratch a livin' out of this shop, and after she went I was doin' the same until you came along with all your daft ideas.' She grinned at Kirsty. 'That's when I began tae enjoy myself instead of just workin' tae keep a roof over my head and food in my belly,' she said. Then the grin faded. 'Now this Hamilton lassie's offerin' me the chance tae make a proper livin' out of the place instead of just scrapin' by. And you could do with more money too, with your man an invalid. If her plans work out the way she seems tae think they will, you'd never need tae beg for work again from the likes of her mother.'

'Jean, it's too much of a risk. What if Rose gets tired of helping us? She'll marry soon; most rich girls do. I don't see any husband agreeing to let her spend her money on a business like this.'

'The only way tae find out the answers is tae ask the questions. When the lassie comes back today I'm going tae tell her we'll talk tae this lawyer of hers.'

'We?'

Jean's determination dissolved. 'You'll have tae be with me, Kirsty, for I couldnae face him on my own. I've given in tae all your ideas. You should be willin' tae stand by me for once, just in case this notion of hers turns out tae be better than we realise. Will you?'

Kirsty hesitated, then nodded. It was true that Jean deserved her support, but at the same time she was wary of trusting Rose Hamilton. She felt that she and Jean were both taking a risk.

John Brodie, a junior partner in the legal firm that handled the Hamiltons' business, had been given responsibility for Rose Hamilton's finances. He was young, efficient and, to Kirsty's surprise, enthusiastic about his client's new venture. He listened patiently, quelling Rose with a glance whenever she tried to break in, while Jean outlined the shop's history, haltingly at first but gaining confidence as she went along.

'And the proposal is that the three of you would be partners in this development?'

Kirsty began to explain that she herself had no money to put into such a venture, but Jean promptly overruled her. 'Kirsty does the alterations, and she's the one that's come up with all the ideas about improvin' the place. I'd not want tae make any changes without her agreement.'

Brodie smiled at her. 'I can understand that, Miss Chisholm. The partnership I referred to would be based on the strengths and abilities of each partner; Mrs Lennox would qualify in terms of her past and, it is hoped, future contributions to the success of the business, you yourself would continue to be the owner and senior partner, and Miss Hamilton's main asset is her ability to provide financial investment.'

'As Kirsty already knows, I can't be trusted near a sewing machine,' Rose Hamilton admitted with a grin. 'But I'd like to do more than just contribute the money.' She sat forward in her chair, looking hopefully at Jean and Kirsty. 'I know I wouldn't be of much help in other ways, but I was good at arithmetic and English at school. I could see to the books for you, and any writing that might have to be done.'

'You'd have to be given a trial first,' the lawyer said promptly, and she shot upright in her chair, glaring at him.

'John Brodie, you've known me all our lives. If I say I can keep books, then I can!'

He smiled blandly at her. 'I don't doubt your word, Rose—as a friend. But this is business. Miss Chisholm and Mrs Lennox have already proved their worth, and you must prove yours. If they are in agreement, I can arrange for a fictitious set of accounts to be drawn up to find out if you can balance them.'

Rose scowled at him then, realising that he was not going to be moved, she muttered, 'Oh—very well.'

'Ladies, are you in agreement?'

'We've not even decided on the partnership yet,' Kirsty objected, feeling that matters were hurrying along too quickly.

'You're quite right, Mrs Lennox. But if the matters under discussion do go ahead, would you be willing to let Miss Hamilton see to the books and any administration that might be required—if a trial proves her fit to do so? We would, of course, appoint a financial auditor to make sure on an annual basis that everything was being done properly.'

Jean and Kirsty exchanged glances, then Jean nodded. 'That'd be fine—if we get tae that stage.'

'And a fair and agreed system of sharing out the profits would be drawn up.'

'Profits? There's never been any of those!' Jean squawked.

'There will be now,' Rose told her confidently.

'If all goes as we hope there most certainly will be,' John Brodie agreed.

'I'll have a look at the place tomorrow, if that suits.'

'That Hamilton lassie'll be the ruin of both of you, Mam,' Alex stormed when he heard the news. 'She had you dismissed from your position as her mother's sewing woman, and now she's out tae spoil the pleasure you get from working in the shop.'

'It's Jean's decision—and Jean's shop.'

He ran a hand through his red hair. 'Could you not have persuaded her tae say no?'

'Jean has a mind of her own, and she can stick her heels in when the mood takes her. The lawyer seems sensible enough,' Kirsty said hopefully. She had fully expected John Brodie to be a male version of Rose but instead had been favourably impressed by the young man.

'He's one of her own kind, Mam,' Alex argued. 'No doubt he lives in a fine big house himself. How d'ye know he's not just as irresponsible as she is?'

'He's got his reputation to think of. I don't think he'd allow Rose to destroy the shop.'

'I'm telling you, she'll ruin everything. I've met the woman—I know what I'm talking about.'

Kirsty's temper began to fray. 'D'you

not think I'm worried enough about how it's all going to turn out without you fretting me as well?' she snapped at her son. 'It's what Jean wants, and we'll just have to hope for her sake that it doesn't go wrong!'

'It's been that long since the place was opened up,' the factor's man said apologetically, struggling to turn the large key in the lock. When it finally gave way, John Brodie was first into the vacant shop's stuffy dark interior. Rose was about to follow when Jean warned, 'There'll probably be rats.'

'Nae harm if there is, missus,' the factor's man said cheerfully. 'They'll be more scared of us than we are of them. But it's best for ye tae wait till we get the shutters down from the windows and let a wee bit light intae the place.' He stamped his feet on the dusty boards as he went to the window, and the three women huddled in the doorway, Rose included, gave out muted squeaks as they heard scuttering sounds from below the floor.

Brodie, looking a trifle apprehensive, rattled a sharp tattoo on the boards with his cane. 'We'll bring in the rat-catcher—and get all this cleared out,' he added as the shutters came away from the large window and autumn sunlight flooded in to reveal discarded rubbish scattered over the floor and the long counter. 'Then we'll get some cleaning women in.'

The factor's employee went into the back shop as the potential partners, keeping close together for comfort, ventured in from the pavement. There came the sound of nails being wrenched from wood, then light broke through the dark oblong of the inner doorway. He reappeared, dusting his hands together.

'I'll just take the upstairs shutters down, then yez can all have a good look round,' he announced.

Twenty minutes later they arrived back in the main shop, dusty but exhilarated. 'It's a grand size.' Jean ran her hand over the long sturdy counter. 'Much bigger than my wee place.'

'We could use this as the shop, and your shop next door as the sewing room,' Rose suggested. 'You'd have better light in there, Kirsty.'

'And if Jean's back shop was cleared it would make a fine wee place for folk to try on the clothes,' Kirsty put in, then they all started talking together.

'What about this back shop and the wee scullery next to it?'

'They'd be for our own use—'

'And there's more storage space up-stairs—'

'And more space in here to display the clothes—'

'The first thing we must do,' Rose said firmly, 'is find a laundry.'

'A laundry?' Jean was bewildered. 'What for?'

'To get the incoming clothes cleaned before we offer them for sale.'

Jean and Kirsty gaped at each other, then at their proposed partner. 'But folk can wash them after they buy them from us,' Kirsty pointed out.

'They ought to be clean when we hand them over. It would be better for the shop and for us if they were dealt with right away. You'd surely prefer to know that the clothes you were sewing were clean, Kirsty.'

'Most of them havenae even been worn much,' Jean argued. 'And they come off the backs of moneyed folk that take baths.'

'Just because people have money it doesn't mean that they bathe regularly,' Rose told her sweepingly, then glared at John Brodie when he turned away and made a strange choking noise. 'Some of the garments hanging in your back shop are badly in need of a good washing, and all the others are dusty. Do stop making that silly noise, John?'

The factor's man obligingly banged the young lawyer on the back.

'But we cannae afford tae have them washed, or tae do it ourselves!'

Rose was adamant. 'We'll find the money.'

John Brodie, his choking fit over, turned back to face them. 'The important question is, do you want to rent this place?'

'Do we?' Rose asked the others, her eyes pleading, her voice hopeful. The moment of decision had come. Jean and Kirsty, taken aback by the suddenness of it all, glanced uncertainly at each other, then Jean gave a faint nod.

'We do,' Kirsty said, and Rose squealed like a child and clapped her hands together.

'Then I'll draw up an agreement for your signatures and see about renting this shop,' Brodie said briskly. 'The next step will be to obtain permission from the landlord to carry out the necessary refurbishment in both premises, but I don't anticipate any problems since this place has been empty for so long.' He beamed round the circle of faces. 'I'm sure, ladies, that your new partnership will do very well for itself.'

'Laundry, indeed,' Jean muttered as they stood together on the pavement five minutes later watching the factor's representative lock the door again.

'It might be a good idea.'

'But think what it'll cost!'

'She's the one who'll have to worry about that—and Mr Brodie. He'll keep an eye on Rose.'

'We'll all have tae keep an eye on that lassie. She's a bossy one.'

'Are you sure you're doing the right thing?'

Jean studied the empty shop then glanced at her own little place. 'I'll tell you better in a few months' time,' she said, her voice sharp with nerves. 'But for now—I just have a feelin', Kirsty, that this is worth the tryin'.'

# 20

Espedair Street was all but empty, Kirsty and a man loitering a few yards further along the pavement being the only people out and about on this wet and windy day. Crossing over from the tobacconist's and walking the last few yards to her door, head down against the wind and a basket in each hand, Kirsty felt that despite the miserable weather the street was cheerier than the shop she had just left, with Beth Laidlaw presiding behind the counter.

The girl's sullen, cold mood never seemed to change—as far as Kirsty was concerned, at any rate. She had just dashed poor Todd's hopes of renting yet another home, on the grounds that it wasn't comfortable enough.

His usual cheerfulness was beginning to fade and might disappear altogether if Beth continued to be so finicky. The truth, as Kirsty saw it, was that Beth had set her heart on Kirsty's house, and nothing less would satisfy her.

The man, well dressed against the weather in a bowler hat and caped raincoat, was glancing in at the mouth of the pend now. She thought of offering her assistance, but just then the rain started to come down harder, so instead she put down one of the heavy baskets and lifted the latch, anxious to get indoors. She pushed the door open and stooped to her basket, then froze as a voice said, 'Kate?'

She straightened and turned to look at the man who had been by the pend. The face was that of a stranger, but she knew the blue eyes that looked out from it. She saw these same eyes every time Alex looked at her.

'Sandy,' she said, the past twenty years tumbling away from her as though they had never happened.

'You've not changed, Kate.' He took off his bowler, letting the rain fall on hair that was still thick and curly, but silver now, with no trace of red. Then, glancing up at the sky and blinking against the fast-falling rain, he said, 'Can I talk with you—away from this downpour?'

Her mind jumped into action. Alex and Ewan would be in the workshop, and Matt, who had had a restless night, was still in his bed and, with any luck, asleep. It would surely be safe for a little while.

She nodded and led the way as he picked up her basket then took the other from her hand. She had meant to take him into the parlour, but while she closed the door he walked ahead of her to the kitchen, the only room he had ever been in.

When she arrived at the door he was setting the baskets on the table and glancing around. 'I mind this place as if it was yesterday,' he said. 'But I don't mind it being so small. We're alone?'

'My sons are in the workshop. My husband's in his bed; he's not well.'

'I know.' He put his hat on the table and unfastened his long raincoat to reveal a well-cut suit. 'You look as if you've seen a ghost, Kate.' His voice was deeper than before, and his speech cultured.

'I have. I thought you were—'

'Dead? Killed by your father? I very nearly was.' He indicated the coat. 'D'you mind if I hang it up? I'd not want it to drip all over your kitchen.'

She nodded, moving automatically to light the gas beneath the kettle as he hung the coat on the back of the yard door.

'How did you know I was here?'

'From Alex.'

'Alex?' She felt as though she was caught up in a dream.

'Your son.' He turned from the door to face her, pausing behind Matt's chair with both hands resting on the back. 'Our son.'

'When did you see Alex?'

He stared at her, as confused as she was, then said, 'I'm sorry, I expected you to know, though I don't see why you should. Alex is making some furniture for my daughter.'

The kitchen seemed to blur for a moment. 'Fiona? You're Fiona's father?'

His head dipped slightly. 'Angus Mac-Dowall.'

'But—surely Sandy's short for Alexander?'

He gave a soft bark of a laugh. 'Red-haired lads are always called Sandy in Scotland—you know that.'

'All these years,' Kirsty said wonderingly, 'and I didn't even know your real name.'

'I was only an orphan, Kate,' he said with sudden bitterness in his voice and his gaze. 'Orphans aren't supposed to own anything, including names. I always had one, though. I suppose that at that time I must have been the only person who knew it. A lot of people know it now.' His fingers had been running over the raised pattern on the back of the chair. Now he looked down at it. 'Is this his work?'

'Yes.'

'He's a talented laddie. You should be proud of him.'

The kettle came to the boil and she made tea, grateful for something ordinary to do. Sandy drew out a chair by the table and sat down, watching her.

'What have you told him about me?'

'I said you'd died.'

'Died? You left him with no hope of ever meeting up with me?'

'I thought you had. Nobody would tell me what had become of you.'

'You could have come to the infirmary and found out. I looked for you, but you never came.' For all his confidence, she heard, for just a few seconds, a trace of the lonely, frightened boy he had once been.

'I wanted to.' The grief she had suffered all those years ago swept back, putting a tremor into her own voice. 'But my father sent me to his sister's in Stirling.'

Pouring tea for them both, she told him briefly about running away from her aunt's house with Alex only days after his birth and about her marriage and, finally, about her return to Paisley. Talking gave her a chance to look at him; although he couldn't be more than thirty-seven years of age, and moved like a young, active man, his hair had nothing left of the original fiery red other than just a hint in his eyebrows and well-trimmed moustache. Prosperity had filled his body out and rounded his features. His mouth was firm, with a slight droop at the corners. Deep lines etched round it, and his nose gave his face a look of severity in repose.

'I'd no knowledge of what had happened to you—or to the child,' he said when she had finished. 'I'd only the one visitor in the infirmary—the old woman that ran the tobacconist's shop at the corner.'

'Mrs Laidlaw? She visited you?'

'She'll be dead now?'

'A long time ago.'

'And rotting in hell, I hope, alongside your father,' Sandy said evenly, and she shivered at the chill in his voice. 'She said that the shock of what she called my attack on your father had caused you to lose the bairn you'd been carrying and that there wasn't an employer in Paisley who'd give me work. She said that if I valued my life I'd get as far away from Paisley as I could.'

He paused, looking back down the years, then went on, 'When I was discharged from the infirmary I walked to Glasgow and found work.'

The tea cooled untasted in both cups as he listed the events in his life as though they had happened to somebody else—hard work and study, clawing his way up the ladder of self-improvement, marriage, the birth of his daughter, the death of his wife.

'I was fortunate enough to find a good employer who taught me everything and left his small business to me when he died. I built it up into a success, for Fiona as much as for myself. Then she brought Alex into my life, and I looked at him and saw myself at his age. That was when I knew that that old bitch had lied to me.'

He looked down into his cup, then across the table at Kirsty. 'He and Fiona are still meeting, aren't they?'

'He's not said anything, but I think they are.'

'I suspected it.' For a brief moment his gaze softened. 'Fiona's like her mother—she needs good reason before she'll agree to anything. And I was so confused with the shock of seeing him after all those years of believing that he had never existed that I couldn't think of any reason to give her. I let her believe that it was a matter of him being working class, while she—I should have known that my own daughter would never accept that,' he said, pushing the cup away, angry with himself. 'That's why I came to see you. It has to be stopped, Kate. We have to stop them meeting each other. D'you not see? They're both my children. They're brother and sister.'

The words stifled the breath in Kirsty's throat. She had been so caught up in seeing Sandy again that the real reason for his visit hadn't occurred to her.

'Oh—dear God!' she whispered.

'Nothing but the truth will do for her—and for him, I've no doubt.' He spread his hands wide on the table. 'We must end this friendship before it goes any further. I'm not saying that it will turn to love, but we can't take—'

'It already has, on Alex's part at least.'

'What?' He blinked at her, then said impatiently, 'No, no—they've only known each other for a short while, and they're too young for strong feelings. It's the future we have to worry about.'

'They're older than we were, Sandy.'

For a long moment they stared at each other, then Kirsty jumped up guiltily as a muffled thumping came from the upper floor.

'My husband—he'll be wanting to come downstairs.'

Sandy got to his feet at once and

collected his coat and hat. 'I'll go. Things are bad enough without making them worse. You'll tell him, Kate?'

'I'll tell him. And the Lord only knows how he'll take it.'

'He'll have to take it. So will Fiona. At least,' Sandy said with a glimmer of cold amusement in his voice as he went into the hall, 'you have the consolation of knowing that he'll not be beaten half to death as I was for looking at a lassie he can't have.'

As usual, Ewan went out as soon as he had eaten his dinner and Caitlin, who found her work in the grocery tiring, went to bed not long after Mary. As soon as she had gone, Kirsty laid her sewing down and said bluntly, 'Alex, Mr MacDowall came here today.'

He was in his usual seat at the table, studying books. His red head jerked up at once. 'He was here? Why didn't you fetch me?'

'It was me he came to see.'

His eyes narrowed. 'About me and Fiona?'

'You're still meeting each other, aren't you?'

'We are, and if he has anything to say on the matter it's me he should say it to, not you!' She could see his temper beginning to rise.

'Alex—'

He scooped the books up and got to his feet. 'He's got no right tae bring you intae it, and he's got no right tae treat me and Fiona like two bairns!'

'He's got every right!' Kirsty scrambled out of her chair and snatched at his sleeve as he brushed past on his way to the door. 'Every right, Alex. He's your father.'

'What?' His eyes widened then glazed with shock. 'What?' he said again.

'He's your father,' she repeated, and saw the colour drain from his stricken face. Slowly he turned back to the table, pulling himself free of her grasp, and put the books down. Then he drew out a chair and lowered himself into it gently, as though his bones had become as brittle as glass and he was afraid of breaking them.

'You said that my father had died.'

'I thought he had.' The wind had died down late in the afternoon, but now it had returned. She could hear it whistling down the chimney and moaning through the pend, a fitting background to the story she had to tell her son about herself and Sandy and her father's vicious assault on his apprentice in that very room, and about her banishment and the cruel lies her lover had been told while recovering in the infirmary. Alex's burning gaze never left her face.

'All those years I was certain that he had died—and he thought that you'd never been born. Then he met you and recognised himself in you.' She waited for a moment, then as he said nothing, 'Alex,' she said gently, 'you and Fiona—'

'Fiona!' Shock suddenly blazed into his eyes and he clapped his hands over his face. 'Dear God—me and Fiona! Wantin' her's the same as lustin' after Caitlin, or wee Mary!'

'It's not like that at all!' Kirsty reached out to touch his hand, but he jerked away, his throat muscles pumping as he swallowed hard.

'Leave—me—be!' he said, and lunged out of his seat and towards the back door, wrenching it open and disappearing into the darkness.

The wind swooped in, setting the curtains at the window into a frenzied dance, sending Matt's discarded newspaper flapping beneath the table, wrapping Kirsty's skirt about her legs. She followed Alex, afraid to leave him on his own.

He was a humped silhouette at the corner where the pend opened into the lane, supporting himself with one hand on the wall as he bent over to vomit on the ruts and grooves carved into the mud by the cartwheels. She waited, the wind's cold bite, more like winter than October, sinking almost at once through clothes and skin and flesh, striking her to the bone, until the paroxysm was over and he had straightened, wiping his mouth on his sleeve. Then she stepped up beside him.

'Come inside—you'll freeze out here.'

Before he could answer, Ewan came whistling through the pend. 'What's going on?'

'Alex's stomach's troubling him,' Kirsty said swiftly.

'Cannae hold your drink? Here—' Ewan protested as Alex pushed him aside roughly, making him stagger, and strode through the pend and out into the street. He made to follow, but Kirsty held him back.

'Leave him—he's not well.'

She urged Ewan towards the back door and he went reluctantly, grumbling. Kirsty followed him upstairs and lay awake by Matt's side, listening. After about an hour, she thought she heard Alex in the kitchen, but he didn't come up the stairs.

When she went down in the morning he was sprawled in Matt's chair, fully dressed and sound asleep, reeking of drink and clutching an empty whisky bottle in his arms.

# 21

Matt, with little else to occupy his mind, picked at Alex's moodiness and his silence as if trying to unravel a tangle of wool.

'He'll be frettin' over that lassie,' he told Kirsty, a thin thread of satisfaction in his voice. 'She's sent him off with a flea in his ear. Didn't I tell ye he was settin' his sights too high?' His voice went on and on until she could scarcely bear to be in the same room with him, while she held her tongue, determined not to make matters worse by lashing out at him and perhaps, in her exasperation, letting slip more than she should.

Ewan complained about his stepbrother's bad temper in the workshop, and on one occasion when Kirsty went to get help to bring Matt downstairs she heard angry voices, which cut off as soon as she opened the door, and found Todd standing between Ewan and Alex, who were scowling at each other from separate ends of the shop.

'What's going on here?'

Alex swung towards the workbench without answering, while Ewan muttered, 'Nothin'.'

'Just a wee argument about work, Mrs Lennox,' Todd said. 'Is the master ready tae come downstairs? Come on, Ewan, we'll give him a hand.'

Once Matt was settled in the kitchen she followed them outside, detaining Todd for a moment. 'Were the two of them fighting?'

'No, no,' he assured her, shifting from one foot to the other, his eyes refusing to meet hers.

'Todd—'

'I've got tae get back, Mrs Lennox,' he said, and slid away before she could say another word.

The shop was Kirsty's rock in the midst of all the domestic turmoil. Whenever she stepped through its door the growing weight of family problems seemed to slide from her shoulders, and for the short time she was there she felt like a different person in a different life. She said nothing to Jean about Sandy coming back into her life; she could tell by the concern in her friend's eyes that Jean knew that something was wrong, but the woman was too loyal a friend to pry. One day Kirsty would tell her, but not yet.

John Brodie had obtained permission to make alterations in both shops and found a builder. At the end of October the 'For Rent' sign came down in the shop adjoining Jean's, and on the same day the partnership papers were signed. Rose, the last to affix her signature, did so with a flourish, then beamed at her new partners. 'A door has just opened,' she announced in ringing tones.

'I've a wee bit of a feelin' that it's opened beneath my two feet,' Jean confided to Kirsty as they left the office.

'It's still your shop. It says so on the papers Mr Brodie drew up, and it'll say so above the new door. We'll stand together, you and me.'

Reluctantly, Jean had had to agree to the temporary closure of her little shop, so that both premises could be refurbished. It had been decided that an archway would be broken through the wall between the new main shop and the former shop, which was to become Kirsty's sewing room, and doors installed between the two back shops and the rooms on the upper floor.

Once Jean's shop was closed, the two of them worked alongside the women who had been hired to clear everything from the new shop before the builders came in. To their surprise, Rose helped as well, wrapped in a large apron and with a scarf tied around her head.

'I want to be more involved with the place than just providing the money. I mean to do something with my life.'

'Your mother won't be pleased,' Jean ventured, and Rose, wringing out a filthy cloth with deft twists of her strong young wrists, grinned at her. 'She's not, but I'm of an age to do as I please.'

Despite her sheltered upbringing the girl wasn't afraid of hard work. Her inexperience caused considerable amusement among the other cleaners, but Rose, fully aware of her own incompetence, was quite willing to be the butt of their jokes and soon earned their respect with her dogged determination and willingness to tackle anything, even the removal of a dead mouse found behind a pile of rubbish. While Kirsty and Jean and the other women pressed themselves in a shuddering, squealing mass against the walls, Rose carried the tiny body out into the overgrown back yard at arm's length by the tail and dropped it into the metal rubbish container, saying, as she returned to the shop, 'Poor wee thing, what a terrible place to die in.'

The restless, mutinous girl Kirsty had known in the Hamilton house had matured overnight. As promised, she found a laundry willing to take on the entire contents of Jean's shop. Despite Jean's protests, everything was whisked off in batches to be washed and ironed.

'She's that forceful I don't know if I'm

goin' tae be able tae stop her from takin' over entirely.' Jean's small round face was puckered with concern.

'You've got a good sharp tongue in your head,' Kirsty urged. 'You'll just have to use it.'

'It's a plain-spoken tongue, though, and she's such a lady,' Jean fretted. 'I know she's worked alongside the rest o' us, and I couldnae have done what she did with that mouse,' they shuddered in unison at the thought, 'but she's that bossy at times.'

Todd and Alex were easing Matt into his chair when Sandy MacDowall arrived at the back door. Kirsty's heart almost failed her when she opened it and saw him standing there. She stared up into his set face and he looked back at her stonily.

'I'd like to see Alex. The lad in the workshop said he was here.'

'Who is it, Kirsty? Bring them in, for there's the devil of a draught,' Matt shouted peevishly, and she had no option but to stand back and let Sandy walk past her into the house.

Alex's face tightened when he saw the visitor. 'What d'you want?'

Matt had taken in the newcomer's good clothes and confident bearing at a glance. 'Alex, that's no way tae talk tae—'

'Angus MacDowall. And you, I take

it, are Matthew Lennox. Don't try to get up—I know from my daughter that you're not so able.' Sandy took Matt's twisted hand in his and shook it gently, careful not to cause any pain. Behind his back, Alex's blazing eyes asked his mother silent questions, and Kirsty shook her head helplessly, unable to supply the answers. Todd, after a swift glance from mother to son, slipped quietly out of the back door.

At Matt's invitation, Sandy sat down on Kirsty's usual chair. 'I came about the work that's being done for my daughter.'

'A bonny lassie, an' kindly, tae.'

'It's good of you to say so, Mr Lennox.' A faint smile touched Sandy's mouth. 'I'll admit to agreeing with you, but perhaps I'm biased, being her father. She's...gone away to visit friends in Fort William,' he added, turning to look at Alex, who stood motionless by the table. 'She'll be gone for some considerable time.' He reached into his pocket and brought out an envelope. 'She asked me to give you this. I promised that it would be delivered, and I thought it best to bring it myself to make certain that it reached you.'

Alex's gaze flickered briefly to the envelope being held out to him, but he made no move to take it. Sandy tossed it onto the table close to the younger man's hand.

'I wanted you to know that the fact that she has gone away will make no difference to her order. We both want you to complete it. When d'you expect that to be?'

The question was directly addressed to Alex, who answered through white, set lips. 'By the year's end.'

'Good. Let Mr Gavin know when it's finished, and he'll arrange to have it collected,' Sandy said, then produced a second, bulkier envelope. 'I'll pay for the entire order now. It's my own experience that folk prefer to wait until the goods are delivered, but I know that you're trustworthy and that you'll no doubt be glad of the money to buy timber and the like.'

Matt took the envelope, his eyes brightening as he felt the weight of it. 'That's generous of ye, Mr MacDowall.'

'I've put something extra in, to show my appreciation.'

'There's no need of that.' Alex's voice cracked through the air like a whiplash. 'I agreed a fair price with—with your daughter, Mr MacDowall,' he almost spat the name out, 'and I've no wish tae take a penny more from you.'

'But I've put you to a great deal of inconvenience,' Sandy told him quietly. 'I want to do what I can to help.' Then, as

276

Alex said nothing more, 'And I'm also here to ask if you'll make more furniture, and decorate it, when Fiona's is done. The new order would be for my shop. I'd like to see what my customers think of it.'

Matt's eyes gleamed. 'We'd be happy tae—' he began, just as Alex rapped out, 'No!'

'Alex! The man's offerin' us more work!'

'The order book's full,' Alex snapped at his stepfather.

'We'll see about that. Kirsty, fetch the book!'

'I said we're too busy. Find someone else tae make your furniture, Mr MacDowall, and tae paint it,' Alex said icily, making for the door. 'Good day tae you!'

As the door slammed behind him, Kirsty noticed that the envelope Sandy had tossed onto the table was gone.

Matt struggled to his feet, gobbling and spluttering like a turkey. 'Come back here! Alex!'

He tottered and almost fell as his bad knee gave way. Sandy and Kirsty both jumped forward to support him and ease him back into his chair.

'Fetch him back this instant, Kirsty!'

'I'll do nothing of the kind. It's Alex who's in charge of the workshop now, and he has the right to decide what orders can be accepted.' She glared at Sandy, who had the grace to look slightly ashamed.

'He'll not be runnin' it for much longer if he cannae learn tae mind his temper!' Matt fumed. 'Ye see what I have tae put up with, Mr MacDowall? That laddie's impossible tae deal with when the mood comes over him.'

'Matt, you know that's not true.'

'Don't you start defendin' him again. Just because he's yer first-born ye think the sun shines out of his arse—beggin' yer pardon, Mr MacDowall,' Matt said, suddenly remembering their caller. 'It's just the way he angers me at times. If I didnae need him so badly because of no' bein' able tae work mysel', I'd take him by the scruff o' the neck and run him out!'

Sandy reached for his hat, his face suddenly wiped of all expression. 'In my opinion, Mr Lennox, he's a very talented young man, who has probably, as he said, got more than enough work to do for the moment. Don't distress yourself; my furniture can be ordered another time—mebbe next year.'

'I'll show you out, Mr MacDowall—by the street door.' Trembling with rage, Kirsty led him through the hall.

'What did you think you were doing, coming here and upsetting the boy like that?' she stormed at him when they were on the footpath, with no danger of Matt hearing them. 'Have you not done enough harm to him?'

His eyes blazed blue fire down at her, just as Alex's did. 'I've done nothing. I wasn't the one who let him think all those years of his life that his father was dead. I promised Fiona that I'd make sure he got her letter, and heaven only knows I've let her down badly enough without breaking my word on that promise too. And I wanted him to see for himself that I hadn't withheld it, or tampered with it. And...' he hesitated, then said with a shrug of the shoulders, 'I wanted to see him again.'

'In God's name why?'

'He's my son,' Sandy said icily. 'Just because I knew nothing of his existence it doesn't mean that he's of no importance to me.'

'And now you've handed the letter over and—' Kirsty stopped and turned, hearing footsteps on the pavement at her back. 'Beth.'

'Mrs Lennox.' The girl swept by, nodding curtly to Kirsty, running her eyes appreciatively over Sandy, smiling sweetly at him when he raised his hat to her.

'Does it not matter that you've upset the boy?' Kirsty asked when Beth had gone out of earshot.

'He'll recover from it. He's got steel in him,' Sandy said, glancing beyond her to the pend. 'A lad to be proud of, Kate. Good day to you.'

Watching his straight back stride away from her, Kirsty knew that there was nothing left of the Sandy she had remembered fondly during all their years apart. The struggle to make his way in a harsh world had taken away the warmth and compassion that had once been at the very core of his nature. She wondered if the death of the lad she had once known had begun with the first blow of her father's fist.

When she went back into the kitchen Matt was counting the envelope's contents clumsily. 'God, Kirsty, the man's been very generous.' His eyes were shining.

'He must like Alex's work a lot more than you do,' she said tartly.

The sarcasm was lost on him. 'He couldnae like him for his manner, that's for certain. Did ye hear the way he spoke tae the man? I'll have somethin' tae say tae the bold laddie about that when he shows his face in here again.'

'Matt, let it be.'

'Are ye daft, woman? What'll happen tae the business if he starts talkin' like that tae every man that wants tae place an order?'

'Mr MacDowall wasn't bothered, and I'm sure Alex'll do his furniture when he's got more time.'

'I'll see tae that. I'm still the master when all's said an' done, and I decide what orders we make. If Alex doesnae like it, Ewan can take over.'

'Ewan can't decorate furniture,' Kirsty pointed out, almost at the end of her tether. 'And it's painted furniture Mr MacDowall wants.' Then, taking advantage of his sudden silence, she said, 'Just be content with the extra money and let the matter end here and now, Matt. Now, is there anything you need before I go to help Jean?'

This was the day the builders started work. When Kirsty arrived, still furious with Sandy for invading her home and her family, Jean and Rose and John Brodie, who was taking a keen and enthusiastic interest in everything that went on, were gathered in the new shop together with the builders.

'There should be a ceremony,' Rose said when the outline of the new archway had been drawn on the grimy plaster wall.

'Like launching a ship?' John Brodie raised his eyebrows while the builders waiting to get on with the work glanced at each other, smirking.

281

'Mebbe.' Rose, used by now to being laughed at, shrugged her slender shoulders.

'P'raps Mr Brodie could say a few words,' Jean suggested, but the girl shook her head.

'No, no, it should be something that comes from one of us. Something...dramatic!'

'Like this?' Kirsty marched forward and grasped a large sledgehammer that had been propped against the wall. It proved to be unexpectedly heavy, and she couldn't raise it beyond knee level. For a moment she thought she would have to let it drop and admit defeat, but determination and the anger still smouldering after Sandy's visit provided the necessary energy. She managed to raise the hammer, clinging with both hands to the shaft and scared to lift it too high in case she toppled over onto the floor in an undignified heap of petticoats and stockings and drawers, then let it fall in a swinging arc.

Jean yelped, and a workman standing by the wall leaped to safety as the hammer head hit the wall with a thud that reverberated up Kirsty's wrists and arms to her shoulders and rattled the teeth in her jaw. Plaster cracked and pattered to the floor, exposing the lathes behind. Jean yelped, Rose cheered and Brodie applauded.

'Here, missus,' the building foreman said respectfully, 'I'd no' like tae go home tae you wi' an opened pay packet.'

Kirsty's arms felt as weak as strips of paper, and her shoulders and wrists and elbows would surely be painful in the morning, but even so she was elated. Letting the man relieve her of the hammer, she turned to beam triumphantly at her partners.

'Another door has just opened,' she said.

# 22

The inevitable quarrel between Matt and Alex erupted that night while Kirsty was tucking Mary into bed, something she still did every night, even though Matt disapproved of what he called 'mollycoddling'.

'This is a grand chance for our workshop—mebbe makin' furniture for a big Glasgow shop,' Matt was saying when she went back downstairs, his voice low but the anger already heating it. 'And you stand there and look the man in the face and say no, just like that?'

'You're not in the workshop—I am, and

it's me who knows what we've got tae do.' Alex's voice was equally low. There was something frightening about the fact that these two, who normally yelled at each other, were being so controlled. Caitlin, who hated quarrels, washed dishes at the sink, her slim back tense with misery.

'Caitlin, pet, away upstairs and tell Mary a story. She's restless tonight,' Kirsty lied, and the girl hurried from the room.

'I'm still the master!' Matt said, as he always did when he and Alex clashed.

'Aye, and you were the one that jeered at the painted furniture. I thought you'd be pleased to hear me refusing to do more.'

Matt was purpling with anger. 'Ye didnae turn it down for my sake—an order's an order, even if it is for spoiled furniture. The man might put in orders for plain furniture afterwards.'

'We're too small tae satisfy the likes of MacDowall. Let him go somewhere else.'

Kirsty interrupted. 'Mr MacDowall said he'd be content to wait until the spring, so there's nothing lost. Matt, d'you not want to go to your bed now?'

'He'll not have tae wait until the spring. As soon as the lassie's furniture's completed, Alex, ye'll find out what Mr MacDowall wants and start on it.'

'And leave the other customers high and dry?'

'For pity's sake, man, there's three of ye in that workshop, an' all time-served. Ye can manage more than one order at a time.'

Alex, too, was angry; Kirsty could almost see fire sparking from the ends of his red hair. 'I'll not do his furniture before others, and that's an end tae it.'

'Ye don't own that workshop yet, my lad, and I'll make damned sure ye never will if ye don't grow up.'

'Matt—'

'Keep out of this, woman,' he snapped. 'It's high time someone told this upstart the truth about himsel'. Can ye not see,' Matt said to Alex, leaning forward and thumping his fist on his knee in emphasis, 'that the man feels sorry for ye?'

'Sorry?'

'Aye. Ye made a fool of yersel' with his daughter, thinkin' she'd fancy ye, forgettin' that when it comes down tae it ye're only an ordinary workin' man. And he could dae nothin' else but put a stop tae it, the way I would if some scoundrel from the gutter started payin' court tae our Caitlin.'

'Matt, for pity's sake leave it!' Kirsty begged, and was waved aside. Matt's temper had eased; clearly he was impressed by what he saw as his own diplomacy and was too taken up with himself to see how white Alex had become.

'An' he's decent enough tae want tae make it up tae ye for yer disappointment, so he's givin' ye this order.'

'You think so?'

'I know so. I'm a businessman, same as him only not so grand. And I've got daughters. I can understand how his mind's workin'. The thing is,' Matt forged on, 'he was awful generous with the payment for his lassie's furniture, for all that she's gone away and doesnae need it just now. That means that we could dae well out of keepin' the man happy.'

Alex's face was now chalk white, contrasting sharply with the brilliant blue of his eyes and his bright hair, and the skin seemed to have tightened over the bones.

'You've told me the truth the way you see it. Now it's my turn tae tell it tae you.'

'Alex, leave it. Just go to your bed and let things be!' Kirsty was beside herself with fear.

'No, no,' said Matt, 'ye've said often enough that ye wish me and Alex could just speak tae each other without losin' our tempers. I've had my say, let him have his.'

'The truth is,' Alex said, his eyes never moving from his stepfather's face, 'that Angus MacDowall isn't being kind to us

286

because he feels bad about coming between me and his daughter or even because he likes the way I paint furniture. It's because the man's riddled with guilt. It's because he's my real father, and he's Fiona's father, and she's my half-sister, and neither of the two of us knew until he came back tae Glasgow.'

He went to Matt's chair, putting a hand on each of the wooden arms, bending over so that his face was only inches from Matt's. The older man stared up at him, mouth agape, trying to make sense of what he had just heard.

'That,' said Alex softly, 'is the truth of it. And if you ever speak of it, or of him, to me again, so help me God I'll take you apart bone from bone, invalid or not.'

He turned away, caught up his jacket from the nail on the back door and went out, closing the door very gently at his back.

'You knew.' Matt's voice was frail, the voice of a very old man.

'I've only known for a week.'

'Ye should have told me.'

'There was no sense in hurting you. I didn't know that San—Mr MacDowall would come back.'

'He's been here before?'

'Just the once, to tell me that—to tell me who he was, and that Alex and Fiona had to stop seeing each other.'

Matt was beginning to rally his thoughts. 'Are ye sure it was just the once? Are ye sure he's no' the reason ye were keen tae get back tae Paisley?'

Kirsty felt bone weary. 'I wasn't the one who wanted to come to Paisley, it was you.'

'Ye didnae try tae stop me.'

'I did. I didn't want to come back.'

'Because ye knew he was nearby. Because ye—'

'I'll not hear any more of this,' she blurted out. 'D'you hear me? I thought the man was dead; I told Alex he was. I never thought to lay eyes on him again—I wish to God I never had!'

There was a long silence, during which they didn't look at each other, then Matt said, 'I think I'll go tae my bed.'

'I'll fetch Al—'

'Ye'll not!' Strength came back into his voice, and he began scrabbling at the chair arms, seeking for a good grip so that he could haul himself to his feet. 'I'll manage alone, without him and without you, if I have tae crawl every inch of the way!'

He reached for the walking stick that was always close at hand now, found that it couldn't give him sufficient support, and threw it aside. While Kirsty watched, not daring to touch him, he got out into the hall. Clutching at the back of his chair, the door frame, the banisters, he managed to get to the foot of the stairs unaided. It took some time, and she could tell by the grunts and stifled moans that it cost him a lot of pain.

The stairs defeated him. Grasping the newel post with one hand and supporting himself on the wall with the other, he made several attempts to put a foot on the first step. Finally, unable to bear his struggles any longer, Kirsty went forward and put an arm about him.

'For pity's sake, Matt,' she said when he tried to push her away, 'is it worth killing yourself just for a bit of pride?'

Realising that he couldn't manage without her help, he gave in and let her ease his crippled body up the stairs, tread by painful tread, then along the corridor and into the bedroom, where he collapsed on the bed. He kept his eyes tightly shut.

'Matt,' she said when she had drawn the blankets over him, 'it all happened years ago. It's been over long since.'

His lids fluttered but remained closed, and he made no answer.

As she reached the top of the stairs Ewan came in at the street door, too late to be of help, Kirsty thought wearily.

'D'you want something to eat?'

He shook his head and began to mount

the stairs, bounding up the treads his father had had so much trouble with. 'I'm away tae my bed.' His hair was rumpled, his shirt collar open. His mouth looked slightly swollen—from kisses, she thought—and as he passed her, brushing against her for a brief moment, she was shocked and embarrassed to discover that she was keenly aware of the strength and virility of the young body so close to her own. Even the smell wafting from him was exciting—a mingling of youth and masculinity and drink, and something else, an underlying whiff of cheap flowery perfume, telling that he had been with a girl.

To her embarrassment and disgust, Kirsty felt colour rush to her cheeks as she continued on down the stairs.

The workshop door creaked beneath her hand. Inside it was pitch dark, and she was frightened to move in case she fell over something.

'Alex?'

There was no answer, but she could tell that he was there. There was a listening, human quality to the air that didn't belong to empty space.

'Did you have to tell your father?' she asked the blackness pressing against her face and body. 'Did you have to hurt him so badly?'

'My father's in Glasgow,' he said from the stairs.

'Matt's been a father to you for most of your life.'

'It was you he wanted, not me. You should have let them take me when I was born.' Her eyes were becoming accustomed to the dark now, and she could just make him out, a hunched shape curled halfway up the stairs.

'I couldn't have done that. You were so wee—there was no knowing what might have become of you.'

'Whatever it was it couldn't have been as bad as what's happened tae me now.'

'If we hadn't come back to Paisley,' she said wretchedly, 'if we'd stayed in Falkirk none of this would have happened.'

'If—if—if!' He almost spat the words out. 'If you and that man in Glasgow had never met, if I'd never been born—I wish tae God I never had!'

'You don't know what's ahead of you. You've got talent, Alex, you can do a lot with your life.'

'Go away, Mam.'

'You'll freeze if you stay here.'

'There's sacking in the loft I can use if I want it.'

Kirsty winced. She knew well enough that there was sacking in the loft, and that it made a passable bed. She'd lain there herself, with Sandy. And because of that one coupling, Alex would lie there tonight, more alone than he had ever been in his young life.

'Go back to the house, Mam,' he said in the darkness. 'If you care for me at all, you'll just let me be!'

The next day Alex was out of the workshop for some time, and at the evening meal he announced that he had found lodgings nearby.

'You don't need to do that,' Kirsty protested, while Matt, who had scarcely said a word to anyone all day, kept his eyes fixed on his plate.

'Don't worry, I'll come to the workshop every day. I'll not let my own family down.' Alex's voice was heavy with sarcasm. Within the hour he had gone, leaving Mary in tears and Caitlin white faced and miserable.

Once he had recovered from the shock, Ewan was envious. 'I'm less than a year younger than Alex—mebbe I should think of movin' out too.'

'You do that,' Matt told him harshly, 'and ye'll have tae find somewhere else tae work as well!'

'Ye never said that tae Alex,' the young man protested.

'Never mind him, we're talkin' about

292

you, an' ye're not movin' out of this house till I say so,' his father bellowed, with a brief return to his old self.

Ewan, his handsome face sulky, pushed back his chair and went out, while Mary promptly burst into tears again, 'I don't want Ewan to g-go too!'

'He won't, pet,' Kirsty soothed the little girl, lifting her onto her knee.

'Ye're damned right he won't,' Matt muttered into his tobacco pouch. 'There's one at least that knows which side his bread's buttered on.'

With her once-secure family life disintegrating around her, the shop continued to be Kirsty's anchor. Despite all her worries, she felt a small thrill of excited anticipation every time she went into her new work room, the original shop. The archway that was to be curtained off from the new shop had been completed and the walls painted, and there would be net curtaining over the small window to ensure privacy. The room was still empty, but a good-sized work table and a second-hand sewing machine, together with a smaller table to put it on, had already been purchased. It was far superior to the stuffy little cupboard she had had to use at the Hamiltons' and, best of all, there would be no Mrs Hamilton sweeping in to harass and harangue her.

This was her domain.

Even Jean's modest little single-roomed dwelling above the former shop had been repainted and the crumbling window sashes renewed to keep out the winter winds.

'Why shouldn't your own home be seen to as well?' Rose had asked in answer to Jean's half-hearted protest about the cost. Then, the businesswoman in her coming to the fore, she had added, 'Besides, it's all part of the building, and we need to keep that in good order.'

Rose had passed the book-keeping test John Brodie had set for her with flying colours and had been officially given the job of seeing to the shop's ledgers. She planned to set aside a corner of the back room as her office.

Standing in the empty sewing room, listening to the other two chattering beyond the archway, Kirsty knew that the first strands of the new three-way partnership had begun to interweave. Morag Bishop was quite right—life was a series of patterns, some able to merge into new and larger designs, while others, like Matt's, remained stubbornly independent. For the sake of the new business, the pattern made up of herself, Jean and Rose Hamilton had to work.

Jean was still in awe of Rose. As well as possessing a strong and confident personality, the girl dominated Jean physically, her tall, lean shape towering over the other's short, dumpy figure. Jean, Kirsty knew, would have to learn to assert herself—after all, she had the most to lose if the new venture failed. The shop was her livelihood, the room above it her home.

The first real confrontation between Rose and Jean came when the second-hand clothing returned from the laundry. Unpacking it, Jean and Kirsty had to admit that there was a considerable improvement. The colours were brighter and the folds free of dust, and when they began hanging the clothes on the rails Rose had bought, their hands were no longer sticky and grimy from contact with the fabrics.

'They look much more attractive, too,' Rose said with satisfaction. 'Folk'll be willing to pay a bit more for them now.'

Jean immediately bristled. 'They're not goin' tae pay more.'

'Only a few pence, or maybe a shilling for something made from really good material.'

'I've told ye before, this isnae a dress shop. It's always been for folk with little money tae their names.' Jean's shoulders squared and her chin came up.

Rose gave her a condescending smile.

'Jean, business is never for the benefit of anyone but the owners and managers—and partners,' she explained.

'Your kind o' business, mebbe, but not mine.'

'But there's the cost of laundering everything.'

'It's nice that the clothes are cleaner, but that was your idea. You never said the cost'd have tae come out of the customers' pockets. If you had, I'd not have agreed tae it.' A faint tremor had come into Jean's voice, and she gripped the jacket she had been unfolding so tightly that her knuckles shone white. Kirsty opened her mouth, then closed it again. If Jean didn't learn now to fight for what she believed in, Rose would always dominate her.

'Surely you realise—'

'This shop was set up by my mother for ordinary folk who cannae afford tae buy themselves new clothes,' Jean interrupted. 'It's true that she made a livin' from it, an' so must I, but if we start puttin' prices up just tae make a profit we'll drive folk away, and that wouldnae be right. They've come tae rely on me for some decent clothes. I've never let them down in the past and I won't start now!'

Kirsty, knowing the effort it had cost Jean to speak her mind like that, could have hugged her friend.

'But if you'd just think about—'

'The prices are goin' tae stay the same, Rose,' Jean said flatly, 'an' that's an end tae it.'

Kirsty, seeing Rose's lips press together, held her breath. Rose was in danger of reverting to the way she had been with her mother. If she gave way to her anger the partnership could end there and then.

Rose appealed to her. 'What do you say, Kirsty?'

'I think Jean's right. We'd be letting our clientele down if we started charging more money.'

Slowly, the light of battle faded from Rose's long face and she nodded. 'I suppose you're both right. It wouldn't be fair.'

Jean's pent-up breath eased from her lungs in a tiny sigh as another strand, fragile but important, was added to the new three-way pattern they were weaving between them.

# 23

Alex, concentrating on the pink rose he was painting, didn't look round when Kirsty went into the workshop. As she had hoped, he was alone. She had left

Ewan eating his midday meal with his father, and she knew that Todd usually went along to the tobacconist's to see Beth during the break. Ewan, who often went to buy tobacco after he had eaten, had frequently jeered about the way the journeyman leaned against the counter, watching Beth at work with, according to Ewan, a look of cow-like devotion on his face.

Kirsty waited patiently while Alex finished what he was doing. He was still working on Fiona's furniture, in this instance a small bedside table. On a chair close to hand stood a half-empty bottle of cold tea together with a half-eaten sandwich. It looked clumsy and unappetising, a thick slice of hard yellow cheese between two pieces of bread hacked, rather than cut, from a loaf.

Since moving out of the house Alex had refused to eat any meals there. He had found lodgings with an elderly widow in the tenement next to where Todd lived with his sister and her husband and family. According to Todd, the woman was a kindly soul.

'Alex'll be all right with her, for she keeps a clean house—not like some of the folk ye get round our area. She'll look after him, and my sister says she'll have him in for his dinner now and then,' Todd had assured her. Even so, Kirsty's heart was broken for her much-loved first-born, living in a rented room, eating alone in a cold workshop, painting roses on furniture he had made for the girl he loved and could never have.

He laid down his brush, balancing it carefully on the edge of the paint pot, and got up from his knees to take the sandwich and bottle from the chair. 'Sit down, Mam.' He didn't smile, but his voice was mild enough.

'How are you?'

'I'm grand,' he said levelly, settling on the stairs, taking another bite of bread and cheese. 'And I'm busy, so if that's all you came tae ask—'

'It's not. There's a whole rack of shelves behind the counter in the new shop, but they're falling down, and some of them are broken. Jean was wondering if you'd put them right for us?'

'Me? You need a joiner for that, not a cabinet-maker.'

'I know, but Jean sees it as putting business your way. It'd be a kindness to her.'

His eyes darkened. 'You've not told her about—'

'I've not said a word to her or anyone else. As far as Jean knows you're still living at home—where you belong,' she couldn't help adding.

He gave her a long look, and she felt as though his eyes were boring into her mind and reading the truth there—that instead of pointing out to Jean that Alex wasn't the right person to repair the shelving, she had seized on her friend's request because it was one way of seeing him, talking to him. Then he shrugged. 'I'll look in at the shop tomorrow.'

Alex had forgotten that Rose Hamilton might be in the new shop. To his surprise, she was talking to a painter and laughing at something the man had said. He stared, surprised to see her looking so animated—and with an ordinary workman, too.

'Alex, it was good of you tae come!' Jean Chisholm called from the other side of the shop, and Rose's head turned swiftly in his direction. The speed with which the warmth vanished from her face at the sight of him amused Alex. It wasn't often, these days, that anything amused him, he thought, as Jean swooped over to lead him to the shelving behind the counter. It was a sorry mess, but the brackets were still usable.

He took measurements, made notes. 'We've got some timber in stock that'd do.' Glancing over his shoulder, he saw that Rose had gone. 'Some of the shelves can be saved. I'll take them back tae the workshop and work on them. Then I'll cut new timber tae the right size and varnish it.'

He was wrenching the shelves free when his mother arrived and insisted on showing him round the place. Despite his doubts about the success of the new venture, Alex was impressed by what had already been done and by the spaciousness now that the two shops had become one.

He was pleased, too, to see his mother so enthusiastic and happy. She had had a lot to contend with since the move to Paisley—probably even before then. She deserved her fair share of happiness, and despite his strong mistrust of Rose Hamilton, he hoped for Kirsty's sake, and Jean's, that the shop would turn out to be a success. Not that he could find the words to say so. His utter despair and soul-destroying misery over the loss of Fiona and the way he had lost her had begun to ease, and he had stopped blaming his mother. She had only been a child when it all happened, little older than Caitlin. She had fought to keep him safe, and it wasn't her fault that he had met and fallen in love with Fiona. But although the first keen edge of the pain had blunted, it was still with him, locking him into a dour silence that prevented him from speaking openly to her. That was why he had agreed to try to do something about the shelving. He had seen it as a way of helping her rather than Jean.

In one of the back shops he spied a battered corner cupboard that had been pushed to one side.

'That's a good piece of furniture.' He squatted down to examine it. 'It's been ill-treated, but it's been bonny in its day.'

'We found it lying here,' Kirsty said. 'We were thinking of just putting it out.'

'Don't do that. It's got a nice shape to it.' Alex studied it from all angles. 'And that's good glass in the doors. It's a wonder it's not been broken.' He straightened up, dusting his hands. 'This would look bonny in a corner of the front shop. You could mebbe use it for displaying wee things like gloves and ribbons.'

Jean had joined them with a mug of tea for Alex. 'It's badly scratched,' she said doubtfully.

'That can be put right. I'll repair it then French polish it and reset the doors with new hinges, if you like.'

Jean beamed up at him. 'You'd not mind givin' the time tae it?'

'Not if it's for you,' he told her, and she giggled girlishly, slapping his arm.

'You're a terrible man, Alex Lennox!'

'Only with beautiful women,' he said,

grinning, and she went into another fit of giggles.

Kirsty and Alex looked over her turbaned head at each other, smiling, and for a moment there was a lightness in the air, then it burst like a bubble as Rose swept down on them, a challenge in her voice as she asked, 'Well now, Mr Lennox, what do you think of the place?'

The laughter went from Alex at once and he buried his face in the mug, taking a long swallow of tea. 'It looks well enough,' he told her coolly, 'but the test's yet tae come.'

'You doubt if the shop'll be a success? Does that mean that I have more faith in your mother than you have?'

'Of course not,' Jean protested, but the smile went from her face as she looked from one young person to the other, puzzled by their antagonism.

To Alex's mind, Rose was reminding him of the day he had told her to leave his mother alone. But she hadn't and she had won. He stared at her, the anger he had been feeling against the entire world ever since Angus MacDowall's first visit to Espedair Street settling back into his heart. 'I've got faith in my mother and in Jean.'

'But not in me.'

'Not from what I've known of you so

303

far,' he said deliberately. Colour swept into her face and her eyes narrowed.

'Rose,' Jean broke in hurriedly, 'Alex says he can repair this cupboard for us.'

'We'll pay you for it, of course.'

'There's no need. I'm doing it as a gift for Jean.'

Her eyebrows rose. 'I thought workmen considered their time to be valuable?'

'I'm not a workman, Miss Hamilton, I'm a craftsman. And friendship's got its value, too—but mebbe you've never learned that.'

'What's amiss?' Jean asked in confusion as Rose flounced away, her narrow back rigid with anger.

'I cannae abide that lassie!'

'Alex feels that after the way Rose lost me my place with Mrs Hamilton she can't be trusted,' Kirsty explained hurriedly.

'Och, that! It was naughty of her, but she's made up for it since, hasn't she, Kirsty?' Jean patted Alex's arm. 'I wasn't too sure of her myself at first, but when you get tae know her, she's a nice lassie at heart. You'll see.'

'I doubt if I will, for she's got as little time for me as I have for her.'

'Why can't you just be civil to the lassie if you should meet her?' said Kirsty when Jean had moved away. 'She's one of my partners now.'

304

Alex took a final swallow of tea then returned the mug to her and wiped the back of his hand across his mouth. 'Mebbe so, but that's no reason for me tae like her. There's somethin' about that lassie that I can't abide, and never will.'

'Mebbe it's because she's as stubborn as you are,' his mother said.

Rose's suggestion that every customer calling in on the shop's opening day should be given a small glass of sherry was quashed immediately by her new partners.

'But my uncle did that when he was auctioning off the contents of his late brother's house, and it worked wonderfully well. It brought in a lot of buyers.'

'It worked for him, mebbe, but round here it'd bring in every drunk in the town,' Jean protested. 'We'd see the same faces comin' through the door time and again!'

'It would help to spread the word that we'd reopened,' Rose explained, and Jean laughed.

'You've no need tae worry about that, hen. Word of anythin', be it good or bad, spreads faster in Paisley than lice on a mongrel. In any case,' she added firmly when the girl showed signs of arguing, 'I signed the pledge years ago and I couldnae possibly permit hard drink on my premises.'

Kirsty shot a startled look at her friend. It was met by a flat stare that defied her to open her mouth.

'You've never signed the pledge,' she challenged when they were alone. 'I mind that whisky we both drank the day Rose came up with the idea of a partnership.'

'I nearly signed it once, but there's been times like that day when I've been glad I didnae take the step. I was just givin' the lassie a wee reminder that she's not goin' tae get everything her own way,' Jean said blandly. 'An' when it comes down tae it, handin' out drink tae every creature that comes in through the door's a waste of good money and a daft idea anyway!'

The shop's reopening in December caused quite a stir. A steady stream of women flowed through the place, some there only to gawk and stare, others intent on buying.

'It used tae be that the only customers were folk who knew where I was,' Jean marvelled, wrapping a jacket for a satisfied customer. 'Now look at the size of the place—and there're women comin' in from all over the town today. The dear Lord knows what my mother'd say if she saw this place now.'

'She'd say that you've made a good

move,' John Brodie assured her. He had insisted on attending the opening. 'I'm hoping that this is the way it'll be from now on, Miss Chisholm. I believe that this shop will do very well for itself.' He bowed to the customer and sprang to open the shop door for her. 'Thank you for your custom, madam. We hope you'll call again.'

'You've got a way with the ladies,' Jean said as the woman went off, blushing and simpering. 'If you're ever turned away from your own place of work we'll mebbe give you a position here.'

He grinned and said, 'I'd enjoy that,' as she scurried away to help someone else.

Thanks to Alex, the shelving behind the counter was broad and sturdy and glossy with brown varnish. Now that the clothes were laundered before going on display, the place had taken on the look of a real dress shop instead of a second-hand clothes store. That, Kirsty thought as she watched the women, most of them shabbily dressed, who milled about the place, would help the customers' morale. Every woman, whatever her situation in life, liked to feel well-treated.

Behind the counter, to her delight, was a drawer just like the one in Mr Laidlaw's tobacconist's shop, fitted with metal bowls to hold the takings. She took great pleasure in dividing a handful of coins into the appropriate bowls. 'There's plenty buying, but in this part of the town you'll find that most of the money coming in's just coppers.'

'Coppers have a way of becoming pounds.' Brodie nodded towards a corner where Rose, in the crisp white blouse and black skirt they had all agreed to adopt as their uniform, was earnestly trying to sell something to a customer. 'I never thought to see Rose Hamilton working in a shop.'

'She insisted, and we're so busy today that we need her help, even though she has to ask Jean or me the cost of everything.'

Brodie watched the long and earnest conversation between Rose and the other woman with interest. 'D'you think they can understand each other?'

Kirsty knew what he meant. Most of the women coming into the shop had shied back in alarm on hearing Rose's clear, confident voice with its finishing-school accent. Some had fled, some had made a point of always being in another corner of the shop to avoid having to speak to her, some had sniggered—although Rose gave no indication of noticing—and some, braver than the rest, had joined verbal battle.

Although Kirsty and Jean had both

found those encounters between the two levels of society amusing, Kirsty was quite offended by John Brodie's attitude. Rose, after all, was her partner. Her voice was sharp when she said, 'I'm sure they can. She's sold quite a few things already. I've come to admire her over the past weeks. She's not afraid of getting her hands dirty—or of being laughed at.'

'My dear Mrs Lennox, I wasn't laughing at her! On the contrary, I share your admiration.'

'Will she get into terrible trouble with her parents, being here?'

'She already has,' he said blithely. 'To their minds it was bad enough that she insisted on putting her inheritance into this place. When they heard that Rose herself intended to spend at least part of her time in the shop her mother had an attack of the vapours and her father threatened to turn her out of house and home. I know because my parents are friends of hers.'

Kirsty felt an unexpected twinge of sympathy for Mrs Hamilton. She well knew, now, what it was like to see a child moving out of the family home. 'Jean and me wouldn't want to cause trouble between Rose and her family.'

'Don't worry about Rose, she can take care of herself. When she told her father that she'd be delighted to find a place of her own he gave in at once, for he knew that she meant it. He's really very fond of her. I think he secretly admires her independence. I understand from my mother that the Hamiltons have decided to let her have her own way in the hope that she'll eventually lose interest in the whole idea.'

'D'you think she'll lose interest?' Kirsty said nervously. She couldn't bear to contemplate what might happen to herself and Jean if Rose withdrew her financial support.

'Absolutely not. Rose isn't the type, and in any case she herself made sure that the papers were worded in such a way that even if she were to walk away from this place she couldn't take her original investment with her for several years. You have to admire her,' John Brodie mused, his eyes still on the tall, thin girl, who looked well in the plain blouse and skirt. 'When it comes to courage and determination there are few women as strong as Rose Hamilton.'

Kirsty looked at him with interest. If there was a romance in the air, it would be a very good thing, she thought. The young lawyer would make an ideal husband for Rose.

'Indeed,' she said encouragingly. 'She's a quite remarkable young woman.'

'Kirsty.' Jean beckoned from another part of the shop. 'Could ye mebbe shorten a skirt for this lassie, and perhaps do somethin' different with these sleeves?'

As she moved away from the counter Kirsty was disappointed to hear the lawyer, his eyes still on Rose, murmur, 'A pity the girl's as plain as a pikestaff.'

# 24

Although Matt was in no mood to celebrate New Year, Kirsty insisted on inviting Jean to share their Ne'erday dinner as before.

'She's got nobody but us, Matt.'

'Och, have it yer ain way,' he said peevishly. 'Ye always do, these days. I'm not master of my own house any more.'

'That's not true.' Since Sandy's last visit Matt had retreated into his own world, only emerging from it now and again when they were alone to ask questions about the days when Sandy had been her father's apprentice. Kirsty had done everything she could to convince him that the past was the past, but Matt refused to believe her.

'The man's widowed, with a fine house needin' a mistress. Ye'd like that, wouldn't ye? Servants tae follow yer biddin', and money tae spend, the things,' he said bitterly, 'that I've never been able tae give ye.'

'I'm content where I am. I'm not interested in San—Mr MacDowall, and he's certainly not interested in me.' She knew as she said it that she wasn't being entirely truthful.

She pushed the memory away and went on briskly, 'As to a mistress for his house, from what I've heard the man's got a very good housekeeper.'

Caitlin, disappointed at the Bishops not being invited this year, took gifts to them from herself and Kirsty and brought back tobacco for Matt and Ewan, a necktie for Alex, a rag doll made by Morag for Mary, and two bottles of raspberries from their garden for Kirsty. Radiant with happiness, Caitlin displayed her own gift, a length of soft, light cloth in checks of misty green and purple, the colours of heather.

'It was made on great-grandfather's loom.' Her slim hands stroked the cloth gently. 'I'm going to keep it for now, and one day I'll make something special from it.'

To Kirsty's disappointment, Alex refused to eat his Ne'erday dinner with his family. 'My sister'll invite him tae eat with us,' Todd assured her. 'He'll not go hungry for food or friends.'

'But she's got enough to do without taking Alex under her wing as well,' Kirsty protested. She knew that Todd's sister, a cheerful, motherly woman, was also entertaining her husband's parents as well as her own children, Beth, Mr Laidlaw and Todd himself.

'She can always find room for another one. We have a grand time at Ne'erday—it's just like the times we used tae have when my own parents were alive.' His eyes sparkled at the memory. 'We usually had that many folk in for their dinner that we'd tae take it in turns tae sit at the table.'

Since Jean was coming to the house, Kirsty had to explain to her in advance about Alex's absence. She didn't mention Sandy, saying only that Alex and Matt had fallen out.

Jean nodded sagely. 'It happens with grown laddies. They say you cannae do with too many women in the one house, but to my mind it's just the same with men. Fathers are used tae rulin' the roost and they take it hard when their sons become men an' start havin' opinions of their own.'

It was a difficult meal. Ewan, fretting to be free like Alex, wasn't good company, nor was Matt. Kirsty wished that, like Alex, she could be in Todd's sister's busy, happy kitchen instead.

As soon as the meal was over Ewan helped Matt to settle in the parlour then went out to meet his friends. Jean offered to help with the dishes, but Kirsty shooed her back into the parlour, where Matt was reading his newspaper and Mary played on the rug before the fire with her new doll.

When she went into the parlour to ask if they were ready for a cup of tea, she found the pair of them sound asleep, and looking like bookends on either side of the fire. Jean's head was lolling on her left shoulder, Matt's on his right. Jean's snores were little ladylike puffs of sound, while Matt's were deeper, longer but, mercifully, lacking the guttural harshness that often kept Kirsty awake at nights. Mary, oblivious to the noise on either side, was holding a long whispered conversation with her doll.

Smiling, Kirsty closed the door quietly and returned to the kitchen.

'They're both sound, but make the tea anyway.' She suddenly realised that Caitlin was standing motionless by the stove, tears rolling silently down her rounded cheeks. 'What's wrong, lassie? Did you burn yourself?'

'It's wee Fergus,' Caitlin's tear-filled eyes were like clear blue-green rock pools, 'and Alex. They were both here with us last Ne'erday, and now—oh, Mam, I want

314

them both back and Father well again. I want everything the way it was!'

Kirsty gathered her daughter into her arms and rocked her gently, noticing for the first time that Caitlin was her own height now. 'Hush, pet. We all want things to go back to the way they were, but it can't happen.'

'D'you think Alex'll come home, at least?' Caitlin mumbled into her neck.

'Mebbe, in a wee while.'

'Why did Father quarrel with him?'

'It's the way of things, Caitlin. Alex is grown up now. He has his own ideas, and sometimes they're not the same as your father's.'

The girl drew away, dabbing her eyes with the dish towel. 'If growing up causes trouble and unhappiness for everyone, I don't want it to happen to me.'

'It's already happening, pet. You're out of school and earning a wage, but even so,' Kirsty said guiltily, remembering that she herself had been too busy with the shop to think of the Ne'erday celebrations, and it was Caitlin who had prepared most of the meal they had just eaten, as well as cleaning the house from top to bottom, 'you're young yet. I expect you to do too much in the house.'

'I don't mind.'

'I'll need to make certain that you get

out with your friends more in the future.'

'I see them often enough.' Caitlin unrolled the sleeves of the high-necked pink blouse Kirsty had brought from the shop for her. The slight swell of her young breasts nudged against the blouse, and beneath her well-cut dark-blue serge skirt, also from the shop, her hips flared sweetly from a small waist. Her hair, looped back with a pink ribbon long enough for the ends to hang halfway down her neat straight back, was like bronze silk, touched here and there with gold in the light from the gas mantle.

Peering at herself in the small mirror, she asked anxiously, 'D'you think they'll know that I've been crying when I go through?'

'Not a bit of it. Crying just makes you look prettier.'

Her soft mouth curved into one of its frequent smiles. 'Pretty? Me? I don't know about that.'

'I do,' Kirsty said. It was true. Instead of reddening the girl's dark-lashed eyes and puffing her oval, neat-featured face, the fit of weeping had merely touched her skin with a pearly sheen and given added lustre to the striking turquoise eyes.

Caitlin was well on the way to becoming a beauty. And while she was proud of the fact, Kirsty found herself hoping that it wouldn't mean more trouble as her daughter ripened into maturity.

Fiona's furniture was completed early in January and collected by a motor vehicle with Angus MacDowall's name painted on the sides in large letters. The sight of the van standing in the street outside while the furniture, carefully wrapped, was carried through the pend, sent Matt into a flurry of questions about Kirsty's past and caused a quarrel between himself and Ewan.

'Just because Alex has managed tae get away from him he's started pickin' on me,' Ewan complained to Kirsty that night. 'I'll not have it. And I know he's in pain and frettin' about not bein' able tae work any more,' he added impatiently as she opened her mouth to speak, 'so don't bother tellin' it all tae me again. It's not my fault that he's got arthritis, and it's not my fault that he's gettin' older. I'm still young—I've got my own life tae think of.'

He thrust his hands into his trouser pockets and scowled at the sink. 'I've got Alex goin' on at me in the workshop and that old bugger narkin' at me in the house—it's no fit life for a dog. I've a good mind tae up and off, and tae hell with the pair of them!'

'That would be daft, and you know it. Your father needs you, and one day you and Alex'll own the business between you.'

Ewan gave a contemptuous laugh. 'What's so grand about ownin' a place like that? A wee wooden shed an' a yard—an' Alex bossin' me around because he's the eldest? I'm goin' out.' He made for the door.

'You've not long come in—it's past time for bed!'

'Don't you start on me now,' he said, and strode out, leaving the door swinging open behind him.

A month after its opening the shop was still thriving. All the regular customers had returned, and now that the place was larger and able to hold more stock, women from other parts of the town had started to call regularly. As Jean was too busy to go round the big houses collecting clothing, a woman had been hired to do it in her place.

The partnership still survived, and Kirsty was pleased to see that having won at least two small battles, Jean was more comfortable with Rose, who was still coming in for a period of time every day and seemed well settled in her new life, with no sign of boredom or regret.

Once, leaving to go home, Kirsty had almost bumped into Mrs Hamilton, hovering outside. The woman, crimsoning when she recognised her former employee, had hurried away without a word.

'I know,' Rose said airily when Kirsty mentioned the meeting the following day. 'I've seen her out there a few times, trying to look as though she's just passing by. I haven't the heart to let her know that she's been spotted, much as I'd like to.'

'Does she still try to get you to give the shop up?'

'All the time, poor thing. They've all had a go at me—Mamma, Daddy, my sisters and their stuffy husbands, but they should all know by now that once I set my mind to something I'll not be talked out of it.' She grinned. 'I hear that poor Mamma has stopped mentioning my name in front of her friends. I think she'd rather see me in prison for committing a crime than behind the counter of a shop selling second-hand clothing. At least there would be no chance of any of her friends seeing me in prison!'

Once Fiona's order was completed Alex turned his attention to the corner cabinet he had agreed to refurbish for the shop. It became a handy excuse for Kirsty to visit the workshop now and again, supposedly to see how the cabinet was coming along but in reality to see Alex and reassure herself that he was all right. He was still cool towards her, and she wondered at times if he would ever forgive her for not telling him everything she knew about Sandy from the start, but at least he didn't make her feel unwelcome.

Almost at once, though, her interest was caught by the work he was doing on the cabinet. She watched, fascinated, as he cleaned and repaired it, then started the long and laborious task of French polishing it, mixing the polish then patiently distributing it evenly over the entire surface, bit by bit, over and over again, building up the layers.

One day he even entrusted the polish-soaked pad to her and let her do some work on the cupboard. Thrilled, she moved the pad over the surface in small even circles as directed, Alex occasionally putting his hand over hers to demonstrate the pressure and movement needed. When she finally handed the pad back, flushed with success, he smiled down at her.

'You did well, Mam.' For a blissful minute he was her Alex again.

'We'll turn ye intae a cabinet-maker yet,' Todd chimed in, while Ewan, glancing up from his own work, said sourly, 'Once is fine—try doin' it day in and day out and ye'll soon wish ye'd taken up another craft.'

To Jean's delight, Alex brought the

completed cabinet to the shop one dark February afternoon and set it up in the front shop.

'Oh, Alex, it's lovely—I'd no idea it could be made so nice! And tae think we were goin' tae throw it out!'

'It's as well you didn't, for it's made from good oak and worth a bit of money,' he told her.

He stood watching while Jean and Kirsty fussed over the cabinet, trying different items in it and finally deciding that it should be used to display gloves.

'You've done a grand job with this place.'

'I never thought I'd see the day when I'd have a shop like this,' Jean told him. 'It's all thanks to Rose. She's a fine lassie,' she added, then, seeing his smile dim slightly, 'I forgot—you don't like her, do you?'

'I don't dislike her, I just don't trust her.'

'That's because you don't know her, Alex. Mebbe the two of you should get to know each other better. Two young things like you might have a lot in common.' Jean burbled on, then, peering up into his face and seeing that the smile had gone entirely, 'Well, mebbe not. So what about yoursel'? Are you happy away from home, or are you missin' bein' looked after by your mam? I know she's missin' you.'

'I'm doin' fine where I am. I'll walk home with you, Mam, if you're leaving soon,' he said abruptly. 'I've got work to finish off before I'm done for the day.'

'Jean means well,' she apologised as they set off. 'I had to tell her at Ne'erday that you were in lodgings, but I didn't say why.'

'I just wish folk didn't always have tae interfere. How can she say you miss me when you see me every day? I'm a man now, Mam, I can't be tied to your apron strings for ever.'

'I know,' she said wretchedly. 'I've never said a word to Jean about missing you. It was her own idea.'

He let the matter drop, but as they crossed the road he guided her with a hand beneath her elbow, as though trying to make up for his sharp tone. At the corner of Espedair Street their eyes were drawn to the tobacconist's lighted window. Above the low partition separating the window display of pipes and packets of tobacco and cigarettes from the main shop they could see Beth Laidlaw handing change to an elderly man, dimpling and smiling at something he had said.

'I don't know what Todd thinks he's about, courting that one,' Alex muttered. 'She's just turned down another place he found for them. She's got no intention of marrying him, yet he doesn't see it.'

'She'll agree to some place eventually. She's young yet.' Beth was only twenty-two, eight years younger than Todd.

They had reached the street door. 'Goodbye then,' he said, and went on towards the pend, waving a hand in acknowledgement when she called after him, 'Thank you for doing the cabinet.'

As she stepped into the hall, lit only by the glow of a gas street lamp through the fanlight above the door, a voice hissed, 'Mam,' from halfway up the stairs.

Kirsty peered into the gloom, and saw Mary sitting halfway up, clutching the rag doll Morag had given her for Ne'erday. 'What're you doing there, pet?' She held her hand out. 'Come on into the kitchen.'

Mary's brown head waggled vigorously from side to side. 'Daddy's talking to a man in there.'

'What man?'

'Just a man. I'll come down when he's gone,' Mary whispered loudly.

'You can't stay—'

'Is that you, Kirsty?' Matt called from the kitchen.

Kirsty looked helplessly from the closed door to the stairs. 'I'll come and get you in a minute,' she told her daughter, and went into the kitchen, where Matt sat in his usual chair and Sandy MacDowall stood by the table.

Her heart sank at the sight of him. 'What are you doing here?'

'I've come to see Alex. I'm told he doesn't live here now.'

'No, but he's still working here,' Kirsty said, and Matt darted an angry look at her, then glared defiantly back at the visitor.

'I...hadn't realised that,' Sandy said slowly.

'Matt—'

'He's caused enough upset in this family,' Matt snapped. 'Why should we tell the likes of him about our affairs?'

'I regret the trouble.' Sandy's voice was cold. 'But I have the right to talk with Alex.'

'Ye've got no rights! Tell us yer business, if ye must, and we'll tell Alex—or his mother will, for the stubborn fool'll not speak tae me.'

Sandy's eyelids flickered. 'All the more reason why I should say what I have to say to his face, in front of both of you, to make certain that I'm doing nothing underhand. I'm not going until I see him or find out where he is,' he added, his voice still mild but with a steely obstinacy creeping in.

'I'll fetch him,' Kirsty said as Matt opened his mouth to argue. The sooner Sandy stated his business and left them all in peace, the better.

'You can tell him to go, for I'll not talk to him,' Alex said as soon as he heard about Sandy.

'You'll have to.' She had called him outside. so that they could speak without being overheard by Todd or Ewan. 'The man won't go until he's said his piece.' Then, as he half turned to re-enter the workshop, she added, 'D'you want me to send him down here where the other two can listen to every word he says? I will if it's the only way to get him out of our house.'

He hesitated, gnawing at his lower lip, then shrugged. 'I'll come to the house, but he'd best be quick, for my patience is short,' he said, and together they turned away from the workshop and went along the lane.

## 25

Alex took up a belligerent stance just inside the kitchen door, his gaze on Sandy. 'I've things tae do,' he said shortly. 'I've not got much time.'

'Then I'll not waste any. I want you to come and work for me.'

'What?' Matt's knotted hands clutched at the arms of his chair.

Alex's expression flickered, then held. 'Why should I?'

'Because you're a fine artist as well as a good cabinet-maker. Because,' Sandy flicked a sidelong look in Matt's direction, 'you should be where your talents are properly recognised and used. And because you're my son. Who else would I leave my business to?'

'You have a daughter,' Alex said harshly.

'I have, but I don't see her wanting to take over a furniture store, and after all the years I've spent building it up I've no wish to leave it to whoever she may choose to marry.'

Alex's face darkened, and Kirsty saw his Adam's apple bob as he swallowed convulsively. Sandy swept on.

'I'll see that Fiona's very well provided for, but MacDowall's matters to me almost as much as she does. I've cherished and nursed that business into what it is now, and when my time comes I want to know that I'm passing it on to someone who cares about it as much as I do. I never thought I'd see the day, but now I've got the chance of leaving it to someone of my own blood.'

'I make furniture, Mr MacDowall. I don't sell it.'

Sandy's silvery head inclined slightly. 'I'm well aware of that. I've had it in mind for a while now to buy over a cabinet-making business so that we can manufacture some of the furniture we sell, possibly to customers' own specifications—as you did for Fiona.'

'By God, ye'll not have my business!' Matt snarled, and Alex took time to flash a cold look at his stepfather.

'It's my mother's, not yours.'

Matt's face flamed and he gurgled with rage before managing to spit out, 'And she's my wife. And I'm tellin' the both of ye, this place is not for sale, so ye neednae think ye can get yer hands on it!'

'I've no intention of making an offer for this place. I already have my eye on a small factory in Glasgow.' Sandy told him without moving his gaze from Alex. 'The owner's looking for a buyer, and I think the business might do very well in the right hands. I'd like you to run it for me.'

'What makes you think I'd want to work for you?'

'From what I can gather you're stifled here. If you agree to work for me the place will be yours to run as you think fit. You'll have the right to make the decisions and deal with the customers yourself.'

A faint cold smile quirked one corner of Alex's mouth. 'And you think you could trust me to do what's best for your precious emporium?'

'I'm sure of it. You're not a fool; you'd not destroy a business that'll be yours one day.'

'You could be making a stick tae lash your own back with in other ways, Mr MacDowall.'

'If you're referring to Fiona, she's settled down well in Fort William and means to stay there for several months at least. I'm told,' Sandy said slowly and deliberately, 'that she's already taken a liking to a most suitable young man.' Then, as Alex drew his breath in sharply and half turned towards the back door, one hand groping blindly for the latch, his voice sharpened. 'I said you were no fool, lad—don't prove me wrong. Before any decisions are made you have to face the truth. You cared for Fiona more than she cared for you. My daughter's young for her age, and I'll admit that I've probably spoiled her, for until now she's been all that I had. She's more like her mother, God rest her soul, than me, in temperament as well as in looks. She's a butterfly, as any girl of her age and her background has a right to be. But you—you're like me,' Sandy said with a satisfaction that made Matt wince in his chair. 'You're ambitious, and too level-headed to let the past get in the way of what you want.'

Kirsty, who had stayed silent because she well knew that she had no part in the scene being played out before her eyes, moved to stand by her husband, a protective hand on his shoulder. Neither Alex nor Sandy seemed to notice the movement; they were still locking gazes, Alex bone white, his hair a brilliant beacon, Sandy calm and collected.

'I shall make certain that when Fiona visits me there'll be no danger of a meeting between the two of you. George Gavin has a comfortable home—he and his wife have offered you lodgings there until such time as you find a place of your own. For the time being, Fiona won't even know that you're working for me.'

'Alex already has work here!' Matt rasped.

'But is he content with what he has?'

'I raised him as my own—I've fed him and clothed him...' Matt's temper began to boil over. Frightened for his health, Kirsty tried to hush him, but he waved her aside. 'For God's sake, woman, think! The man fathered a child on ye and left ye tae take the consequences alone—'

'He didn't know—'

'And now, when he walks intae my house bold as brass and talks of taking

329

Alex from us, ye want tae treat him as a guest? I've had enough of this. Get out of my house,' he roared at Sandy, who calmly picked up his hat and cane.

'I've had my say, and I'm going. Take a day or two to make up your mind,' he told Alex. 'When you have, come to the shop and ask for me.'

'I might—and I might not.'

'Whatever your decision, I surely deserve to be told man to man.'

'Out!' Matt erupted, struggling from his chair. 'Or by God I'll—'

'Leave it.' Alex went to his stepfather and eased him back down. 'It's no business of yours.'

'No business? After all I've done for you?'

'I can understand your anger, Mr Lennox,' Sandy said from the door. 'But at least I made the offer in front of you and not behind your back.'

Leaving Alex to deal with his stepfather, Kirsty followed Sandy into the hall. 'Why have you done this to us?'

He loomed above her, the silver of his hair haloing his face in the light sifting through the fan window. 'I want to help Alex.'

'You want to have your own way—and you'd hurt a sick man to get it!'

'Kate, I've already heard from your

330

husband's own lips that he doesn't give a damn about the lad's ability, let alone encourage it,' Sandy's voice was low and fierce.

'There's more to it than that.'

'Of course there is. I want my son.' The words dropped from his lips with cold deliberation. 'That man's called Alex his son for most of his life, and he has a lad of his own besides. I've had none, and now I want what's mine. D'you not see, Kate—I have a right to him!'

'He's a person, not a possession. Nobody has any rights to him.'

'At least I have the right to try to make up for all those years. As to whether or not I'll succeed, let the lad decide that. I'd not want him to come to me unwillingly. It has to be of his own free will.'

'M-mam?' Mary quavered from the stairs, and they both whirled, startled.

'It's all right, pet—everything's all right. I'm coming.'

'It's only fair,' Kirsty heard Sandy say as she moved towards the stairs, 'to let him make the decision.'

The street door opened and closed, letting a breath of chill air into the hall.

When, Kirsty reached Mary she had to coax the little girl to let go of the wooden balustrade she clutched tightly with both arms. In the kitchen, Matt and Alex's voices were raised in argument. For once she felt no desire to intercede and try to stand between them. They must each come to terms with this latest situation in whatever way they could. And so must she, for she knew that Alex would choose to follow Sandy. It was the only road for him.

Sitting on the stairs, holding Mary's trembling body tightly, she wondered if life would ever settle down instead of whirling around their ears like the cold wind Sandy had let into the hall, and into her life.

It started to snow heavily on the day Alex went to live in Glasgow. When he came to the house to say goodbye to his mother, white flakes lay thickly on his shoulders and tangled in his eyelashes and his fiery red hair. He had said his farewells to Caitlin and Mary the day before.

'You've got everything?'

He glanced at the bag on the floor. 'All my worldly possessions.'

'I made you some sandwiches.'

'I'm only going to Glasgow, Mam,' he protested, laughing. 'I'll not starve.'

'Take them anyway,' she insisted. She had known while making them that it was foolishness, but to her mind he wasn't just going to Glasgow; he was setting out on a journey that was taking him from her for good.

Perhaps he sensed this, for when he had stowed the packet in his coat pocket he said, 'You know I have tae go, Mam.'

'I know.'

'It'll make things easier for you in the long run. No more quarrelling between him and me, and he'll get his own way about Ewan inheriting the business. It'll be for the best all round.'

'Are you not going up to see him?' Matt had taken to his bed since Sandy's visit.

'Best not.'

'You can't just leave without a word.'

'Mam, you know he'll only snarl at me, and I'll snarl back. And I'm sure he won't want to see me any more than I want to see him.' Then, glancing at the clock, 'I'll need tae go in any case, or I'll miss the train.'

For a few seconds Alex hesitated, embarrassed and unsure of how to say goodbye, then Kirsty opened her arms and he went into them. For a moment his cheek was pressed to hers, the snowflakes in his hair icy against her warm skin, before the contact was broken and he picked his bag up and opened the back door.

'I'll not be far away. I'll write and let you know how things go, and I'll see you often.'

'Yes, I know.'

He stepped out into the whirling snow, and was gone.

Matt made no mention of Alex when she took his midday meal upstairs. 'Tell Ewan tae come up. There's things we have tae talk about.'

'He's just started on his own food.' She spread a clean towel over the bedclothes then laid a tray holding a bowl of soup and a plate of bread on his knees. 'He'll come upstairs when you've both eaten, and not before.' She held out his spoon, which had strips of cloth bound round the handle to thicken it and make it easier to grip. 'Take your soup before it gets cold.'

He picked up the spoon, dipped it into the plate, then muttered a curse as his hand jerked and some of the soup splashed back into the dish before it reached his mouth. Kirsty wiped the splatters from his nightshirt and the covers, then laid the cloth by his other hand and left, knowing that he hated anyone, even her, to see his clumsiness.

'Mind now—you've not to say anything that'll worry him,' she instructed Ewan

334

when he went up to his father later.

He scowled. 'I wish he'd just leave us tae see tae the business and stop interfering.'

'Listen to him and agree with him, and if necessary, just go your own way,' she said wearily. 'It's what Alex did to keep the peace.'

'If Alex did it, then it must be right,' he snarled, and trudged off.

With Matt upstairs and not knowing what was going on in the kitchen, she had insisted on Todd coming in for his midday meal with Ewan. Now he got up and reached for his jacket.

'That was a grand dinner, Mrs Lennox. My thanks tae ye.'

'You're welcome, Todd. I want you to eat in here every day with Ewan, during the winter, at least. I won't have you sitting out in the workshop in this weather.'

'It's no hardship, but there's nothin' like a cooked meal.' She was stacking dishes at the sink, and he came to stand behind her, peering out at the snow. 'It's comin' down hard again,' he observed, then fumbled in his pocket and laid a parcel wrapped in greaseproof paper down on the draining board.

She opened it to find some neatly cut sandwiches. 'Don't be daft, Todd!'

'Since you've given me my dinner it's only fair that you have the food I brought to eat, Mrs Lennox. I don't like tae take yer hospitality and give nothin' in exchange,' he added as she began to refuse. 'Ye'll mebbe be able tae use them.'

Perhaps it was Todd's kindness, perhaps it was because the little parcel was so like the one Kirsty had given Alex not two hours ago; she would never know. All she did know was that she tried to say something but instead, to her horror and embarrassment, started to weep.

'What's wrong? Is it the master?' Todd asked in alarm. 'Has he got worse?'

'It's—it's Alex—' She turned blindly, reached out for the dish towel. It wasn't there.

'Here.' Todd thrust his own handkerchief into her hand. 'It's all right, it's clean.'

'I know I'm making a fuss about a grown man,' she said shakily. 'It was time he went off on his own. It's just—it was a year ago today that we lost Fergus, only with all that's been going on nobody's remembered.'

Mention of her dead baby's name was her undoing. She lurched forward towards the comfort and security of Todd's shoulder, and felt his arms go around her. He held her, one big hand patting her back, as she wept for Fergus and for

336

Alex, and for poor crippled Matt, and for herself.

'I'm such a fool,' she said shakily when she finally drew back.

'No ye're not. Everyone needs tae have a good cry now and again.'

'But I shouldn't have landed you with it all, Todd.'

'Of course ye should. What else are friends for?' He peered down into her swollen face, then said awkwardly, 'If ye're all right now, Mrs Lennox, I'd best get along tae the workshop.'

'Of course—on you go, Todd, I'll be fine. And thank you,' she said, as he opened the door. He gave her a quick smile and stepped out into the snow.

She barely had time to thrust his handkerchief into her apron pocket and rinse her face before Ewan clattered downstairs and erupted into the kitchen, muttering under his breath. Kirsty pretended to be busy with the dishes in the sink so that she could keep her face hidden, but she needn't have worried, for he stormed through the room and out of the back door without a glance or a word.

From the window she watched his broad back disappear into the whirling snow, shoulders hunched and hands thrust deep into his jacket pockets.

# 26

Once the snow melted, pools of dirty water were left on the shop floor each time customers came in, and a mop and bucket had to be kept in a corner at all times. Whenever any of the staff had a moment free they ran the mop over the muddy, dirty floor. Jean was shocked the first time she saw Rose wield the mop.

'I'll do that.' She tried to take the mop from Rose, who held onto it.

'I can manage fine.'

'But it's not seemly, you cleanin' up after folk.'

'It's perfectly seemly. Anyway, I enjoy it.' Rose pushed the mop vigorously around the floor. 'There's something pleasurable in doing things that I know would shock my Mamma.'

She had lost none of her enthusiasm for the venture and continued to spend time in the shop every day despite her mother's opposition. To everyone's surprise, including her own, she had begun to reveal a hitherto hidden sense of humour, sharp as a honed blade, which made her popular with the regular customers.

338

'There's always been things I've wanted to say, but I couldn't, for they'd have shocked everyone,' she admitted to Kirsty and Jean. 'But here it's different. I can say whatever comes into my head, and people know what I mean. Ordinary folk have a much better sense of humour.'

Winter gave way to spring and spring to summer, and Kirsty was kept busy between the shop and the house. She was surprised, in June, to realise that it had been four months since Alex's departure. He had never been back, but he wrote now and then, brief letters indicating that he had settled down in Glasgow and was busy reorganising the small factory Sandy had bought. Matt professed to be uninterested in the letters, but Kirsty made a point of telling him of their contents, and he didn't stop her.

'I think he's sorry now that he let Alex go so easily,' she said to Jean, who had been told long since of the reasons behind his sudden departure, 'but it's too late now, so he'll not admit it. He quarrels with Ewan just as much as he did with Alex—probably more, since Ewan's heart isn't in the business at all.'

'He's young yet.'

'There's more to it than that, Jean. Ewan's restless, and he doesn't like the responsibility, or having to answer to Matt

339

all the time. And we've lost some regular customers since he took over. I notice these things now I'm doing the books.'

'Did you ask the laddie about it?'

'He just shrugged it off, so I asked Todd.' She smiled faintly. 'Poor soul, he hated having to talk about Ewan. He squirmed as if I'd been trying to pull a tooth from his jaw.'

'So it's Ewan's fault?'

'He gets impatient easily, and folk who're willing to spend good money to get what they want don't take kindly to being treated harshly.' Ewan, she thought, was too like his father.

'Are you going to say anything to Matt?'

Kirsty shook her head. 'It would only make him worry, and cause another row. It's Ewan I'll have to—'

The door flew open and Rose burst in, glancing round the empty shop. 'Thank goodness there's nobody here!' She began to haul her jacket off.

'What's wrong?'

'Everything. John's sister's engaged to be married, and her parents are holding a party for her.' She tossed the jacket over the end of a rail. 'And John's asked—'

'Rose,' Kirsty said patiently, 'your jacket belongs in the back room.'

'I'll put it there in a minute. I'm trying to tell you—'

'You know what happened the last time you left it there for a minute.'

Jean's lips twitched at the memory. They had had a sudden rush of customers that day, and a determined woman had tried to buy the jacket, which was expensive and almost brand new. Even worse, she had wanted Kirsty to alter it for her. They had had quite a bother rescuing it.

'Oh, very well!' Rose snatched the jacket from the rail and flounced into the back room.

'She's burstin' tae tell us somethin', poor lassie,' Jean whispered. 'Sometimes you're awful hard on her.'

'I'm just reminding her that she has to follow the rules like the rest of us.'

Rose shot back into the shop, smoothing her black cravat. 'As I was saying,' she took a second to glare at Kirsty, who smiled back, 'John's invited me to be his partner at this party for his sister.'

Jean beamed at her. 'That'll be nice for you.'

'That's what Mamma said when I told her.' Rose paced the shop. 'But it's not nice at all, it's terrible. She wants to help me to choose a gown, and I know that she'll choose some dreadful, silly, fussy thing.'

She looked at them both, her eyes tragic. 'And I can't bear the thought of

341

embarrassing poor John in front of his family and friends after he's been kind enough to invite me.'

'You make it sound as if he's doin' you a favour,' Jean said.

'Of course he is! He knows that nobody else will invite me.'

'Mebbe he just thinks that he'd enjoy your company.'

'Good heavens, no,' Rose said at once. 'We've known each other for years, and believe me, it's kindness and nothing else. And as a kindness to him,' she reverted back to her former panic, 'I have to find something to wear before Mamma does. She's still got this bee in her bonnet about marrying me off, and she's quite certain that if she leaves it to me to find something to wear I'll look a fright and spoil my chances completely—not that there are any.'

'Why not?' Kirsty asked, and Rose gave her a withering look.

'I'm not wife material, you know that. If I ever do marry, it will be to some old and ugly man from mutual despair.' She scanned the nearest rail, then detached a dress and held it against herself. 'What about this?'

'You can't wear something from here,' Jean said, shocked.

'Why not?' asked the girl who had once

shuddered at the thought of people wearing second-hand clothes.

'Because it might be recognised. What if the woman it used tae belong tae was at the party?'

'I never thought of that.' Rose put the dress back reluctantly. 'What a bind!' Then, brightening, she said, 'There's that little cream gown I brought back from France. The one Mamma hated because it had no frills or ribbons. D'you remember it, Kirsty?'

'I do, but you'd need something more elaborate than that for an engagement party.'

'I have to think of something!'

'That dark-blue lace your mother refused to let me put over the pink silk,' Kirsty suddenly remembered. 'Is it still in the sewing room?'

'Probably. I haven't dared to set foot in there since...' Rose stopped suddenly and gave Kirsty a sidelong look. 'Since that day.'

'P'raps it would do over the cream.'

'I'll bring it in,' Rose said at once. 'And the dress too.'

The cream satin dress, Kirsty recalled as she lifted it from its wrappings the next day, was the very garment that had set off the first quarrel she had witnessed between

Rose and her mother. Mrs Hamilton, maintaining that it was far too old for her daughter, had made Kirsty add a frill round the skirt, puffed sleeves, and a bunch of flowers at the low rounded neck. The result had ruined the simple lines of the gown and made Rose look, as she herself said at the time, like a carthorse decked out for a parade.

'I couldn't take all that rubbish off by myself,' she said, stepping out of her skirt in the fitting room. 'I'd probably ruin the material if I tried, and the sewing woman Mamma hired after you left knows nothing.' The cravat was draped over the back of a chair and her long fingers seemed to flow down the front of her high-necked white blouse, leaving buttons undone in their wake. Watching, Kirsty thought of poor Matt, scarcely able to hold a newspaper.

The blouse was whipped off to reveal a round-necked sleeveless petticoat in snowy white nainsook, with narrow lace round the bodice, armholes and hem. Watching Rose reach for the cream gown, Kirsty realised that although the girl was gawky and normally strode about like a man, her bare arms and black-stockinged legs were nicely rounded and her movements, controlled by the size of the little room, were surprisingly graceful as she lifted the gown over her head and let it fall into place down the length of her body.

The shop door bell gave its melodious chime, so unlike the former flat clang, and Jean came into the room. 'How are you gettin' on? Here, Rose—you've got a nice figure.'

'Nice? I'm a beanpole! No hips to speak of,' Rose clamped her hands over her chest, 'and I'm flat as an ironing board.'

'But you've got nice lines,' Jean said, then nodded approval as Kirsty unrolled the blue lace and held it against the gown. 'That'd make a bonny overdress.'

'One that follows the simple lines of the gown itself—'

'With wee sleeves,' said Jean, 'and a rounded neckline, following this one—'

'And just a little fullness in the skirt, and perhaps a short cape of the lace at the back.'

'You'd want a narrow sash—'

'But not too high—mebbe coming down low at the front, to a point—'

'And little crystal beads down the front of the bodice,' Jean said. 'Or wee pearls.'

'Or both.'

Rose was looking from one to another. 'I'd not want anything too fancy,' she warned anxiously.

'Just enough to make the gown a wee bit more...interesting,' Kirsty assured her, reaching for the box of pins. 'Hold that lace at her shoulder for me, Jean.'

'There's not much time before the party.'

'I'll manage. I'll work on this dress at home as well as here.'

'You shouldn't have to do shop work at home,' Rose protested.

'I can't give more time to the shop because of Matt being the way he is,' Kirsty said through a mouthful of pins. 'I don't mind taking work home with me. You'll have tae stand still if you don't want a pin stuck in you.'

'D'you not think we should bring in another seamstress?' Rose asked. 'There's enough work now to warrant one. Someone who could do some of the plain work under your instruction, Kirsty.'

'There's Teenie Dunbar in Mary Street,' Jean said thoughtfully. 'She's a widow woman, a respectable sort of body, and good with a needle. She'd be glad of a wee job that'd bring in some money. She could help behind the counter too, when we're busy.'

'But it'd mean another wage,' Kirsty protested, removing the pins. 'And another sewing machine.'

'You have to put money into a business to get it going, just like priming a pump,' Rose told her. 'We'll find the money, John

346

and me. Business hasn't been too bad in our first six months. Ask your friend to come in and have a word with the three of us, Jean.'

Teenie Dunbar, a scarecrow of a woman with anxious brown eyes, was waiting in the shop when Kirsty arrived a few days later.

'I've brought samples of my work.' She delved into a large carpet bag and pulled out several items of clothing, a clean, nail-bitten finger indicating the small neat stitches on this hem and that seam. 'They've all been done by hand.'

'Can you use a machine as well?'

'I can that.'

Kirsty led the woman into the sewing room and found a blouse that needed taking in for the undernourished woman who had bought it. Teenie whipped off her coat, revealing a neat apron over a grey blouse and black skirt, and set to work, spinning the wheel and pumping the treadles until Kirsty feared that she would send the machine whirring free of the screws that held it down.

The woman was accomplished, there was no doubt of that. She was also a dedicated worker; on being told that Jean and Kirsty would have to wait for Rose's arrival before making a decision, she turned down the suggestion that she might like to return in an hour.

'I'm not doin' anythin' else. It'll save the walk home an' back again if I just get on with some work here while I'm waitin',' she said, and off went the sewing machine again.

By the time Rose arrived Teenie had shortened one skirt and was working on a second. It was agreed, on Kirsty's recommendation, that she should be hired for two hours every afternoon.

When Teenie had departed, beaming from ear to ear, the three partners looked at each other.

'Well,' Rose said at last. 'We've just engaged our first employee!'

'Don't start on me,' Ewan said when Kirsty brought up the subject of the fall in orders. 'I've got enough of that with Father naggin' away at me day after day.'

'He only wants to make sure that everything's going well.'

'Everythin's fine. We've got enough work tae keep the two of us busy.'

'But you've not got many orders in hand.'

They were sitting at the table; Kirsty pushed the opened order book over to him, but he only glanced at it and said,

'There's enough, surely.'

'I thought Mr Wilson was supposed to put in an order for another two chairs last month. He said he would when his last order was completed a year ago.'

'Two chairs won't bring in much money.'

'It's better than nothing.'

Ewan shrugged. 'He's forgotten.'

'He's given the order to someone else, Ewan. He told me that when I spoke to him the other day.'

His handsome face flushed. 'So you're spyin' on me now? Goin' round askin' folk why they're not rushin' tae give us their business?'

'I met the man in the street and I reminded him about his promise, that's all.' She hated having to confront him like this, but there was no other way. 'He says he came to see you about the chairs, but you didn't seem to be interested.'

Ewan pushed his chair back abruptly. 'I've got my father goin' on at me, and Todd, and now you. Alex did the right thing when he walked away from this place!'

'Ewan—'

'I've got work tae do,' he said, and slammed out of the back door, almost knocking Mary over as she came in.

'Get out of my way,' he snapped at

349

her, and she stared up at his angry face and said at once, 'It wasn't me that told.'

He swept on without a word and she came into the kitchen, her face wrinkled with concern. 'You know it wasn't me that told you, don't you?' she demanded of her mother.

'Told me what?'

'About seeing Ewan walking in Brodie Park with Beth when he should have been wor—' Mary stopped abruptly, with one hand flying to her mouth. 'Now I've told,' she said between her fingers, her eyes wide with horror. 'Will he want the penny back?'

'What penny?'

'The one he gave me when I promised not to tell. And I didn't, but now—'

'Sit down, Mary.' When her daughter had obediently perched on the edge of a chair, Kirsty said 'Now, tell me what all this is about—you might as well, now,' she added as Mary began to argue, 'since you've already said so much.'

The story came out reluctantly, a few words at a time. Mary, playing in Brodie Park with friends the previous week, had seen Ewan out walking with Beth Laidlaw.

'He was probably in the park alone, and so was she, and they met up with each other.'

350

'That's what he said, and I pretended that I believed him because he was angry about me seeing him. But he was holding her hand, and you don't do that when you're alone,' now that she had started confessing Mary seemed to be unable to stop, 'so I promised not to tell in case Father gave him another row because he should have been working and not in the park at all and he gave me a penny.' She stopped and sucked in a great lungful of air, then finished, 'And now he might want it back and I've spent it!'

When the little girl had been reassured and sent out again to play, Kirsty closed the order book and put it away. Her mind kept returning to Mary's story as she peeled the potatoes for the evening meal. Ewan had an eye for a pretty girl, but he knew well enough that Beth Laidlaw was promised to Todd. They must have met by accident, she decided, and Mary was confused as to what she'd actually seen.

But even so, why had Ewan been walking in Brodie Park when he should have been at work?

# 27

Thanks to Teenie, who freed Kirsty by taking over most of the alterations, Rose's dress was completed a few days before the party. She gasped as she looked at herself in the full-length mirror.

'It's beautiful!'

Kirsty felt her mouth curve in a satisfied smile as she saw how well the dress and its wearer complemented each other. There were no ribbons, no flowers, no frills. The cream satin underdress showed as a pearly glow through the blue lace overdress, which followed the lines of Rose's long, slim body. A slightly gathered bodice led the eye down to a skirt just full enough to allow for easy movement, with a slight flare at the bottom, where Kirsty had inserted a deep panel of flower-patterned lace in the same shade of blue. Flowered panels had also been inserted at each side of the bodice, and seed pearls scattered over the flowers echoed the undergown's pearly sheen.

'I must let Jean see it.' Rose made for the main shop.

'There might be a customer in.'

'Then we'll give them a treat.' But the shop was empty, giving Rose room to parade up and down while the other three watched. 'You're striding out too much,' Kirsty said. 'Take smaller steps. That's better.' The small steps made Rose look as though she was gliding across the floor, and set the dress floating easily around her feet.

'It feels so...free!' She spun round, and the flare at the bottom of the skirt swung out, then fell back. 'It's as if I'm not wearing any clothes at all!' she exulted, and Teenie blushed.

'Long gloves—dark blue, not cream,' Kirsty suggested. 'And a necklace round your throat.'

Jean disagreed. 'A blue velvet ribbon'd be better. She's got bonny shoulders—a ribbon'd show them off better.'

'You're right.'

'Mamma has a nice sapphire brooch I could fasten the ribbon with—and earrings to match,' Rose said eagerly, caught up in the excitement of the moment. 'I'm sure she'd lend them to me.'

'Yer hair's too tight,' Teenie put in. 'Here.' She whisked the girl back into the fitting room and sat her down in front of the mirror. 'Let me have a try at it. I used tae be a lady's maid,' she added, her fingers already busy with the grips and combs that strained Rose's hair back from her face. 'There now.' The last grip came out and a cascade of reddish-brown hair tumbled down to fall softly about Rose's shoulders. It curtained both sides of her face, softening the strong bony features. All at once she didn't look much older than Caitlin.

'It's a sin tae treat bonny hair so badly, like tyin' a dog up an' never lettin' it run free.'

'I don't like my hair loose.'

'At least ye could put it up in a more kindly way,' Teenie lectured, no longer in awe of the girl and her money now that she was able to use some of her own skills. 'Someb'dy find me a hairbrush.'

Five minutes later her nimble fingers had swept Rose's hair into a soft, full roll framing her face then sweeping back into a single thick plait that sat snugly at the nape of her neck.

'Oh, Rose, you look lovely,' Jean said, awed, while Teenie studied her own handiwork critically from all sides, then nodded.

'Yer maid'll need tae use pads tae get the right fullness, but that's the general idea. Let's see ye walkin' up and down again.'

The overall effect was much improved, but once again Rose had broken into her usual long stride. They all tried to show her the right way, mincing up and down the empty shop and scattering each time a customer came in, but it didn't work.

'You're ruinin' the line of the dress,' Jean lamented.

'I can't help it—it's the way I've always walked. I'll never remember to take short steps!'

'We could mebbe tie each end of a ribbon round her knees under the dress so's she can't take long steps,' Teenie suggested.

'And what if I forget about it and try to step out? I'd fall over!'

'Your Caitlin moves like a princess, Kirsty,' Jean said. 'It's half-day tomorrow—d'you think she'd mebbe come in and teach Rose the right way of it?'

Caitlin did indeed move well, Kirsty realised as she watched her daughter walk easily up and down the shop on the following afternoon, hand in hand with Rose so that she could hold the older girl back each time she tried to stride ahead.

'I feel like a gun dog being trained to walk to heel,' Rose said, starting to giggle.

'Now try it on your own.' Caitlin stood back, watching. 'You're stepping out again.'

'It's no use, I'll never get it right.'

'Music,' Caitlin said suddenly. 'If you could learn to walk to music, you could sing it to yourself in your head.'

' "The Man Who Broke the Bank at Monte Carlo",' Teenie said at once. 'I like that one.'

Caitlin shook her head. 'That'd just encourage her to stride.' She thought for a minute, then suggested, ' "Two Lovely Black Eyes". Come on.'

She seized Rose's hand again and then started to walk her up—and down, singing. The others joined in. 'Two lovely black eyes, oh, what a surprise...' they carolled, Jean sweeping Teenie into a dance around the room.

The song seemed to do the trick. Within ten minutes Rose was gliding up and down on her own, the lace overskirt flaring out neatly with each step.

Rose beamed at them all. 'It's all going to work, thanks to you. You're the best friends anyone could ever have, and I'm lucky to have found you. And never mind the maid, Teenie. If I get the pads, will you come to the house to do my hair for me on the night?'

'Your house? I couldnae do that!'

'Yes you could—you must, Teenie!' Rose took the woman's work-worn hands in hers. 'If you don't, Mamma will get her maid to do it, and she's sure to get it wrong. Please! Kirsty knows the house; she'll come with you,' she added as Teenie began to shake her head. 'Won't you, Kirsty?'

The thought of going back into the Hamilton house made Kirsty's knees feel weak, but Rose's eyes were begging her to agree. Against her own will, Kirsty nodded.

'Oh, thank you! I'll send the new car for you,' Rose promised, and Teenie almost fell apart again.

'I couldnae go in one of those things—don't make me do that! I'd be much happier walking on my own two feet!'

'Rose is nice,' Caitlin said as she and her mother walked home. 'Nicer than I expected. It just goes to show, moneyed folk can be just as friendly as anyone else when they put their minds to it.'

Kirsty sent word ahead to Bessie, the Hamilton's cook, and she and Teenie were given a warm welcome when they arrived in the big kitchen. Teenie, clasping a worn bag holding all that she needed and looking anxiously back over her shoulder at Kirsty, was led off to Rose's room by a maid, while Bessie, waving to one of the two comfortable armchairs in the room, said, 'Sit yerself down and tell me what ye've done tae tame Miss Rose.'

The chair was deep and soft and comfortable. 'You should try to get a sight of her in her party gown tonight,' Kirsty told the cook as she sank into its welcoming depths. 'She's far prettier than she allows herself to be. And she's done well by the shop. She's not afraid to do her share of the work.'

Bessie chuckled. 'Ye should have heard the rows when she first came up with the idea. Her and her parents went at it hammer and tongs, then finally the master gave in and said that Miss Rose could do whatever she wanted as long as she took the consequences—only he put it more strongly than that. Between ourselves, Kirsty, I think that lassie's the one he likes the best, because she's got more backbone in her than the other two. She was his mother's favourite an' all.'

'She was a lovely lady—a real gentlewoman.' Kirsty thought of her first employer with fondness. Slender and elegant, her back as straight as a stair rod, the woman had been firm but fair with her servants and had earned and held their respect and loyalty.

'She was that. Not in the least like that...' Bessie glanced round to see if any of her staff were within listening distance, then elaborately mouthed, 'that bitch,' before reverting to her usual speaking voice. 'As I was sayin', old Mrs Hamilton aye had a soft spot for Miss Rose when she was a bairn. That's why she left money in trust for the lassie—an' that caused quite a stramash when the will was read, I can tell ye. This Mrs Hamilton and her older daughters made such a fuss, but Mr Brodie—that's Mr John's father—said there was nothing they could do but accept it.' She gave a sudden bellow of laughter. 'I cannae tell ye how pleased I was when I heard what she'd decided tae dae with it. Her grandmother would've approved.'

'I'm not so sure about that—but I'm glad it happened, for my sake as well as Jean's.'

'It's worth all the money if it keeps Miss Rose happy, I can tell ye.'

Although it was a warm evening and the kitchen was hot after a day's cooking, Bessie, who felt the cold keenly, always had a fire going in the grate. Now she turned her skirt back to let her knees have the good of it. 'The mistress must have bought out Paisley's entire stock of smelling salts, and at one point she took tae her bed and said she wasnae gettin' out of it until Miss Rose saw sense. That was a nice few days for us, for it meant she couldnae come down here and make a nuisance of herself. But she soon got tired of bein' an invalid—and she soon saw that she wasnae goin' tae win that way.'

'Has she accepted it?'

'No' entirely, but she's havin' tae live with it. Young Mr Brodie bein' involved helps, for the mistress is very friendly with his mother, and she's got faith in him. She was fair excited about him askin' Miss Rose tae this party. Now, how's that poor man of yours?'

'No better, Bessie. Worse, if anything. He scarcely comes downstairs at all now.'

'Poor soul. I've got some things for ye tae take home tae him.' Bessie nodded at a bag on the table.

'You can't—'

'Now don't start talkin' with yer conscience instead of yer tongue again, Kirsty Lennox! It's just a wee mouthful here and a wee mouthful there. Ye'd not grudge an invalid a few tasty bites, would ye?'

Kirsty smiled at her old friend. 'You've got a good heart, Bessie.'

'Not a bit of it! There's a cake I baked with my own hands too. It must be hard tae see yer man in a state like that.'

'It is. I think the fight went out of him when Alex left.'

The cook's eyebrows shot up. 'Yer eldest? He's away from home?'

Kirsty had forgotten that Bessie knew nothing of what had been happening. 'Alex got the chance of a good job in Glasgow,' she said casually. 'He's been gone four months now.'

'Ye'll miss him, but I suppose the business is a bit wee for him and his brother. An' how're the lassies? Is Caitlin growin' up tae be a beauty like I said she would?'

In no time at all Teenie was back, flushed and fluttery and too excited to bother with a cup of tea. After the warmth of the kitchen it was pleasant to walk down the tree-lined driveway in the cool evening air.

Now that her ordeal was over, Teenie chattered like a parrot all the way back to the town. 'Mind Rose said her mother had a sapphire brooch she could use? I've never seen anythin' like it. The gems sparkled that much they could have put yer eyes out. It looked just right on a blue velvet ribbon, and the earrings were dangly. She's got just the right neck for them, long and slim.'

'You didn't have any trouble doing her hair?'

Teenie shivered. 'There was this woman that turned out tae be Mrs Hamilton's maid fussin' round the place all the time and givin' me black looks. Rose told her more than once that she could go, but she'd not budge—just kept makin' excuses about things she was doin' for the lassie.

She was fair eaten up wi' jealousy because it was me doin' Rose's hair and not her. Oh—and ye should have seen the look she gave me when I called Rose by her name the way we do in the shop, without the "Miss" in front of it. I just gave her a nice smile back, and she flounced her head in the air and looked as if she'd been suckin' on a lemon.'

'Did you see Mrs Hamilton herself?'

'A fat woman that looks as if someone had let off a bad smell right under her nose? She came in when I was nearly finished and said, "Not like you at all, Rose." ' Teenie did a good job of mimicking Mrs Hamilton. 'So Rose says, "I thought that was the idea, Mamma," and Mrs Hamilton went red. Then Rose made me wait behind tae see how she looked in the dress, and—oh, Kirsty, she was a picture!'

'What did her mother say?'

'Her eyes nearly came out her head. She said, "Very nice, Rose," and Rose said, "Thank you, Mamma," as if butter wouldnae melt in her mouth. Then when her ma turned her back Rose winked at me in the mirror and that snide maid saw it and nearly swallowed her own teeth. And Rose gave me a pound note for my trouble—imagine, a pound!' Teenie said as they turned out of the gates and onto the road. She halted and began to fish in her large bag. 'That's ten shillin' for me and ten shillin' for you, when I get it changed.'

'You keep it, Teenie; you earned it.'

'But you walked there and back with me. I'd never have had the courage without you.'

'Even so, I spent a nice hour with an old friend, and I'll not take a penny of—what's amiss?' Kirsty asked, startled, as Teenie, who had found the note and was smoothing it out carefully, gave a sudden scream.

'Kirsty—it's five pounds, not one!'

'That shows how pleased Rose was with her hair.'

'But—but...' The woman was gabbling, her agitated hands screwing up the note she had just smoothed out. 'It's too much!'

'It's what she wanted to give you. Put it in your purse before you tear it.'

'But you made that bonny dress for her—'

'And I was well paid for it,' Kirsty assured her. 'So we're all happy.'

'Happy?' Tears stood out in Teenie's eyes. 'I've never had so much money in my life!'

They didn't expect to see Rose the next day, but she swept in at her usual time, looking radiant. Her hair was no longer strained back tightly; instead she had piled it on top of her head in a soft bun, similar to the style Kirsty had adopted.

'It was the best party I've ever attended, and everyone admired my gown—and my hair. John's eyes almost fell out of his head when he first saw me, and even Mamma thought I looked passable for the first time in my life. Several of the ladies asked where I had had the dress made.'

'What did ye tell them?' Teenie asked.

'The truth, of course.' Rose gave a gurgle of amusement. 'It caused quite a stir. I'm surprised your ears weren't burning, Kirsty, for your name was being passed around quite considerably.'

'What did your mother say to you telling the truth?' Kirsty was half amused and half horrified.

'She didn't care for it, but she herself raised me to be honest, so she couldn't object.' Rose giggled again. 'I overheard her tell one friend that she had employed you at one time, and found you to be a skilled dressmaker.'

'And you managed to keep yourself from striding out?'

'Oh yes. Your Caitlin's a genius, Kirsty. That song worked very well, though I haven't been able to get it out of my mind since!' Rose broke into 'Two Lovely Black Eyes', sweeping Teenie into a waltz round the empty shop. Then, sobering for a moment, she said, 'I was thinking when I looked at the ladies gathered there from all round the town, we should be spreading our net and collecting used clothes from other districts. We've got enough room for them now, and two seamstresses.'

'You were thinking about that while you were enjoying yourself at a party?' Kirsty asked, and Rose's vivid blue eyes sparkled at her.

'Why not? I'm a businesswoman now. Anyone object to the idea? No? Then I'll draw up a notice asking for collectors and put it in the window.'

# 28

In September Beth Laidlaw's father decided that since Beth and Todd still hadn't found a place to live, they should share his flat above the tobacconist's shop.

'It means that we'll be gettin' married at long last,' Todd told Kirsty exultantly. 'And I'll be just across the road from my work.'

'I didn't think Beth would want to stay in her own home, since she's turned down all the other tenement flats you've found.'

'She'd as soon have somewhere with her own front and back door,' he agreed, 'but that'll come one day.'

Todd seemed to be the only one who approved of the plan. 'The man's clean daft, agreein' tae it,' Jean said flatly. 'Andra Laidlaw's never done somethin' for nothin' in his life—this'll be him makin' sure there's someone there tae look after him in his old age.'

'I don't see Beth doing that.'

'She's probably got little choice. From what I hear, Andra's promised that if she stays with him she'll inherit the shop when he goes, instead of havin' tae share it with her sister that lives in Glasgow. That'd be enough tae bring her tae heel, for she's got his love of money.' Jean sniffed and shook her head. 'Her and Todd'll pay a heavy price for the inheritance, bein' at that old miser's beck and call for as long as he lives. The day might come when she'll wish she'd not done so much hummin' and hawin' and turnin' her nose up at all those places Todd found.'

'D'you think Todd knows what he's letting himself in for?' Caitlin asked that evening. 'I'd not want to live with Mr Laidlaw. Have you seen the way he counts out the money when you pay for something?'

'I have.' Kirsty hated it when the man

was in the shop. He always counted her money out carefully at least twice before tucking it tenderly into the till, as though suspecting her of trying to cheat him.

'You can see the pain on the man's face if he has to give you change.' Caitlin shivered. 'I don't know how Todd can think of living in the same house as him.'

'It's because the man knows which side his bread's buttered on,' Ewan broke in. 'He'll do very well for himself, marryin' a woman who'll have her own wee business one day.'

'That's nonsense,' Kirsty said. 'All Todd wants is to be married to Beth. Goodness knows they've been engaged long enough.'

'Only because he's a fool. A lassie like Beth needs a man who'd just make the decisions and tell her about them afterwards. Todd's not got the first idea of how tae treat women.'

'And I suppose you have,' Caitlin jeered, and he gave her a long cool look.

'I certainly know a lot more about them than the likes of Todd Paget. He's just a carthorse without a brain between his ears.'

'He is not,' Mary flared. She was devoted to Todd, who always had time to talk to her when they met. 'He's the nicest person I know—nicer than you!'

Ewan laughed and reached out to pull

the ribbon from her long brown hair, something that he knew infuriated his little sister. 'You're a trustin' wee soul, aren't you? Goodness knows what you'll end up walkin' down the aisle with.'

'That's enough!' Kirsty caught at Mary's arm as the little girl flew at Ewan. 'Stand still, Mary, and I'll put your ribbon back in. And you should have more respect for Todd,' she added to Ewan as Mary, scowling, snatched the ribbon from her half-brother and handed it over. 'He does a grand job in that workshop. I don't know where we'd be without him.'

Ewan got out of Matt's chair and tossed Matt's newspaper down on the floor. 'He's certainly not lost for admirers in this family,' he muttered, then grabbed his jacket from the nail on the back of the door and went out.

'There.' Kirsty gave the ribbon a final tweak and patted Mary's arm. 'As good as new.' As she picked up the newspaper and folded it, she fretted about Ewan. Matt had been convinced that once Alex was out of the way his own son would enjoy taking control of the workshop. Instead Ewan had made no secret of his boredom and his resentment of the way Alex had, as he saw it, escaped from the family business.

Matt, who knew nothing of the way Ewan's lack of interest was beginning to affect the order book and the ledgers, and who would never know, if Kirsty could help it, had recently begun to depend more on Todd, summoning him for consultations rather than Ewan.

Perversely, Ewan resented his father's growing dependence on the journeyman and seemed to blame Todd for it. When it was time for the midday meal, they arrived in the kitchen separately and kept their eyes on their plates, not looking at or speaking to each other, their mutual dislike thickening the air. The situation had become so fraught that when Todd had found a lame reason for spending the midday break in the workshop again Kirsty had accepted it without protest.

Only the other day, going to ask if Todd would help Matt to get to the bathroom, she had heard the two of them in the workshop, voices raised in anger. Silence had fallen as soon as she put her hand to the door latch, and when she went in both men were busy at opposite ends of the shop. She was convinced, though, that they had sprung apart when they had heard her at the door and that she had unwittingly prevented a violent confrontation.

There was nobody to confide in. She didn't want Matt worrying about something he couldn't control, and she was afraid that if he did get to hear of it he would solve the matter by dismissing Todd. Without him, she was convinced that the business would collapse within weeks.

When she tried to find out the truth of the situation from Todd, he was evasive and so uncomfortable with her questions that she gave up. She could only watch, and wonder and worry.

She thought, briefly, of confiding her fears in one of her letters to Alex, then discarded the idea, realising that it was no longer his concern and that he probably had enough on his hands forging a relationship with his real father and establishing himself in the new business.

The wedding dress came into the shop a few weeks later, a great billowing mass of oyster satin and corded silk with knots of orange blossom scattered over the vast skirt. Rose spent some time wrestling it onto Aggie, the dressmaker's dummy, who had been rescued from her precarious existence on the pavement and given her own corner in the front shop.

'It's probably the sort of gown my mamma might have worn. Isn't it frightful?' She lifted a great armful of satin train, then let it fall. 'Such a weight to drag around.'

'There would have been several pageboys

carrying the train.' Teenie stroked the skirt. 'I wonder what happened tae the bride it was made for?'

'She's probably a grandmother by now. We'll never be able to sell this,' Rose said dismissively. 'We might as well let the ragman have it.'

Teenie was shocked. 'But it's beautiful material!'

'It's served its purpose—and lain in a trunk for about thirty years,' Rose scoffed. 'Nobody round here's going to want it.'

'Beth Laidlaw will be looking for a wedding gown,' Kirsty said thoughtfully. 'She'd look lovely in something like this.'

'You'd need to do a lot of work on it, Kirsty,' Jean warned. 'Why go tae all that bother for a lassie that'd pass you in the street without a glance if the mood took her?'

'I'd not be doing it for Beth, I'd be doing it for Todd.' Kirsty could imagine the pride on the journeyman's face as he saw Beth come up the aisle in a beautiful gown like this. 'It could be my wedding gift to them both.'

Beth came to the house reluctantly, but her green eyes filled with avarice when she saw the gown Kirsty had brought from the shop. It fitted her slim figure almost perfectly, and the ivory satin emphasised

371

her smooth creamy skin. Studying herself in the long mirror Kirsty had brought down from the bedroom, the girl became almost animated.

'None of my friends has ever had such a bonny gown.' She moved a few graceful steps about the room, twisting her head so that she could continue to watch her mirrored reflection.

Kirsty studied gown and wearer from all angles. 'The train and the bustle will have to go, of course. I'll use some of the material to make a back panel with a wee train to it, and I'll take away some of the fullness in the sleeves and use the extra lace from the skirt to make a higher neckline.'

'Will that not spoil the dress?'

Kirsty shook her head. 'Its lines could be seen better without all the frills and fuss.'

Beth's cheeks glowed and her eyes sparkled. 'I cannae—can't,' she corrected herself swiftly, 'wait to see folk's faces when they see me in this!'

It wasn't until the girl had gone and Kirsty was carefully wrapping the dress in an old linen sheet to keep it safe from harm that she realised that not once, in all her prattling about how much she would be envied for her fine wedding gown, had Beth made any reference to what Todd might think of it.

Beth's dress took up all the spare time Kirsty had. There was so much of it that she took her old sewing machine into the parlour rather than having to carry the great bulk of the dress from room to room. Caitlin helped in the evenings. Together they stripped the bustle and train away and removed the elaborate bows on the bodice and the knots of orange blossom scattered over the skirt.

'It looks prettier already,' Caitlin said as they surveyed the result. 'A girl with Beth's looks doesn't need all those additions.' She rescued the train from Mary, who had wrapped it around her shoulders and was walking about the little floor space left, her head twisted back over her shoulder to admire the great stretch of satin trailing behind. 'Don't spoil that; we'll be able to make something else out of it.'

'My dolly wants a wedding dress.'

'She'll get one, when I've got the time,' Caitlin promised. Ever since Mary's babyhood, Caitlin had made doll's clothes for her from scraps that Kirsty didn't need.

'I thought I'd take this deep lace frill off the skirt altogether and gather it into a high neck using some of the material I'll take from the sleeves. It'd look better than this round neck.'

Caitlin nodded. 'Much better.'

Once the gown had been stripped of all its embellishments it was easier to work with. Rather than ask Beth to come in to try it on as it went through the various stages of alteration, Kirsty used Caitlin, who was about Beth's height and just as slender. For the final fitting before Beth herself was invited back to the house, Caitlin brushed out her hair, normally hanging down her back in a single plait, and pinned it up out of the way before slipping into the gown.

Kirsty fastened the row of tiny buttons that ran up the length of the spine and hooked the high, severe satin collar, then shifted the sewing machine to one side so that Caitlin could move about.

'You're like a fairy princess!' she heard Mary say in awe.

Caitlin laughed. 'What d'you think of it, Mam?'

Kirsty glanced up, then stared. 'You look beautiful!'

'It's worked out well, hasn't it?' Caitlin agreed, all her attention on the dress. She was oblivious to the picture she herself made with her glowing auburn hair piled on top of her head and her turquoise eyes sparkling. 'It feels grand, too.' She moved a few steps, and the skirt seemed to flow around her. 'It's just a wee bit too long. She might trip over the hem when she's walking into the church.'

'I'll finish off the hem when Beth herself tries it on. Turn round and I'll unfasten the buttons.'

Studying herself in the mirror, Caitlin said almost wistfully, 'Beth's lucky, marrying in such a lovely gown.'

Kirsty swallowed the lump in her throat and wondered what on earth she'd be like when Caitlin's own wedding day arrived. 'I'll see that you get one just as nice when your turn comes,' she promised.

Caitlin flashed a wide smile at her over her shoulder. 'Oh, that'll not be for a while yet,' she said.

Two weeks before the date set for the wedding, Beth came to the house for another fitting. Her eyes widened when she saw the dress spread out over an armchair, and she gasped when she put it on. 'It's the most beautiful gown I've ever seen!'

'You look lovely in it.' But not, Kirsty thought, as lovely as Caitlin had. She had a fresh innocence that complemented the gown, whereas Beth's beauty was already slightly flawed by the discontent round her mouth and a hardness in her green eyes. 'I've still to get the hem right. I'll fetch a stool for you to stand on.'

Lifting the skirt delicately in both hands,

Beth followed her. 'It'll save you bringing the stool through,' she said, looking openly about the kitchen while Kirsty brought the stool from the corner and moved one of the armchairs back to make room.

Glancing at her, Kirsty saw the girl's lip curl contemptuously as she took in the worn chenille table cover, the old chairs set round the table, the shabby rug before the grate. She knew fine and well that Beth was thinking of the way she herself would have furnished the room if she had achieved her ambition and become its mistress.

'Can you step up here?' she asked levelly, picking up the old tobacco tin she kept her pins in. As she worked, Beth kept up a constant chatter about the wedding gifts she and Todd had already received and those she still hoped to get. Kirsty had pinned up a third of the hem, shuffling uncomfortably round the stool on her knees, when the door burst open and Ewan came in.

'Mam, show me that order—' He stopped suddenly. Peering round folds of oyster satin, Kirsty saw him framed in the doorway, motionless, staring at Beth. After her first surprised squeak, and a sudden start that almost toppled her from the stool, she too was as still as a statue.

Kirsty tried to speak, and almost swallowed the pins between her lips. She spat them into her palm and scrambled to her feet. 'Ewan, did you have to come bursting in like a—a bull in a china shop?'

He shut his mouth, swallowed, then said, 'I didnae know—I wanted to see Rab Leitch's order.'

'No harm done,' Kirsty said as she fetched the book from its drawer. 'It's the bridegroom that's not supposed to see the bride in her wedding dress. Not a word to Todd, mind.' She leafed through the book. 'This is the order you want.'

'What?'

'Rab Leitch's order. You can take the book to the workshop, but don't let it get dirty.'

'I'll do that.' He turned to go, then looked back at the girl on the stool. 'I'm sorry if I frightened you, Beth.'

'D'you like the gown?' she asked, preening, and he ran his tongue round his lips before saying huskily, 'Aye. It's...very grand.'

'Mind now,' Kirsty called after him as he left, 'not a whisper about it to Todd.'

To Kirsty's relief, Beth's nonstop chatter dried up after Ewan had gone. When the hem was pinned, she hurried back into the parlour to change into her own clothes.

'I'll have it ready by Sunday,' Kirsty said, and the girl nodded. She looked pale, and there was a worried frown between her well-shaped eyebrows.

'Are you all right?'

'I'm fine,' Beth said swiftly.

'Did Ewan upset you, bursting in like that?'

Beth shook her head. 'I'm just in a hurry to get back to the shop. My father doesn't like being behind the counter.'

Going back into the parlour to cover the dress with its protective sheet, Kirsty thought uneasily about the way Ewan had gaped at Beth in her finery, and the way Beth had gone quiet afterwards. It occurred to her that it was just as well that Todd was finally about to claim his bride.

## 29

Someone was banging on the street door, an ominous pounding that reverberated through the house and sounded like an attempt to smash through the panels. Kirsty, setting the table for breakfast, let a handful of cutlery clatter to its surface, her mouth dry and her heart fluttering at the urgency of the racket.

'I'm coming!' she called as she hurried through the hall, but the words either weren't heard or weren't heeded, for the pounding continued until her trembling fingers managed to raise the latch.

'Where is he?' Todd Paget demanded to know, bursting into the hall, almost knocking her down.

'Who?'

'Ewan—who else?' His face was distorted with rage.

He pushed her aside and started for the kitchen, then swung round when she said, 'He's not up yet. It's Sunday—he always lies abed on a Sunday.'

'Is he in the house at all? Have ye seen him?'

'Of course he's in the house. Where else would he—'

He was already halfway up the stairs, taking them two at a time. As she followed she heard him say, 'Where's Ewan's room?' and arrived in the upper corridor in time to see him throw the door open so violently that it banged against the small chest of drawers behind it. Caitlin and Mary, still in their nightclothes, were huddled together at their own door, Caitlin white as a sheet, Mary dissolving into frightened tears.

'Mam, what's happening?'

'Take Mary into the room and shut the door, Caitlin. Wait there till I come to you.' Kirsty could hear Matt calling from the front bedroom, but she went on past the door. For once, he would have to wait. Todd must have taken some sort of seizure, she thought in a panic. She had to get him downstairs and out of the house and away from her family.

He erupted from the room just as she reached it, almost knocking her down for the second time. Only his hands, fastening hard on her upper arms, saved her from falling to the floor.

'Where is he?' He shook her, his face, suffused with blood, close to hers.

'He's not in his room?'

'See for yersel'.' He thrust her through the door. It was true—Ewan wasn't in bed after all. He hadn't risen early, because the bed was still made. She pulled back the curtain that shut off one corner as a wardrobe, then looked through the little chest of drawers while Todd watched, filling the doorway with his body and the entire house with his smouldering rage.

'His things are all gone.' She stared at the journeyman, trying to make sense of the situation.

'When did ye last see him?'

'Last night, when he came in late and went to his bed.' Pretended to go to his bed, she thought, looking again at the smooth coverlet, the plumped pillow. He must have packed his clothes and crept out once the rest of the household was asleep. 'But why—?' she began, then, sharply, 'How did you know?'

'Beth's gone too.'

'Beth?' For a matter of seconds, Kirsty couldn't think why Todd should link his fiancée with her stepson; then the truth hit her, and she had to sit down suddenly on the bed. 'Beth and Ewan?'

'Ye didnae know?'

She shook her head, but already her mind was filling with pictures—Ewan lounging against the tobacconist's counter, Ewan's expression a few days earlier after he burst into the kitchen and saw Beth standing there in her wedding gown, Beth's sudden silence afterwards. She remembered Mary, too, calling after Ewan, 'I didn't tell!'

Todd was still speaking, his hands running through his hair, over his face, continually moving as if they couldn't, daren't, be still for one second. 'I guessed about him—the things he said, the sly wee glances at me, the grins when he thought I wasnae lookin'. He thought I hadnae the wit tae know what he thought of me, but just because I'm easy-goin' it doesnae mean I'm daft!' He slammed one fist hard against the doorframe, oblivious to pain. 'I faced him about it—I warned him that I'd kill him if I ever got proof of anythin'.'

'Did Beth...was she—?'

'Beth flirts with every man she sees,' Todd said bluntly. 'She swore tae me it was never anythin' more than that, an' I believed her. I thought with us gettin' wed at last that there was nothin' tae fear. But I was wrong!' Again his fist thudded at the frame. 'Where d'ye think they might have gone?' he demanded of her.

'I don't know.'

'Because it's not over,' Todd said thickly. 'I'm goin' tae find them, and I'm goin' tae kill him for this!' Suddenly he turned and went storming along the corridor and down the stairs. By the time Kirsty was halfway down to the hall, he had gone, slamming the door hard behind him.

The smell of burning porridge was beginning to seep into the hall from behind the closed kitchen door. Mary was screaming with fear now, and Matt was bellowing, demanding to know what was happening. 'I'm coming!' Kirsty shouted for the second time that morning, and took time to hurry into the smoke-filled kitchen and heave the burning pot out into the yard. Back in the kitchen she halted and took down the old ginger jar from the mantel shelf. She always kept some emergency money in there, but now it was empty.

Upstairs, she put her head into the girls' room, where Caitlin was hurriedly dressing herself and Mary was huddled on her bed, curled into a ball, rocking herself to and fro, the screams pouring from her.

'Take her downstairs, Caitlin, and try to quiet her while I see to your father. It's Ewan and Beth,' she added quickly to the girl's questioning face. 'It seems that they've run away together.'

Matt had got out of bed and was standing clutching the bedhead, trying to find the courage to attempt the few steps across the linoleum to the door. 'A body could die in here and still never get help,' he started raging as soon as Kirsty went in. 'Is the house on fire? Is it the workshop? For God's sake, woman, will ye tell me what's goin' on? Who was that bangin' at the door and chargin' about the house?'

She pushed him back onto the bed and sat beside him, taking his hand in hers. 'It was Todd. He's gone now.'

'Todd Paget? Right, that's the end of it—he'll not ever work for me again after makin' all that stramash an' frightenin' the lives out of us.'

'Matt, he came about Ewan.'

He stopped his blustering at once, the colour draining from his face. 'Has he been hurt? Is he...?'

'He's fine, as far as I know. He's gone,

and so has Beth Laidlaw. That's why Todd was so upset.'

He stared at her, the angry colour draining from his face as he took the words in. 'Ye mean...our Ewan's run away with Todd's woman?'

'It looks as if he's done just that.' For a moment she thought that he was going to collapse completely. He turned from pale to a sickly grey colour, and she ran to fetch the bottle of sal volatile that she kept in one of the two smaller drawers in the tallboy. He pushed her away when she unstoppered the bottle and tried to hold it under his nose.

'Get that filthy stuff away from me,' he said, his voice weak and thready. 'And for pity's sake bring out the chamber pot before I wet this bed.'

Kirsty felt as though she was living through a nightmare.

Ewan hadn't left so much as a note, and nobody seemed to know where he and Beth might be. When she went down to the workshop on the following morning hoping against hope that Todd might be there, the place was empty, the tools stacked neatly where they had been left on Saturday, a small table abandoned half finished in the middle of the floor.

At the flat where Todd lived with

his sister and her family the door was opened by a woman who bore a striking resemblance to him. She had his thick brown hair and grey eyes set in a face that, like his, was naturally cheerful, though on that day it was drawn. A flicker of a smile appeared when Kirsty introduced herself.

'Todd's talked a lot about you and your family, Mrs Lennox. I'm his sister, Marion Lang.' Then she asked hopefully, 'Did he turn up for work today?'

'No, I thought he might be here.'

'Ye'd best come in,' Marion said. 'Let the lady in the door, Tommy,' she added to the toddler clinging to her skirt, sweeping him up and stepping back to let Kirsty pass. The door opened into a fair-sized kitchen, warm and comfortable and spotlessly clean. A little girl slightly older than Tommy played with a kitten on the rug before the grate.

'These are my two youngest.' She put the little boy down. 'Ella, take Tommy and Tinker intae the bedroom tae play, there's a good lassie. Sit yourself down, Mrs Lennox. You'll have some tea?'

When Kirsty explained that she had very little time, Marion seated herself opposite and said, low voiced, 'Todd's not been home all night and I'm worried out of my mind about him. I thought he might have gone tae work but Archie—that's my man—said he didnae think so.'

'You've no idea where he might be?'

'Archie went round all his friends last night, and one of them says Todd was with him till mid-evening, then he left. He'd had a fair bit tae drink by then, and that's not like Todd at all. I've never once seen him the worse for drink.'

'D'you think he's out looking for Beth and Ewan?'

'That's what I'm afraid of,' Marion admitted. 'Normally I'd say that he'd never hurt a fly, but this time...' She had taken up some knitting when she sat down; now she glanced at it and saw that several stitches had slipped off one of the needles. 'He worships Beth. I've never seen him as happy as he was when she agreed about the two of them stayin' with her father. Not that I was happy about him havin' tae live under old Mr Laidlaw's roof, but Todd was all for it, for it meant bein' married tae Beth at long last.'

'What happened? Todd was in such a state when he came to the house that I couldn't get any sense out of him.'

Marion gave up her attempt to salvage the dropped stitches and put the needles aside. 'He was supposed tae see Beth on Saturday night as he usually did, but she sent word round that her father was poorly and she was stayin' in tae see tae him. Then on Sunday mornin' when he went round as usual tae walk with her tae the church for the mornin' service he found Mr Laidlaw in a fine takin' because he'd got up and found the lassie gone.'

'He'd not been ill at all?'

'Not a bit of it. Beth had gone out as usual and let him think she was with Todd. She came back and went to her bed just like any other Saturday, but she must have slipped out when he was asleep.'

'They'd planned it all, then.'

Marion nodded. 'All Beth's clothes were gone, and some jewellery belongin' tae her grandma and her ma that was tae go tae her on her marriage. And some money, seemingly, that Mr Laidlaw'd put by for the weddin' too. She must have packed her clothes and hidden them in the shop ready tae pick up on her way out. They'll likely have caught the train tae Glasgow. They could be anywhere by now.' The woman got up and went to the window, peering out into the street below. 'I just wish I knew where our Todd was. I'm sorry he's let ye down, Mrs Lennox, it's not like him at all.'

'It's us that have let him down by the sound of it.'

'Folk cannae be held responsible for what their grown weans do. If he'd just come back, so's I know he's all right.' Marion Lang turned back to the room with a shamefaced smile. 'Here's me sayin' folk cannae be responsible for other folk, and I'm frettin' about Todd as if he was one of my own weans.'

'Have you gone to the police office? They might be able to help you to find him.'

'We cannae do that,' Marion said at once. 'What if he's found the pair of them and—' She broke off abruptly, then said, 'If he's done somethin' wrong, even out of grief, he might end up in trouble. I'd not want tae be the one tae bring him tae the law's attention in the first place.'

Kirsty got up. 'I must go, my husband's not well. You'll let me know when he turns up? Just so that I know he's all right?'

'I will that. And I'm sorry,' the woman said as she opened the door, 'for all yer own trouble, Mrs Lennox.'

To Kirsty's surprise, the tobacconist's shop was open, and Mr Laidlaw, looking even more pinched and skeletal than usual, was behind the counter.

'Ye can just get out of my shop,' he said as soon as Kirsty went in, 'for I'll no' serve ye.'

'I'm not here for tobacco, Mr Laidlaw, I came to ask how you are.'

'How I am? How d'ye think I am?' he said harshly. 'I'm grievin', that's how I am. Grievin' because I've been robbed of my daughter. Grievin' because she's been thieved away from me by your son—and you come in here and ask me how I am?' His voice, which had been rising with each word ended in a falsetto shriek.

'Mr Laidlaw, we knew nothing about—'

'Get out!' He moved to the end of the counter. 'I mind you—don't think I don't, just because I held my tongue like a good Christian and said nothin' when ye came back! I know all about yer whorin'!' He had rounded the counter now, and was advancing on Kirsty as she backed away. 'My mother said this town was well rid of ye, and now ye're back, bringin' yer spawn with ye tae curse my family...'

He raved on, out of control, while Kirsty groped for the door handle, turned it, and escaped from the shop, running across the street and into the house, pushing the door closed and leaning against it until her heart stopped pounding in her ears and her breathing slowed. Matt was shouting for her.

'I'm coming!' she called, and started up the stairs, climbing slowly, clinging to the banister and dragging herself from step to step.

She couldn't go out that afternoon, for there was nobody to look after Matt. Not that she wanted to leave the house; the scene with Mr Laidlaw had so unnerved her that for that day, at least, she couldn't face the prospect of leaving the safety of her home. When Mary got home from school, Kirsty sent her to the shop with a note for Jean briefly explaining what had happened and promising that she would call on her friend on Tuesday afternoon. That was the town's early closing day, and Caitlin would be at home to see to Mary and Matt.

Matt had retreated from the world. He scarcely said a word to anyone, and Kirsty had trouble coaxing him to eat that evening. Gloom hung over the house and seemed to seep in beneath the doors and through every crack in the window frames.

'I want Alex,' Mary said suddenly as her bedtime approached. 'I want him to come home!' Tears sparkled on her lashes.

'Mary...' Kirsty stopped ironing and sat down, pulling her youngest onto her lap. Mary was growing so fast that it was like trying to cuddle a daddy-longlegs, but they both needed the closeness and the comfort. 'Alex's all grown up now, pet, and grown-up folk need to go away from their mams and their dads and find places of their own and meet other folk.'

'Is that why Ewan went away?'

Over the brown head, Kirsty's eyes met Caitlin's. 'That's why.'

'And Todd? He's not in the workshop; I looked when I came home from school,' Mary sniffled.

'Todd's just taking a wee rest. He'll be back.'

'Can you be certain about Todd coming back?' Caitlin asked when Mary, reassured, had trotted upstairs to get ready for bed.

'I can't be certain about anything any more. But I hope he will.'

'If he doesn't, we'll have to close the workshop, won't we?'

'Unless you've been secretly learning how to be a cabinet-maker all this time,' Kirsty said, and surprised a spurt of laughter from her daughter.

'I only know how to weigh lentils and slice ham. Mebbe we should tell Alex about this, Mam.'

'Where's the sense in that? He has his own life now. He's not going to be able to come home and take over the workshop.'

'What're we going to do?'

'We'll manage. We always do.'

'Ewan never was one to think of the way the things he does might hurt others, was he?' said Caitlin.

# 30

'Everyone knows about Ewan and Beth,' Caitlin burst out as soon as she came in the back door on Tuesday afternoon. 'Folk have been staring at me and pointing me out to their friends and whispering all morning.' She bit her lip to hold back the tears glittering in her eyes. 'I'm sure that some folk came into the shop just to look at me!'

'It'll pass, pet. Empty-minded folk always behave like fools when something like this happens. They'll be off gawping at some other poor soul soon enough.'

'If Ewan was here right now I'd—I'd smack his ears for him good and hard for the trouble he's causing us!'

'If Ewan was here right now folk wouldn't be gawping at you, would they?'

'I can't understand why Beth went off with him—from what I've heard of her, all she wants is money and a nice house and nice things. How can the likes of Ewan give them to her?'

'He probably gave her more attention than Todd did.'

'Todd worshipped her,' Caitlin protested.

Kirsty reached for her coat. 'Mebbe Beth needed something more than worship. I'll try not to be long. Will you wait in for Mary coming home?'

'I've got no notion to go out again—not until folk find something else to talk about.'

'Your father's had his dinner and I think he'll sleep for a wee while. I've put something in the oven for you. You'll be all right?'

Caitlin nodded, but glancing back from the door, Kirsty was struck to the heart by her wan face. It wasn't right that Caitlin or any other innocent soul should have to suffer just because Ewan had taken what he wanted.

Although the shop was shut for the afternoon, Rose and John Brodie were crowded into Jean's tiny living room.

'We agreed that it was best not to come to your house,' Rose said, 'but we wanted to find out what we could do to help.'

'Jean's told you?'

'There was no sense in keepin' it from them with all the folk comin' intae the shop knowin' the story,' Jean said defensively. 'And Rose is our partner.'

'I know.' Kirsty was glad to see the three of them.

They represented an increasingly important part of her life, and it was comforting just to know that they were there. 'I'm not going to be able to come to the shop for the time being. Matt's taken Ewan's disappearance hard, and I'm worried about him.'

'If it would help, I'd be happy to pay for a private nurse,' Rose offered.

'It's kind of you, but he'd not hear of it. Nor would I, for that matter. It's my duty to look after my own husband. I'd not feel right if someone else was being paid to do it.'

'What about the business?' John wanted to know.

'The workshop's closed at the moment, but I'm hoping that Todd might come back. Nobody knows where he is—it was his fiancée Ewan ran off with,' she explained as John looked puzzled.

'I didn't realise that. Quite a mess.'

'And one that we have to help Kirsty to sort out,' Rose told him firmly.

'I could do some work at home. I've got my own old machine, and I'll have time in the afternoons. I just have to be there in case Matt needs me. We can trust Teenie to take folk's measurements.'

'That's what we'll do, then,' John said.

'Perhaps the women who bring in the clothes could deliver work to you.'

'I've already got work in hand at the moment. It's just a case of going downstairs to collect it. I brought this.' Kirsty unwrapped the parcel she had brought with her and lifted out Beth's wedding gown. Jean helped her to spread it out over the table.

'It's bonny!'

'It's beautiful,' Rose corrected Jean.

'The bride it was made for won't be needing it now—she's the one who eloped with my stepson.'

'Poor bridegroom,' Brodie murmured, his eyes travelling over the detail of the gown. 'It's a lucky man who'd have watched his bride coming up the aisle in a gown like this.'

As soon as the evening meal was over Kirsty left Caitlin in charge again and set off to call on all the customers on the workshop books. She was exhausted when she got back.

'I've managed to persuade them all to wait a wee while longer for their orders, but if the workshop's not opened by next week I'll have to ask another cabinet-maker to take them on. It'd not be fair to keep them waiting any longer than that.' She eased her shoes off and groaned with pleasure at the relief. 'Did Mary get off to sleep all right?'

'It took a while, but she went over at last. And Father's sleeping too. I had to give him some of his laudanum. Archie Lang came to see you—Todd's sister's man. He said to let you know that Todd came home this evening.'

'Is he all right?' Kirsty sat upright, glancing at the clock, scrabbling for her shoes. 'I'll go round...'

'He said not to, not tonight. Todd was very drunk, and they had to put him to his bed. Archie says you could try him in the morning, though.'

Todd came to Espedair Street before Kirsty was ready to visit his sister's house. She had settled Matt and was washing her face at the kitchen sink before fetching her coat when she saw a man pass the window on his way to the kitchen door, then almost immediately pass back again towards the pend. She snatched up a towel and dabbed the water from her eyes, then looked again.

At first she thought that the figure standing in the lane, shuffling from one foot to the other, wavering very slightly, was a tramp who had wandered in from the street. Then he half turned and she got a glimpse of the side of his face.

Running to the back door she threw it open. He jumped, then swung round guiltily to face her.

'Todd!' His face was unshaven, his eyes bloodshot and his clothes looked as though they had been dragged on.

'I thought...' He stopped, then tried again, pointing down the lane, his outstretched arm wavering so that the stiff index finger drew patterns in the air. 'I thought I'd just go down tae the workshop...'

'You'll do no such thing. You'll come in here.'

He shuffled over to her like an old man and said almost pleadingly, 'I'm no' decent for visitin'.'

It was true. His clothes and his hair and even his skin stank of stale tobacco smoke and stale drink and other things she preferred not to try to identify.

'Never mind about that. Come on in,' Kirsty said mercilessly, pointing to Matt's chair when she had got him into the kitchen. 'Sit down, Todd.'

He flinched away from the chair and had to catch at the edge of the table for balance. 'Tha's th' master's chair.' His voice was still slurred with drink. 'I'm no' fit tae sit in th' master's chair.'

'Sit down before you fall down, man!' In the past, Matt had been fond of a drink, and on more than one occasion he had come home the worse for it. Kirsty had learned then that some inebriates responded, like children and dogs, to a sharp command. Luckily Matt was one of them and Todd apparently another, for he collapsed untidily into the chair without further argument.

Kirsty threw a handful of leaves into the teapot, asking, as his stomach rumbled noisily, 'When did you last eat?'

He waved his hand vaguely. 'Yesterday— mebbe. I've no' had the stomach for food.'

She cut some bread and buttered it, then thrust it into his hand. 'Eat this.'

'I'm feared I'll mebbe—'

'You'll keep it down—and if you can't there's a privy just outside the back door.'

She bullied him into eating the bread in small, reluctant mouthfuls, and swallowing down hot strong tea. He managed to keep it all down, and a tinge of colour came into his grey stubbly cheeks.

'Now, what have you been up to, Todd Paget?'

He looked up at her pathetically. 'I cannae mind, but it had somethin' tae do with drink. Then I woke up in a ditch outside of the town, and a carter brought me back.' He belched hugely, clapped a hand over his mouth, and said through his fingers, 'I didnae mean tae disturb ye. I just came for my tools.'

'What d'you want your tools for? You're in no fit state to use them.'

'A craftsman needs his tools, Mrs Lennox. How else am I tae get work?'

'You've got work here.'

He blinked at her, then began to shake his head, stopping immediately and wincing with pain. 'I cannae come back here—no' after the way I behaved, shoutin' at ye an' all.'

'I'd have shouted myself if I'd been in your place. And of course you'll come back.'

'Ye mean ye'd still employ me?'

'Todd,' Kirsty said patiently, 'right this minute I'd employ Beelzebub if he was a time-served craftsman.'

'But what'll the master say?'

'I'm afraid the master's not well enough to decide what's to happen in the workshop. I'm having to do it for him, and I've got orders waiting to be filled. You'll be on your own, but we'll talk about getting help for you later.'

'I'm grateful.' He struggled to his feet, beginning to look better already. 'I'll just away down tae the workshop, then.'

'And gash your hand with a chisel and be no use to me for weeks? You'll do nothing of the sort, Todd Paget. You'll get yourself back home and get a decent meal in your belly. Then you'll have a good sleep and tomorrow you'll wash and shave and make yourself presentable. Then you can come back to work—but not until then.'

Muttering his thanks, he made for the door, looking back at her before going out. 'I didnae find them,' he said, 'but I have tae tell ye—if I had, I'd've killed Ewan for what he's done.'

'Then I'm glad you didn't find him, Todd, for your own sake as well as for his.'

When he had gone she propped the door open to let the cool wind scour the smell of him from the kitchen and poured herself another cup of tea, her spirits beginning to rally. The workshop, at least, had been taken care of and the customers assured of their orders. And Todd, who had begun to matter to her just as much as any member of her family, was home and safe.

Kirsty waited until Todd returned to work the next day, washed and shaved and penitent, before telling Matt that the journeyman was back in the workshop. As she had expected, his temper erupted.

'D'ye mean tae tell me that he's workin' down there as if nothin' had happened after the way he came chargin' in here, wakenin' the whole household and threatenin' tae do harm tae Ewan? I'll not have that rascal on my premises, and ye can just go out this minute and tell him tae take himsel' off!'

'Matt, we've got orders to fill and customers waiting.'

'We'll employ someone else!'

'We've not got the time to interview men, and even if we had, I know nothing about the work and you can't go down to the shop to keep an eye on them. Todd knows the business—he's the one who kept it going before we got here. He cares about the place.'

'Cares? He wasnae doin' much carin' when he went off after...' he paused, searching for the right words, then said, 'after that woman of his. Two, three days he was away from the place. He wasnae carin' then about what happened tae it, was he?'

'He was upset—what man wouldn't be with his bride running away the week before their wedding?'

'More fool him for ever havin' trusted her. I knew from the start, that time you insisted on them visitin', that she was a sleekit lassie. Did I not tell ye at the time that no good would come of treatin' an employee like a friend?'

Kirsty opened her mouth to point out that Ewan had some blame in what had happened, then closed it again, realising that they were on dangerous ground. Matt was in a mood to blame everyone—Beth Laidlaw for tempting Ewan away, Todd for letting it happen, Kirsty herself for trying to be friendly towards Beth. But never Ewan, his beloved son.

'What's done's done, Matt,' she said instead. 'I had to try to keep the business going, and Todd's the best man to do that just now.'

'If Alex hadnae gone waltzing off—'

'But he did, and there's no sense in crying over spilled milk.'

He tried to clench his hands into fists, but couldn't. 'D'ye mind when these hands were able tae do a good day's work?'

'I mind it fine.' She touched one hand gently. 'You did your share of work, Matt. There's no shame in not being able to do it any more.'

'Don't talk nonsense, woman,' he told her roughly. 'When a man like me loses the ability tae work, he loses everythin' that makes life worth the livin'. Damn this arthritis tae hell!' And he turned his face away and closed his eyes against her and against the entire world.

Going downstairs, she suddenly recalled those same hands of his, gentle enough for their size and the rough skin, fondling and pleasuring and rousing her. Their marriage had come about for practical reasons rather than love. Matt had wanted a mother for Ewan, she had wanted security and a father for Alex. They had both wanted a home, a hearth, the comfort of marriage.

But through the years it had become more than that—for a while, at least. A yearning she hadn't experienced for a long time stirred deep inside Kirsty—a need to be held and touched and loved again before it was too late.

'This business of you working at home isn't any use,' Jean said on the following Tuesday. 'Teenie's willing, but she hasn't got your flair for knowing what suits folk and what can be done tae make the clothes look right for them.'

'And you're looking strained, Kirsty,' Rose butted in. 'You need to come here and meet folk and be yourself for a few hours.'

They were both right. Kirsty was missing the shop, and she hated being in the house all day, but she couldn't see any way out of the problem.

'Matt can't be left on his own, and I can't ask Todd to keep an eye on him, for he's working alone.' Matt had finally had to give in and let Todd help him into the bathroom every day, but it went against the grain, Kirsty knew. Ewan's ghost seemed to stand between the two men, and always would. Matt certainly wouldn't agree to being left in the journeyman's care, and she'd not ask Todd to take on the added burden in any case.

'What about Caitlin?' Rose asked tentatively.

'She's got her job at the grocer's shop, and her own friends. I'll not ask her to give up either to look after an invalid. And Mary's very good at starting the dinner and seeing to her father's needs when she comes home from school, but she's too wee to take on more responsibility. There's only me.'

'What sort of help does he need?'

'It's mostly just being there to fetch and carry for him, or pick up his newspaper or his tobacco pouch if they fall off the bed. And making tea, and sometimes just giving him a bit of company.'

'I could do all those things.'

Jean and Kirsty both gaped at Rose. 'You?'

'The shop can manage without me better than it can manage without you, Kirsty. I could fetch and carry for your husband and give him a bit of company if he wants someone to talk to.'

'But...you and Matt don't even know each other.'

'Every friend used to be a stranger. And

if it's...the more personal side of things that you're worried about,' Rose said delicately, 'we've got a commode at home that you could borrow. I've been meaning to offer it to you. And there's the man in the workshop to call on if I need help or advice.'

Jean and Kirsty looked at each other, then Kirsty said, 'I couldn't ask you to do a thing like that for me.'

'Why not? We're partners.'

'But you're—you're—'

'Upper class?' Rose asked with a wry grin. 'Maybe I am, but I've got two arms and legs and hands like you, and a brain—and a good Scots tongue in my head. And you'd not be all that far away if you were needed.'

'What would your parents say if they found out?'

Rose batted the words away with a wave of one hand. 'They stopped trying to tell me how to live my life a while ago.'

As far as Kirsty and Jean knew, that was true. John Brodie had told them that Mr and Mrs Hamilton had grown weary of continually arguing with their daughter and continually losing. Since his sister's engagement party, the young lawyer had frequently invited Rose to be his escort at various social occasions. As he was an eligible bachelor, her parents took some comfort from her relationship with him.

'Let's see what your husband thinks before we make any decisions.' Rose unfolded her tall and lanky body from the chair she had been sitting in. 'I'll call round tomorrow morning, and the three of us can talk it over.'

# 31

The commode Rose had promised arrived in a chauffeur-driven car on the following morning, to Kirsty's embarrassment. It wasn't the commode that worried her, for Rose had had the forethought to have it carefully wrapped, but the handsome car and its uniformed driver.

A group of stragglers hurrying along Espedair Street on their way to the South School just as the vehicle drew up at her door immediately forgot about their teacher's wrath and their teacher's cane in their delight at being so close to a motorcar.

The chauffeur insisted on carrying the commode upstairs and into the bedroom, where Matt sat up in bed staring, his hair awry.

'What in the—'

'I'll be back in a minute,' Kirsty told him hurriedly, sweeping the man out of the room. In the hall, overwhelmed by his smart appearance and his experience with motor vehicles, she asked timidly, 'Will you have a cup of tea?'

'Best not, missus, not with these wee toerags out there up tae God knows what wi' the master's precious motorcar.'

Outside on the footpath the youngsters, who had been admiring but not daring to touch, scattered like flies as he emerged and touched the shining peak of his cap to Kirsty. 'Miss Rose asked me to tell you that she'll be along in the middle of the afternoon, madam,' he said, reverting to his official working voice, then gave her a huge wink and left.

In the bedroom Matt was squawking and fussing like a shedful of hens. 'It's a commode,' she told him as she started stripping off the wrapping paper. 'Rose Lennox thought it might be of help to you while you're in bed.'

'We don't take charity!'

'It's not charity; it's a loan made out of kindness. She's—oh, my!' She broke off as the last of the paper fell away to reveal a handsome carved wooden chair. 'I didn't realise it'd look so grand.'

She stepped back, as intimidated by the chair as she had been by the chauffeur in

407

his finery. 'Bring it closer,' Matt ordered, and when she had summoned up the courage to do as she was told he leaned across the pillow to touch it. 'It's oak—an' made by a craftsman. Lift the lid.'

She did, and withdrew a large, deep, cream-coloured chamber pot, tastefully decorated with painted strands of ivy.

'I'd be feared tae pee in a pot like that, let alone shit in it,' Matt said, awed.

'You'll have to—that's what she sent it for. And think how useful it'll be instead of always trying to get to the bathroom.'

'Right enough,' he said thoughtfully. She could tell by his expression that he had realised that the commode would mean freedom from dependence on Todd's strong, gentle arm. 'I suppose it was a kindly thought,' he acknowledged, and she seized the chance to break her next piece of news.

'Rose was talking about coming round for a wee while this afternoon, to see what we think of the commode.'

'Comin' here?'

'She'd like fine to meet you, Matt. She'd not stay long,' she added as he started to object. 'I'd best get you settled, just in case she does come.'

By the time Rose knocked at the door he was washed and shaved and in a clean nightshirt. His hair had been brushed, his moustache combed and the bed remade.

'Did the commode arrive?' Rose asked in her clear voice as soon as the door was opened.

'It did—we're both very grateful. Come on in.'

'I decided to wait and walk round this afternoon instead of coming this morning in the car.' Rose stepped into the hall. 'I thought it might be too much for your poor husband, me and the commode arriving together.'

'He's nervous about meeting you.'

'I'm nervous about meeting him,' Rose confessed. 'Should we both get it over with at once?'

At first Matt treated the visitor as though she came from a far land and spoke a foreign language. But when Rose launched into an amusing and faintly bawdy story about the commode's history he began to thaw, and even to smile a little. Kirsty left them together while she made tea, and when she went back upstairs with the tray Rose, using her ability to laugh at her own faults, was deep into another story, this time concerning some confusion she had caused in the shop because of her ignorance of the local dialect. Matt was listening closely, and even chuckling now and again.

Rose had more sense than to outstay

her welcome. 'I was wondering,' she said casually as she got up to go, 'if I could call on you again, Mr Lennox—mebbe on Friday afternoon?'

'If ye like.'

'If I'm going to be here, Kirsty, you could go to the shop. We'll be fine together for an hour or so, won't we, Mr Lennox? I'd like to hear all about the trade you were in,' Rose swept on as a flicker of uncertainty came into Matt's eyes, 'and about the training you had to do.'

Before Rose left, Kirsty took her to the workshop to meet Todd, then led her back into the house through the kitchen without thinking twice. To her, Rose was a friend, not a visitor who should only see the parlour and visit the workshop via the pend. Mary, who had just arrived home from school, was introduced, then before leaving Rose paused to admire the fireside chairs.

'These are very pretty—the flowers look real enough to pick. Who did them for you?'

'Our Alex,' Mary said proudly, and Rose shot her an astonished look, then said, 'Oh.' It was a flat, negative sound.

'He's a decent lad, Alex,' Kirsty said at the front door. 'I think you and him got off on the wrong foot the first time you met.'

'Maybe we did,' Rose said distantly. 'Why isn't he here, helping you to manage everything?'

Kirsty hesitated, aware of Mary in the hall behind them. 'It's a long story,' she said at last. 'I'll tell you about it one day.'

'Father's agreed to let Rose sit with him?' Surprise sent Caitlin's voice soaring up the scale when she heard the news that evening.

'He's willing to give it a try. I've not said to him about next week, though, we'll just take each day as it comes.'

'She was asking why Alex wasn't here to help us,' Mary chimed in, 'but Mam wouldn't say.'

'There's nothing to say, lady. Alex is grown up and off leading his own life, that's all.'

'I want to see him again. I've nearly forgotten what he looks like!'

'You'll see him one day, Mary. But we don't want to bother him just now when he's so busy.'

Caitlin shot a look at her mother and opened her mouth to speak, then closed it again. Later, when Mary had gone to bed, she said quietly, 'Mam, I wrote to Alex today, to tell him what's happened.'

'Wrote to him? Have you posted it? Why?' Kirsty asked as her daughter nodded.

Caitlin looked guilty but defiant. 'He's got a right to know what's happening here, Mam—about Ewan and Beth, and Father being worse. He's still part of this family.'

And a fast-shrinking family it was, Kirsty thought. All three sons had gone for one reason or another. Apart from Matt, the house had become a place of women. Aloud she said, 'Alex has his own life now, and his own work to do. We can't expect him to come back and run the workshop for us.'

'You never know—he might think of something,' Caitlin argued.

As soon as Kirsty stepped into the shop on Friday afternoon her domestic worries seemed to drop from her shoulders. She revelled in it all—the sewing room, the demented whirring of Teenie's hard-worked machine opposite her own, the frequent summonses to the front shop to give advice, the customers' chatter, the cups of strong tea, the stolen moments when the shop was empty and Jean came into the sewing room to perch on a stool and talk.

'You look the better for your outin' already,' Jean commented when Teenie had gone off home and the two of them were alone together.

'It's been grand, being back. I've never seen anyone work as fast as Teenie. I keep thinking that she'll end up with crooked seams, going at that rate, but she never does.'

'You and me can put in a peck of work ourselves, when we put our minds tae it.' Jean looked round the shop with satisfaction. 'D'ye realise it's near enough a year since this place opened? I couldnae sleep at nights at the time for worryin' about what I'd let myself in for, but it's turned out well.'

'I was certain that Rose would lose interest long before the summer and be off on a new ploy.'

'Not that lassie. You have tae give her credit for her determination.'

'D'you know what she brought with her this afternoon?' Kirsty asked. 'A big blanket made into a cape thing that one of her uncles brought back from South America. There's a hole in the middle for your head, and slits to put your arms through. She says there's a lot of bits and pieces in their attic that were brought from foreign parts.'

Jean's eyes widened. 'She's never expectin' you tae wear the thing!'

'Not a bit of it—it's for when Matt's on the commode.' Kirsty felt a broad smile begin to spread across her face. 'By her way of it, when he puts this thing on it covers him and the commode, so's he can attend to his business without fretting about being seen. She thought it would make it easier for him to let her help him on and off the thing if Todd wasn't to hand.'

'Fancy,' Jean said weakly. There was a pause, then she caught Kirsty's eye and the two of them went into peals of laughter.

'I'm quite sure it'll work, too,' Jean said when she had sobered up. She pulled a handkerchief from her sleeve and mopped at her eyes. 'Once that lassie makes up her mind tae somethin' she'll make it work. She'll not let anythin' put her off.'

'I just hope,' Kirsty said as she made for the door, 'that Matt hasn't been the one to finally put a dent in her determination.'

But in fact Rose's first afternoon with Matt had been quite successful. They both seemed to have enjoyed their time together, and it was agreed, before Rose left, that she would return on Monday to let Kirsty go to the shop again.

It seemed to Alex, as he turned the corner from Causeyside Street, that Espedair Street was smaller than before. So was the house. He smiled faintly, remembering the first time he had seen it and how large it had appeared to him then. But that had been before he knew Glasgow, with its broad, busy streets and its handsome, airy buildings. He hesitated at the door, and almost turned towards the pend instead, then, deciding that he no longer had the right to go round the back, he put a hand to the latch.

The hallway, too, had shrunk, and was darker and narrower than he remembered. As he closed the door the kitchen door opened.

'Who's there?'

'It's me, Ma—' He stopped halfway along the hall, staring at the girl framed in the doorway. 'What are you doing here?'

Rose Hamilton was clearly as dismayed to see him as he was to see her. 'You'd best come in. Your father's asleep and we don't want to disturb—oh!' She whisked back into the kitchen, and he followed in time to see her snatch a flat iron from where she had left it, on one of his father's shirts. She examined the material anxiously. 'Thank goodness, it's not burned,' she said, then wet one finger and dabbed gingerly at the flat of the iron. 'It wasn't hot enough to burn.' She put the iron on the lit gas ring.

'What are you doing here?' Alex asked again from the doorway. His abrupt tone was enough to bring her head up sharply.

'I'm looking after your father.' The hostility that always came between them sparkled in her eyes.

'You? But where's my mother?'

'At the shop.'

'She should be here,' Alex said without thinking. He had come home eager to see his mother again after all those months apart, and he was almost childishly disappointed to find that she wasn't where he had expected to find her, where he had pictured her during his self-imposed exile—in the kitchen, the heart and the core of the family.

Rose interpreted his sense of loss as masculine selfishness. 'She's not a prisoner.' She smoothed the shirt she had been ironing on the blanket-covered table with angry sweeps of her hands. 'As you once told me yourself, nobody owns her. She surely has the right to go out now and again. I'm trying to help because nobody else seems to be willing to share the burden she's having to carry.'

Alex coloured angrily. 'Why else d'you think I'm here?'

'It took you long enough.'

'I didn't know about Ewan until the other day!' he snapped, then wondered why he was justifying himself to this arrogant intruder.

For a moment they scowled at each other, then Alex asked, 'When will she be back?'

'In an hour, maybe.'

'I'll look in at the workshop,' he said, and escaped outside.

When he returned to the house he had simmered down.

'Todd tells me you've been doing what you can to help my mother. I'm...grateful.'

'I've made some tea,' Rose told him stiffly. She was still ironing, her movements clumsy and uncertain. He filled a cup for himself, grimacing when he saw how weak it was, then lit another gas ring and put the teapot on it.

'You'll boil it.'

'That's what it needs. It's far too weak as it is.'

'I've never heard of boiling tea.'

'You've probably never made tea before,' he said dryly. 'Or ironed. Here.' He went round to her side of the table and took the iron from her. 'Longer strokes and a bit more pressure. And this end's pointed so's you can push it into the gathers. See?'

'I've never met a man who could iron clothes,' she said, faint respect creeping into her voice, as he relinquished the iron. He drew a chair out from the table and sat down.

'I had to learn when I moved into lodgings in Glasgow. That's when I learned how to make tea too,' he added.

In the silence that fell, he stared at his clasped hands on the table, sneaking brief glances at her from beneath lowered lids. Her face was flushed from the heat of the room, and her hair was different—softer round her face instead of being scragged back. It improved her looks.

'There.' She finished the shirt and shook it out. In places she had ironed creases in instead of removing them, but Alex, who had heard a glowing report about the girl from Todd, held his tongue. Her effort reminded him of his own first attempt, but at least she hadn't burned the material, as he had.

She folded the blanket and put it away, then poured tea for herself, grimacing at its strength.

'I'll take that one,' Alex offered, 'and you can have mine. I've not touched it.'

He watched her adding milk and stirring in a spoonful of sugar, liking the deft, feminine movements of her hands now that she was doing something familiar. It occurred to him for the first time that he missed feminine company in his new life. Until then he had been too busy to think of it.

A thumping on the ceiling brought both their heads up. 'That's your father wakened. He'll be ready for a drink.' Rose put her cup down and got up to pour more tea. She put some biscuits on a plate, then settled cup and plate on a small lacquered tray Alex had never seen before. 'Are you coming up to see him?'

He hesitated, then shook his head. 'Best not.'

Censure came back into her eyes. 'He's a sick man, and he's your father.'

'My stepfather.'

Her lips tightened. 'From what I've heard he's the man who raised you. You owe him the courtesy of a visit.'

'He'll not want to see me any more than I want to see him.'

'You should let him decide that for himself instead of skulking down here out of sight.'

The open challenge brought warmth to Alex's face. He pushed the chair back noisily and got to his feet. 'Give me the tray,' he said, and followed her from the room.

# 32

At the top of the stairs Rose halted and turned. 'He's taken your brother's disappearance very hard,' she said, low voiced. 'You have to make allowances for that.' Then before he could answer she whisked round and went off along the corridor, carolling, 'You've got a visitor. Mr Lennox. Someone you'll be pleased to see.'

Alex's first sight of his stepfather gave him a shock. The man had aged far more than the nine months since they had last met, and he seemed to have shrunk in on himself. But his glare was still the same, and so was the antagonism in his voice when he said, 'What're you doin' in this house?'

'I came to see how you were.'

'Came tae gloat, ye mean.'

Alex almost gave an angry reply, almost walked out of the room and out of the house to wait for his mother on the footpath, but just then Rose moved between him and the bed to take the tray from his hands. With her back to Matt she stared up into Alex's face, shaking her head very slightly. He took a deep breath and moved past her to look down at the man in the bed.

Pain had used a blunt knife to carve deeply into Matt's forehead and cheeks and round his nose and mouth. His eyes were dull and the clawed hands lying on the bedcovers were little more than lumps of bone enclosed by shiny red skin stretched tightly, as if it was having a struggle to contain them.

'No,' Alex said, pity tempering his dislike of the man. 'I just came to see you.'

'I'll sort your pillows.' Rose had laid the tray down on the bedside table; now she put an arm behind Matt's shoulders and eased him forwards, using her free hand to rearrange the pillows. When they refused to go where she wanted, Alex went to the other side, of the bed and freed her by supporting his stepfather's shoulders. The man felt like a bag of bones. When he was settled, Rose wrapped some cloth round the cup to make it easier to hold, then placed it carefully into Matt's hands.

'Drink it while it's hot. Kirsty'll be home in a wee while.' She had a special voice for Matt, soft and light and reassuring; a voice Alex had never thought to hear from the likes of Rose Hamilton.

Matt slowly lifted the cup, bending his head until his lips touched the brim, and sucked the strong tea in noisily. 'That's a good cup o' tea. Ye're learnin', lass,' he said, and Rose blushed.

Alex stayed in the room for five minutes, during which, with Rose's help, he and Matt managed to make conversation of a sort. It was a relief to him—and, he was sure, to his stepfather—when Rose sent him back downstairs while she washed

Matt's hands and face and made him comfortable.

'You're very good with him,' he acknowledged when she came into the kitchen.

'I feel sorry for him, having to end his days like this. And I like him,' she said, then added, with a sidelong glance, 'I've got the freedom to like him, for I've not had the experiences of him that you've had.'

'You know about it all?'

'Kirsty told me as much as I needed to know. Thank you for not losing your temper upstairs. He's not strong enough to manage a quarrel, and there's no sense in it anyway, is there?'

'It wasn't easy.'

'Doing the right thing's never easy,' Rose told him briskly. 'I'll be off now, since you're here to see to things.'

'You don't have to go on my account.'

She shook her head. 'They'll all be pleased to see you. I'll just get in the way.'

Mary, who got home from school before Kirsty arrived from the shop, met her in the hall, her small thin face glowing. 'Alex is home!'

He appeared behind her, laughing, scooping her out of the way so that he could take his mother's bags from her. 'I've not come home, Mary, I told you that. I've come for a visit, to see you all—hey!' he protested as Kirsty threw her arms round him, 'You're crushing me!'

'I've got every right to crush you—I'm your mother. Let me look at you.' She drew back, drinking in the sight of him in his good suit and white shirt and neat tie. 'You look...all grown up!'

'Mother, I'm twenty years old now!' That wasn't what she had meant. There was a new maturity about him, an air of confidence. His hair, normally tousled, was shorter than it had been, well cut and almost smooth, with just enough of a wave to break the perfection. It was as red as ever, though, and the colour was echoed in his new, neatly trimmed moustache. Even his speech was different, just a little more refined. Most important of all, the pain and bitterness of Fiona's loss had gone from his eyes, and they were clear and steady, the eyes of a man who had found himself and liked what he had found.

Caitlin arrived home, and Kirsty left brother and sisters together while she went up to see Matt.

'Yer prodigal son's returned, then,' he said as soon as she went in.

She refused to rise to the bait. 'It's nice to see him after all this time.'

'And lookin' so prosperous.'

'You've seen him?'

'Rose brought him up.'

'Come downstairs and eat with us, Matt. Todd'll still be in the workshop and he and Alex could help you.'

'I'm no' able,' he said, and turned his head away.

'He's gone downhill fast,' Alex said later when they had eaten and Mary had gone to bed.

'It's losing Ewan that's done it, and the way he lost him.'

'Has there not been any word? You'd think,' Alex said angrily when Kirsty shook her head, 'that he'd at least write to let his father know he was all right.'

'Ewan's always acted without thinking of the consequences,' Caitlin put in.

'He's taken on a deal of consequences this time. D'you think he and Beth'll stay together?' Alex wanted to know, and his half-sister shook her head firmly.

'They're too like each other. And Ewan's not got what Beth wants. He's helped her to escape from her father, and from poor Todd, but to my mind she'll be off with the first man who offers her more than Ewan can give her.'

He laughed. 'You seem to know a lot about how folk work.'

'You learn a great deal behind the

counter of a grocer's shop,' Caitlin told him solemnly, then leant forward. 'But never mind Ewan and Beth—tell us all about what's been happening to you.'

He launched into the story, glowing. 'It's been hard work, but the wee business I took over's beginning to show results. I've got two men in the workshop making the furniture—both good at their trade and able to take responsibility—and we've taken on an apprentice. We've just finished our first big order, and there are others waiting their turn.'

'You're doing the decorating yourself?'

'For the moment, but we're talking of bringing in an artist, to free me for the office work. There's a deal of that. I'm going to night school to learn about book-keeping and the like. And I'm in lodgings now. Two nice big rooms, and the landlady's a decent enough body.'

'She seems to look after you,' Kirsty said, and he laughed.

'I'm learning to look after myself. You'd be proud of the way I can iron my own clothes, Mam, and do a bit of cooking.'

'D'you get on well with...with Sandy?'

He nodded. 'Better than I thought I would. We're alike in many ways, and he's pleased with my work.' He hesitated and stared for a moment at his hands, then looked up. 'I've got something to tell you, Mam. I'm changing my name from Lennox to MacDowall.'

'Oh.' She couldn't think of anything else to say.

'It's what he—my father—' he said, flicking a swift glance at her, then looking back at his hands, 'wants, and it makes sense, for all going well I'll be made a partner when I'm twenty-one. He'd like to make it public knowledge now that I'm his heir.'

'Did you say anything to...' she hesitated, about to say 'your father', then realising that to Alex the title no longer meant Matt.

He understood at once. 'I didn't, and I don't think you should.' He looked from her to Caitlin. 'He'll never know, and it's best that way, for it'd only hurt his feelings. I just hope,' he touched Kirsty's hand lightly, swiftly, 'that it doesn't hurt yours.'

'It doesn't. You're as entitled to call yourself MacDowall as Lennox.'

Kirsty wanted to ask about Fiona, but couldn't bring herself to. It was Caitlin who finally said baldly, 'What about Fiona?'

Something flickered across Alex's face and was gone. 'She's still in Fort William, and engaged to be married to a man who lives there. We've not set eyes on each other, though she knows now that

426

I'm working in Glasgow, and that I'm changing my name. She wrote to wish me well. Now,' he said briskly, without giving either of them time to comment, 'I spoke with Todd this afternoon. You'll need to get another journeyman in, Mam, for he can't manage for long on his own.'

'I know. The orders are beginning to pick up again, and with the shop doing quite well, and Caitlin earning, we could manage to pay another wage.'

'You should let Todd pick a man for himself,' he advised.

When he left, Kirsty walked through the cold November night to Canal Street Station with him, their breaths rising into the air in white clouds that met and mingled as they spoke, then dissolving into the darkness.

'The old man's deteriorated a lot. I don't see him getting better, Mam,' Alex said as they waited for the train.

'I know that. He's in such pain now that he can't sleep without laudanum. I have to dole it out carefully.' Kirsty sighed. 'It's hard to see him suffering like that.'

'I'm glad you've got the shop, and Jean.'

'We're doing well. Rose's daft idea worked after all.'

He gave a short laugh. 'She's changed

too. I couldn't believe my eyes when I walked into the kitchen and found her doing the ironing.'

'I've lost a few garments since she decided to try her hand with the flat iron. But her heart's in the right place.'

'I mind you telling me once that you needed some independence, and I couldn't understand it because I thought that having the house and us to look after should be enough.' His eyes glittered in the gaslight as he looked down at her. 'I know better now. I'll try to visit more often, but it's not easy with so much to see to.'

She patted his hand as the train hooted in the near distance. 'You've got your own life, Alex, and I'm glad it's a success. We'll be fine, me and Caitlin and Mary—and Matt. And there's Todd in the workshop if I ever need him.'

'I'm glad he came back to work for you. He'll never see you lost for a friend.'

The train came charging into the station, huffing steam, impatient to be on its way to Glasgow. Alex gave her a brief peck on the cheek. 'You know where I am if you need me,' he said.

Heedless of the cold, Kirsty stood on the platform and watched the train's lights until they vanished before walking slowly home.

# 33

Kirsty ran out of the shop without stopping to fetch her coat or hat, heedless of the March rain soaking her hair and her blouse. The child who had been sent to fetch her pounded along at her side, pointing as they turned into Espedair Street. 'There, missus,' he gasped, 'the house where the car is, and the folk standin'. That's where the lady is that sent me tae fetch ye.'

She fumbled in her skirt pocket and found a coin to press into his hand, then pushed through the small knot of people who had gathered at the door, drawn there by the sight of the doctor's car.

Todd was in the hall, his arms about Rose, who was white faced and shaking. 'Oh, Kirsty...' At the sight of her, Rose broke free and ran to take her hands. 'I thought he was just having a good sleep for once. He said he didn't want to be disturbed, so I just left him...' She started to weep, and Kirsty put an arm round her.

'Come into the kitchen and sit down.'

Todd followed them in, his face drained.

'I'd have fetched ye mysel', Mrs Lennox, and tried tae save ye some of the shock, but I felt I was needed here.' He nodded at Rose.

'You did the right thing, Todd.' Kirsty eased Rose down into her own chair, then asked the journeyman over her bowed head, 'Is he—?'

He nodded, then swiftly pulled a chair out from the table. 'You should sit down too. You've gone white as a sheet.'

'He said he was tired and I was just to leave him be,' Rose said. 'Then I began to wonder...'

She began to cry again, and Kirsty was comforting her when the doctor came downstairs.

'I'm very sorry, Mrs Lennox. He just slipped away in his sleep.'

He offered to take Rose home, and Kirsty managed to persuade her to go. 'I'll manage fine, with Todd's help, and you've had a bad shock. I'll see you tomorrow.'

The doctor went ahead to open the car door for Rose, and Todd stayed in the kitchen. For a moment the two women were alone in the hall. 'Kirsty, I found this by the bed and put it into my pocket before I went to fetch Todd.' Rose slipped a small bottle into Kirsty's hand.

'It's all right, I gave him the last of it before I went out because the pain was bad,' Kirsty said, and relief came into Rose's reddened eyes.

'I didn't say anything to the doctor because I wasn't sure if it...I wondered...'

'There's nothing to worry about,' Kirsty soothed, walking with her to the pavement.

'About the layin' out,' Todd said awkwardly when she went back into the kitchen.

'I'll see to it myself.' Once or twice she had helped her mother to prepare bodies for burial, and she herself had assisted neighbours in Falkirk when the need had arisen.

'My sister could give ye a hand if ye want. She knows about these things.'

She thought of Marion's calm warmth. 'I'd be grateful for her help. Could you fetch her, Todd—and notify the undertaker while you're at it?'

'I'll send Davie.' Davie was the new journeyman he had hired to take Ewan's place.

'I'd as soon you went yourself, being as near to one of the family as anyone could be.'

Concern came into his smoky eyes. 'I'm not leavin' you on yer own at a time like this. If I must go, I'll ask one of the neighbours tae sit with ye while I'm away.'

'I'll be fine, Todd. I just need to have

431

a minute on my own with him before—'

'I should've thought of that,' he said gruffly. 'I'll not be long.'

'Todd,' she said as he headed for the back door. He turned, and she stepped forward into his arms, resting her head on his shoulder, as she had done just over a year ago, on the anniversary of Fergus's death. He stood rigid for a moment, then his body relaxed and his arms enfolded her. She leaned her weight against him for a full minute, drawing strength and comfort from his support, then drew back and looked up into his face, her hands on his chest.

'You're a good friend, Todd Paget,' she said gently. 'On you go now. Mebbe you could look in at the grocer's and tell Caitlin to come home,' she added as he turned away. 'It would help me if she was here for Mary coming home from the school.'

When she was at last alone she went upstairs to a bedroom that was strangely empty now that everything that had been Matt had gone, leaving only his body behind. After opening the window to release his soul, she went to the bed and lifted the sheet back from his face. He lay on his back, his eyes closed as though in sleep, but when she bent and kissed his forehead the skin was cold against her lips.

His hands, which had been feverishly hot from the arthritis for the past few years, were also cold. She smoothed a strand of grey hair back from his forehead then took from her pocket the small brown bottle Rose had given her.

It hadn't been completely empty when she had left for work; there had been some laudanum left in it; just a few drops, but enough. Only she and Matt had known that the bottle was in the bedside drawer instead of in the bathroom, out of his reach. At Matt's request, she had put it in the drawer on the first day of the new year. It was his key to the final door, should the pain become too much for him. Their final pact, their secret, and something nobody else would ever know about.

She put the bottle back in her pocket and drew the sheet over his face. Clearly he had hoped that Rose would leave him to sleep until Kirsty came home. Instead the poor girl had caused herself anguish by trying to make sure that he was all right.

In the back yard she pushed the bottle deep into the rubbish container then stood for a moment, breathing in the cold air. The rain had stopped, but there was more to come. The skies were grey and lowering, the wind heavy with moisture.

She had left the house that afternoon a wife and returned to it a widow. Kirsty rubbed a finger over the broad gold wedding ring she had worn for the past sixteen years. It would take a long time to get used to the change in her status.

Matt's funeral was well attended, and the house was packed with mourners after the burial. There was a buzz of interest when people realised that the tall, thin, brisk young woman helping to prepare and serve the refreshments was none other than Rose Hamilton, from one of the big houses in Thornly Park, and another buzz at Alex's smart and prosperous appearance.

'My...Angus MacDowall would have liked to attend,' he told his mother at the gathering afterwards, 'but he felt that it might not be proper. He sends his deepest condolences.'

'Thank him for his thoughts—and his consideration.'

'I'm surprised to see him here.' Alex nodded over at Mr Laidlaw, standing in a corner devouring a plate of ham sandwiches.

Kirsty had been surprised, too, in view of the way the man had ordered her out of his shop, but nobody else knew about that. 'He's a local businessman, and so was Matt. It's the done thing for them to attend each other's funerals.'

'And get a good feed,' Alex commented.

'Who are the two sour-looking folk with him?'

'That's Annie, Beth's older sister, and her husband. They came back to Paisley to live with Mr Laidlaw after Beth—went away. Annie's taken over the shop, and when Mr Laidlaw's time comes she'll inherit it instead of Beth.'

'If Ewan's wed Beth he'd be well advised to stay right away from this place,' Alex murmured. 'Imagine marrying into a family like that. You'd think they were trying to stock up their bellies before a famine.' Then, voicing Kirsty's own thoughts, he said 'It doesn't seem right, Ewan not knowing his father's gone. If we only knew where he was...'

Morag Bishop had hurried over from Kilbarchan as soon as she heard of Matt's death, and she and Todd's sister, both strong and caring women, had done a lot to help Kirsty and her daughters through the days before the funeral. All three members of the Bishop family were present that day, although they had only met Matt once.

'The arthritis is beginnin' tae bother Geordie's hands now,' Morag told Kirsty. 'It happens as often as not with weavers when they get tae his age. I doubt he'll be able tae work his loom for much longer.'

'What'll you do?'

435

'We'll go back north, tae our own folk, when the time comes,' Morag said.

The hours dragged by, and at last the mourners departed. Rose and Jean would have washed all the dishes, but Kirsty, wearied to the bone, dissuaded them.

'We'll see to it in the morning—me and the girls. For tonight I just want to be quiet for a while.'

John Brodie, who had also attended, offered to take Jean and Rose home in his new motorcar. Alex would have escorted Jean on the short walk to her home above the shop, but she shook her head at him and went on tiptoe to whisper in his ear, 'No offence, laddie, but I've never been in a motorcar before and I'd fairly like tae try the experience!'

Todd would have left with his sister and her husband, but Kirsty detained him with a hand on his arm. 'We'll be talking about the future, and I'd like you to stay,' she said, and his face, already flushed from the warmth of the small crowded house, the funeral whisky and the pressure of his tight high collar, reddened a little more.

Kirsty had decided that Mary, tearful over the loss of her father and yet another bewildering change within her family circle, should be allowed to participate in the funeral gathering. 'Mary needs to say goodbye to her father,' she said when

Alex and Caitlin argued with her. 'If she's shut out of what's going on, she'll mebbe feel cheated in later life when she thinks of him.' She knew what she was talking about—she herself had suffered, and always would, because she hadn't been able to take part in her beloved grandfather's funeral.

Dressed in a black dress her mother and sister had hurriedly made for her, Mary had worked hard, scurrying to and fro among the guests like an ant in a patch of tall grass, burdened with plates of sandwiches and sausage rolls and biscuits and cake. Now, with the visitors gone, she was white with exhaustion and could scarcely keep her eyes open.

'Bed for you, miss.'

'Can I not stay up...' Mary began, but was interrupted by a jaw-cracking yawn. 'Will you be here in the morning, Alex?' she wanted to know when she had regained the power of speech.

'No, pet, I've got work to do tomorrow,' he said, glancing apologetically at his mother and other sister. 'I'll have to take the train back to Glasgow tonight.'

Fresh tears were added to those brought into her eyes by the yawn. 'But you'll have to come back now that Ewan's gone and Father's...' Her voice began to wobble, and he picked her up and hugged her, his face drawn with misery and guilt. 'Mary, love...'

'We'll be fine, you and me and Caitlin.' Kirsty patted her young daughter's hand. 'You're old enough to do your share of looking after the house, and Todd's never far away.'

'I'll carry you upstairs,' Alex offered, and Mary blinked the tears away and nodded, wrapping her arms round his neck and laying her head on his shoulder. He well knew that ever since babyhood she had loved the sensation of being carried upstairs, her head bumping and rolling against some adult's shoulder at each lift and step.

He lingered while Kirsty helped Mary, now stupefied by fatigue, out of her funeral clothes and into her nightdress. She was asleep before the two of them reached the bedroom door.

'I want to stay, but I have to go back, Mam,' Alex said as they began to descend the stairs. 'I've to see an important customer tomorrow morning and he's off to Carlisle at midday, so...'

'You've got your own work, Alex, and your own life. We'll manage fine.'

'Are you sure? I'm not all that far away if you need me. And Father,' he said the word easily without even noticing that he had used it, 'says that if there's ever

438

anything he can do to help you, he will.'

'Don't forget to thank him for his kindness—and say I'll not hesitate to accept his offer if I need him,' Kirsty told him, knowing that the time when she had most needed Sandy, and he had needed her, was long past. She would not ask for his help.

Caitlin had made a fresh pot of tea, and she and Todd had made a start on gathering up the cups and saucers and glasses and plates scattered over the kitchen and parlour.

'What's to be seen to?' Alex asked when the four of them were seated round the table.

'Nothing much, to tell the truth. Poor Matt was housebound for so long that we all got into our own ways of coping. I just wanted to make sure that you knew how well we could manage. Then you'll be able to get on with your own business without fretting over us.' Kirsty stared at her cup, realising with a stab of guilt that life without Matt would in fact be easier, since she would no longer have to worry about him being left on his own. 'I've got the shop, Caitlin has her work, and when Mary's on holiday from school she can come to the shop with me. She's a good lassie, and the others won't mind.'

'What about the workshop?'

'I'm going to keep it on. We've got our

regular customers, and I'd not want to let them down.' She smiled across the table at the journeyman. 'Todd's been the master there since Ewan left. Since you left, Alex, if the truth be told. Now the title's his, for all to see, for as long as he wants it.'

Todd glowed with pleasure. 'I'll be there for as long as ye need me,' he said, and for a moment Kirsty thought of Beth, who had so wanted Todd to become the master of the little workshop. Now it had happened, and she knew nothing about it.

'The new man's good?' Alex wanted to know.

'I picked Davie mysel'. He's a fine craftsman, and a reliable worker.'

'If there are problems, you'll both let me know?' Alex looked from Todd to Kirsty.

'We will, if we need you. But there'll be no problems,' she told him firmly. 'If there are, I'm sure we can see to them—Todd and me.'

## 34

Rose, who, thanks to Caitlin, had learned how to walk properly in an evening dress, had still not mastered the art of walking like a young lady at other times. She burst into the shop in her usual way to announce excitedly that John Brodie's mother wanted Kirsty to call on her.

'Me? What for?'

'She's having problems with some outfit she bought. She's like me, entirely the wrong shape for clothes, and she remembered the nice dress you made for me for her daughter's engagement party. Please, Kirsty,' she hurried on as Kirsty began to shake her head. 'It's not like Mrs Brodie to ask for our help, and she'd pay you well—I'd see to that. And since she's a close friend of Mamma's, it would give me so much pleasure,' she added with a wicked grin. 'Do it for John if you won't do it for me. Think of all he's done to help us.'

She and John Brodie were now spending quite a lot of time in each other's company, so much so that they were usually linked in the minds of the local hostesses when they issued invitations. Kirsty had made or adapted a number of outfits for Rose in the past few months, and from what she heard, each one had been well received.

'She's right about John. You should go and see the woman, Kirsty,' Jean said, and Teenie nodded vigorously.

'Oh, very well.'

Rose hugged her. 'Bless you! She's a

dominating woman, but quite nice in her own way,' she added casually, to Kirsty's alarm. 'Assert your authority if you must—she caves in if she's challenged.'

Carriagehill Road, where the Brodies lived, was familiar. So, when Kirsty reached it, was the Brodies' gate. She looked along the length of the driveway to the house and remembered all at once that she had indeed walked along that road before, and in at that gate and up to that door.

On her last visit to the house she had been shown from the back door into the sitting room. This time the uniformed maid led her upstairs and into a large carpeted front bedroom, complete with a hand basin and vast wardrobes along two walls.

'Mrs Brodie will be along in a moment,' the maid said, and withdrew. Nervously, Kirsty took her jacket off and studied her hair and her clothes in the full-length mirror. Although only four months had passed since Matt's death she had recently decided that she and her daughters should dispense with the usual year of wearing nothing but black. To her mind it served little purpose, and heavy mourning had a depressing effect on the wearers and all those who came in contact with them.

She had reverted to the shop uniform of white blouse and black skirt, but today, since she was outside the shop, she wore a grey skirt and jacket over a lilac blouse with slightly puffed sleeves and a high neck with a flounce of lace at the throat. She nodded approvingly at her reflection and had just moved to the window when the door opened.

'Mrs Lennox?' Mrs Brodie swept into the room, followed by another uniformed maid, presumably the servant who helped her to dress and attended to her clothes and her hair. 'Miss Rose Hamilton assures me that you will be able to assist me with a slight problem.'

'I'll do my best, Mrs Brodie.' Kirsty took a step or two away from the window, and the woman's eyes narrowed as she saw the caller's face more clearly.

'Don't I know you?'

'We met once before, Mrs Brodie.'

'Where?'

'Here in your home, almost two years ago. I was looking for work as a sewing woman, but I didn't find it here.'

'Good heavens!' Red patches flared high on the woman's cheekbones. 'You're the woman who used to sew for Mrs Hamilton.'

'Yes.'

'And now you're working for Rose?

443

What a small world.'

'Now Rose and I are partners, together with Miss Jean Chisholm.' Kirsty corrected the woman gently but firmly. Then, as Mrs Brodie, taken aback, blinked and stuttered, she introduced a businesslike note to her voice. 'You mentioned a problem?'

Mrs Brodie managed to collect herself. 'It's this costume.' She indicated the outfit she wore—a flowery silk-taffeta dress, the skirt embellished with two deep frills of the same material, and a matching bolero jacket thick with dark-blue braid. 'I'm accompanying my husband on a business trip next month, and I planned to wear this at an important afternoon gathering. For some reason he doesn't care for it.' She twisted and turned before her full-length mirror, frowning at her own reflection. 'The question is, can something be done with it?'

'Perhaps your own dressmaker—'

'She made it, and she thinks, like me, that it looks quite all right as it is. Then dear Rose suggested that I should consult you. I must say that she has been looking quite elegant recently. Something of a revelation, in fact. I'm hoping that you can do as much for me.'

Glancing at the maid, Kirsty read the slight flicker of the woman's lips accurately.

It was one thing dressing Rose's long, angular frame and quite another dealing with Mrs Brodie, who was built like a box—square and solid and quite wrong for the frills and flounces and cummerbunds of modern fashion.

Kirsty took a deep breath. 'To begin with, Mrs Brodie, I think you should replace the bolero jacket with something longer, perhaps, and looser.'

'But that would require more of this patterned material. It may not be easy to find now.'

'I would suggest a jacket in one colour that picks up a shade from the dress—grey, perhaps, to match the background of the dress material.' The background could scarcely be seen behind the large, rioting flowers, but it was there.

'Grey?' Mrs Brodie was shocked. 'How dull!'

'Grey can very fetching, and excellent for offsetting colours and patterns. A grey sash too—not a cummerbund, something narrower...'

Mrs Brodie clasped both hands protectively over the broad sash about her generous waist. 'I insist on retaining the cummerbund. It's very fashionable.'

Kirsty began to wonder how a nice man like John Brodie could be the son of this overbearing woman with not the slightest understanding of colour or style. 'Mrs Brodie, you asked for my advice, and that's what I'm giving you,' she said as politely as possible.

'My dear woman, you must bear in mind that she who pays the piper is allowed to call the tune.'

For a moment they eyed each other, then Kirsty, remembering Rose's advice about asserting her authority, shrugged and picked up her jacket and bag. It took all her courage, but she managed to do it with an air of finality. 'Then I'm afraid I can't help you, Mrs Brodie. I'm a seamstress and, as you say, you pay the piper. Perhaps a piper can be of more help to you than I am.'

'Wait,' said Mrs Brodie.

It took an hour, and all the tact and firmness Kirsty possessed, to persuade the woman to allow her to strip the outfit of its cummerbund and puffed sleeves and bolero jacket. Even the starched maid was wilting by the time Mrs Brodie conceded defeat.

'Oliphant, help me off with these things so that Mrs, er, Lennox can take them away,' she commanded. Kirsty watched, fascinated, as the servant removed the dress and jacket to reveal a meaty torso so well corseted that it was a wonder that Mrs Brodie could draw breath, then eased her employer into a pretty lacy tea gown, fastening the buttons and tying the sash. She had never before seen a grown woman being undressed and dressed like a doll. Mary was far more capable than this woman when it came to looking after herself.

'If I don't care for the changes you've suggested once they're done,' Mrs Brodie said as the maid carefully packed the clothes into a small travelling bag, 'I shan't pay one penny.'

'As you wish, Mrs Brodie.' Kirsty had used up a month's supply of firmness and was too drained to argue.

'And if you spoil the dress I shall expect you to reimburse the cost. It was very expensive. In fact before you start cutting into it I want to see a sketch of your proposed changes.'

'Certainly, Mrs Brodie,' Kirsty agreed. Anything to escape from this house and get back to Causeyside Street, where folk were able to do up their own buttons.

Although it was half-day, the others had all waited in the shop to find out how she had got on. 'I'll never forgive you for this, Rose Hamilton,' she said when she arrived back.

'Oh dear, was she in one of her ladylike moods?'

447

'I'd say she was in one of her Queen Victoria moods.'

'She can be quite a nice woman really,' Rose said helplessly, then went red when Kirsty retorted, 'Mebbe so—if you've got money and you're walking out with her son.'

It was generally agreed that Kirsty's ideas would be a great improvement. 'We'll charge her for the time you spend on it,' Rose promised. 'She can afford it, and she'll pay happily if she likes the changes.'

'If she doesn't, it'll cost us money.'

'That's my problem, not yours.'

'The thing is, I've agreed to let her see a sketch first, and I can't draw.'

'Nor can I,' Rose said at once, while Jean added, 'I mind I was good at drawing wee houses at school, with daffodils in the yard and chickens scratching about. But not dresses.'

Kirsty began to fold the dress and jacket up. 'I'll have a word with Caitlin. She was quite good at drawing at school.'

'Here.' Rose snatched up a handful of fashion papers and put them on top of the clothes in the travel bag. 'Perhaps these will help her.'

'But I was going to spend the evening working on my new jacket,' Caitlin protested. She was walking out with the new apprentice Todd had recently taken on and had started making herself a jacket from the length of woollen cloth the Bishops had given her almost two years earlier.

'I'll do some work on the jacket for you if you'll try the drawing,' Kirsty coaxed, and the girl shrugged and agreed. She spent some time frowning over the fashion papers strewn across the kitchen table, then trying out some sketches on an old sketch pad Alex had left behind, working with colouring crayons borrowed from Mary. Kirsty, busy at the sewing machine, glanced up at her now and again. Caitlin, at fifteen years of age, had all but blossomed into womanhood and was clearly going to be beautiful in another year or so. Bryce, her new sweetheart, was a year older, which meant that they were the ages Kirsty and Sandy had been when Alex was conceived.

Strongly aware of that from the first, and remembering how mutual loneliness and lack of security had catapulted her and Sandy into each other's arms, Kirsty had made certain that Bryce, a likeable lad, was made welcome in her kitchen. Caitlin was going to be given all the time she needed to make decisions about her future.

'I went to Kilbarchan this afternoon,' the girl said just then. 'Mr Bishop's going to give up work in November, and they're all going back north.'

'You'll miss them—we all will.'

Caitlin nodded, then said, 'I think I can start trying the sketch now. Come and tell me what it is you want.'

'This is very well done,' Rose said, awed, when she saw the sketch the following day. 'I'd no idea that two of your children were artists, Kirsty.'

The sketch was good, but Kirsty did her best to conceal her maternal pride, saying casually, 'Caitlin's scribbled out ideas from time to time for clothes she wanted to make, but that's been all up until now.'

Rose herself took the sketch to show Mrs Brodie and returned to report that the woman was impressed by it and had agreed to let Kirsty proceed.

'We'll need to buy material for the jacket.'

'We can hardly make it out of something from the shop,' Rose agreed. 'We'd best go shopping.'

After a lifetime of unpicking and remaking second-hand clothing it was a joy to Kirsty to see so much virginal cloth in all patterns and colours, and of all materials. She moved from one shelf to the other in the draper's shop, drinking it all in while Rose watched her, amused.

'You look like a child let loose in a sweet shop for the first time.'

'It's—it's like being in heaven!'

'We should buy new material sometimes for the shop.'

'Our customers couldn't afford to pay for it.'

'Then we'll think of other ways of using it,' Rose said, a light in her eye.

Kirsty finally settled on a pale-grey silk taffeta for Mrs Brodie's jacket. She bore it almost reverently back to the shop, where the first cut was a nerve-wracking moment.

'What if she doesnae like it once it's finished?' Teenie quavered. 'Ye'll have tae pay the full price of it.'

'If we must, we must—but she will like it,' Rose told her firmly as they stared at each other over the expensive material. 'Look at us—we're like the witches in Macbeth. For goodness' sake, Kirsty, start cutting!'

'Well begun,' Kirsty said with a bravado she didn't feel, 'is half done.'

'Or you could say, another door opened...' Rose put in as the scissors plunged into the material and started snipping.

# 35

Mrs Brodie was delighted with her new outfit and almost at once asked Kirsty to alter another dress for her.

'Please,' Rose coaxed when Kirsty firmly refused.

'It's not what we're supposed to be doing, Rose! I've got enough work on my hands without becoming Mrs Brodie's personal dressmaker. Isn't that right, Jean?' Kirsty appealed to her friend.

'Well, the thing is...' Jean said evasively, and Kirsty looked from one partner to the other.

'What have you two been plotting behind my back?'

'Not behind your back, Kirsty, it just came up in conversation when you didnae happen tae be in the shop.'

Rose grasped the nettle with both hands. 'To tell you the truth, Kirsty, I knew from what Mrs Brodie said after her first fitting that she was delighted with your ideas for that outfit, and I was certain she'd want to use your talents again. And you know how much pleasure it gave you to buy that material for her jacket. So Jean and

I thought that if she did ask you to do more work—'

'It wouldnae be a good idea tae turn the likes of Mrs Brodie down,' Jean broke in. 'We think you should do it, Kirsty.'

'As a sort of sideline.'

'It wouldnae take away from the other customers.'

'But it would,' Kirsty protested. 'It would take up too much of my time...'

'Not if we brought in another employee,' Rose said. 'Not if we asked Caitlin to come and work for us.'

'Caitlin?'

'I first thought of employing her when I saw that drawing she did for Mrs Brodie. And I made up my mind the day she came in wearing that bonny jacket she had made for herself. She's wasted in that grocery shop, Kirsty.'

'I had it in mind to try to get her into Cochrane's sewing room one day.'

'And let someone else get the good of her when she could work for us?' Rose almost exploded. 'With us she could sew, and mebbe even try her hand at some designing—'

'And help behind the counter if she had the time,' Jean broke in. 'Say yes, Kirsty.'

'Can we afford another wage?'

'Yes we can—and Caitlin would more

453

than pay her own way,' Rose assured her.

'We'll need to see what Caitlin thinks of it,' Kirsty said, already knowing the answer, and already looking forward to bringing her daughter into the business that had come to mean so much to her.

A pale autumn haze was lying over the park and the quarry and the row of old terraced houses when Kirsty walked up the park on her last visit to the Kilbarchan house that had once belonged to her grandfather. Mary ran ahead, scuffing her booted feet through the gold and red and brown leaves by the side of the path, while Caitlin and Kirsty followed behind, talking about the shop. Caitlin had just completed her first month there and had already settled in and become an integral part of the place.

Geordie and his daughter, Ellie, had completed their final orders, and the two looms on the ground floor were silent, waiting to be taken apart and crated for the journey north.

'There'll be work for Ellie, for the weavin's still goin' on up north,' Geordie said as they stood in the silent shop. 'And I'll still do some work, but not so much. There'll be others tae take over if my hands decide they cannae keep goin'.'

'I'll be sad to see you go.'

'There's nothin' sad about it,' Morag said robustly. 'It's only another change, and life's full of those—as you should know, Kirsty.'

They walked up the garden, still rich with autumn fruit and flowers, to the shed where the old loom stood, it's rollers empty of cloth. Geordie took a parcel from the shelf. 'This is for you, Kirsty. I made it specially on this loom.'

Kirsty unfolded the wrapping and found herself looking at all the colours of the Scottish moorland—russet and gold and yellow, and every shade of brown, all intermingled in a pattern that seemed to flow like a burn purling its way down through the bracken moors to the river.

'Geordie, it's beautiful!'

He nodded with justifiable pride. 'I think it's one o' the best pieces of cloth I've ever woven. Caitlin here helped me tae decide on the colours.' Then, laying a hand on the loom, he said, 'The thing is, lass, what's tae be done with this machine? I cannae take it with me, for the two I already have are more than enough. And if it's left here it'll mebbe end up the way it did before.'

'We have to think of somewhere to keep it, Mam,' Caitlin said anxiously. 'I couldn't bear to think of it being abandoned again, not after seeing it working.'

'We won't let that happen,' Kirsty assured her, stroking one of the big rollers gently. 'I'll speak to Todd about it.'

'It seems only fitting to bring it back to the store by the pend,' she explained to Todd the next day. 'After all, that was once a loom shop, before my father's father started up his cabinet-making business. But I'll not allow the loom to be put into a corner in pieces the way it was. I want it to be set up properly, even if it's never used again.'

'Ye never know, ye might be able tae find a weaver one day.'

She smiled at him, struck by the way their minds often seemed to be in tune. 'I'd wondered about that myself. Caitlin's got an idea in her head about making clothes from material woven on it, but we'll have to wait and see. For the meantime, I just want to know that it's safe and it's being looked after properly. It would mean you losing some of your storage space,' she added anxiously.

'We can manage without it,' he said easily. A year had passed since Beth had run away with Ewan, and for Todd, the wounds appeared to have healed. He had thrown himself into his work and had reverted to his usual cheerful self. 'It's just a matter of makin' certain that the finished furniture's removed right away so that it doesnae have tae be stored. There's no worry about that.'

'Are you certain? I can try to find somewhere else for the loom if you want.'

'You own the place, Mrs Lennox,' he said simply.

'Mebbe I do, but you're the master.'

'Even so,' he said, his eyes holding hers, 'it's what you want that matters tae me.'

Geordie arranged to have the loom taken apart, delivered to Paisley and reassembled, while Todd and Kirsty cleared the store out and prepared it.

There was an air of celebration about the place on the frosty November day the loom arrived back in Paisley. Even Alex had arranged to be there. Once it had been reassembled and settled, they held a gathering in the kitchen to celebrate—Todd and the other two men from the workshop, Alex and Kirsty and Caitlin and Mary, and the Bishops.

In the evening, when all the visitors had gone and the workshop was closed for the day and Caitlin was out with Bryce, and Mary in her bed, Kirsty took a lamp into the store to look again at the loom, strong and sturdy in the store that had, in a way, become a loom shop again.

It was true what some folk said, she

thought, running her fingers over the timber. Things did have a way of coming full circle. The storms of yesterday were over, and today here she was, back in her old home, reunited with her grandfather through the loom that had been an almost lifelong companion to him. Alex was well settled with his father; Ewan, wherever he was, had chosen his own road; and she and Caitlin and Mary were at peace with their lives. As for tomorrow, it would take care of itself, for as her mother had always said, tomorrow is another day.

Morag had had the right way of it with her sayings, too. Kirsty felt that this very loom had somehow woven her own life pattern, a pattern that brought together all her children, and Sandy, and Matt, and Jean and Rose and the shop.

A step sounded in the pend and the door creaked slightly at her back.

'Come on in, Todd,' she said without looking round.

'I'm not disturbin' ye?'

'Not a bit of it.'

'I just wanted tae have another look at it, without all those folks around,' he said, coming to stand by her side, his big hand landing gently on the loom close by hers. 'It's a beautiful piece of machinery.'

'It is.' His presence, in the flickering shadows of the shed, was comforting as always, but at the same time being alone with him in the calm darkness sent a very faint tingle of pleasure dancing along her veins. It was a sensation she had first noticed only weeks earlier while talking alone with him in the workshop. She suspected that it had been with her, unnoticed, for much longer.

Kirsty was well aware that she was nearing her fortieth year and that Todd was a few years her junior, and that she hadn't been widowed a full twelve months yet. But something whispered to her that one day, perhaps quite far in the future, Todd might just become an important part of her own particular life pattern.

Then again, she thought, standing by the loom, Todd close by her in the store's silence, it might not happen.

But the possibility that it might, distant as it was, filled her with happiness.

The publishers hope that this book has given you enjoyable reading. Large Print Books are especially designed to be as easy to see and hold as possible. If you wish a complete list of our books, please ask at your local library or write directly to: Magna Large Print Books, Long Preston, North Yorkshire, BD23 4ND, England.

This Large Print Book for the Partially sighted, who cannot read normal print, is published under the auspices of

**THE ULVERSCROFT FOUNDATION**

---

## THE ULVERSCROFT FOUNDATION

. . . we hope that you have enjoyed this Large Print Book. Please think for a moment about those people who have worse eyesight problems than you . . . and are unable to even read or enjoy Large Print, without great difficulty.

You can help them by sending a donation, large or small to:

**The Ulverscroft Foundation,
1, The Green, Bradgate Road,
Anstey, Leicestershire, LE7 7FU,
England.**
or request a copy of our brochure for more details.

The Foundation will use all your help to assist those people who are handicapped by various sight problems and need special attention.

Thank you very much for your help.

PORT TALBOT LIBRARY
INFORMATION SERVICES

| | 73 | |
|---|---|---|

2000128388

NEATH PORT TALBOT LIBRARIES